Ghost Emerald

Ghost Lovers – Book Two

SALLY SWANSON

DEDICATION

To all of the purveyors of the unexplained
who lived to tell their tale.

ACKNOWLEDGMENTS

Cover art: Eros by Dan Houston
http://www.architecturalwalldecor.com/home

Cover design: Andrew Swanson

PROLOGUE

The Mid-Atlantic
March 1, 1780

Felipe didn't hesitate. Using the long afternoon shadows, he slipped from one to the next progressing stealthily down the pristine deck. Upon skirting the foremast, his pulse heated with boyish anticipation when he saw the young beauty standing still and alert like the figurehead of their commandeered ship. The wooden likeness shared the same curves of the waist and alert breasts, the serene face and flowing hair. Felipe would never be able to look at the tall ship Immaculata again without thinking of Vivian Dufrense.

"Lieutenant Cordova, how long were you planning on staring at me without announcing yourself?" Vivian didn't move; her statuesque profile was a perfect complement to the starched novitiate dress.

Felipe had over a decade of experience in seducing women, yet his heart leapt at the sound of her seductively smooth voice. "Señorita, I was admiring true beauty. For a moment, I thought you a watery mirage, a figment of my imagination, for on a calm and endless sea, men have been known to see visions. Most certainly, you are a vision too beautiful to be real."

"Your compliments are as smooth as the sea and equally as empty Lieutenant. I suggest you take your leave." Slowly she turned away from the radiant sunset and cast her tempting emerald eyes over his face.

The hypnotic sweep from his chin and lips to his rich brown eyes made a genuine smile crease his well-rounded lips, deepening the dimples which he had hated as a boy, but at court too many women found them irresistible. However, none of the courtesans compared to Vivian Dufrense, who would be the greatest conquest of all.

"The sea is anything but empty, Señorita. Every manner of creature exists in its depths." He took a step, close enough to touch her, and yet she didn't back away. Defiant and proud, her nature was even more compelling than her beauty. "It is as full of life as are my compliments, for you are of the sea. Your hair shines like smooth midnight waves. Your skin is fashioned from its finest pearls." The temptation was too great, and he lowered his gaze. Under the fine Spanish lace, her breath made the gentle mounds rise, rocking the simple wooden cross. "Your every breath breathes life into the wind."

"If that were true, we would be flying across the sea with a single puff from my lips." With the overt exaggeration of a stage actress, Vivian blew a stirring breath.

Her fragrant essence slipped into his lungs, kindling the slow burn. His lustful eyes remained on her tempting mouth; if he didn't taste it soon, he would go mad. "Your lips are the color of the sea rose blooming along a reef, where secretive creatures spark when touched, and the spark when I touch your skin is just as mystifying." He lifted her hand, allowing his lips to linger on the gentle swells, and then raised his gaze ever so slowly. "Your eyes are the shade of water surrounding Caribbean shoals and just as dangerous to a man." He had already run aground and was afraid he would remain trapped there forever.

She laughed, but stopped quickly, casting a cautious glance toward the cabin where her cousins and Sister

Marguerite napped. "Dangerous? Me? You are mistaken. I am the best behaved young lady in Spain."

"And according to young Tomas one of the best at swordplay, though I have yet to see your skill. I would love to fence with you."

"I'm sure you would." Vivian flounced her glance back out to the sea where the sun's waning glow touched the horizon, brandishing the flowing crests with undulating fire. "I've been warned about rakish lieutenants bearing skillful compliments."

Leaning forward, he placed his mouth next to her ear. "By the good and pious Sister who keeps you locked away?"

She sucked in a quick breath. "If it wasn't for Marianna's betrothal, she and I would have remained at Las Monjas. I hoped this trip would bring a respite; unfortunately, the stateroom aboard ship is even more confining than the convent."

"Yet you found a few moments to steal away. This is only the third time we've spoken; although, I've waited for days, watching for you from the wheel." He rubbed the sensitive flesh behind her ear with a fingertip, and although she visibly stiffened to resist the gesture, the slight rise of her chin indicated his touch did affect her. The desire to press his lips to the very same curve inched him even closer. "Your father must receive betrothal offers daily."

Gasping in surprise, Vivian swung around, absently brushing her hips past his muscled thighs. "You forget yourself. That is mine and my father's business, not yours Lieutenant." Her eyes shifted quickly side to side, but he had grasped both railings and boxed her in. With no means of escape, she retreated until her back pressed into the hard rise of the bow.

Inching across the renewed distance, Felipe's determined fingertips began stroking her once more, continuing their sensual path over her cheek to the loosely curling tendrils of dark hair framing her face. Her eyes widened and lips parted as if to ask a question, and then paused still gently spread. Of course his sexual need grew, yet more than just lustful desire flowed through him, tinting that familiar craving with an even deeper longing. With other women he would satisfy himself within a single night, but once he had a taste of Vivian Dufrense, one night would never be enough. Although these new thoughts and feelings frightened him more than steering the ship into a raging hurricane, he pressed forward. "What would you think if I decided to make it my business?"

In the waning evening glow, her innocent eyes glittered lovelier than jewels and held power in their indeterminate depths, oh yes, just like the dangerous shoals. "I think you are rash and spout whatever needs to be said in order to win my favor. You have plenty of time to determine the verity of your impulses, for we have such a distance yet to travel and then the same back to Cadiz to speak to my father. In those long weeks, one has time to contemplate the difference between love and lust." As the final words passed her lips, her breath quickened again, caressing his cheek and neck.

Sensing victory, he moved even closer until his lips whispered against her ear. "Do you contemplate such thoughts of me?"

"That, Lieutenant, is a rakish question and not appropriate to ask a lady." Yet her words didn't match the huskiness in her voice or the sudden smoldering in her bewitching eyes. "Lust is a sin, while love is divine. I have given neither to any man."

"While you were gazing through the window today, can you honestly say you didn't think of me even once?" He watched her eyes widen again with a refreshing combination of shock and wonder, and found them even more appealing. "Why don't you answer? May I guess it's because lying is a sin as well."

Vivian scoffed, "Who are you to lecture me about sin?"

"Ah, your avoidance has answered my question. Shall I give you more than just thoughts to confess?" As he formed the last word, his lips brushed lightly over hers. Starting with a spark, the contact sizzled, more, ever so much more than any of his former conquests.

Although she stubbornly refused to respond, he continued plying his skill. Sliding his hand to the base of her neck, he wove his fingers into the downy hair and held her firmly. A tiny gasp opened the seal upon her mouth, but he did not press inside. Instead, he tasted her lips, rounding the delicate petals, awakening them to know passion. Perfectly soft and extremely feminine, her mouth was full and ripe, and just as sweet as exotic fruit.

His arm rounded her waist, drawing her away from the railing and into vibrant contact with his arousal. Before she could protest, he brushed his tongue across the opening of her mouth. There, right then, the tension eased from her muscles, and she became pliant in his arms.

Once victorious in an initial campaign upon a lady's virtue, a true gentleman would pull away, but Felipe had earned his reputation. This time languidly, he traced the moist edges of her lips until they parted and then deepened the kiss, sliding into the softness. On a quiet moan, Vivian shifted toward him, inviting something she didn't understand, yet nonetheless fueled his longing. She tasted like the sea just as fresh as he had imagined all those lonely hours at the ship's wheel, yet he hadn't prepared for the intoxicating effect. As every nerve hungered, the fledgling sensation grew powerfully compelling. It wasn't lust, for he had lusted a thousand times while at court. This curious emotion was sharper than simple desire, biting into his flesh like a blade, yet smoothly coiled, winding its way into his heart.

With a low groan, he pulled away from the sweet lips no other man had ever tasted. Felipe knew he would find treasure at sea, he just had no idea the prize would be of flesh and blood with emerald eyes.

CHAPTER 1

Puerto Rico
March 16, 2015

The mofongo Juan Carlos Diego Calderon ate at lunch was even better than he had remembered, rich and thick with chunks of shrimp. His grandmother proudly served him two platefuls of the unique Puerto Rican delicacy before he was able to leave the house in Bayamon. Now as he approached San Juan, the delicious meal hovered at the top of his stomach.

J.C. thought he could do it. He was a man for Christ's sake, not some teenage kid. Yet just like the mofongo, the haunting memory uncomfortably slid up, evoking the fear which fueled his nightmares for far too long. Although he had been away from the island for fifteen years, every detail of that night flooded his mind.

Hell, *Ghost Lovers* took him to dozens of haunted locations. Some of them definitely had vibes going on, yet most phenomena were benign in comparison to the associated legends. His hand passed to his abdomen, covering the scar he received as an unexpected souvenir from his last encounter with the paranormal. The belief in they couldn't hurt you was a load of shit. Not every ghost interacted with the living, but the powerful ones could and would.

Even with it being mid-afternoon, cars crept along the congested freeway toward the heart of San Juan past walls decorated with urban art. If it hadn't been for the stifling heat, he would have thought he was back in Brooklyn. At the exit with the national park icon, he sucked in a deep breath and took the ramp to the left, curving away from the modern condos in tall glass towers and toward the ancient history of Old San Juan.

He never told his grandfather what had happened that night or anyone else for that matter. At the time, he and Andres were out to see what they could see. It was just too easy to swipe his grandfather's keycard and head off in search of… What had they been looking for? Why had they gone into the fort that night? J.C. now knew some places were locked for a reason.

The massive stone wall grew out of the landscape before the road even curved toward San Cristobal hill. The fortification used the naturally uneven terrain and the seacoast to its advantage. Thomas O'Daly, the most famous military engineer of his day, had done his job well and built a fortress to watch over the island for at least a thousand years. To date, his architectural masterpiece remained the largest fort in all the Spanish Main. Hundreds of years resonated there. The hidden vibrations accumulated within the stones themselves, channeling the power and enmity deep into the inner tunnels, the bowels of the beast.

J.C. concentrated on the street ahead of him, but the gray fortress grew uncomfortably in his peripheral vision. He felt it there, the embodiment of evil hidden in perpetual darkness waiting for him to return. Unconsciously, he eased his foot off the gas. Momentum carried the car forward, yard after yard, foot after foot, then inch after inch, yet even with the lack of intentional propulsion, he eventually reached the main entrance as if drawn by some unseen tide.

After giving his name and relationship to Eduardo Calderon, the guard released the gates and motioned toward the employee's parking area. The long moment grew painful while J.C. stared at the steep drive. The guard started to walk back toward him, so he gunned the motor and insanely zoomed up the ramp.

CHAPTER 2

The stone wall was hot from baking in the relentless Caribbean sun. Pressing her palms against the rough surface, Fara Trotter felt something pulse into her inner awareness, more than just the sizzling heat. Nothing truly tangible, yet something she couldn't ignore. She trusted her sixth sense just as strongly as her verifiable senses; in too many circumstances, intuition was what had kept her alive. Kicking off her shoes, she easily scaled the stone blocks, and bracing herself against the anticipated burn, leaned her torso over the wide wall. She couldn't quite see down the other side, but in the frothy surf, the rough peaks of jagged rocks were about sixty feet below her. Jumping from San Cristobal wouldn't be a pleasant way to die.

The words from the park ranger continued to ease across the grassy expanse on the warm ocean breeze. "...This area was also used for public executions. The Spanish utilized all of the island's natural resources and enslaved the indigenous Taíno and Caribe Indians to mine gold. When the resources dwindled, the Spanish found a new fortune in sugar cane and rum and conscripted African slaves to work the fields. At the time, less than a third of the population was Spanish, who lived in constant fear of uprisings. To maintain control, the Spaniards demonstrated their brutal might by publically- Hey chica! Lady, get off from there!"

Fara shot a look at the old tour guide and then down to the younger man who had followed her away from the group. There was a strong resemblance, but that was true with most Hispanic men.

The younger man shielded his eyes from the sun as he looked up at her. The wind caught the edge of her skirt, and his eyes widened. "Lady, you're going to give my grandfather a heart attack. Why don't you just hop down from the wall?"

She locked eyes with the man who spoke English like a New York. Another tug pulled within her, but this time, it wasn't paranormal intuition. With agile grace, she landed silently. "I was just looking at the rocks."

Turning toward the old man, the New Yorker held up his hand. "You can slow down Abuelo. She was just looking at the rocks."

"Dios mío, chica." The ranger doubled over panting. After catching his breath, he wiped the beads of sweat from his brow with a quick flick of his wrist and closed the remaining few yards. "Please," he laid his hand gently on her arm, "come back to the group."

Fara could break more than just his grip easily, but she patted the aged hand and slipped softly from the unwelcomed touch and back into her sandals. "Are the ghost stories true? Did a girl really jump near here?"

The younger man visibly paled. "Abuelo, the tour's waiting, and a few of the cruise ship gorditos look like they're ready to drop dead from the heat." He motioned to the group with a tip of his head, and his shoulder-length hair rippled. "I'll answer the lady's questions, and then we'll catch up with you."

While the crowd meandered toward the shadowy lower levels, Fara leaned against the heated wall and watched the man whose dark hair was slick with perspiration at the temples. The edge of the wind started to shift, yet she didn't try to maintain her modesty, allowing the wrapped dress to catch in the breeze. She watched for a change in his eyes, but his expression remained tense without even a glimmer of manly interest. Perhaps, she had been wrong about her initial impression and started to resent how her pulse was dancing, anticipating what she wanted.

When the tour began, something about him appealed to her, yet she really didn't know what it was. He was attractive, every inch macho Latino, with a rugged been-around-the-block edge. Over the past thirty minutes, he hadn't interacted with anyone, hanging back like her. He'd been looking around corners and inside rooms, clearly searching for something that he was afraid to find, or she thought a moment, would find him.

Whisking the heavy locks of long hair over her leeward shoulder, Fara cocked her head to the side. The lengths caught in the breeze and soared above the blue silk. A faint glimmer of interest darkened his chocolate brown eyes as he stared at her legs. She had been told by more than one man her legs were flawless. Spreading her knees slightly, she watched his mouth open, as if ready to speak but without finding the words. His left hand swept the hair out of his eyes, and his ring finger was bare.

There was hope to divert his attention to something much more enjoyable than a moldy fort. Fara's instincts started humming, and whenever that happened, she knew her life was about to change. It was time for a new beginning on a multitude of levels, and she would start by fulfilling her most basic need.

His gaze rose back to her face. A sly smile creased his lips, and desire heated her in places where the sun didn't shine.

CHAPTER 3

The brilliant light swept through her hair, burning radiant highlights into the dark mane, and her skin shone with a fine luster, imparting the color and sheen of melted caramels. J.C. chastised himself for forgetting a camera. The shot was as good as some swimsuit edition, with her striking legs crossed at the ankles, relaxed yet sexily poised in unspoken invitation.

Her radiant face was long and artfully proportioned with a prominent nose and chin, gracefully crafted and beguiling. J.C. didn't think she could get anymore sexy, but then she took off her sunglasses. Dreamy green eyes started at his face and swept over his shoulders and torso, taking time upon his midriff and then quickly down his legs. As if her eyes physically touched him, every inch of J.C.'s body tingled.

The raw sensual power she emitted caused his brain to go numb while other parts of his body grew acutely aware. He ran a hand through his hair, watching her watch him. If his grandfather hadn't interacted with the dazzling beauty, he could have imagined she was a new ghost trapped within the historic fort. Still, ghosts didn't have real eyes, at least not the ghosts he had encountered.

"My plans fell through for today, and I noticed you weren't with anyone during the tour. You got plans?" Based solely upon her looks, he thought she would have a Middle Eastern accent. Instead, she spoke with a mid-west American lyricism which melted like chocolate in the heat, just as rich and sweetly decadent.

"I came to see the fort, haven't been here since I was fifteen." The fearful memory crept back, and he crossed his arms tightly, glancing over his shoulder across the parade grounds. "You?"

"I'm taking in the sights while I have some free time. Do you have somewhere to go this evening? Someone to spend it with?"

Startled, he spun back around and couldn't believe the words actually fell from his gaping mouth. "You asking me out? I don't even know your name."

"I don't know yours either. Isn't it more exciting that way?" She replied slowly, fixing her eyes upon his. After licking her lower lip, she affected a little pout. "I would prefer spending my first night in the Caribbean with someone, rather than being alone in my hotel room. Want to join me?"

J.C.'s brain toggled between his very real fear of the fort and the sudden invitation that brought an odd fear of its own. He hadn't had sex in over a year, not that he didn't have opportunities, but he was selective. He liked long limbs and long hair, but a pretty face and body weren't enough to hold his interest. A woman needed to be assertive yet not overbearing, intelligent and quick-witted.

As he kept thinking, a hand swept over the two days of stubble on his face. "I'm being set up for the show, aren't I?" He glanced around for a video camera. The fort would cause some logistical issues but wouldn't be impossible. "You're too beautiful to be alone, and if you are, you could have any man you wanted. You wouldn't be looking at me. Did Luis, put you up to this?"

"This isn't a set up." Her eyes narrowed. "If I can have any man I want, I choose you. For tonight. So will you?"

"If I say no, you'll be offended." His mind sped up and then slowed down, trying to process while his body smoldered with edgy desire. "If I say yes, you will think I only want to end up in bed with you."

"There are more creative ways than having sex in bed, but we could start there and see where else we end up. One night only. My hotel is just a few blocks from here." She didn't move, and her expression didn't change, except those emerald eyes sparkled brightly with tempting inner luminescence. She licked her naturally red lips, feeling the smooth curves under her tongue.

"No strings, no tricks, no commitments, and no questions. First names only. You can call me Dahlia."

"Juan Carlos, ah, J.C." His eyes skimmed over her body, imagining the feminine possibilities of what he hadn't yet seen under the wispy dress. "Which hotel you staying at?"

"El Convento." Slowly and seductively, those full lips smiled.

"The old convent." He laughed, knowing it had to be a set up. He'd be on the next season of *Gotcha*. Luis and the other guys with the show decided to send him off in style. Jesus, it would mean his grandfather was in on it too. He hadn't expected anything so creative out of him. He hadn't even let on with a quirky smile or sideways glance as he walked away.

"Former convent. Why not help me add to the irony?" She pushed away from the wall and balanced on impossibly high heels. With the grace of a dancer, she reached out toward him, sliding her long fingers across his shoulders, allowing them to linger over the curves of his biceps.

"What the hell, I'm game." He smiled cheerfully. There wasn't any reason he shouldn't go along with the gag since the guys did a remarkable job on the set-up, and the woman they found fit his ideal to a tee. "Should be fun."

Slipping out of the fort's upper entrance, they cut across the elbow in the busy two-lane street. It had been years since he spent any time in Old San Juan and definitely never hung out at an ancient convent turned elegant hotel. Yet Old San Juan wasn't a big place. He knew where the hotel was basically, and she was definitely heading in that direction. "Are you going on a cruise?"

Her eyes flashed and then she touched a fingertip to her lips. "No questions, remember?"

Rush hour was backing up the narrow streets. Of course, the old city wasn't designed with accommodations for modern conveniences, so parked cars choked the roads and jumbled electrical lines hummed overhead. They walked down the cracked sidewalk of Calle Sol with a slew of other pedestrians, tourists and locals alike. An old woman with a few bags of groceries in a wire cart rattled down the slope of the hill, making them slow their easy yet deliberate strides.

J.C. and Dahlia walked side-by-side, close enough to touch, but they didn't. To a casual observer, they were just two adults walking down the sidewalk, not even a couple, which wasn't the normal M.O. of *Gotcha*, but the guys would have to be creative to fool him. He'd worked too many set-ups to fall for some hackney standard.

They reached the intersection, and the traffic light changed while cars still blocked the crosswalk. Horns blared as if that could clear the congestion of the overcrowded street. When the cars finally moved, the old lady hesitantly started across the street, but a delivery truck turned in front of her, cutting her off, causing a hasty retreat.

"Excuse me ma'am." Dahlia tapped the fragile shoulder. "Would you like some help?"

After receiving a quizzical look for an answer, J.C. translated the question into Spanish. She gave them an odd stare before nodding her head. He took the woman's arm, and Dahlia grabbed the two-wheeled cart. One of the worn tires fell into the cracked pavement, so she hefted the basket against her side and carried it across the street. The woman thanked them in Spanish and turned right, while they continued straight toward the inlet to the bay.

One of his last locations with *Gotcha* was New Orleans. He hadn't noticed before how much the two cities resembled each other. This section of San Juan was older than New Orleans but not by much in the overall scope of time. The aged buildings maximized every inch of the long blocks, built side-by-side, with iron balconies jutting overhead. Many were still residences, and like New Orleans, most of the buildings had street level businesses with apartments on the second or third floors. None of the buildings was taller than that, not like the high rises in the newer sections of the city.

Shade stretched lazily across the street, and the relief from the blistering sun was immediate but limited. Partially concealed in a doorway, a beggar with a one leg rattled change in a cup. Dahlia stopped and withdrew an old-fashioned coin purse. Squeezing the corners made the center gape, and she emptied the contents into his outstretched palm. J.C. watched in amazement as the pleasure spread across her features, enjoying the deed even more than the beggar. Definitely not the standard *Gotcha* scenario, the guys had really outdone themselves with the fine details of the set-up.

He thought of it like a game and expected the *Gotcha* moment around every corner. The closer they got to the hotel his heightened anticipation sizzled hotter than the blistering day. They stepped within the air conditioned lobby, and the chill had no effect on his residual heat, which was tangible, as real as the lamp on the table or the polished brass bell on the glossy front desk.

Although there were plenty of locations for hidden cameras, there was so sign of anyone. *Gotcha's* schemes ended in a crowded place, but there wasn't a soul in the lobby. Glancing over his shoulder, he stumbled over his own feet before following Dahlia into the old Spanish-styled corridor complete with sweeping arches. Without a word, she slipped the keycard into the slot and pushed open the door to a suite. The spacious sitting room had two distinct living areas. Closest to the door was a full-sized table with four chairs, and near the window, a comfortable sitting area overlooked sculpted gardens. The late afternoon tipped the flowers in brilliant shades of red, but she didn't seem to notice. The shapely woman walked through the open bedroom door and untied her wrapped dress. "There's some vodka and orange juice in the ice bucket if you want a drink."

He followed her gesture. "I'm good." He looked back in time to see the dress puddle at her feet. She stepped out of the silk and kicked off her heels. Strips of lace posing as a bra covered pert breasts and a matching swatch of black cloth swept between her legs.

"I have a feeling you will be." Those incredible eyes swept over him. "I'm clean, disease free, and plan to stay that way. Got something with you?"

His mouth went dry as all of the blood drained from his brain. This was real. Up until this moment, he didn't think it could be. With shaking fingers, he pulled his wallet out from his back pocket, sliding a condom from the inner fold. He held up the cellophane package and wiggled it between his fingers.

After wetting her lips, she used the same graceful stride, closing the distance until he could feel the heat radiating from her. She was more than muscular. Her body was carved and lean, yet soft feminine curves rounded all the right places. With shattering dexterity, she unbuttoned his cotton shirt. He closed his eyes, squeezing them for a second. Instead of her disappearing as he almost expected, she was staring at him, her eyes narrowing cautiously.

"You okay Slick?" She ran her hands over his chest, easing the shirt from his shoulders before tossing it casually aside. "The answer to your unspoken question is no."

"Question?" He couldn't even think never mind formulate a question.

"Oh, I imagine something like, 'Will this woman fuck my brains out and leave me for dead?'" Her fingers were strong with natural nails, and dear God, she knew how to use them, leaving molten heat in their path. Nimbly she unbuckled his plain leather belt. Before she even unzipped the loose cargo shorts, they were sliding down his legs. "Although I will fuck your brains out, I have no intention of killing you, beating you, robbing you, or leaving you maimed in any way. Your legs may be wobbly for a few hours, but I guarantee you'll fully recover."

"Why me?" Right after the words left his lips, shame heated his face, but he was already so flushed she wouldn't notice. But she would notice his erection, suddenly alert and arching away from his body.

"Do you like women?"

"Yes." His senses went into overdrive. She smelt intoxicatingly fresh, like the sea and sky.

"You like sex?"

"Yes, but it's been…" Dear God, he couldn't even remember the last time. It had to be before the *Ghost Lovers'* shoot at Fyvie Castle had left him in the hospital.

"Me too. When I noticed you staring at me, I got the idea we would both enjoy each other's company. Like I said, no attachments or expectations." She snatched the condom from his fingers and tore open the edge of the square envelope. Sliding the lubricated membrane between her fingers, she hummed before unrolling it down every long inch of his rigid length. "It couldn't have been that long for a good-looking man like you. Come-on Slick, it's like riding a bicycle. You never forget, and if you do, I'll be more than happy to remind you how it's done."

She turned toward the bed, and his breath caught. The scars looked like a burn, but the torn flesh had been scored into a lopsided grid. The wounds were still bright as if the rough damage had enough time to heal but not fade. "What happened to you?"

Her shoulders stiffened. "Most people have a few scars. I just happen to have more than others. You have a few too." She twisted quickly and slid her fingers over his abdomen, fingering the sensitive mark. "Stab wound. Small blade, probably a pocket knife. I'd say about a year ago."

"Year and a half, and the knife was a Scottish dirk." He sucked in his breath as her fingers artfully wound lower, around his hardened shaft, and stroked in long and easy movements. The inner hardness swelled even tighter inside the latex.

"If the scars bother you, you don't have to go through with this." She deliberately felt the weight of his package, rolling his hanging testicles lightly along the ridges of her fingers, just enough for them to jiggle. Her eyes drilled into his. "I'm not looking for a pity fuck."

"Look, I don't pity you, and I'm not disinterested." Shooting his hand to the back of her head, he captured her mouth with a kiss full of raw and turbulent emotion. All of the anxiety J.C. had built up during the day, all of the fear and guilt stormed out of him, tearing into the moment. The charge provoked him, and his body throbbed with fevered urgency. The desperation was new, challenging and astounding; he had wanted other women before, but never with this disturbing anxiety. He broke off the kiss, and with her taste still clinging to his lips, J.C. pushed her upon the bed roughly.

Laughing, she fell back against the pillows. "Now, that's the way I like it." Her lips were even darker red and had swollen from the contact, and she licked them slowly in an enticing invitation. One of those alluringly slow and feminine smiles slipped over that incredible mouth, and looking him dead in the eye, she unhooked her bra. Her breasts were small and perfectly rounded, topped with dark, tight nipples. Smoothly, she tossed the lace aside and then hooked her thumbs in the panties, arching them from her hips and down her legs. One at a time as if in slow motion, she spread her thighs, opening the delicate pink folds to the early stages of sunset shining through the window.

Her hands slipped over her body, slowly rounding her breasts. She stroked and kneaded the flesh, pulling on each nipple until they stood hard and tall. Sliding downward, her fingers caressed her ribs and then the concave slope of muscled abs. He held his breath as the motion continued, circling lower until finally her fingers dipped into those incredible hidden depths. They circled the tight opening, expanding the moist sheen across rich, pink flesh. She paused, and he moaned out loud. Embarrassment tinged his face, but she smiled that same temptress smile he had only ever seen on late night TV.

Removing the two damp fingers, she glided them over her clitoris, turning and thrusting in tight circles. Pleasure spread through her eyes and then unfolded across her face. While her fingers circled at a frantic pace, her back arched, spreading her thighs even more widely. Licking her lips, she sucked the lower one into her mouth and released a guttural moan. Tiny spasms visibly rippled between her legs as her fingers continued to squeeze. Her breath panted in ragged gasps. Shudders convulsed, causing her body to writhe upon the disheveled bed.

"Come on Slick, join in." Placing her fingers to her mouth, she licked her own flavor from them, gently suckling upon the tips one at a time.

J.C. realized he was just standing there, staring. The simple motion of her lips rounding her fingertips kept him mesmerized while wondering what it would feel like for her to taste him like that.

Removing her fingers with a final pucker, she pouted, "If I had wanted a party of one, I wouldn't have invited you."

With a final glance at the window for a camera's lens, he couldn't reflect on the how or why he was here when a sensual goddess was spread eagle on the bed. Keeping his eye on her prize, he climbed over scattered covers. In his quickly formulated plan, he meant to ease up one thigh and down the other, nipping and suckling his way, but one simple touch incinerated his thoughts. Jumping on top of her, he buried his face in her breasts. His mouth was desperate with impatience, sucking and nipping at the crests and rises. With each nibble, she writhed, enlivening the tussle between her flesh and his teeth and tongue. Each time his mouth tasted her he felt a new kind of desperation, one that only she could fulfill, the woman whom he could only possess for a single night.

Their ardor rose, engulfing the room with the heat and scent of sex while encasing their skin within a fine sheen of lust. Charging and changing, their ranging touches built just like a rising inferno, raging and jumping, pinching and consuming, continually escalating in intensity. Body parts entangled. Mouths fed. Strong fingers dug into his shoulders, kneading the muscles down his back, until she rounded his ass. Grabbing him firmly, she pulled him closer and raised her hips.

In a single thrust, J.C. dove into her heat. With other lovers, he would enter them slowly, allowing them to open and adjust to his size, working patiently into the fine petals of flesh. With this woman, the foreplay had prepared her, so wet and hot. In that initial stroke, she took his entire length, every last inch of him. She gasped with surprise, but it was a good sound, filled with sultry exaltation.

Withdrawing until just his tip stroked her, he entered again pounding into her heat. The pressure forced her deeper into the downy pillows. "Oh yeah Slick, give me all you got."

J.C. threw his head back, arching to bury himself to the hilt, and more than just warmth surrounded him. Her inner muscles grasped and tugged, binding around his shaft. Every time she was even wetter and hotter until the contact of their damp flesh slapped and sucked. The frantic sexual rhythm filled the room and reverberated off the walls, along with their breathy cries.

Thrusting harder and deeper than he ever had with any woman, he released his inhibitions, penetrating into his own psyche as readily as the woman below him. Fucking her as fast and hard as he could was his only concern. She was tightening around him, the muscles constricting the passage until he had to push harder. The tightness was like nothing he had experienced while inside a woman; it was more like a hand job, grasping tightly all the way along his shaft.

Impatient and gasping for air like a drowning man, he was poised to go over the edge until she magically slipped out from under him and mysteriously flipped him onto his back. Just as ruthlessly she clasped his wrists and dragged his arms over his head, pinning them against the headboard. Her shins pressed his thighs into the bed. Literally immobile, he was stunned. Ruthless desires begged for release, too close to the brink of orgasm to be stopped cold.

"What the fuck?" Never had J.C. hungered as he hungered now. Violent desire pulsed with needy heat, and each breath inhaled heady temptation still sizzling in the air.

The vixen smiled with devilish delight, clearly enjoying his torture. One breast came close enough to his mouth for his lips to catch. He tugged on the taut nipple, suckling hard lest he lose his hold. Arching her torso toward him, a deep and throaty moan curled out of her, feminine and feline, like a leopardess growling to attract a mate. Opening his mouth, he arched his tongue over the delicious curves. She didn't pull away, but shifted, taking a moment for the victor to assess the conquered. The green of her eyes had deepened into a luscious shade of jade, with a thin golden band highlighting the dilated pupils. For years to come, he would remember those glazed eyes and equate them with passion.

"Too nice a ride to rush." A silky smile slipped over her lips, and her syrupy voice rolled from that rosy mouth. "Ready for round two?"

In a long and agonizingly slow stroke, she slid onto his straining shaft, all the way down, consuming every inch of him. Her inner heat was blazing and still perfectly moist. As agile as a gymnast, she rose and lowered her body, constricting and loosening her inner muscles purposefully in an erotic wave.

Being too much of a control freak, he had never been into the bondage scene. Even while a lover was riding him, he used his hands to help lift her for the maximum effect. This woman didn't need any help. With almost no effort, she rose and dipped, gliding her body along his entire length. Still close to the edge, he craved the madness she was driving him toward, and his greed shocked him. His body demanded the mystery and suspense, especially the danger. Danger of what, he didn't know, but he felt it just the same. Being dominated had an edge, and trusting a stranger was never easy. This went way beyond trust.

While keeping the steady pace, her lithe body bent forward taking his nipple between her teeth. Reflexively, J.C. cried out, but she didn't stop. The temptress drew his nipples firmly into her mouth, scraping her teeth around the edges and feeling the rippling flesh respond. This time when he screamed, it was low and guttural, beyond salvation.

The tension between her legs mounted along with the rhythm. Leaning back, she focused on riding him in long and deliberate strokes. He felt her anger surging to the surface, and it drew more from his body than sheer lust ever could. The urgent excitement raged unleashed, fighting within them both. The battle wasn't one of the flesh. This was deeper, as if their immortal souls struggled among the surging power, fighting for domination, appealing for submission. The confusing combination merged within their union, fueling the challenge. The struggle was on her face, in her scent, while her body blazed in sensual fervor.

His hands were free now. J.C. couldn't remember when she let them go, but it didn't matter. Even without the bondage, she dominated him, racing him up to the slashing crest. Waiting, destroying the rhythm, she let his urgency ease back without culminating his orgasm, and with each trip, her eyes glowed with defiance.

While his blood fired even more violently through his veins, he finally roused his need for control. While distracted with her own orgasmic shudder, he reclaimed possession of their covetous battle. Throwing her to the side, he pinned her shoulders firmly against the edge of the downy bed.

Craving the madness, the turbulent hunger raged like a starving wolf ready to devour. He drove into her, and she matched him, bucking her body up to meet him in a frenzy of speed. Her long legs banded around his waist, and her fingers dug into his hips, holding on, gripping deeper and harder, until a shattering moan screamed from her soul. The sound rang in his ears triggering the white hot essence to surge from his body. The violent and turbulent energy drained until he shuddered final ragged groans. Still gripping her shoulders, he struggled to catch his breath. Nothing in his life had prepared him for this moment. None of J.C.'s fantasies had ever come close.

CHAPTER 4

Sinking into the glorious satisfaction, Fara allowed all of the tension to flow out of her body like melting wax. She didn't move, not wanting him to leave her, not wanting this moment to be over. When she first saw him, something stirred, signaling her need, but never in Fara's wildest imagination had she expected such physical delight.

J.C. shifted, and she made a small sound of protest but didn't reach out. She continued to stare at the ceiling while his weight spread out on the bed beside her, and a contented moan slipped into the rapidly fading twilight. She felt the heat of his body radiating from the culminated pleasure.

She hadn't thought about the after, but now the moment was upon her, and she didn't know if she could just walk away.

"Dahlia?"

With an unuttered sigh, she rocked to her side. Even though she told herself she was a free and unattached woman, a smidgen of guilt swept through her. It left nearly as quickly as it came, but even though fleeting, left its mark, which he must had seen skim across her features.

His eyes were wide and expectant. "I didn't disappoint you, did I?"

She chuckled with what limited energy remained. "After what we just shared, I'm surprised you have to ask. Oh Slick, you were more than I expected, and just what I needed." She gave him a quick smile. "I'm going to have to eat something and regain my strength."

"How about having dinner with me at the Blue Parrot? It's just a few blocks. I don't know if I can walk that far right now, but I could drive-" The color drained from his face. His features tightened as he glanced at his watch. "Shit!"

He leapt off the edge of the bed. Like a caged animal, he paced the room twice, and with each turn, glanced into the darkness consuming the courtyard. "Damn it, my car is in the employee lot back at the fort."

"And it's closed now?"

"Closes before dark. Fuck!" His breath came shallow and quick, and a shaky hand swept through his hair, grabbing the thick waves by the roots. Frantically, he snagged his shorts off the floor and started to dress.

She propped herself onto an elbow, poised to jump off the bed if necessary. "Was that ranger really your grandfather?"

His lips drew into a tight line. "Yeah."

"Why don't you give him a call? He has an access card, doesn't he?" She resisted the urge to try to soothe his discomfort. Whatever he feared was definitely at the fort and in the night. "He could use it to get your car out."

"No!" The rugged growth of beard provided a stark contrast, his face so very pale under the dark stubble. The despised horror returned to his eyes, violently livid. "He can't go in there, not at night. It's too- Fuck!" In a swirling sweep, he grabbed the tourist magazine from the small table and threw it across the room.

"Okay." Fara knew better than to press. "What if we order room service? We can regain our strength. Have a few drinks. I don't know if we can top this, but I'm willing to try. What do you think, Slick?"

His expression tightened into a frown. "I think you have to quit calling me Slick. My name is Juan Carlos, or don't you care what my name is? I'm just another man you've fucked."

His comment stung deeper than she was willing to admit. She slipped over the edge of the bed and picked up her dress, sliding it over her vulnerability. "I didn't force you to come with me, and despite what you think, this is the first time I've done something like this."

"So I was your fucking Guinea pig, literally."

Her thin resolve cracked. "Why is it when a woman takes the initiative, a man assumes she's a slut?"

"You certainly fuck like one."

"Okay fine, Juan Carlos. I don't know what's wrong, and I don't care. Thanks for the entertainment. There's the door." She jabbed her index finger to the left. "Get out." She remained poised but motionless as he stormed past her and out of her room.

The violent ending to her return to sexual activity stirred too many dormant emotions Fara didn't want to acknowledge. She had sex before to fill an inner hunger, and with Jason, making love brought with it a gentle essence to the physical act. What she experienced today was neither. Compelling and stormy, the sex fed upon anger and trepidation from them both. When she first saw J.C., something had connected. Something she would never have again, which at this point wasn't a bad thing, yet was still pathetic.

She had a new job to start in the morning and should get more than just a few hours of sleep. But she was accustomed to getting by on just a few hours for far too long, and it felt strange not sleeping in shifts, taking turns with her crew to maintain a constant vigil. With the time difference, live reports for the evening news occurred at about dawn after a long night of rocket fire. Kabul, Qandahar, Pnajab, Jalalabad, Baghran, unlike other war zones she covered for CCN, each city in Afghanistan held distinct memories, separating the sights and sounds from the constant wind and harsh desolation. The severity of the Afghanis' austere existence added to the inhospitable environment, yet they survived and fought for their way of life with undying and unforgiving severity.

Her command of several Arabic dialects allowed her to pass unnoticed to gather information which was valuable to more than just the news. She had the correct skin tone, and once covered head to toe with a burqa, she was almost indistinguishable from the Islamic women, except for her eyes. Fortunately, Fara's green ones weren't immediately noticeable, especially once humbly cast to the ground.

When she had touched the wall of the ancient fort, the heat reminded her of the desert cities where pise held the temperature like the fort's stones. During the summer, there never was sanctuary from the damned heat. Even if her crew was lucky enough to find a room with A.C., the measly unit could chill the air, but the walls would only begin to cool in time for dawn to begin the heating process all over again. She pressed her hand to the exterior hotel wall, and a sad smile creased her lips. Despite the fact she was halfway around the world, it was the same, and she was just as alone.

After dressing in jeans and a loose cotton shirt, Fara decided to wander around Old San Juan, eat some dinner, and maybe do some window shopping. Two cruise ships were in port. She was good at getting lost in the crowd, nameless and faceless, one of many, or at least she had been. The flesh on her back crawled as the vile memory tried to take root, but she forced it back into the recesses of her former life.

Each locale had its own personality, and Old San Juan was no exception. The air was thick and pungent, carrying the decaying scents of an old city. Uneven shadows stalked hidden doorways. An armed guard, dressed in black lurked in a dark corner with an AK47 strapped around his shoulders. Fara would have carried a MP5, which had a selection of single or three-round bursts and was more selective in crowds, picking off the targets while lessening the chance of wholesale slaughter, with an option of a fully automatic thirty-two round spray if the situation deteriorated.

None of the tourists seemed to notice of the man with the gun. As if she belonged, she wandered with the nameless others milling from store to store, but she had no home to shop for, no family to bring gifts to. Her few possessions were in North Carolina, locked behind a steel door in a mini storage unit. Just like while in the military, she paid for a year in advance, just in case she was out of pocket when the monthly charge came due. With her new job, she didn't know where she would be, and she needed that, especially now.

She walked back onto the street. Hearing music she headed toward the sound, but before the end of the block, a narrow corridor caught her eye. Instinctively, she cast an experienced glance at the potential points of a concealed attack and then sauntered casually through the doorway. The tiled hall was dimly lit, not that there weren't sufficient lamps affixed high up on the walls, but they were covered in yellowed haze, trapping most of the light inside of smoky glass. Hazy incense drifted, clouding what light seeped through with ghostly waves, and pressed the lingering sewer scent back toward the gutter.

Fara paused in the first open doorway and then stepped up a few steps to go inside the shop. The clothing was stylish, made of soft cotton fabrics. She fingered the dress on the mannequin in a gorgeous shade of violet.

"That would look beautiful on you." The middle-aged woman spoke English easily. "It needs someone with a lithe figure."

"I don't care for halter tops. Do you have something with a back and short sleeves? Preferably in this same color and fabric."

The woman bustled to the other racks. In her sensitive fingers, Fara fingered the flowing scarf-point hem while trying to decide if she should wear a suit to the morning meeting or get something more temperature appropriate. She'd met Robert Hartz only once when she interviewed at his Miami office. He hadn't worn a suit then, and she doubted the executive producer would be wearing one tomorrow. She was supposed to meet her co-worker who had been with *Ghost Lovers* for some time. She didn't remember his name. More than likely Rob never mentioned it, for she had a phenomenal memory.

The woman came back with a top and skirt in the same violet, but the fabric had a slightly different pattern. Standing in front of the mirror, Fara held the shirt up to her chest. The classic princess line would be flattering. The skirt had an elastic waist and would definitely fit.

In a slightly better mood from indulging in shopping therapy, Fara continued down the tiled hall. The light at the end of the passage was oddly compelling, jumping, and golden. On a whim, she walked into the tiny store. The glowing light emanated from an ancient lamp, something right out of a museum. The warm radiance glittered brightly upon several polished coins left on the counter, dating back to the 16th Century. Their condition was immaculate, as if they had been pulled out of circulation centuries ago. Fara had inherited her dad's love of coins. The thought brought the loneliness back and sanded the bright edge off of her refreshed mood.

The display cases formed a boxy U and barely provided enough room to turn around in the tight space. In the very last case, several delicate pieces of jewelry caught her eye, definitely old, estate sale types. Although the ivory broaches were beautiful, they weren't Fara's style. She laughed quietly, not knowing if she had a style in jewelry. The only ring she had ever worn had belonged to Jason's grandmother and was one of the items her ex-mother-in-law demanded along with Jason's personal effects. Each stage of her life ended up kneeling in front of a cardboard alter and the scent of packing tape.

"Ah Dios, chica, no te escuche." An ancient man hobbled from a back room. "Que querías?"

Although Fara spoke Spanish, she answered in English, "You have some beautiful coins."

The man's shining gray eyes widened. "Ah, you like to see?"

"No, not really. I enjoy looking. I can't afford to buy such lovely antiques."

His eyes glassed over while he stared at her face.

At first, she thought he didn't understand her and would have to start speaking in Spanish after all.

"I make good deal. I know what needs you. Match your eyes." At the end of the case in the bottom back corner, he removed a velvet tray. In one of the small squares was a delicate emerald ring. Even before the old man turned up the flame in the old-fashioned oil lamp, the emerald glittered and glowed, radiating an inner luminescence. With bent fingers, he scooped it up and held it out to Fara.

The stone was a traditional cut with a polished flat top and several bevels around the edges. Four gold prongs secured the gem to the delicate gold band with two small linked hearts on either side. Arching around the top and bottom were two sets of five diamonds, offset slightly, supporting the curvature of the oval stone. The lime green gem had a singular irregularity, a tiny fissure within the emerald. Realistically since it didn't go all the way through, the fracture had to have been there when the jeweler originally cut the stone.

"There's a crack." Leaning against the edge of the aged counter, she held the ring up to the lamp, and her eyes narrowed, examining the inside of the stone. It wasn't really a crack. Blemish didn't adequately describe it either. Something seemed to be trapped within the gem, like an insect in amber. She couldn't quite make it out yet seemed hauntingly familiar and enigmatically compelling.

The tiny Puerto Rican man squinted and then retrieved an ancient jeweler's glass. Just like the coins, the old brass shone with care. He removed the ring from Fara's outstretched palm and carefully examined the stone. "Old stones have character; that how you tell real from fake. Fakes no have character." The bent fingers put it back in the young woman's palm. "This ring wants you."

Catching herself, she decided not to correct his grammar and took the ring from him. "How old is it?"

"Let me call the sister." Like a Billy Chrystal caricature, he waddled from the room. Her fingers closed around the ring still in her palm, amazed such trusting people still existed in this age.

A few moments later, a woman of indeterminate years emerged. Her hair was pure white and hung to her shoulders in glossy waves, making her Hispanic complexion even more dramatic, yet very few lines creased the pleasant face. With some brightly colored silk scarves, she would have epitomized the Hollywood cliché of a gypsy fortuneteller. "You are making a wise purchase, Miss. This is a special stone cut right here on the island hundreds of years ago. The raw gem made another ring; the male match was lost. Love lost with this single reminder that it did exist and endured over time. That's what you see in the stone."

Love lost, so sad and perfectly befitting. Fara nodded and turned it over again and again in her palm. Warmth and power radiated into her, lulling her into wanting the ring more than anything she ever wanted in her life.

"You should try it on." The woman held her breath in anticipation.

"Oh I can't," she extended the ring toward the clerk. "I was just looking."

The glow from the lamp reflected in the ageless eyes. "I know you want to."

Every finger on Fara's right hand had been broken twice, and even though they healed well the second time, the knuckles were larger on her right hand. The delicate ring wouldn't fit on any of them, even the pinky was clearly too large.

"Here, allow me," the woman took Fara's left hand and slid it down onto the finger which had worn Jason's diamond. "I knew it would fit perfectly, like it was made for you."

As soon as the emerald encountered her flesh, warmth and love radiated into Fara's body, not a real heat, but the sizzle of energy and power filled the void she stubbornly refused to acknowledge. "How much is it?"

The woman smiled, showing off a perfect set of teeth, especially for someone her age. "Two hundred."

"One fifty," Fara replied quickly.

The woman stared her in the eyes. "I didn't notice until now the stone," she paused, "matches your eyes. Because of that I'll let you have it for one seventy-five."

The sensation emanating from the ring was overtaking Fara's judgment, driving her to make a rare, impetuous decision. "Alright, one seventy-five." She went to slide it from her finger, but the woman stalled the process with her cool hands.

"This ring needs you, and you need the ring. The match is made. Don't take it off."

CHAPTER 5

When J.C. rushed out of El Convento, he didn't know where he was going or even why he was going. The moment he slammed Dahlia's door behind him, his mistake slammed into him just as harshly. There wasn't any going back, especially not after being a raving lunatic.

"J.C.," his grandfather approached with two tumblers that looked like cola but smelt strongly of rum. "Want to talk?"

"It won't change anything, Abuelo. I'm resigned to my fate in this world, and I prefer not to talk about it."

"Life sometimes has to get harder before it gets easier, but no matter what it is, talking relieves the soul." Eduardo handed him a glass that was already slippery with condensation from the clinging heat.

J.C. drank the cool sweetness. Puerto Rican rum was just too smooth, and this was the good stuff. Although his grandparents lived in a modest home, they spent money on the comforts in life. "I need to apologize for something that happened a long time ago. I wanted to do it this afternoon, and I ... well I got sidetracked."

"With that beautiful woman?" Eduardo's voice always had a soothing quality, smoothly flowing like an endless river.

"Yeah," his mind shifted into the sound and lost what he was going to say. He didn't want to think about her but couldn't help it while his body hummed with sexual satiation. Her touch was still on his skin, her scent still in his mind. Inadvertently, his tongue brushed over his lips where he could still taste her.

"I don't quite know how she could have got up the wall like that." His grandfather leaned back in the wooden chair on the tiny patio. Even though it was nearly ten, he still wore his tan ranger uniform.

J.C. closed his eyes, remembering the vision of the woman who would now haunt him just as readily as the demon, and both were associated with the damned fort. "She kicked off her shoes and climbed, scrambled up like a squirrel."

"Can't blame your interest, Nieto. Did you take her for dinner and then she went back to the cruise ship?"

"Not exactly." He groaned before draining his glass. He'd just had the most incredible sexual experience of his life and felt miserable. "I can't believe I'm talking about my sex life with you."

His grandfather started chuckling. "I might be old but I'm not stupid. That woman wanted you, and you wanted her."

"Yeah, Abuelo, you're right; you're not stupid."

The old man broke into an all-out guffaw which rumbled in his chest, and with a quick glance back toward the house, he took a cigarette from his upper pocket. The end flared bright red against the darkness. "Regardless how old you are, you'll never figure them out, so a wise man quits trying and goes with the flow."

"I'm not a wise man. Actually, I'm about as stupid as they come." J.C. sank into the chair, mirroring his father's father. "Did you ever have a moment when you said the absolutely worse thing in the worst way?"

"Every man has at one time or another. If you really want this woman, go after her, charm her until you seduce her."

"There's no fixing this one." He stared at the ice cubes and felt the first glorious wave of the rum begin to dull the inner pain. "She's gone."

"Then it wasn't meant to be." A weathered hand reached across the small plastic table and patted the younger one.

"You're probably right but doesn't feel that way."

"Although this one inflamed your desire, she wasn't a keeper, Nieto. You need to find a nice Taíno girl. About time to think about settling down, raising a family, finding a mate to be by your side for all eternity."

J.C. set the tumbler on the table, needing to change the subject. "Thanks for picking me up and letting me stay the night. In the morning, I have brunch with Rob and the new producer for the show. She's some big time war correspondent who quit after being taken hostage. I don't know why she settled on *Ghost Lovers*."

"Why did you? After Alex stabbed you, I thought it was over." His voice grew louder to talk over the Coqui's chirping.

"Me too. But with the publicity from the Fyvie episode, *Ghost Lovers* reruns have rocketed in the ratings. I was part of that, and now Rob's offered me a bigger role and a huge raise. I can't say no. This is my shot and a hell of a lot better than operating a camera for *Gotcha*. I hated hiding in hedges or jumping out from behind doors."

"Traveling the world to historic locations on the company's dime isn't a bad way to make a living, Nieto. You ever seen a ghost?"

"Yeah, which brings me back to why I needed to see you today. Fifteen years ago, I took the keycard out of your wallet and snuck into the fort." Instead of feeling better, the confession churned inside of him, insisting he let the rest of it out like a sickness unsettling his stomach. "I saw something. Not just me, Andres was there too. We both saw it. Abuelo, I swear it was a demon or maybe even the devil himself. That's why I couldn't go back and get my car tonight. It knows I've come back."

The pause grew as both men stared out into the hazy sky. The little house sat behind Rio Hondo Mall, and the parking lot's sickly orange glow was stronger than any stars. The only celestial body visible from the city was the moon, which hadn't risen. There was just nothing but hazy orange blankness.

Finally, Eduardo cleared his throat. "Is that why you took off to New York?"

"Yeah, but no matter where I go, the nightmares follow."

"An experience like that stains the soul, and once it has touched you, there's no cleaning it off. It's there for all eternity." Eduardo took a long drink and settled back into his chair. "Spirits of the dead haunt this world of that I have no doubt."

CHAPTER 6

Holding the cup of coffee in both hands, Robert Hartz absently gazed across the ocean from the balcony of his penthouse suite. Stretching one leg at a time, he balanced the heels of his glossy wingtip shoes on the railing. He had come a long way for a punk kid from Detroit. Four days after Rob's eleventh birthday, his dad got fifteen years for larceny, and Rob's mom took off. She always claimed she'd come back for him once she got settled, but then the phone calls were fewer until he never heard from her again. Somewhere deeply hidden in his heart, he expected her to come find him, but as the years slipped by, hope faded until it was just a vague reminder of what had been. Overall, it probably saved his life.

His mom had dumped him and two cardboard boxes onto the doorstep of his grandmother's house in the thriving metropolis of Ypsilanti. The middle-aged woman didn't seem too surprised and adjusted her regular schedule to ensure Rob had a decent upbringing. He had to go to school every day, and on Wednesdays, the church bus picked him up in front of Estabrook Elementary and took him to Catechism class at St. John's.

Rob put up with the good intentions because every Saturday afternoon, his grandmother would go play bridge and ditch him at the movies. There was only one theater in Ypsi, next to the K-Mart on Washtenaw Avenue. The theater was huge with rows upon rows of seats and a balcony that stunk of sweet bubble gum and stale popcorn. Saturday afternoon matinees played one film after another, and they hooked him. Hollywood was the business for him, and with a direction, he made good. Well, maybe not feature length films, but he had a name in the business. *Ghost Lovers* pushed him to the top, and he wasn't about to let it turn into a ghost itself.

"Come-on baby, come back to bed." The smooth, feminine voice eased through the thin opening in the sliding glass door, breezy as smoke floating across water. "I'll make it worth your while."

An all-out grin covered his face, but he didn't let her see it. He was right to bring Carolyn with him, definitely better than sleeping alone. "Got to work today, doll. Going downstairs in ten. Not enough time to enjoy a beauty like you." The sliding glass door scooted open, and a blast of air conditioning escaped.

Just like the cool air, the blond slid into his lap. "You work too much."

"Yeah doll, I like it that way." He slipped his hands over the satin of the teddy he bought her yesterday. "I think you like it too. If I didn't work, I couldn't buy you all those nice presents, now could I? Anyway, you talked me out of meeting with my producers yesterday. Every day is money, and I can't push it back again. The faster they get started, the sooner the dough starts rolling, and *Ghost Lovers* is primed for the top."

"Alright sugar," she pressed her ample breasts against his cheek, and the delicate scent of Chanel drifted. "I understand."

He mumbled into the soft flesh. "I thought you would."

Exactly ten minutes later, he walked through the hotel lobby, his polished shoes resounded off from the equally polished floor. He wished his grandmother could see him now, rich, successful, respected. People opened doors for him, rather than having to open them on his own. Filled with buoyant confidence, he stopped at the edge of the outdoor dining area. The cultivated space overlooked the pools, designed within lush gardens to enhance the tropical paradise.

J.C. rose from the table near the balcony with a great view of two lovely ladies out for an early tan. "Good to see you, Rob. How was the flight?"

"Smooth as the scotch."

J.C. laughed easily. "Between you or Lily, I don't know drinks the most scotch."

"Heard from Lady Sloan lately?"

"Yeah, she called on Christmas day. They decided to stay in Scotland this year." J.C. settled back into his chair with a glass of orange juice in hand. "She's expecting again, another boy in June."

Before he could control it, his face smirked. "When I saw her in November, she didn't mention it."

"You know Lily. She keeps her cards close until she's ready to play her hand; although, she did tell me how you tried to get her back."

"The fan mail for Lord Sloan was so hot I had to try, but he wouldn't budge. It's hard to influence someone who has everything he wants." Savoring the scent, he took a swallow of the fresh coffee, dark and rich, just how he liked it. Oh yeah, this was the life. Maybe not everything he wanted, but pretty damned close.

J.C. saluted him with the juice. "I'm glad they turned you down, so I could have my turn at bat."

"You've got talent. Let's see how you use it. Your co-producer got skills too. Straight out of high school, she went into the military. Don't remember which branch, but she studied linguistics, can speak damn near every language on the planet. Then, she started working for CCN. Don't know how she managed that jump, and when I asked, her references clammed up, like after the Army she turned into a spy or something. You know how other countries are always accusing the media as being spies; well her last gig in Afghanistan got the better of her. Taliban abducted her straight out of the market in broad daylight, and they questioned her the Taliban way. Special ops rescued her, and she ended up marrying the guy who carried her out. For the past six months, she's been sitting stateside going stir crazy while he finishes his last tour of duty."

"She's not going to bolt once he gets out, is she?"

"Don't think so. She thrives on action, has to be on the move. You can tell just looking at her. She's got an inner need, like an adrenaline junkie." He liked how her skills stacked up with J.C.'s. "She's real good in front of the camera; makes you feel like she's talkin' straight to you. We weren't hitting the male audience demographic, so she's the key to expanding our market share. Has an incredible voice, the kind who would make a fortune on the phone late night, if you know what I mean." He thought better of what he considered a compliment because she might not take it that way. "Don't you dare tell her that though. From what I heard, she could break just about every bone in your body in less than ten seconds, and I believe it. This one is tough, can protect herself."

"Yeah boss, that's up there with a great personality and strong work ethic." J.C. glanced at the bathing beauties who just turned over onto their stomachs and untied the strings to their bikini tops to expose their smooth backs to the brilliant sun, and the sight triggered thoughts of Dahlia. He'd never find out what had happened to her. "What's Rambo's name?"

"Fara Trotter."

While both men were entranced with the nearly naked women, neither saw Fara approach from behind them. "Are you discussing me?"

They turned around, and Rob saw Fara's face flush when her gaze shot to J.C. She tried to cover it, but recognition had been there just the same. If he knew anything about people, these two had met, and his mind ran wild with speculation as to the where and how while he pressed his palm against hers in a steady handshake. "Fara, good to see you. Let me introduce you to J.C. Calderon, your co-producer."

Fara leaned forward taking J.C.'s outstretched hand. "Hello."

"Hello Fara." His voice was more than tense, as if his throat was forged steel. "It's good to see you again."

Rob glanced back and forth. Both of their faces were stern, breath elevated, glaring eyes bordering on the edge of hostility. Whatever was going on, the feeling was mutual. "You've met?"

J.C. took a quick breath and let it out slowly. "We were on the same tour through the fort. Strange how life circles back around at times."

"Like a Greek tragedy." Instead of sliding into the available chair, her eyes landed on the buffet. "Mind if I grab a plate? Smells delicious."

Rob waved absently. Something had happened between them, something personal. He groaned, desperately hoping the issues wouldn't spill over into the show. He couldn't afford any more delays.

CHAPTER 7

J.C. pushed away from the table while seething at his own gullibility. All last night he couldn't sleep thinking about how he reacted irrationally and hurt her feelings. The married bitch used him.

"What are you doing here?" Fara hissed as he stepped close enough not to be overheard.

"My job. Seems like you and I are going to be working together for awhile. Hope your husband won't mind." He whispered through gritted teeth. "Even if you have one of those don't ask, don't tell marriages, I don't do married women."

"I'm not married." She spat back. "This isn't the time or place to discuss personal details. Honestly, I never wanted to see you again."

His heart strained. All last night he wished for a way to run into her again. The scenarios were fanciful. Somewhere he would be setting up a shot in a foreign land, and she would walk by and notice him. They would laugh about the stupid way he overreacted about leaving his car at the fort. But his growing anger continued to spike and pushed all of those syrupy daydreams from his mind. "Likewise."

Defiantly, she set her feet shoulder length apart, pure military. The eyes he once thought of as inviting and sensual were cold as stone. "I'm not giving up this opportunity."

"Neither am I." Even though her gaze was heartless, he still remembered how she had looked at him last night, how he had felt with her, and hated himself for it. "I have more right to remain with *Ghost Lovers* than you. You're the one who has to leave."

"Leave? What the hell? You're under contract, both of you." Rob roared from behind them, and they both spun around. "Look, I don't know what's going on, and I don't give a damn.

We're going to discuss the details for your first show, set out the timeline and deliverables, and then you two are going out that door to make it happen. Together. I'm giving you fifteen minutes to settle whatever the hell it is, and when I get back, we're getting down to work." Other than his footfalls snapping across the tile, there was silence.

"Shit!" J.C. wanted to throw the plate across the gardens like a discus, while he battled internally against his lingering need for her and the disturbing fact she belonged to another man. "Get some breakfast and sit down. Like he said, we're going to have to find a way to make this work."

Without the slow and seductive flair she employed yesterday, Fara tossed the hair off her shoulder and then stormed back to the table. Her filmy lavender dress flowed with the long strides. With a lady-like flair, she tucked the back edge of the skirt before sitting down at the table. When he finally sat across from her, she stared at him but didn't say a word.

"I'm not the villain here. After leaving last night, I thought I was. I berated myself for losing control and ... well for running out like that, but now, this ... this changes everything." He tried to keep his voice in check but felt it rising along with his resentment. "Why didn't you tell me you're married? Or are you going to deny it again? Rob may leave off a lot of details, but he was pretty damned sure you had a husband, had a story to go with it and everything."

"I had a husband." Her breathing hissed through clenched teeth.

He reached for his glass of juice and brought it to his lips but couldn't drink. "Rob said he saved your life in Afghanistan."

"What else did Rob say?" Finally, she glanced at him with those incredibly green eyes which were blazing with fury and softly wilted, a disturbing and confusing combination. He had trouble maintaining his shield of anger while she was looking at him like that.

"You were military, then worked for CCN. Taliban abducted you." He remembered the scars on her back and nearly winced. "Special-ops saved you, and you married your savior. Have anything you want to add?"

She pushed the plate away with clenched fists. "Nope, pretty much sums it up."

He choked out the words he had to say but didn't want to know. "Tell me about your husband."

"Last night, we agreed to no questions asked." Her lips tightened into a pale red line.

"It's not last night any longer." His hands were starting to shake, so he pushed his palms onto the table and leaned forward, staring her down. "You married this guy six months ago, but now you're not married."

As she inhaled, her entire expression hardened. "That's right."

"Only a heartless bitch divorces her husband while he's serving overseas." He let his voice carry, not giving a damn if everyone on the veranda heard what a bitch Fara Trotter was.

"I didn't divorce him." She stared him straight on, and visible pain expanded through the corners of her eyes to her drawn brow and pursed lips.

"Well, that only leaves…" He broke off his ranting and wanted to melt under the table but managed to find the chair as his legs gave way.

"Leaves one option, a very permanent one." Fara looked down at the table and pulled her cup of coffee closer, staring into the dark liquid. "I buried Jason in Arlington National Cemetery. If you feel the need to verify, his full name was Jason Derrimore Trotter. And just to put your childishness behind us, my full name is Faradahl. My parents called me Dahlia. I didn't lie to you."

"Shit!" He tossed his head back and wished he could evaporate. "Now I'm the bad guy again."

"You're an insane asshole, but that doesn't change the fact we're under contract. I've learned how to work with people I don't like. We focus on our assignment, not each other." She slid a piece of bacon off her plate and looked at it with surprise. "Now that the inquisition is over, I'm hungry and going to get an egg-white omelet. When I get back, we'll behave as co-workers, nothing more, nothing less."

Before Fara returned to the table, Rob had rejoined him. For the rest of their meeting, J.C. couldn't get past the look of pain creasing her face. She was a fucking widow who had been brutally tortured, and he brought up both, callously wanting to hurt her. He really was an asshole, and the revelation tugged at his inner sense of humanity.

Rob bluntly issued commandments regarding preproduction planning, timeline, and what he called the deliverables, which ultimately equaled forty-two minutes of pseudo-erotic programming. J.C. definitely knew he had an advantage since he understood the production values and wanted to get down to the specific assignment, while Fara asked questions at every turn regarding resources, policies, applications, and equipment, like she wanted a manual with step-by-step instructions.

He was now saddled with a recent widow who hated him and would follow every regulation and instruction to the letter. If Rob had told her to use 1.5 pieces of toilet paper to wipe her ass, Fara would measure before tearing the squares from the roll. J.C. knew it was an absurd example, but at least it made him smile.

CHAPTER 8

Focusing on the specifics, Fara listened actively, absorbing the field directions. At times Rob veered off onto a nonessential tangent, so she processed, organized, and categorized the information in her notebook. Producing a television program was more complicated than shooting footage for the news, and she wanted to ensure she had the requisites because she definitely didn't want to ask her co-worker any questions. The more she could limit her involvement with that crazy man the better.

"Alright boss," she shot a cutting stare at J.C. when he groaned. "I've got it. What's the first assignment?"

Rob smiled. "Carolyn and I went on a ghost tour last night and heard a local story about a girl who committed suicide because her lover shipwrecked. I've already researched, and you won't find any info on the Internet so don't waste your time. Not much is known about her other than she was the niece of some official, and he covered up the whole incident, which leaves the show wide open. I want this show hot. I want her to be this poor little rich girl, far away from home while visiting her uncle in Puerto Rico. A handsome sailor seduces her, takes her virginity, and leaves her. When she hears his ship foundered, she launches herself off the fort. You have full license, so make up the rest."

J.C. paled, rubbing his face before speaking. "You're talking about the Pink Lady at Fort San Cristobal."

"Yeah, that's the one." Rob did a double take. "That's right. I forgot you're from around here. That's great, maybe you can fill in the details, but remember has to be hot and sultry."

Fara knew they just couldn't waltz into a U.S. government installation and set up equipment. "I'm sure there's an approval process through the U.S. National Park Service."

"I'm a step ahead, doll." Rob handed her a packet of documents. "Permits and access card is in there. You only have one card, so keep good tabs on it. You have full access to the fort, both day and night."

"What?!" J.C. jumped out of his chair, rattling the dishes and nearly tumbling the glasses. "You can't possibly expect night scenes inside the fort."

"Why not? Some ghost shows only shoot at night." Rob finally looked at J.C. "You sick or something? You look like you're going to hurl."

"I'm not taking a crew into the fort at night. It's not safe."

"What, you afraid of the ghosts? Jesus Christ man!" Rob stared. "Fyvie Castle was an isolated incident, nothing more, and you told me you were over it. Tell me now if you can't handle it, and I'll find someone else. I hired you because you know *Ghost Lovers* as well as Lily did, but if you can't handle being in a scary place at night, you're fired."

"I'll watch out for the crew, make sure they stay safe." Fara's comment visibly surprised both men.

"I bet you will." Rob's grin smirked across his lips.

She didn't have much time to process before Rob suddenly departed, so methodically flipping back in her pad, she had noted to secure the location, which he had assigned and arranged access. Now, she needed to define the characters and scenes, and after that write the script.

"What the hell are you doing?" J.C.'s contempt hung over him like a black shroud. "Are you going to tell me you never produced a television show before?"

"I'm not going to tell you any such thing." One of her natural abilities skills was avoiding the truth, and she kept it honed. "Sounds like your job's in jeopardy, not mine, so get off my ass."

"Alright then, come-on. We're a team, remember?" He walked a few steps and waited, blowing out a huff before turning around. "We don't have much to go on, but there are some people who know more than I do about the legend. Even though the details aren't plastered on the Internet, we have to stick to the historic timeline because viewers love to point out a mistake, something even as minor as it was September 1619, not August 1619, and once they start picking it apart, Rob starts picking it apart. Lily was a real history buff and wanted to be as accurate as possible."

"I'm not Lily." Fara hissed, hating to be in the shadow of anyone, especially a woman who had everything she had ever wanted; even worse, Lily had everything Fara wanted.

"Don't I know it!" He crossed his arms contemptuously. "If you were, I'd be chasing after you to catch up." With that, he walked briskly to the glass door, displaying the same economical ease of motion she had noticed while walking with him in Old San Juan. His body was finely tuned, and he knew how to use it, which irritated her even more.

Tipping her head back, she stared up at the cloudless sky, trying to convince herself to cut her losses and seek a different job, but this was all she had at the moment and wouldn't let some insane bastard get in her way. Gulping in a deep breath, she steadied her mind and rose as if she had all the time and patience in the world.

After awhile one hotel looked like another, but this locale was memorable. Reminiscent of a 1920's gangster movie, small round tables filled the sunken bar area made of warmly-colored wood, which had a considerable number of patrons for late morning. Some drank coffee. Others were hitting the alcohol early. If she had been here on vacation, she would have relaxed in one of the chairs next to the wall and enjoyed watching the activities. Vicariously, she enjoyed the experiences of others, which is what had initially attracted her to the news, but it turned out to be unlike anything she had imagined. She recorded death of the guilty and innocent alike and the despair of the survivors for the rest of the world to experience vicariously, but she had to live it.

Her days spent interrogating apprehended Taliban still haunted her; even though, a lot of life had passed since then. Interrogation was nothing like the movies depicted. Most of the rooms were brightly lit and small, barely large enough to walk around an adjustable metal gurney, similar to a medical examiner's table. One thing they did have in common was a drain in the center of the concrete floor. The human body held so much blood.

Fara hated when those memories bubbled up, usually at the worst fucking time. She wondered why now, but there never was an answer. The shrink told her certain stimuli triggered the reaction. J.C. had made her angry enough to slip back into that world, but when she was the interrogator, she was an ice queen. Nothing got through.

Leaning against a chair inside the comfortable lobby, she waited close enough to watch J.C. at the valet stand, yet was far enough away for him to be wondering whether she would come with him. Although she didn't want to admit it, he was right. They needed as much information as possible to create an accurate outline. She may not have produced television shows or be a history aficionado, like the unstained Lily, but Fara did know accuracy and understood why it was important. She also knew the importance of teamwork, and whether or not she liked J.C. was a moot point. They would work together. They would produce the show, a hot and sultry show, and that was something she did know.

The valet pulled up the neon green sub-compact. J.C. rushed around to the driver's side, but before he could take off, she slipped into the passenger seat. "Thinking of leaving without me?"

He cast a begrudging smirk without really looking at her. "I figured if you didn't want to come with me you'd find your own way."

"It's hard to get somewhere if I don't know where you're going. I'm not a mind reader."

"Damn good thing, because you wouldn't like what I've been thinking." He stopped at the traffic light next to the circular cock fighting arena. "Okay miss big time news reporter, where would you start?"

"With your grandfather and then work through the hierarchy of fort employees, especially security. If people had seen a woman jump from the fort, even if she was a ghost, they would report it." Picking up her purse from the floorboard, she pulled out a piece of gum and reconsidered offering one to J.C. He could suffer through morning coffee breath. "I'm also going to find out where the governmental archives are and get access to them. I don't have security clearance any longer, but I know ways to get information." She kept the cold thought at bay. "So where are you headed?"

"Bayamon. It's not far, but it may take a while because of traffic. A Dios, it's gotten even worse since I lived here." Focusing on the road, he merged into the line of cars heading toward the tunnel. "When I told Abuelo about sneaking into the fort, he didn't say anything for awhile. There's something there," the traffic flow stopped dead; only the blue tiled walls seemed to move in hazy waves within the exhaust fumes, "and I think he knows what it is."

"What does that have to do with our story?" She settled back, glad to focus on work. When he acted professionally, J.C. was actually a semi-intelligent human being.

"Everything and maybe nothing," he inched forward with the other cars, glancing at her occasionally with eyes a Labrador puppy would envy. "I know some of the history, so let's talk it out. Boy and girl meet and have a shipboard romance. They get to Puerto Rico, and she stays behind. Why? Why didn't she remain with her lover?"

"She probably didn't have a choice. Women rarely had a voice in the seventeenth, eighteenth centuries." Hitching the seatbelt under her arm, Fara scooted to face him. He had great hair, long but not too long, on the lighter edge of black, thick and with just enough wave to make a woman want to run her fingers through it. She couldn't remember if she did that last night, probably not since they went after each other like two dogs in heat. She caught herself before the groan left her throat. Why did her carefully calculated one night stand have to get so complicated?

"Which opens the storyline to insert the villain or outside evil influence." He glanced at her again, this time longer; so long in fact, she wondered if he was going to wreck the car.

Knowing it irritated him, she pulled out her notebook and jotted down the chronology. "The villain has an alternate plan for the girl. Perhaps her uncle, the official dude, wanted her to marry someone else."

"So, in keeping to Rob's requirements, the boyfriend makes a promise to marry her and physically takes her to seal the deal so to speak. I would conclude he was a sailor and had to sail when the ship did, but he had to be pretty high up, at least a lieutenant, maybe the captain, to have had access to her in the first place, and she was too high up to marry without her father's permission."

"Makes sense." She nodded absently. "If the boyfriend had been a passenger, he would have stayed in Puerto Rico for a few weeks anyway. People didn't go sailing across the ocean for pleasure in those days."

"Can you just imagine what conditions were like on one of those boats? I wouldn't sail back and forth once, never mind repeatedly. Thank God I'm alive during modern times."

"From their perspective, they were living in modern times too."

J.C.'s quiet chuckle stirred her inner senses. Regardless of how hard she shielded herself, something he did every few minutes triggered how she had felt when he was inside of her. "Shit," Fara mumbled not loudly enough to be heard over the blowing A.C.

"He makes it to Cadiz and speaks with the girl's father and then heads back across the Atlantic. His ship sinks." Sticking the bumper of the rental car precariously into the other lane, J.C. edged his way past the stalled car with steam billowing from under its hood. "Why? Was it a hurricane, a pirate attack? Did it founder or run aground?"

"Someone had to know his ship sank and how, which would indicate a flotilla, and records. Ships were expensive."

"The Spaniards fortified their fleet in the Caribbean during the U.S. Revolutionary War. They said it was for protection, but they had plans to raid and capture English ships, back then everyone hated the English. It would put the timing in the late 1770s or early 1780s, which corresponds with the completion of San Cristobal." J.C. paused. "This is the part I don't get. If

Rob was right and her uncle was a government official, she would have everything she needed."

She followed the logic easily enough. "Why would she commit suicide in any scenario? For a Catholic, it's an instant ride to the gates of hell."

"Puerto Rican history wasn't my best subject in school; actually I hated it because the textbooks presented the Spaniards' perspective. I'm one of the few descendants from the native Taínos, and the Spaniards enslaved and subjugated them to the point of genocide. My grandfather's an expert on the subject." J.C. passed a hand over his face, rubbing his chin. He had shaved since last night, and his moustache and trim beard added dimension to his angular jaw line. "But if I remember right, during the Eighteenth Century, Spanish men outnumbered women on the island, at least ten to one. It would have made her a hot commodity, and with lofty connections, the entire husband market would have been at her disposal. So why did she jeopardize her immortal soul?"

"Maybe she couldn't see herself living without him." Instead of her voice wilting, Fara grew stronger. After Jason died, killing herself had never even entered her mind, despite what the shrink might have thought as he broke the news to her. "Perhaps she was being forced to marry another man, another villain opportunity." She thought for a moment. "But you're thinking an exterior force drove her to it. The evil that lurks in the dungeons of the fort."

"Why not? It adds an element of horror to the story of a tragic young woman." He chanced a glance at her. "The evil corrupted her and found a way to trap her soul."

"Makes for an interesting show." She flipped back through her notes. "How would we shoot the shipboard scenes?"

"There're some museums with Spanish ships, and with a decent backdrop, we could recreate it pretty well. Or shoot the actors on a set and drop in the background digitally." After glancing at her notebook, he ran his hand through his hair. "An old-fashioned excursion ship would serve as well. It would be pretty nice to be out on a big sailing ship and do some snorkeling. The reefs off St. John are incredible."

"Sounds like fun, not work." *Hell of a lot better than being in the sandbox,* she thought while tapping the pen against the edge of the spiral binding. "Rob would approve the budget for something like that?"

"If we stay in budget, Rob doesn't care. We're on our own now. As long as we bring him his deliverables on time, he understands locations cost. Although I'm sure there was red tape, I doubt the fort is charging much if anything. *Ghost Lovers* would be able to pay for a few days aboard ship."

"The foundering would be an issue, but there may be some stock footage to use."

"Since other ships come back to port and tell the girl, we may not even have to shoot it as a scene. But we're getting ahead of ourselves." He chanced another lengthy glance; long enough for Fara to see him thinking behind those warm eyes. "I only have pieces of the story. Let's see what we can verify before going too far in one direction."

Since his outburst last night, she had been itching to ask, and now that he opened the door to the topic, she decided to take a chance. "Did you see the Pink Lady that night at the fort?"

"No." The shroud descended again, but unlike last night, his rational mind appeared to remain in control. "There're two types of hauntings, intelligent which interact with you, and residual. If she's a ghost, she's a residual haunting, one that repeats like a recording, trapped to relive the same moments over and over again. When the circumstances align just right, she appears. The cleaning crew has reported hearing a voice in her bedroom, carrying on a one-sided conversation about not being able to live without love, or at least something to that effect. The sightings are of her running toward the garita and launching herself onto the rocks. You're right on target about talking to security. Whether they keep the reports, I don't know."

"I'm sure your grandfather knows the head of security. Do you think he will help us?"

"Abuelo's odd when it comes to the fort. He skirts around topics or just flat out changes the subject. Maybe with you there, he'll behave. He knows I left with you yesterday, but I didn't mention our … our …"

Several words came to mind, but only one of them was a polite description of their lustful intercourse. "Intimacy."

"Thanks. That's sounds much nicer than I was thinking."

She smiled. Good to know their situation was unnerving him as well. "He'll be surprised to see me."

"To put it mildly." J.C. tapped both hands against the steering wheel and then gripped it tightly. "The night I went to the fort I wasn't alone. Andres Figueroa was with me. Actually, going there was his idea. He had talked about the ghost stories and legends, and like an idiot, I didn't believe any of it. What I told you about the maids hearing voices and the tourists' reports, all of that came from him via his dad, who was head of security. We both promised not to say anything to anyone, but if he told his dad, Señor Figueroa may not be too inclined to help us."

She understood more than what he said. It wasn't a simple case of them taking a quick tour about the fort at night. This was about trust and a bond shared between men on a multitude of levels. The band of brothers was more than just a saying; it was a link, a bond that held them together, a shared mind.

Fara took a hard look at J.C. and saw the same elements that had attracted her last night. His looks were on the edge of harsh with a dash of boyish charm to soften the effect, but it wasn't just his looks she had noticed originally. At the time she hadn't known why, but his intensity was intriguing and vulnerable. At least his paranoia about the event had subsided to the point where he could talk about details. "If I can get my hands on the records, I can determine if there's a pattern with her appearances. I'm good with encryptions; by finding the commonalities, I can break the code. If nothing shows up or if I can't get my hands on the records, I could always hack into the system."

"Were you really a spy?"

His question caught her off guard. Normally she was really good at blank face, but the truth showed in her surprise. Whether he noticed was another story all together. "I guess you heard that from Rob as well."

J.C. just kept driving. "Breaking encryption codes and hacking systems aren't normal skills. So were you?"

Leaning back against the seat, she closed her eyes against the memories of her captors asking the very same question but in a much different way. "The Taliban seemed to think so."

"Jesus Fara, would you just answer my question?" J.C. snapped.

She didn't move, didn't want to acknowledge their conversation had just detoured once again. "I don't see how it's relevant to our working relationship."

"Okay, if you're not going to tell me, I'll assume by evading the question you were a spy, and the C.I.A. got you your job with the news to get you into war zones. Constant Cable News is big league, and someone just doesn't become a field producer without any production experience. You took so many basic notes this morning I know you don't know shit about TV production. Are you still an active agent? That is my business."

"I'm not an agent or a government spy, so just get that out of your head. I take notes out of habit. I produced the news for over two years after working as a linguist in military field communications, both require copious notes." Squeezing her eyes shut, she fought for control, but the seething bubbled out of her anyway. "You're right, okay I admit it. I haven't produced a full television show with actors and stuff, but I'm a fast study. One thing I do know is that I'm not going to take any more shit about it from you. Clear enough?"

"For now." He clenched his teeth.

CHAPTER 9

J.C. was irritated about being irritated and would have liked to have blamed it all on Fara, but he just couldn't get a handle on his emotions, which was his own issue. Things were going along just fine until she mentioned the fort, and then one thing just seemed to end up grating into another. He couldn't figure out why her being a spy would matter and felt ridiculous for asking. How could she still be a government agent and work for *Ghost Lovers?* They did nothing secretive. They didn't go near sensitive installations. All in all, *Ghost Lovers* was about as far away from the C.I.A. as someone could get. Perhaps that was why she applied for the job in the first place.

Cars backed up from the drive-thru lines for KFC and McDonald's into the main thoroughfare in front of Rio Hondo Mall. At the second traffic light, he turned right, and in the next block, parked in front of the house where he grew up.

The steady schedule never changed. His grandfather painted the white exterior walls in March and September and always made J.C. help. Like any kid, he complained about the chores, but secretly he liked painting. He also fondly remembered planting flowers around the patio and mowing the small patch of grass in front of his bedroom window. Once he moved to Brooklyn, he lost all of that and never got it back. Even though he now kept a small apartment in Miami, he didn't have a home, not like this was. Unfortunately, he never would.

He didn't rush around the car to open Fara's door or even look in her direction. All he could think about was how Lily hated Rob's edicts and inflexibility, but J.C. hadn't really understood until Rob had saddled him with a female incarnation of Rambo. One thing he was right about was her voice. The verbal silk would earn her a lot more money doing phone sex than producing *Ghost Lovers*, but perhaps money wasn't her primary motivator. If not, what was? He shook the thought out of his head. He didn't want to know. He didn't want to care, but somehow every thought came back to her and how he felt when he was buried deep inside of her.

She followed him down the short, single car driveway toward the front door and waited a couple of steps behind him while he rang the doorbell. Even with the threat of rain clouding the sky, the carport radiated heat which shimmered in the tangible humidity. Sweat slipped down J.C.'s spine while fumbling in his pocket for the key his grandfather had given him last night. Pushing hard because it had a tendency to stick, he opened the door, and the A.C. blessedly welcomed him to the cool inner darkness.

"Abuelo, Abuela, soy Juan Carlos. Están?" He almost let the heavy door swing closed behind him, but as an afterthought, he caught the edge with his heel. "I guess they're not home."

"You think?" Fara's voice pulled harshly, nothing syrupy or sexy about it. "I might be mistaken since I don't have your years of television production experience, but I would have called before driving out here."

Swiveling quickly, he backed her against the door, pinning her shoulders against the heated steel. "I'm not going to constantly fight with you."

"That's good because you won't win." She quipped.

"I've never hit a woman, even if she was a bad-tempered bitch, but I'm tempted."

"Oh I'm so afraid." She facetiously shivered. "There's nothing you can do to hurt me physically or verbally, J.C. I never give up, never surrender."

The cocky grin curled his lips before he could do anything about it. "You surrendered to me last night. You liked it when I got tired of your teasing and finally took you." He stared into her remarkable eyes and suddenly grew rock hard. Yesterday, fear had fueled his passion, and today chaotic anger charged need through his veins. "I know it doesn't make sense for either of us, but it's real and tangible. We can't continue pretending it didn't mean something to us both."

She clenched her fingers into fists. "We had decided we wouldn't talk about-"

His mouth silenced any debate. He knew this was a mistake, which only heightened the inherent urgency. Nobody had ever made him feel true chaos. He didn't want to comprehend why she made him turn into a lunatic, flipping through his normally well-structured feelings as easily as leafing through a book. Regardless, anger, fear, and desire blazed, burning in unison. Charring his mind into incomprehension, the need resonated until overwhelming sensations hammered him, too fast and sharp to think of anything other than having her. Yesterday was just a prelude to the staggering and phenomenal things he planned to do to her today, right now in his old bedroom.

CHAPTER 10

Fara braced against the sudden onslaught. Her fists started to press against his chest, but before she pushed him away, physical need overcame emotional resolve. Her fingers uncurled to grab his shirt and hauled him closer. Rationally, she knew this was a mistake, but she couldn't think clearly while the explosive battle raged inside of her, driving her to strain against him while his mouth continued to demand more. His taste was enough to drive her mad with hunger.

Desperate for control, her mouth fought to conquer rather than be conquered, but he wouldn't relinquish his domination. He pressed his heated erection against her thigh, and the quiver within Fara hummed like a plucked string, vibrations spreading until she unwittingly trembled. Charged with heat, the burning consumed her remaining defenses degree by flaming degree.

The sound of a key scraping in the lock rattled her conscious mind. She tried to spring forward, but his body blocked her. The heavy door flew open. The few inches provided just enough space to allow the momentum of the steely edge to hit her in the back of the head. J.C. was still in front of her, and she fell into him. He lost his footing, and the bewildered couple crumpled into a tumbled heap.

"J.C.? What the hell were you doing behind the door?" His grandfather quickly set down the armload of groceries and went to help Fara back to her feet. "I'm so sorry. Are you alright?"

While holding the back of her head, she took a few seconds to focus on the soft brown eyes. She had noticed the familial similarity between the two men at the fort, yet their subtle differences only seemed to add to the likeness. She groaned and closed her eyes; that didn't make any sense.

"Come and sit down." A gentle feminine voice cooed at her. The resonance flowed within the waves cascading inside of her head while her brain tried to order her feet to move.

Behind her calves, she felt the sofa and eased backwards into the softness. The initial blast of pain merged into a continual throbbing, resounding like native drumbeats. The sofa leaned moments before an ice pack pressed uncomfortably against the growing lump on the back of her head.

"Fara, sweetheart. Keep your eyes open and stay awake." J.C. shouted excessively loud. "Do you think we should call an ambulance?"

"No," the sound of her own voice wanted to make her head explode. "No hospitals. I just need a couple of minutes. I'll be fine."

J.C.'s body pressed close. "Can we get you anything?"

"Some quiet." She tried a smile. Even though her eyes were still closed, she could envision the tense line forming between J.C.'s brows, deepening the angles of his chiseled face. She blinked and realized she was right.

"Sorry love, but that's one thing you can't have. You could have a concussion and need to stay awake. How about a couple of Tylenol?" His narrow beard accentuated his square jaw and covered the almost unnoticeable cleft in his chin. There was nothing soft about his face except for his eyes that were the color of chocolate milk. Those eyes searched her face and then stared directly into her soul. She needed to do something to break the contact, but mesmerized, she just stared back and allowed him to enter her inner self. Only once in her life did she have such a connection with another person, and it led to disaster. Yet here she was, staring into a man's eyes that melted more than just her resolve.

In her peripheral vision, an older woman approached with a glass of water. Her face wavered on the edge of Fara's memories. "Here. It will help with the headache." She wrapped Fara's fingers around the glass. "Just what were you doing behind the door?"

Fara accepted the two white tablets in her other hand and sat up straighter, swallowing them with the cool contents in the glass. "We came here to talk about the fort."

"Our first *Ghost Lovers* episode is about the Pink Lady." J.C.'s voice was returning to a normal tone rather than booming inside of her head.

"You two are working together?"

Fara's eyes followed the sound. "We're co-producing the series. I'm Faradahl Alecto Trotter."

"Faradahl Alecto? You were on CCN." The woman leaned forward to stroke her cheek and then took the glass from her fingers. "I couldn't even begin to imagine all those bombs and gunfire. Were you really captured?"

For months the psychiatrist had tried to pry the information from Fara's mind, but now the memory popped into her head and flowed out of her mouth effortlessly. "I was just buying some bread. While listening to the women's idle chatter, hands came out of nowhere. They pulled the burqa tightly, binding my limbs with straps or maybe belts with broad metal buckles. Although I tried to fight, they carried me out of there like a rolled up carpet. No one even shouted out against them. The hood had twisted, hiding my face behind the dark fabric. I couldn't see anything, and the harder I struggled, the tighter the bindings became, cutting into my flesh.

"None of them said a word, but by counting the footsteps, I determined there were three men. I felt the heat of the sun, and then the sounds of the market faded into the rumbling of a diesel motor. They threw me, and I hung in mid-air before slamming into the bed of the truck. The tires spun as it launched forward, which sent me rolling. I used the momentum hoping to fall out the back. The dirt crunching under the tires grew louder. I knew I was almost there. Then, someone kicked me, crushing my right hand in the blow..." As Fara's fist curled, her thoughts drifted back.

The woman's unsettling eyes were huge and round, so dark they were almost like pieces of coal. "How did you get away?"

Shedding the odd feeling, Fara blew out a breath, coming back into herself. "An old beggar woman risked her life by going to the base. It's ironic. I gave her a few odd coins every day, and she repaid me with my life." Leaning forward, she removed the ice pack and gingerly felt the bump. "It's not that bad."

"You're keeping the ice on for at least another ten minutes." When she didn't do as he asked, J.C. took the bag out of her hand and pressed it to her head, making her wince.

The white-haired woman leaned forward. "If you don't keep it on, I won't answer your questions about the Pink Lady."

"You're ganging up on me." Fara searched the old woman's face for a glimmer of assistance and noticed something, something very familiar and haunting. She was the woman from the store, the one who sold her the ring.

"You've been through a terrible ordeal, which brings you closer to God. You are his agent." She answered while stroking Fara's hair back from her face.

"God had nothing to do with it." Fara answered bluntly. She tried to soften the harshness, yet her words were edgy. "What do you know about the Pink Lady?"

"Unfortunately, I don't have any solid evidence." Eduardo's voice was distant and echoing, yet still biting and harsh. "No solid evidence at all."

"That's funny," J.C. chuckled. "Most of the time with ghosts, you don't."

His grandfather shot a wry grimace. "A woman visited the fort about a year ago and wanted a private tour. She declared she was psychic and immediately picked up on lots of vibes, that's all."

The woman continued as if the man had never even spoken. "The Pink Lady was Vivian Dufrense, the niece of Captain General Dufrense. Under his heavy hand just about every prisoner perished, especially the native Taíno Indians, who started the legends of the dungeon being a portal to hell."

Eduardo shifted uncomfortably and pulled a blue velvet pillow out from behind his back, clinging to it protectively against his chest. He wore a large ring on his center finger which glimmered with silver light.

"Vivian was vivacious, especially compared to her cousin, Marianna, who was getting married to a friend of her father's whose wife and infant died in childbirth. When Don Miguel de Ustariz saw Vivian, he wanted to change his betrothal offer from the Captain General's daughter to his niece. This infuriated not only Dufrense but also Vivian, for during the voyage she had fallen in love with Felipe Cordova and promised to ..."

The woman's words faded as Fara's head spun suddenly, pounding with sound which was in rhythm with the throbbing ache. Lying still, she waited for the dizziness to lessen. Opening her eyes, she found herself lying on the couch. She struggled with the change as readily as she struggled to sit up, but a firm hand held her.

J.C. stroked her cheek softly. "Jesus, you had us scared there for a minute."

"What are you talking about?" Wrapping her fingers around his outstretched hand, she sat up. Her temples pounded.

"The door knocked you out." J.C. squeezed her fingers. "The ambulance is on its way."

"I told you I'm not going to the hospital." Biting her lip, Fara glanced around the room. It had changed somehow, yet nothing had changed physically. J.C.'s grandfather was in the chair across from them, leaning forward with his hands clasped over the blue velvet pillow. Her vision blurred, so she looked in the direction where J.C's grandmother had been sitting. "What else do you know about Vivian Dufrense? What happened to her?"

"Who?" J.C. reached across her lap and snagged the ice pack off from the pillow, which had left a wet spot on the fabric.

"The Pink Lady. Your grandmother just told us about her." She glanced across the coffee table.

The old man's eyes were no longer gentle, rather filled with something cold and menacing. The corners tightened, as if he was looking directly into a bright and blinding light. "What? The Pink Lady's a legend. None of us know any details."

"Eduardo, leave her be. Can't you tell she's disoriented?" J.C.'s grandmother extended a glass and a pair of white aspirin. She was different than the woman who was here only moments ago. This one had red hair dyed in a purplish shade that didn't occur in nature and light brown eyes, almost amber, nothing like the other woman. "The paramedics will check you out. Then you can decide if you will go to the hospital or not."

She didn't reach for the glass. "I just took two a couple of minutes ago."

The woman exchanged glances with both men and set the glass onto a coaster, laying the pills alongside. "They will be waiting for you right here if you change your mind."

Fara swiveled toward J.C. and felt a painful tug behind her eyes. "What's going on?"

His face wavered in and out of focus. "We had just come inside, and you were behind the door. The edge of it hit you in the back of the head as my grandparents came inside."

"And I fell down on top of you."

"Yeah, you were knocked out cold." J.C. stared into her eyes warily. "We laid you on the couch. You woke up just now."

"No!" She dropped the volume of her voice to lessen the echo inside of her head. "I don't know what you're doing, but it's not going to work. I've been sitting right here listening to the story about Vivian Dufrense, how she came to Puerto Rico with her cousin, Marianna. Her uncle, Captain General Dufrense, hated her because Marianna's betrothed wanted to change his mind and marry Vivian instead, but she was in love with the lieutenant from the ship."

Eduardo shifted back into the chair and set the pillow on the floor awkwardly. "There was a Jose Dufrense who was the Captain General in the late Eighteenth Century, but I haven't heard about a Marianna or Vivian."

"What else do you remember?" J.C. set his hand on her shoulder. "Any other names?"

She closed her eyes and tried to remember. Her normally crisp memory only held blurry details. "Vivian's lover was Felipe Cordova. Marianna's husband was Don something Ustariz."

"Miguel Antonio de Ustariz was also a Captain General, like Jose Dufrense." Eduardo clapped his hands. The sound rang harshly, vibrating like a gong within Fara's head. The vibrations coursed through her recent memories, feeling them, massaging them.

"Anything else?" J.C. tugged on her arm.

She started to shake her head no, but it pounded fiercely. "Not really. Now tell me what's going on." As the pounding grew, she stared at the little white tablets. "Tell me honestly. Did I already take two Tylenol?"

"No, you didn't." J.C. and his grandmother answered in unison.

Fara removed the icepack. The bump was right where she remembered. With an indignant grunt, she swept the tablets off from the table and set them in her mouth. Clasping the glass in both hands, she swallowed the chilled water.

CHAPTER 11

The glass was still in hand when the paramedics arrived. Although J.C., his grandparents, and both paramedics insisted she go to the emergency room, Fara refused. J.C. didn't even know how to begin to describe her. Stubborn, pig-headed, intractable, none of them could do her obstinate inflexibility justice. It would have been so much easier if she had remained unconscious for just a few more minutes. They would have packaged her onto the stretcher and delivered her to the emergency room. He would have hated the ride and the waiting until the doctors had their fill of tests, but this was worse.

By the time Fara convinced him to take her back to the hotel, red and gold beams lanced the storm clouds that had drifted toward the western horizon. Sunsets normally filled him with a pastoral rightness with the world, a glorified end to a busy day. He hadn't felt at peace since he first laid eyes on Fara, and his discontent only grew.

Every now and then, he chanced a glance at her in the passenger seat. The sun's lengthening rays brushed color into the ribbons of hair dangling around her face. The highlights danced with the movement of the car, accentuating her feminine features. Thankfully he was driving, which limited his intense scrutiny, yet while stuck behind the machine that scooted the freeway's changeable concrete median, he allowed his eyes to linger and visually touched the angular curves of her cheeks and brow. Regardless of where his eyes started, they always ended on her lips. Their kiss, his kiss, he reminded himself, ignited something powerful and dangerous. He didn't know how long he could hold it inside. Eventually, his ardor would break down the inhibiting barriers. Worse yet, he wasn't sure if he wanted to control it.

Perhaps the names Fara imagined were gibberish, but a deep and penetrating fear roiled in his gut, tightening like fists until he felt sick. Something odd and compelling was at work here, something beyond rational explanation. He had witnessed a similar scenario in Scotland. Events channeled them onto a tragic path, and once they had realized the depth of their involvement, it was too late. If the oddities of Fara's revelations were true, if she had tapped into the past and discovered the name of the amorphous Pink Lady, Fara was already involved, perhaps beyond the point of no return. If it had anything to do with the demon hidden in the bowels of the fort, it would use her to get to him. J.C. had a difficult time reconciling Fara to a pawn being manipulated. She was valiant, a force to complement and foil rolled into one. He thought for a moment. That was how he would have described Lily Cameron, and even with her strong will, the ghosts at Fyvie Castle nearly killed her.

He chanced another glance. Fara's face was flushed, much better than the deathly paleness as she lay unconscious. Her disheveled hair fell in sexy chords over her shoulders. Her eyes reflected the sunset's hues in the golden flakes around her fathomless pupils. It was impossible for him to know what thoughts transpired behind those eyes. They guarded her like a shield when she didn't wield them as a weapon, but their power wasn't absolute. When he kissed her, he witnessed the fleeting weakness. A small wonder, for he had forced himself upon her, allowing the disconsolate force take hold of his faculties and take hold of her just as readily. Unfortunately, he remembered the moment all too clearly, especially since her taste was still clinging to the edges his lips.

Letting the valet take the car, J.C. wrapped his arm securely around Fara's waist and led her toward the suite. Yesterday, he had been so involved with looking for the hidden *Gotcha* cameras he failed to notice the beauty of the ancient building. He loved the old Spanish design, the arched doorways and textured ceilings with polished wooden beams. All of the wood was dark with age and had absorbed hundreds of years of humidity, exuding a scent that triggered something in his mind, yet he wasn't sure why.

He had seen a ghost show on El Convento. The hotel had been a nunnery, but modern renovations converted the buildings into elegant luxury. He loved to learn about the history through the tragic stories, which was the main reason he had accepted the *Ghost Lovers'* offer originally. The fact he felt like a protective brother to Lily was a close second; although, he didn't do anything to keep her safe in Scotland. He found her dazed in Lord Sloan's office and should have removed her from the castle, forcibly if necessary. Instead, he focused on the final shots of their final scene. If he learned anything second guessing himself those long subsequent weeks in the hospital, it was to act upon his instincts, and right now, they were humming with just as much warning. Unfortunately, there was nothing supernatural about it, unexplainable, unfathomable, but not ghostly. He was falling in love, hard and fast, and didn't know what to do about it.

Closing the hall door behind them as softly as possible, he followed Fara to the bedroom. It looked exactly as it had yesterday, and a lump grew in his throat as he fought against the consuming need.

She stood just inside the bedroom doorway, blocking it with her body. "I want to take a shower and get some sleep."

Swinging the laptop bag off his shoulder, he set it onto the table in the sitting room, waiting to respond until he could ensure his tone would be just as easy and even. "Sounds like a plan."

He approached her, and her palm met his chest. "Which means you should go."

"Nope." J.C. hitched a shoulder in the doorframe matching her defiance for defiance. "The EMTs said you needed surveillance for at least twenty-four hours, so you're stuck with me. Do you need help getting undressed?"

Casting a devilish smirk at him, she competently sauntered to the edge of the bed, but as she leaned forward to remove her shoes, her balance wavered.

"Whoa chica, you're still not too steady." In two strides, he was across the room, kneeling at her feet and unbuckling the straps from around her ankles. He hesitated, sliding off the sandals with a lingering touch. "You have beautiful feet."

"I don't think anyone's ever told me that." She reached out and touched his hair, running the wavy strands through her fingers. Tenderness lingered in her features, soft and extremely feminine. "Thank you."

The gesture was innocent enough but still had his blood pounding. He resisted the urge to smooth closer to her, to scoot forward between her parted legs and press his cheek to her breast. "It's just a silly compliment."

"No, not about my feet." Her smile was mystical and affected more than a casual ease. "I still don't understand what happened this afternoon, but you were really decent about it all."

"I was decent?" J.C. choked back an amused chuckle along with his raging hormones. "I don't think anyone's ever told me that." While they were smiling at each other, a current flowed like a riptide pulling him under. He had to force his lungs to breathe, in and out, in and out. Striking an informal appearance was even more difficult when he witnessed the change come over her as well.

She cleared her throat, "I'm going to take a shower. You really can go. I'll be fine."

Rocking back onto his heels, he stood with a swagger on weakened knees. "Not a chance. I can be just as persistent and tenacious as you." He took her hands into his and gently rubbed the backs. She really was delicate; no one would convince him differently. He continued to hold them as he guided her to her feet. "Keep the door ajar, so I can hear you if you need me."

"You going to peek?" A coquettish flash of green swiftly darted as a warning or perhaps an invitation.

Since he wasn't sure, his brows rose along with a quirky smile. "Maybe."

Languidly, she chuckled and then closed the door behind her, but he didn't hear the lock click. The thought crossed his mind to follow her, yet he stopped himself. If he saw her naked, he didn't know if he could retain his composure.

Returning to the other room, he removed the laptop and stared at the blank screen while it booted up. Fara Trotter was an enigma, a puzzle without an easy solution. He couldn't get her bewildered and angry confusion out of his mind while she was arguing about not having passed out. He saw it again while she adamantly refused to go with the EMTs, yet she succumbed to him staying with her with only a paltry show of defiance. She needed him even if she only recognized the fact on a subconscious level. He was sure of that. They would spend the next twenty-four hours together, and then he would know what his true feelings were.

The wireless Internet connection was fast, much faster than he expected, but Puerto Rico wasn't some backwater nation. His homeland had all of the modern conveniences of the states and the historic traditions of his people. He had missed the island. For fifteen years, he had been hiding from his fears that had patiently awaited his return. Meanwhile, he had denied himself the comforts of home and family.

Struggling back to reality, he typed the names into a search engine, and they registered with dozens of hits. Both Dufrense and Ustariz were precisely what Fara had described. The Smithsonian site even offered a portrait of Ustariz. As it downloaded, J.C. rubbed the scar on his abdomen. The nagging tightness had returned.

Kicking back in the chair in order to see the bathroom door, he wondered what was happening. He had only known Fara for a day, but he trusted her and her instincts. Somehow that hit on the head tuned her into the paranormal connection. Most people would scoff, but he didn't need to believe. He knew ghosts could manipulate the living, but it required a connection. For Lily, it was genetic, being the descendent from the long established bloodline. Fara definitely wasn't Puerto Rican or even Spanish for that matter, but there had to be something to tie her to this piece of the past. They had to figure out what it was and how to use it before it figured out how to use them.

The bathroom door opened. He got up and stood in the bedroom doorway. Delicately, Fara padded into the room with a white hotel towel wrapped around her head and another around her body. Even though the towels were the king-sized variety, long legs branched down, making him break out in an instant sweat. He desperately wanted to run his hand along the shapely curves of her ankles to her calves and then thighs. Being on his knees to remove her shoes had him remembering how he hadn't spent sufficient time to enjoy those delicious legs last night.

All he had right now was time. He shouldn't push his advantage, especially not tonight while she was fragile. "How are you feeling?"

She inhaled deeply, and the towel pulled tautly across the tops of her breasts. "You don't have to keep asking me that."

"You better get used to it because it's become a habit." Despite his best intentions, his eyes followed her to the dresser. "You hit pay dirt with the names. Do you mind telling me again, with as much detail as possible, regardless of how inconsequential it may seem, what you remember from this afternoon." She waved her hand in a little circle, and he turned his head. "Don't you think it's a little late for modesty?"

"If I had known we would be working together, I wouldn't have seduced you."

His hackles rose without warning. "Would you have asked someone else?"

"No."

He caught himself before turning around. "Why not?"

"That question doesn't deserve an answer. Just like this afternoon, you can come up with whatever ridiculous conclusion you like, but I'm not going to discuss it. You can turn around now."

Even though she was wearing a faded Army t-shirt, Fara looked as seductively lovely as a lingerie model. Her damp hair hung in loosely twisting chords, dripping slowly, darkening the gray shirt near her breasts.

He swallowed, trying to remember what he had wanted to say, but lost his opportunity. Smoothly she passed him and sat at the table across from the laptop. She proceeded to describe the conversation that only she heard, and he focused on the keyboard, typing frantically.

"Anything else?" He waited. A guilty look creased over her eyes, and he dared to hope it was about their kiss. It was driving him crazy not knowing if she remembered, especially after the way her body responded with that hot and sultry flash. "Fara, don't hold back. This is important."

"It's going to sound crazy." She bit her lower lip hesitantly.

His stomach tightened. "I need you to tell me, especially the crazy stuff."

"The woman I was talking to wasn't your grandmother. I thought she was, but when I woke up, your grandmother was a totally different person. The other lady had recognized me from CCN and asked me about Afghanistan and how I had been captured." Fara held out her right hand, absently clenching and flexing her fingers while she recapped the story. "I used to play the piano. Actually I was more than pretty good at it, but the fingers on my right hand just don't move like they used to." She held both of her hands out to him, side to side. "See how the right is larger than the left? By the time I got to a hospital, the breaks had already started to mend, so they had to break it again to align the bones correctly."

A misty wetness rose to J.C.'s eyes. Before his resolve completely cratered and every emotion he had been feeling came pouring out, his gaze focused on the ring. "What's that?" He reached out and gently cradled her left hand. "You didn't wear a ring last night."

"It's not what you're thinking." She didn't struggle or pull away from his firm touch. "I bought it last night in a back alley shop. There's something hidden within the stone, a flaw, but I can't make out why it's familiar. I'm not an impulse buyer, but I just had to have this ring."

"Do you mind?" He watched her slide it off and took it from her. It was light and delicate, with an emerald as green as her eyes. He switched on the desk lamp and stared into the stone. "You know what it reminds me of? It looks like a garita standing off the side of the fort."

She leaned against his side, and the scent of coconut and lime drifted. "It could be like one of those psychological tests that each person sees what they want to see."

"What do you see?" He shouldn't have looked at her. The angelic face was free of any cosmetics, yet her lips were still strikingly red and inviting as they curved into a smile.

"A lady dancing with her skirts twirling out to the side."

As he ran his finger absently over the emerald, he felt the connection. This had to be the trigger object. "Where did you say you bought it?"

"Does it really matter?" She shrugged while slipping it back onto her finger. "The woman who sold it to me was odd, reminding me of a gypsy. She told me the ring needed me and not to take it off. She's the person I saw when I was unconscious, the woman I thought was your grandmother."

"Tomorrow, would you be able to take me back there? I need to buy Abuela a present. She likes vintage jewelry." He couldn't look into her eyes; although, it wasn't really a lie. His grandmother's birthday was months away, but there was no reason not to give her an impromptu gift.

"I guess I can. I was out wandering, more like meandering with the crowd, not paying too much attention. But, I should be able to find it again." The color was draining from her face, and she sank into the closest chair. "What's on the agenda for tomorrow?"

"I'm going to meet with Andres and his father. Eduin Figueroa retired a few weeks ago and lives on the northern shore of Lago La Plata."

"Living on a silver lake sounds nice." Her eyelids looked heavier.

"Why don't you go lay down for a few minutes while I order some room service? Want anything special?"

"No, I'm not hungry. Just tired." Standing, she wavered, and he was immediately at her side, nearly holding her off her feet while guiding her to the bed. As she stood on unsure legs, he drew back the sheets and stacked the downy pillows, helping her into the softness.

With a final glance over his shoulder at her in the king-sized bed, he closed the adjoining door not wanting to disturb Fara with the call for dinner. By the time he got back to his laptop, he had to refresh the screen. Flipping back over to the Internet, the portrait of Ustariz greeted him. The middle-aged man wore the formal layers of a Spanish military general, which in Madrid would be appropriate, but wearing those clothes in Puerto Rico would be a form of suicide, or at the very least, personal torture. The man's face was thin, along with the rest of his body, not very foreboding to today's standards, but in his role, he held the power of a tyrant. If he wanted Vivian Dufrense, he would have found a way.

After researching the women's names without luck, J.C. gave up the search to eat his steak alone. He thought about waking Fara, but since she didn't wake up naturally when the service cart arrived, he couldn't bring himself to disturb her. After researching more dead ends, he closed the laptop and checked on the woman in the huge bed, allowing his memories to blur into those of last night.

He had never expected to feel so strongly for someone, especially so quickly. It was more than physical; although, the sex was damn memorable. There was an emotional tie to her as well. He should turn away and walk out that door, for every minute he stood watching her, he fell even faster. This time he couldn't keep the groan at bay, but he ran a hand over his face to muffle the sound.

Walking to the other side of the bed, he slipped off his shirt and shoes, unzipped his jeans, and then eased into the bed without her even murmuring. Even though it was by far the softest bed he had ever slept in, his hardened emotions fought against sleep.

CHAPTER 12

The first light of dawn poured orange streaks through the window brightening the room, and the glare hit Fara right in the eyes, instantly sparking one hell of a headache. She rolled over to cling to the dusky shadows. Her arm stretched lazily to gather another pillow, and she encountered a firm shoulder attached to the naked torso of a man.

A strange and unaccustomed surge warmed her, and she sighed while reaching out to stroke the hair back from his face. Even though J.C. said he was going to stay with her, she had expected him to go back to his own hotel. Juan Carlos Calderon was an enigma compared to other men she had known, and that wasn't a good thing. In her world, men were predictable. They focused on immediate pleasure, because tomorrow was never a foregone conclusion.

In stark contrast to the white duvet, J.C.'s tanned skin was the warm color of burnished oak. Just like a man, he was sprawled on top of the covers, consuming at least two-thirds of the giant bed. His chest lifted, rhythmically expanding with each easy breath, slowly and smoothly under the broad muscles. Some men were born with the genetics of a flawless body, while others waged a constant war against the creeping effects of weight and age. J.C.'s physique appeared to be a natural manifestation. At least she hadn't seen him workout.

She chuckled inwardly at her own naiveté. This was their third day together. She had no way of knowing his habits, but somewhere inside of her, she knew he was a decent man. He wouldn't have stayed to sleep beside her if he wasn't.

Softly she sighed and cuddled closer. The point of the seduction was to take him for sex, but somewhere along the way, he met her warring need and battled past it into her heart. Oh, he definitely could be infuriating, yet there was a gentler side she doubted he let many people see. The sex had been monumental; still it was a mistake they couldn't make again. They were coworkers, and a personal relationship would leak into their professional involvement, equaling a recipe for disaster. Her heart twisted. It was better not to get involved; losing another man was a pain she couldn't survive again.

Inside the pulsing headache, she could hear Jason's mother screaming at her just after his casket lowered into the ground. Edith blamed Fara for his death, for getting into Jason's head, which the woman swore clouded his judgment in the field. Even though Fara knew it was ridiculous to blame herself, the thought was always there, just under her skin, pricking her conscience. If Jason hadn't met her, would he still be alive? It was one of those questions that would never have an answer, but underneath it all, Fara knew Edith was right. Jason was just her most recent casualty. Anyone she got close to died. She wouldn't, couldn't allow it to happen again.

Under heavy lids, J.C.'s eyes twitched with a dream. He had gloriously long lashes that would make any supermodel envious. His lips were naturally rosy. She remembered how their attentive fullness awakened her skin, tasting and nibbling with heated passion. They had shared a few hours of pleasure, and that would have to be enough. Because of, not in spite of her feelings for the man, she had to stay away from him.

Just outside the window, the birds began their morning chorus, darting and flitting between branches filled with purple flowers. The young sunlight blazed in the red and green feathers, regaling the beauty of a new day.

Fara eased her body off from the bed and silently tip-toed to the bathroom. When she returned, J.C. had rolled over, absently shielding his eyes with a forearm. Quietly, she drew the drapes and cast the room back into darkness.

About an hour later, a busload of tourists arrived at Fort San Cristobal minutes before Fara peeled the backs of her legs off from the plastic seat of the cab. Her head still hurt with an uncomfortable fullness, enough that she didn't want to walk the few blocks in the growing heat. Although she went on technically the same tour, the younger ranger's speech was more generic and less sensationalized. Unlike J.C.'s grandfather, he didn't mention anything about the Taíno natives and their persecution.

Although the fort had a definable purpose, the stronghold had been a showplace, a testament to power and wealth. Part impregnable fortress and part fancy castle, spiral staircases and maze-like corridors connected the lofty opulence of the commander's wing to the lowly bowels of the dungeons, yet the standardized tour took her to neither of those extremes.

She continued with the group to a tunnel the guide termed the dungeon, but a dungeon was something altogether different. There wasn't space here designed to inflict pain, no manacles set into the walls, no place to hold the specialized tools designed to open a body while still keeping the victim alive. This was more like a holding cell. Names and dates decorated the walls, and one of the tenants had sketched a ship, definitely a sailing vessel from the era of the Spanish conquests. Hanging back, she hastily sketched the boat in her notebook. If they could locate something that looked like this to shoot the shipboard scenes, it would add veracity to the overall production.

The guide took his final leave in the middle of the parade grounds, and Fara sauntered to his side and gave him a more than average tip. The heat caused a trickle of sweat to glide uncomfortably down her back and under the waistband of her miniskirt. She explained who she was and that *Ghost Lovers* was going to be filming at the fort. Lightly attaching herself to his arm, she swayed purposefully. Within the first ten seconds, she had the young man's undivided attention. Unfortunately, he had only been in his position for six weeks and knew nothing other than what was printed in the guidebook.

He led her to the offices, which were next to the employee parking area where J.C. had left his car that first night. Her mind drifted to Lago La Plata, imagining J.C. on an elegant veranda sipping a frosty beer from a pilsner glass. Last night he didn't include her in his plans. It was better this way. She'd been right to come here on her own. She knew how to seduce information from men and sharpened her rusty skills on the young ranger.

Before he left to retrieve the head of security, he asked Fara out to dinner, to which her only answer was a coy smile.

The ranger left her in a waiting area. She imagined J.C. and his friend, Andres, sliding the access card into the electronic lock on the wall. If Andres' father had been the head of security, it would have made more sense to swipe his card rather than the ranger's. She doubted Señor Calderon's card had total access. Perhaps it was the easier of the two to obtain, and the boys went with the path of least resistance. Curiosity and sense of adventure lured them to explore the fort at night, and they probably were drunk or buzzed, or both.

One thing she noticed when she arrived in Puerto Rico was the availability of liquor, and during her stroll through Old San Juan, the scent of other substances hung in the air. With the high cost of living, the only way many folks could survive would be fueling the black market with contraband and drugs. Being local high school students, J.C. and Andres would have been able to access anything they wanted. But that wasn't her problem, and it certainly had no bearing on her quest for Vivian Dufrense.

While seated in a utilitarian plastic chair, Fara stared at the tiny red light glowing on the edge of the electronic lock, which was out of place on the ancient stone wall, holding tightly to a twisted anachronistic imbalance. Closing her eyes, she tried to imagine what the entrance would have looked like back in Vivian's day. When her ship docked in Bajia de San Juan, Dufrense would have met his daughter's entourage with a carriage to bring them to the fort. Would the horses have pulled the carriage up the steep stone drive, or would they have used another entrance, something more secluded?

The door clicked, and her eyes sprung open to view a man in an impeccably tailored charcoal suit. The first impression reminded her of Guy Carver, her former lover who died in a car bomb explosion.

The man's impatient brown eyes immediately stared at her crossed legs and then floated up her body to her face. His irritated stance relaxed, and a haughty smile grew across clean features. Flawless from the perfectly groomed closely-cropped black hair down to the toes of his sparkling Italian leather shoes, a man awaiting a general's inspection couldn't have been better prepared, and subsequently, he seemed even more out of place than the lock on the wall.

After introducing herself, Fara sidled to his side, purposefully brushing the tip of her right breast against his arm. She clung as delicately as a Southern belle and felt his pulse quicken under her fingers. Power resounded through her veins, infusing her faculties with the heady mix of endorphins and adrenaline. She inhaled deeply, savoring the powerful rush.

Señor Muñoz slid his card through the slot in the side of the electronic lock. Like an old-school gentleman, he escorted her into the security room which was organized as efficiently as a fortified bunker in a war zone.

She had learned how to observe critical information quickly and efficiently, and when paired with her natural feminine wiles, she slipped into areas men would have no other options to get into other than fighting their way through the front door. This door definitely wasn't the front door. The gun-metal steel was thick and heavy with a small reinforced window at the top.

Fara's eyes flicked across multiple security monitors noting not much could go on within the fort without some type of recording. Watchful guards followed the tour groups from the upper left, across the row, and then down to the next line, through standard locations, starting at the entrance, and going through the casemates, the battery, Devil's garita, plaza de armas, chapel, barracks, great moat, the Caballero, and then across the expanse of the defense depth. In addition to the cameras, motion sensors covered critical junctures. Camera number four would have documented her climb up onto the exterior wall.

The predominant screens at eye level displayed four areas she had not seen during the two tours, and she quickly identified the real dungeon. The camera's lens wavered slightly as if trying to focus on something in the darkness shifting behind the massive iron-barred gate. She had the uncanny feeling something was watching her through the camera's lens, rather than the reverse. A shiver inched up Fara's spine, far too slowly to be an innate reaction, like an unseen tongue damply lapped over her damaged flesh. Ignoring the sensation, she smiled a practiced grin and flapped long lashes toward Señor Muñoz as she shuffled a half-step to the left. Purposefully, she had positioned herself for his back to be toward the monitors.

One camera was at the juncture of two hallways, and what appeared to be the administrative wing was to the left. The doors were rectangular, definitely not Eighteenth Century, but not really modern either, rather a period of governmental utilitarian that spanned the ages. The walls were barren of ornamentation except for rectangular sodium vapor lamps near the ceiling. Even though the monitors were black and white, in her mind's eye she could see the orange light emanating in waves. Ranking officer quarters branched to the right. On the tour, she remembered looking into the hall from the opposite end where there was a chain with a small "No Entrada" sign.

The next monitor covering a long tunnel was green and grainy. Throughout the fort's design, the architects had used daylight to illuminate the corridors and rooms. Even most of the tunnels had some sort of ambient lighting at regular intervals. However, this corridor ended in a point that was blacker than black, like an endless void or black hole that absorbed all light. Even the night-vision camera was unable to penetrate the depths. This area had to be at the very bottom of the fort. The roman-arch design would support the superstructure's massive amount of weight. But if that were true, what or where would it be sloping toward? The architects built San Cristobal on a rocky hill, perhaps it was an evacuation route, a last ditch escape in the case the fort fell to the enemy. But why would something so potentially obscure and meaningless in these days and times still need to be monitored constantly?

The final screen displayed a hallway with antique furnishings and a carpeted runner down the center of a broad and highly polished floor. Fara felt her eyes widen as one of the doors swung open, not a few inches, but wide enough for a person to pass through easily. The motion alarm sounded, yet no one, no one visible anyway, had stepped into the hall. Acutely aware, she observed the protocol of which buttons the young security guard pressed to deactivate the alarm. While committing 8-4-6-3-1-2-

4-8 to memory, she passively waited for the guard to inform Señor Muñoz. The look of impatience and irritation returned to the man's charcoal eyes. On the main computer keyboard, Señor Muñoz typed in a security code, B-4-t-i-m-e-2-b. The 3-D display of red dots throughout the complex turned green with the exception of one.

Señor Muñoz opened the disabled door without swiping his card. Without asking, Fara swept into stride beside him. As they left the administrative hall, the modernizations immediately fled back into the Eighteenth Century. Fara continued to follow him up a tight spiral staircase, designed for an upper-level defense with a sword. At the top, Señor Muñoz expertly thumbed through the keys and found the one for the upper passageway. He held the door, and with a hand on her waist, ushered her into the expansive hall.

A faint whisper had Señor Muñoz turning an ear as well. Although slight, the whisper would speak and then pause, as if carrying on a one-sided conversation. They were close enough now to localize the sound, yet not close enough to determine what the feminine voice was saying.

Fara entered the large bedroom. The air was frigid, as if an air conditioner had been pounding out cold for hours. Directly in her ear, she heard clearly however faintly, "I will not live without you," spoken in Spanish with an old-fashioned Castilian lisp. The hairs on her body rose with a consuming tingle which pressed into the place where Fara had hidden her own sense of loss.

An unseen hand parted the draperies near the window. Compelled with the parallels, Fara followed the motion, exposing the doorframe that had several oddly placed nail holes which had been driven in and then removed. They were parallel on each side of the jam, like these doors had been boarded up for a time.

The small balcony had a spectacular view of the northern wall, securely dividing land from sea. In the center was the garita, where the young woman had taken her life.

Señor Muñoz's footsteps approached; even though, the circular rug muffled the sound.

She asked, "Does that happen often?"

He stopped. "I don't know what you mean."

With a hand still clasping the leafy print, Fara turned to face him. "The door opening on its own. The chill. Voices. Those are classic symptoms of a haunting." Allowing the fabric to trail through her fingers, she stepped past him toward the massive canopy bed with carved bedposts the size of tree trunks. Oddly, the bed was turned down. The linens were fine quality in a soft green, elegantly complimenting the flower and vine patterned fabric draping from the canopy's overhead folds.

Out of the corner of her vision, Fara caught her own reflection in the oval mirror atop the dresser. Someone else was there, and then she wasn't. Yet even a glimpse of the raven-haired beauty left a lasting impression, especially in the eyes where swirling fog replaced the actual eyeballs. A swish of intense cold then led to an immediate change, stirring a warm current into the air.

Señor Muñoz's tone was even, however perturbed. "So, we're back to the ghost business?"

Seductively, Fara's light chuckle carried through the rapidly warming room. "At the moment ghosts are my business." Draping her arm around the carved pillar, she leaned against the footboard, "And I always put business before pleasure."

He stopped abruptly before crossing into the band of light stretching through the gap in the drapes. "I'll keep you true to your word and remind you when it's time for pleasure, Señorita Trotter."

Casually, she tipped her head and with a sweep tossed her hair over her shoulder. "We are both practically-minded individuals and know a draft blew the door open, but that doesn't make for an interesting television program. So, why don't we let our imaginations run wild? A beautiful young woman was staying, let's just say, in this room. She lived a sheltered life and was innocent in the ways of men."

"Hopefully you don't suffer those same challenges." Seizing her arms, the man turned her firmly toward him. "You are an incredibly attractive and sensual woman, Señorita Trotter."

With manipulative glee, she noticed his eyes had darkened, yet not necessarily with desire. Instead of sensing pheromones rising, her intuition kicked in. Something was off, unnaturally out of balance. Not allowing her uneasiness to show, she stroked a finger along his smoothly-shaven cheek, which was cool, a little too cool to the touch. "Señorita Trotter sounds so formal, especially attached to such a lovely compliment, Señor Muñoz."

His rich laugh reverberated off from the smooth walls. "Let's overcome that barrier at least. Call me Fernando, and I will call you Fara."

With a smooth breath, she cooed a low and guttural moan. "I like that. It's so much … friendlier." Too many men had told her that her voice made them weak, and she poured the smooth charm into well-accentuated words. "You know, if we could set aside all of my business questions, we could focus on those of a more pleasurable nature."

His body visibly tightened, and his clothing adjusted automatically with the change. Not once did a button pull, a lapel buckle open, or even the collar gap. "What do you want to know?"

"Well, I try to be thorough in every aspect of my life. I have a very passionate nature, you see, throwing myself fully into each endeavor." She shrugged and affected a little pout with her bottom lip and watched his eyes carefully, which didn't show any tangible sign of alacrity. "I have such little information to build upon, and as I explained, this is my first assignment for the show. I want all of the details to rise and stand out, to be ardently compelling." She skimmed her fingers along the well-muscled arm and felt his flesh quietly shudder, still not in a sensual way. Just hidden beneath his smooth façade, something rough and disjointed bided its time, just inside the overly cool exterior. "This innocent young woman, just old enough to feel the compelling desire to know a man, arrives at the fort. Would she have come up the main drive or would they use a secret entrance?"

"The fort is full of secrets, but for her to have stayed in this wing, she would have been a visiting dignitary or blood relative of someone very important, so her arrival would have been regaled with full honors. The Captain Generals would receive her entourage in the reception hall."

"Were Captain Generals known for their hospitality and generosity?"

His eyes darted to the doorway as if he worried to be overheard. "Not particularly."

"So if her uncle discovered her interest for a sailor, she would be...?"

"It would depend on whether or not she had been compromised." The cool, factual tone drifted.

"Let's take it from the perspective of both scenarios, and tell me which you would find most compelling, for the show of course. She is a pious girl, well-bred from a good family. A handsome sailor captures her attentions during their voyage to Puerto Rico. She remains chaste; although, her young body yearns for something she doesn't understand. The sailor, being an honorable and well-bred man himself, courts her as a gentleman should, adhering to appropriate social norms. Shelving his sexual needs, he returns to Spain to gain permission to marry her from her father. At the time, I believe men outnumbered women on the island. Suitors of the highest echelon seek her out, yet she remains committed to her promise to marry her one true love. Once she discovers he has perished on his journey back to her, she," Fara paused allowing the words to linger on her lips. "This is where I need you Fernando. How does the story end?"

"People have seen a woman in a pink nightdress run out of the stairway and toward the garita, jumping to her death." His eyes darted to a muffled sound coming from the veranda. "Without a scream."

"Oh," Fara exhaled, slowly blowing the breath between her parted lips. "That would be a tragic sight for some poor tourist. Whoever saw it would certainly report the story to security. Hopefully, it doesn't happen frequently."

"More frequently than you would expect. I inherited a file at least an inch thick of documented sightings since the fort became a national park."

"Oh my," she dramatically glanced over her shoulder and shivered as if the ghost was only inches away. "Is she the only ghost at the fort?"

His hands immediately clasped her by the waist. "How could someone as sensitive and beautiful as you chose such a macabre profession?"

"I guess deep-down I love to be scared." She assessed the odd sensation, which continued to heighten her unease, but she didn't let it show. "You know, it's like going to scary movie with a strong man to keep me safe and then take my mind off from the movie. The Pink Lady isn't really scary. I'm sure there are plenty of other stories you could tell me about the fort that would set my pulse on fire."

"First, tell me the other scenario. The one where she was chaste and virtuous was so compelling I want to hear you tell the other." He drew her closer. "I love how you tell a story."

"It would start the same way." Again, his touch stirred her anxious awareness, and warning shot into her system. "She is sailing toward Puerto Rico, and the lieutenant, a rogue in every sense of the word, makes physical advances, breaking down her traditional and pious defenses. She is innocent to the ways of men and doesn't know about bodily pleasure, so little by little, the good lieutenant introduces his plan calculatingly. He measures each move and adds more influence with each encounter. First, by whispering about her beauty. Then his hands caress her body."

Fernando's hands urgently plied over Fara's lower back, skimming the rounded tops of her derriere. Although she knew he intended his touch to be sensual, the stroking missed its mark, irritating rather than arousing.

"With each delight, he eases her to his will. Since she is an honored guest of the ship's Captain, the lieutenant's behavior is proscribed aboard ship, so he has to wait and plans to demonstrate his love once they've arrived. Even though the fort is so large, it's busy with people, so the lovers arrange a liaison outside of the city walls, which would mean she requires a secret tunnel to escape from the ever watchful eyes of her uncle, which takes precious time. The night before the lieutenant's ship sails for Spain they meet at a prearranged rendezvous. She's so happy to see him she collapses into his arms. He lowers her to the soft grass under a shady tree and," she stopped and linked with Fernando's eyes. They should have been broiling with desire. Although banked flames were present, passion wasn't driving them. "Well, I'm sure a man of your experience knows what comes next."

"I certainly do." He drew her hard and fast against him, pressing his mouth to hers.

Normally she would have been amused to know her seduction was working, but she barely tolerated the challenging embrace. While struggling to wriggle free, she tried to make it seem playful. "Fernando, you are going to make me lose track of why I came here in the first place." She eased out of his grasp and sauntered toward the doors that closed off the small veranda. Drawing back the draperies, the afternoon sun spilled across the floor, and Fernando shrank from it, edging back to the far side of the circular rug.

"Promising to be ever faithful and to take her as his bride, she relishes in the physical sensations coursing through her body, and he teaches her what it means to be a woman. With their culminated passion now spent, they still cling to each other, somehow knowing this would be the only pleasure they would ever find together. Alone, she weaves her way back through the labyrinth of tunnels and sneaks back to this room, patiently awaiting her lover to return. When she learns of the shipwreck, she is inconsolable, so her uncle quickly promises her to another man. But she is no longer a maid, and in all honesty, she could never give her heart to another, so she runs out of the stairwell and slips through the narrow opening of the garita, throwing herself into the surf foaming on the rocks and thereby joining her lover in the sea." She glanced over her shoulder. "So which do you find the most compelling?"

His eyes glint darkly from the shadows. "There's no comparison."

Allowing the draperies to fall back in place, she glided across the room, pausing in the doorway, knowing she would now be visible on the security cameras, which should preclude any other personal embraces. "But the second scenario will require so much more information about the fort. I will need full access to the records and learn its innermost secrets. The show's executive producer is steadfast on maintaining the schedule, so I must start writing the script today to email at least the outline to the studio tonight. It would be such a help to review the files about ghost sightings and any maps of the complex. You've no idea how grateful I would be."

"Come back to my office, and I'll give you what you need." With a sidelong stare, he moved past her into the hall, closing the door securely behind them.

Delaying for a moment, she tugged on the ornate handle. The door didn't budge. She looked back toward the man, and the dark eyes seemed to swirl momentarily with a rainbow of color, sweeping under heavy lids.

They retraced their steps back to the administrative corridor, and Fara followed Fernando into the barren office. No knick-knacks or other non-essential items warmed the enclosed space. The bone-colored paint was fresh, and the scent hung in the ever damp air. "You've recently moved in I see. Where are the pictures of the wife and kids?"

"My predecessor recently retired, and I've only been here a couple weeks." He chuckled while sliding into his chair, "As to the pictures, I've focused on my career. Spent the past few years overseas, so I haven't any family pictures, yet." Fernando smiled and then opened the lower desk drawer. Not watching what he was doing, the large silver ring on his index finger snagged the edge of the drawer as he pulled out the file.

Multiplying in the other incongruities in Fernando's behavior, warning bells resounded, exponentially magnifying Fara's initial qualms. She had been in enough government offices to last a lifetime, and the files in the lower desk drawer were for daily access. Somehow, he knew she would be coming here and requesting the file. Her mind whirled through the possibilities. If his personal interest had been sincere, he might want to expose what had been happening at the fort. The second, and more likely scenario, was he made a fake file to mislead her.

Both led her to question who was Señor Muñoz, and what did he really want?

CHAPTER 13

While waiting in the tranquil serenity within the immaculate garden of El Convento, J.C. should have been relaxed; however, with each passing minute, his fingers drummed faster on the side of the chair, keeping time with the headache pounding inside his temples. He didn't want to be obsessive, worrying about Fara's disappearance, yet ugly thoughts popped into his mind with aggravating frequency of Fara having lost her memory, wandering around dazed and confused. However, those were better than thinking about her inviting another man to play a new round of sexual roulette.

He saw her step through the lobby doors, alone and apparently unharmed, and his heart skipped a beat. He didn't want to get involved, not now, not ever, and especially not with someone who saw him as a damnable inconvenience, yet just like the time he'd gone skydiving, the sensation of the wind and speed flowed through his body, engaging all of his senses. Yet instead of being able to pull a shoot and glide back to earth, his heart was going to hit at a hundred and twenty miles an hour, shattering into a million pieces at Fara Trotter's feet.

Absolutely inconsistent with his turbulent mood, Fara smiled. "How were things at the lake?"

The words skidded through his dry throat. "You should have been there."

"Must have been beautiful. Did you get a chance to visit with your friend?" She glided into the rattan chair next to his, sliding her right calf down the glossy flesh of her left. She was wearing the same shoes she had on last night, and he hated the way he wanted to take them off from her again.

"Yeah, he brought the wife and kids, and we went out on his new boat." His eyes burned, but he told himself it was from the sun and wind. Trying to add every ounce of frustration to clue her into his mood, he repeated more vehemently, "You should have been there."

She shifted uncomfortably. "Last night you said you were going to the lake, not us, so I decided to check out the fort again."

"You went to San Cristobal?" Jesus, even saying the name made his palms sweat. "By yourself?"

"I met with the head of security, the new guy who took Señor Figueroa's place."

"Fernando Muñoz." J.C.'s eyes narrowed, watching for any reaction.

"Yeah, that's him." She shifted again and then rose. "I'd like to hear more about your day, but I need to go to the bathroom. Why don't you come inside?"

Instantly deflating his effort to make her uncomfortable, he got up and followed her, heeling like a fucking puppy. Quickly he approached the door before hers in the hall. "I got tired of not spending time in my own hotel room, so I checked in. We're neighbors."

Not catching her expression, which he wanted to do, he entered his room and knocked on the smaller adjoining door. In a moment, it swung open. He stepped through and caught Fara's backside as she slipped into her bedroom and heard the bathroom door close.

His hand wound into his hair and twisted the roots sharply. This isn't what he had envisioned, not at all. His blistered ego was ready to get into a full-blown fight when she breezed in with the *I didn't think I was invited* bull-shit. Like hell!

She came around the corner and went straight to her massive hobo-style purse she had tossed onto the table and withdrew a file. "I had a productive day." She glanced over her shoulder, and her stare lingered when he didn't say anything. "What's wrong?"

The thin leash holding back his rage snapped. "Take a fucking guess. I stayed last night because I was worried about you and was supposed to watch out for you today, and you trip out on me. Didn't know where you went or who you were with. You just fucking disappear."

She swept the piece of paper off from the top of the closed computer. "I left you a note."

"I didn't want a fucking note." He snatched it from her hand and read it hastily.

> *Dear J.C. – Thank you for watching out for me. You are an angel in disguise. I feel fine and decided to go ahead and start the day. Have fun at the lake with your friend. I'm going to the fort and hope to discover more about the sightings. See you this evening or in the morning depending on how your day goes. Call me later.*
> *–Fara*

Defiance stretched into her voice. "Then what the hell did you want?"

"You. I wanted to spend the day with you. I wanted to introduce you to Andres, and I was hoping you'd charm some information out of his dad. Instead, my grandfather and Andres' father spent the afternoon discussing the fort's maintenance plan." He stomped, not knowing how to express all of the challenges screaming through his brain. "Damn it Fara. Why'd you skip out on me?"

She settled into the chair and leaned back, her eyes narrowing dangerously into thin slits of piercing green. "Some of the details from yesterday are a little fuzzy, but I clearly remember you saying you were going to the lake, not us."

"Yeah, well, we're a team. I had expected you to go with me." He wanted to growl out a slew of raging derogations, but anything he said would just backfire and make him look ridiculous. How could he tell her he was worried about her? He wanted to show her off to Andres and his father, and even worse, he wanted to wake up beside her. Instead, he was alone and felt like an outsider while kids ran around the yard and played in the water.

"Okay, I didn't realize you wanted to stick together; although, we covered more ground separately." With a huff, she swept the file off from the table. "I did get my hands on this."

He barely looked at the file. "What else did you get your hands on?"

Fara sneered. "Is that what you're worried about? Are you jealous of a six-foot three wall of muscle who wears a designer suit in this heat and doesn't break a sweat?"

"Of course not." The blood rushed to his face, and he knew the start of a sunburn turned even redder. "I was worried about you. How's the bump on your head?"

She sat at the table and gazed up with two doses of emerald fire. "My getting hit on the head wasn't your fault."

Jesus, she didn't remember their kiss, but unfortunately, he did. How he pushed her up against the door and took her lips was omnipresent all day, making the need to do it again churn in his stomach, tying it into knots. Perhaps it was better for him to have awakened alone. If not, he would have rolled over and drawn her against him, kissing her face and gloriously long neck.

"I saw Vivian's ghost."

The simple words snapped J.C. out of the intimate details of how her breasts felt cupped in the palms of his hands. "You did what?"

"I was in the security room; the bottom right monitor is the upper residential wing. A door opened without explanation. I went to investigate with Señor Muñoz, and I saw Vivian in the mirror. Her face was slender, really too thin, and framed with dark hair. She wore a pale pink nightdress, even the bed was open as if she was ready to slip between the sheets."

His misery and discomfort instantly fled. "Did you see her eyes?"

"Vivian looked straight at me, acknowledging I was there, but she didn't really have eyes." Fara sucked her lower lips between her teeth. "It's hard to describe."

"Like foggy swirling mist?"

"Yeah." She perked, nodding slowly. "You know the saying that eyes are the gateway to the soul? I got the feeling her eyes were reflecting the void where she's trapped." She lifted the hand that still held the file. "Supposedly, this is a record of the sightings. I haven't had a chance to look through it. I came right back here."

With his curiosity peaked, he walked behind her and leaned over the back of the chair. "What do you mean supposedly?"

"There're a few things that just don't add up." She opened the file and thumbed through the pages clipped to the top with standard two-hole prongs, punched in perfect alignment, as if they were drilled in a single stack. "More so feelings."

"What feelings?" He wished she hadn't glanced up. Her eyes were too bright. Her lips too close. All he needed to do was lean forward and taste them.

"Let's just call it intuition." She looked back to the papers, skipping to the very back. "A bunch of weird little anomalies. Each on its own doesn't mean anything, but they add up to strange. Like this," she rubbed the edge of the paper between her fingers, "white bond paper, twenty-weight, extra bright." She held it up to the light. "No watermark, but back then most paper had one. The date on this report is 1983, the year the fort became a national park, almost thirty years ago, but this sheet of paper is just as white as the top page, indicating a sighting not quite two weeks ago. Yet the file folder itself appears to be original. See how the drab green is yellowed at the corners. Oils from the skin absorb into paper whenever it's handled." She flipped over the last page and ran her fingers across the back of the paper. "In 1983, this would have been typed, but there aren't impacts on the page from typewriter keys or even a Selectric cartridge ball."

J.C. ran his own hand over the back of the smooth paper. "He could have run a copy to keep the original. I wouldn't give out an original file."

"On a copy, the yellowed age would come across as gray at the corners, and the typeface would still show deviations, shadowing where some keys would hit harder than others. This was printed out, recently, on an ink-jet printer." She thumbed through the reports. "Each page is exactly the same, except for the dates. And there're only about the Pink Lady. There aren't any other reports, even though the file's entitled, 'Unexplained Occurrences.' When did you and Andres visit the fort? What was the date?"

"February 29th, 2000."

"Leap year. People tend to do strange things on leap year day. Like it's a bonus free for all." Fara continued through the pages. "Nothing's noted in 2000."

As soon as his curiosity started to fade, the gnawing jealousy returned. The emotional tide ebbed and flowed, but regardless, it was omnipresent. "Why would he go through so much trouble?"

"That's the question now, isn't it?" With a huff, she closed the useless file and shoved it across the table.

Seeing her exasperation and disgust made J.C. wonder what she had to do to get the file in the first place. "We're talking about a ghost from the late Eighteenth Century for Christ's sake. What difference would it make?"

"When we find out the answer, we'll resolve more than just the mystery surrounding Vivian Dufrense. It has to be tied to whatever you saw that night in the fort." Fara twisted in her chair, bringing her face too close. "What did you discover?"

"Nothing." God, he needed space. J.C. paced across the room, but something kept pulling him back to her, dragged by the force of some inner tide. "My day was bizarre as well. Andres and I had promised never to tell a soul, so I waited until we were alone to ask him about it. He didn't remember. Not like he didn't want to talk about it, not remember. It was as if his memory had been erased, like it never happened in the first place." He wouldn't forget Andres' blank stare without any inkling behind the gray eyes. "Later, I asked his dad about the sightings of ghosts, and he joked it away with stories of drunken tourists in the heat. My grandfather didn't help either. Every time I brought up the subject, he would detour. Close, but not really what I was looking for."

"Well, at least he admitted there were sightings. Even a drunk tourist would throw in an occasional truth, and no two people would describe the situation quite the same way." Rocking her head side to side, she stretched her neck, and he resisted the urge to lay his hands on her shoulders and massage the tension. "So why make up a dummy file? Señor Muñoz could have told me he didn't have a clue about any file regarding ghost sightings. He's so new would have been plausible. Much more realistic than creating a," she broke off and held up a single finger to her lips, which had J.C. stopping dead in his tracks.

Quickly, she retrieved the folder, slipped the small metal slides off from the tips of the tines, and lifted the rectangular metal plate off from the first page. Turning it carefully, she noted no deviations in the standardized design. She made a little circle with her index finger. "God J.C., that bump on the head really must have got to me more than I was willing to admit. I don't know what I was thinking, how ridiculous all of that sounded. I'm sorry. I'm paranoid and crazy, which is why they kicked me out in the first place. You know, I have a very interesting theory on who shot J.F.K. Not many people know Jackie was suffering from post partum depression..." Fara continued to babble about the presidential assassination conspiracy theories while examining each prong with the tell-tale bends that demonstrated how the file grew over time.

The uppermost grooves were higher than the height of the current stack, indicating it had been significantly larger than what it was at the moment. Finally, she slid each single page of paper off from the metal tips. At the end she pushed the prongs to disengage them from the folder, but they didn't budge. She flipped the ensemble over and stared at the new piece of tape holding the base of the prongs secure. From her purse, she withdrew a tiny pocket knife and slid it along the edges of the metal, releasing the clasp from the aged folder. Hiding inside was a tiny metal dot, smaller around than a pencil's eraser and thin, barely perceptible, as small as a chad of punched paper. Carefully sliding the blade of the penknife under it, Fara balanced the chip on the tip.

He leaned in closer, cheek to cheek, looking at what he assumed was a bug. He had never seen one before but knew enough not to ask if that was what this was. Falling in line with her game, he added with a full dose of masculine machismo, "That's okay sweetheart. You know babes are pretty to look at, but most of the time, I'm not expecting much upstairs. You can babble about Kennedy all you want. I still think you're gorgeous."

He watched in amazement while she reassembled the pieces perfectly so that no one would even begin to think they had taken it apart, including putting the bug back where she had found it.

Contemptuously, she rolled her eyes and shook her head. "I guess I'll take that as a compliment. To stay on schedule, we have to get started. When we get back from dinner, I'd like to start on the outline of the script."

"Is that an invitation?"

"Baby, you were pretty damn clear about us being a team." She walked the file into her bedroom and closed the door. Taking him by the arm, she led him into his bedroom and shut the connecting door. Before saying anything, they continued into his bathroom where she turned on the faucet.

"Was that what I think it was?"

"Yeah, not cutting-edge technology but pretty damn savvy. I should have thought to check the file before saying anything. Shit! Muñoz set me up, and I don't take that lightly. I knew it was too easy."

"What do you mean too easy?" He stared into her uncanny eyes. "What were you prepared to do?"

Tipping her head back, she regarded him impassively for a few seconds. "My plan was to get him interested in me personally, enough to where he would give me the file to help me with my new job, explaining I would express my gratitude once the shoot had concluded."

"Shit, that's what I expected you to say." His stomach churned. "So what did you do to engage his interest?"

"You really want to know, don't you?" She ran her fingers over his cheek like sensual ribbons. "Nothing except some seductive words, but he," she pulled her hand back, "oh, I don't know. It's like he was trying to seduce me in the same manner, but not really. Two shams equal an even bigger anomaly."

He closed his eyes but couldn't close off his mind to how her simple touch brought his senses to life. "So what do we do now? Hide in the bathroom all night?"

"We'll take the file with us to dinner and drop it off in your car. It can stay outside until morning. Its internal battery should die by then. The tiny ones don't last long." She huffed. "I'll take it back to Muñoz tomorrow." She hastily stood, and then with a twist, she scanned J.C. with her eyes. "Did you take your clothes off today?"

"Did you?"

Fara laughed, and the simple shake of her head didn't really answer his question. "Did you change into a swimsuit or perhaps leave your shoes on the dock?"

"Yeah, so?" He felt stupid as she raised her brows, and understanding flooded into his mind.

"Take off your clothes."

Although he had wanted her to say those words to him for hours, he hesitated.

She leaned against his body and whispered, "If you want privacy, I can go into the other room."

"Hell no." With a skewed grin, he started unbuttoning his shirt and then handed it to her. With each piece of clothing, she examined the seams and felt every inch of the hems, even tried to peel off the tops of the coconut husk buttons. He had lost any hope for this being arousing when her attention was on what had covered his body, rather than what it had been covering.

She took his shorts from him, and he watched her eyes skim over his naked torso that was standing less than two feet from her. Unfortunately, just her looking at him was enough for heat to grow within his loins. "What about you?"

She pulled her eyes away. "Hmm?"

"It's your turn. I show you mine, you show me yours."

"Hate to disappoint you, but it's not gonna happen." Not even phased, her fingers continued down the length of his belt. With an indomitable look furling her brows, she strode out of the bathroom and back to the table, twisting the three-way bulb onto its highest setting and angling the lamp shade for its full effect. Changing the blade to a tiny flathead screwdriver, she worked it into the tight leather loop wrapped around the base of the buckle. With the precision of a surgeon, she worked it from both sides but wasn't able to dislodge whatever was there.

Still naked, J.C. had followed her and watched her work. Her hands were steady as if she had been disarming a bomb, trying one angle then another. Only once she exhausted the options within her mini toolkit, she finally took out the tiny blade, slicing open the thick leather as easily as a scrap of paper. There on the inside, was another little disk. Without a word, she held it up like the first, balancing on the tip of the knife to examine it carefully. For what, he wasn't sure he wanted to know. What he did want to know was why they would go to all of that trouble. Worse yet, who were *they*? Amazed, he watched her set the bug back onto the leather.

She pulled the thin plastic liner out of the trash can under the table and set the belt inside. Drawing J.C. aside, she whispered directly into his ear. "Put the rest of your clothes in the bag, and I will too, just to be on the safe side. We'll keep them and the file in the trunk of the car until tomorrow."

"You did, didn't you?" He haughtily stepped back. With the same gentle patience as she exhibited in the bathroom, she reached out and set her palm against his bare chest, but just like before, she didn't answer.

CHAPTER 14

J.C. and Fara looked like any other couple while strolling into the parking lot. To a casual observer, Fara was completely at ease, but J.C. could see her eyes. Vigilant as a hunting falcon, she scanned each vehicle for signs of a transmitter link. She said the hidden devices had a very limited range. J.C. had to take her word for it. At least he had his answer; she was a spy. He envisioned the women in James Bond movies, seductively luring men into their beds to find out their secrets.

She didn't look like an international spy in her tennis shoes and denim shorts, which made it all the more plausible. For the late afternoon, Calle de Cristo surprisingly wasn't very crowded. She walked in her normal leggy stride, not quite as edgy or deliberately as when she led him to the hotel for the first time. Their first and only time.

He didn't want that memory to go the way of Andres' recollection of the fort, which bothered him more than he wanted to admit. He had heard of internal defense mechanisms blocking out negative memories that were too violent or painful for the conscious mind to process. Although he would be better off to block the image of those whirling demon eyes, he just couldn't do it.

The street ended in Parque de las Palomas. He hadn't been in this section of Old San Juan since he was a kid, when his mother's parents had visited from Brooklyn. They had done the tourist things, including the tour of the fort. In his gut, the memory resonated in that weird preternatural way. Events in his life revolved around contact with San Cristobal. That Sunday had been the last time his family was together. He was only six and was tired, acting up like any cranky young boy. He went home with his Calderon grandparents while his parents took the Goyas to the airport. On the way back home, his parents ran headlong into a truck that had jackknifed inside the tunnel. In a flash, he was an orphan. Even so long ago, the pain of knowing he'd never see his parents again still existed; although, the burning edge of it had dulled over the years. No one else would ever understand what it felt like to have everything suddenly change. No time to say goodbye. His last words to them were angry, saying he hated them for making him go home. Just that fact had saved his life. If he had been in the car with them, he would have died too. Sometimes he wished he had.

Shaking it from his mind, he followed Fara along Calle Tetuan, listening to her passive account of the night after he stormed out of her hotel room. She pointed out the doorway where the armed guard stood with an AK47, vigilantly watching the tourists and the shops.

About every four steps, he had to tug the waistband of his shorts. Although pants hanging onto the rises of a guy's butt were in style, he couldn't stand how it felt. He also couldn't remember which boxers he had worn. He thought they were the black ones with gray plaid, but he wasn't sure and didn't want to look.

They ducked inside the store on the corner. In between the t-shirts silkscreened with drunken frogs playing guitars and the display of shot glasses, they found a rack of leather belts embossed with the Puerto Rican flag. Turning one over in his hands, J.C. examined the pattern warily and kept telling himself it was only temporary until he could go to the mall and buy a plain brown leather belt, but he'd have to wear it to keep his pants from sliding.

Dusky twilight was falling, braiding the lazy shadows with brilliant streaks of red sunset. Just like in the car, the light filled Fara's face and hair with heavenly light, highlighting her features with rosy softness. She was more than beautiful. She was a goddess.

Just when she started to describe the music, a lively Latin rhythm officially welcomed the night. He slipped his hand into hers as they crossed Calle Tanca, and then she turned into the nearly concealed alleyway between the buildings. The yellowed lamps glowed with hazy softness, but incense wasn't adding to the drifting haze. They walked past the shop where she bought the violet dress continuing to the end of the corridor, but the door to the jewelry and coin shop was closed.

Fara's knocks brought out the shopkeeper next door.

J.C. answered him in Spanish, "We're looking for the little coin shop."

"Hasn't been a store there for at least fifteen years."

Fara tipped her head, adding a Castilian lisp to her Spanish. "Does a woman live here with long white hair and a young face?"

"You're confusing this with someplace else, mujer." He crossed his arms tightly. "Like I said, no one's been there for years. We use the place for storage, nothing more."

"Can you describe the people who used to be here? Have you seen a woman with pure white hair here?"

The brawny arms pulled tightly like the lines at the corners of his eyes. "No one's been there. There's no one to see. Why don't you come in my store? I got some nice carvings."

"No thanks. I had my eye on an antique coin." She turned back down the tiled hall and paused in front of the clothing store, staring at the purple top and skirt on the mannequin near the door. She didn't say another word, not even once they emerged onto the street.

J.C. watched as the line between her brows furrow even deeper. Taking her hand, he stopped before heading into the next block. "I believe you."

Her eyes widened. "What?"

"I said I believe you." He stroked her fingers casually, giving him a reason not to let them go.

"I don't know why. I just led you to a place that doesn't exist."

"It had been a store, just not in this time." He held up her hand. "You were meant to have that ring, and somehow the ghosts got it to you."

She scoffed. "I want my money back then because they won't need it."

He chuckled at the incongruent parallel of practicality and fantasy intertwining into a single concept. "If they had tried to give the ring to you, would you have taken it?"

"No. I would have thought it was some scam." She looked at her finger. The final light of the day hit the emerald, making it glow, radiating bands of wavy green light.

Securely, he wrapped his fingers around hers, drawing her closer to admire the glowing ring. "I think this was Vivian's ring, the one Lieutenant Cordova gave her."

"The lady did say there was another ring, with a matching stone, one that was lost." She closed her eyes tightly. "She said this was a reminder of love lost, love that would endure over time."

He raised her hand gingerly to his lips, kissing the back gently, yet she didn't open her eyes. "Anything else?"

"The emerald was cut here on the island hundreds of years ago."

"Who knows, it could have been cut right there in that shop. Jewelers kept their stores off the streets to reduce theft. Lots of gold and gems would pass through the islands on the way to Spain. Most of it went through Hispaniola, which is now the Dominican Republic, but San Juan had a safer port in a storm. And once El Morro and then San Cristobal defended the island, there wasn't a safer harbor."

"Did people give engagement rings back then?" Opening her eyes, she shrugged to reclaim her hand, but he didn't relinquish his hold. "As you astutely pointed out, I'm not a history buff, but I don't think a woman wore a ring until she was married. Do you know?"

"That sounds right. Why?"

"If this was Vivian's ring, and the other was Felipe's that was lost at sea, it would mean they were married and not just lovers."

For a moment a strangely powerful pause hung in the air. Startling them both, the stone began to vibrate. They looked up to each other, confirming with their eyes what they were experiencing was real, while an audible hum encased them.

SALLY SWANSON

CHAPTER 15

Pungent scents drifted from the docks, ripe odors mingling
sweat and watery decay. A horse-drawn buggy wheeled past
with a barefoot black boy perched on the rear rigging. On the
opposite side of the cobblestone street, a lady in a sunny yellow
dress rounded a puddle. Every man stopped to stare. Yet they
bustled past J.C. and Fara, ignorant of their anachronistic
presence.

The hum continued to envelop them while J.C. led Fara back
to the tiled hall. The door to the little jewelry shop was standing
open. Hand-in-hand, they entered the room, filling the tiny
space. A tall man fidgeted with excitement, eagerly pressing his
thighs against the glass display, examining the rings carefully in
the light of the same oil lamp. He wore a tailored coat with
black knee-high boots and had a saber strapped to his hip. The
broad man shifted, and Fara saw the same old man behind the
counter, the one who had waited on her just two nights ago.

She glanced down at the ring. Deep pulses emanated from
the emerald, starting in the very fissure she had thought a flaw.
Desperately, she edged closer, trying to think of a way to
examine the other emerald to see if it bore the same mark.

After kissing the stones, the soldier set the rings on the
counter and proceeded to sign Lieutenant Felipe Luis Morgan
Cordova in a bold script. He counted out several gold coins and
exchanged them for the rings. While turning, he flashed them
directly in front of Fara's face. The man's ring had a plain wide
band of gold into which the large emerald was set without any
frilly ornamentation like the other. Even with her quicker than
normal perception, she still couldn't tell if Vivian's ring bore the
mark.

"Your wife will be a lucky lady, Lieutenant." The old man's
voice was exactly the same as Fara recalled.

"I guarantee no man could ever love her more." With that, he slipped the rings into an inner coat pocket and then patted his heart.

A woman slipped through the curtain with graying hair pulled back from a tight face and slid the coins into a velvet purse. Fara stared blankly, wondering why the woman wasn't the same.

J.C. tugged her hand. Hastily, they followed Lieutenant Cordova out of the alleyway and onto the street, catching up to him on the same corner. Growing louder and louder, the buzzing in her head was maddening; suddenly, a small motorcycle zipped past.

Jerking Fara back from the edge of the street, J.C. drew her against the building. "What the hell?"

"Please tell me you experienced that too."

"You're not crazy." Leaning against the building next to her, he drew a shaky breath. "Holy shit, I need a minute."

"Me too." She dropped her head onto his shoulder. "What? Why?"

"I don't know. I've never experienced anything like that before. The closest was when Alex... Oh never mind. It has no bearing on what's happening here."

"Doesn't it?"

"The ghosts were mirror images of them, who used them, used their bodies to establish a new timeline. None of that holds here. I don't look like Lieutenant Cordova, and you don't look like Vivian Dufrense. Do you?"

"No."

"I believe our link centers around your ring. Maybe you should take it off."

"No." She sighed wearily and pushed herself up onto her feet. "The white-haired lady told me not to. I don't know who she is, but I have a gut instinct to trust her. I've learned to trust my instincts."

He slid beside her, absently drawing her arm around his. "She may be the ghost that's causing this all to happen."

"Then it's happening for a reason." Stopping short, she perked. "You said you needed to buy your grandmother a present. Do you want to go back to the tourist shops?"

"No, I think I've had enough shopping for one night."

CHAPTER 16

After eating a quiet dinner in the hotel's restaurant, Fara and J.C. returned to their rooms. As soon as they walked through the door, Fara's intuition singed, not the standard wary but a full-blown nervous alert. Nothing looked amiss, but she didn't dare dispute the veracity of the feeling churning inside her. She tugged J.C. to her and whispered, "Stand very still," and switched on the light.

While wishing she had a gun, she improvised. Taking the miniature hotel coffee pot by the handle, she engaged all of her senses and went room to room. To the visible eye, nothing seemed out of order, but she knew someone or something had been here. If nothing else, the scent in the air felt disturbed.

She lightly lifted the ornate iron handle on the armoire and slid out the drawer. Her clothes were disarrayed. She waved J.C. over. "Someone's been here, either looking for something or bugging us again, perhaps both. Why go to all this trouble?" The ring hummed on her finger, and the emerald began to glow.

"I think you should take the damn thing off. What could it hurt?"

"Nothing, maybe everything. It may be protecting us. It's probably what they're looking for." She drew him closer to the window and opened it. The Coqui frogs chirped loudly. Anyone trying to listen through that interference would get a hell of a headache.

"Should we change rooms?"

"Whatever we do, they'll come back. Someone wants to hear what we have found out very badly."

"So what do we do?"

She glanced toward the sitting room. "We give them something to listen to."

Out of the laptop bag, he removed a packet of yellow sticky notes and scribbled in almost unintelligible scrawl the scene headings. Felipe meets Vivian aboard ship. He falls in love with her. They arrive at PR. Meet her uncle. Other men want Vivian. Vivian marries secretly. Leaves for Spain. Other men continue seduction. Vivian hears of shipwreck. Mental breakdown. Jumps out of garita. "That's eleven scenes, about five too many."

"Doesn't give us much time, does it? I could put the non-visual elements into my narrative. We want the on-camera scenes to pop."

"To pop?" He stretched his shoulders. "How would you describe pop?"

"Seductively sizzling. If the scene doesn't sizzle, it goes." She arched her brows. "Let's take each one. I'm Vivian. You're Felipe." She walked to the middle of the room, and then changing her mind, sat back into her chair. "Vivian would be in her cabin, under the watchful gaze of the chaperone because well-bred young ladies wouldn't be allowed to venture across town alone, never mind the ocean. Let's say the chaperone is an elderly nun."

"Oh yes, I would call an elderly nun sizzling." He pretended to throw the packet of the yellow squares at her and laughed as he palmed them.

"Give me a minute. I'm just setting the scene." Taking a breath, she started again. "Glancing back into the stale heat, Vivian makes sure her cousins are sleeping. She never quite trusts whether Sister Marguerite is really sleeping, for the woman has an uncanny sense for mischief, which is what she calls anything other than prayers. Gently, slowly, as to not even stir the heavy air, Vivian smoothes across the room and silently turns the brass handle, slipping out of the uneasy tomb. She slides through the long shadows cast by the still sails, their rigging at the ready for even a hint of wind." Fara whimsically flowed toward the window.

He chuckled, and then shaking out his limbs, sobered. "The lieutenant spies her from the ship's wheel, and after waving a mate to his post, he follows her. Instead of speaking, he waits, taking in her astounding beauty, noting how similar she is to the masthead."

She spun around, hands on hips. "Spanish ships didn't have mastheads."

"Alright, they were on a ship that the Spaniards had raided and repurposed." J.C. smiled. "It has a masthead."

Shrugging, she gazed toward the window. "Vivian doesn't turn yet knows he's there. She says, 'How long were you planning on staring at me without announcing yourself?'"

"I was admiring true beauty, my lady." J.C. mimicked the voice of the ghost they saw in the coin shop. "For a moment, I was afraid you were a mirage, a figment of my imagination, for on a calm and endless sea, men have been known to see visions. You are a vision too beautiful to be real."

"Secretly Vivian is pleased. We'll cut to a close up as a sly smile creases her lips, yet she continues to stare out across the water and says, 'Your compliments are smooth as the sea and equally as empty Lieutenant. I suggest you take your leave.'"

"'It is as full of life as are my compliments, for you are of the sea. Your hair shines like smooth midnight waves. Your skin is fashioned from its finest pearls.' The temptation is too great, and Felipe lowers his gaze. The camera will follow zooming in. Under the fine Spanish lace, her breath makes the gentle mounds rise, rocking the simple wooden cross. Then he says, 'Your every breath breathes life into the wind.'"

"'If that were true, we would be flying across the water with a simple puff from my lips.' She inhales deeply and blows a stirring breath along his neck." In character, Fara blew a whisper.

Inhaling her essence, J.C. shivered. "Your lips are like the sea rose blooming along the reef where secretive creatures spark when touched." He lifted her hand, and his lips lingered. "And the spark when I touch your skin is just as mystifying. Your eyes are the shade of water surrounding Caribbean shoals and just as dangerous to a man."

"Vivian would laugh and stop just as quickly, casting a cautious glance toward the cabin. 'Dangerous? Me? You are mistaken; I am one of the best behaved young ladies in Spain.'"

"And one of the best at swordplay according to young Tomas, though I have yet to see your skill. I would love to cross swords with you."

"I'm sure you would. I've been warned about rakish lieutenants bearing skillful compliments." Fara flounced her gaze back toward the window, where the night sky took on the features of a dark, boundless sea.

"By the good and pious Sister who keeps you locked away?" J.C. leaned forward, placing his mouth next to her ear, blowing on the delicately swirling curves.

Feeling more in the past than the present, she sucked in a quick breath. "If it wasn't for Marianna's betrothal, she and I would have remained at Las Monjas. I had hoped this trip would bring a respite; unfortunately, the stateroom aboard ship is even more confining than the convent."

"Yet you found a few moments to steal away. This is only the third time I have spoken with you alone; although, I have waited for days." He rubbed the smooth and sensitive flesh behind her ear with a fingertip. "Your father must receive betrothal offers daily."

She gasped in surprise, and forgetting herself, swung around, absently brushing her hips against his thighs. "'You forget yourself. That is mine and my father's business, not yours Lieutenant.' Her eyes shift quickly side to side, but Felipe boxed her in. With no means of escape, Vivian retreats until her back pressed into the hard rise of the bow."

His fingertips continued their sensual path over her cheek to the loose tendrils of hair framing her face. "What would you think if I decided to make it my business?"

"I think you are rash and spout whatever needs to be said in order to win my favor. If your intentions are genuine, you have plenty of time to determine the verity of your impulses, for we have such a distance yet to travel and then the same back to Cadiz to speak to my father. In those long weeks, one has time to contemplate the difference between love and lust."

He leaned closer to whisper in her ear, allowing the rapid whisper of her breath to caress his cheek and neck. "Do you contemplate such thoughts of me?"

"That, Lieutenant, is a rakish question and not appropriate to ask a lady. Lust is a sin, while love is divine. I have given neither to any man."

"While you were gazing through the window today, can you honestly tell me you did not think of me even once? Remember, lying is a sin as well."

She scoffed, "Who are you to lecture me about sin?"

"Your avoidance answers my question, so I will give you more than just thoughts to confess." He brushed his lips lightly over hers.

Wiggling, Fara tried to break his hold, but J.C. embraced her firmly. She didn't want to acknowledge the ache stirring within her, especially as it jumped and danced through her pulse. Wondering whether their kiss behind the door was real or just part of her unconscious fantasy was more than Fara had wanted to bear. That kiss had stirred her, deeply rousing hidden emotions she had locked away, never wanting to reawaken. And just like that kiss, Fara now met J.C.'s urgency with her own.

J.C. pulled away and licked his lips. "Dear God, I want you."

She felt the heat of his need growing, pressing into her flesh, and the tell-tale wetness between her legs grew, preparing for him. "I, I can't." She leaned away.

Releasing her, he smiled coyly. "Do you think Vivian would say that? I would expect her to slap his face. Or if she did enjoy it as much as he did, she would be silent, not knowing how to express the moment. But if you think she'd say that, we can keep it in the script."

A flutter passed over Fara's heart. "Oh no, you're right. I think she'd stay silent, and move away from him as quickly as possible." She retreated to the safety of the chair and swiveled the laptop toward her.

"She couldn't go too far." Oozing arrogance, he sidled toward her. "They are on a ship."

She busily opened the script template. "I'll jot some of this down."

"While it's still fresh. Another great idea." Just like a man, he twisted the other chair around and straddled it backwards, folding his arms around the upper spindles.

109

She tried to cover her unease with a firm voice. "You're awfully agreeable."

"Although I felt stupid at first, it was a great way of working the scene."

"Hmm, I see." She couldn't bring herself to look at him and mention the word at the same time. "The kiss had nothing to do with it?"

"Not one bit."

Fara mulled over his answer. Either it had nothing to do with their personal past, or it had nothing to do with their professional assignment. After glancing upon his still smug expression, she decided to concentrate on typing. After setting the page break, she typed Scene Two at the top of the page. Warily, she looked up at him, who had been staring at her this entire time.

"Ready?" With a quick flick, he snagged the second note and read it aloud, "He falls in love with her." Those soft brown eyes smoothed over her face, touching it as easily and readily as fingers. "Do you think it's possible for two people to fall in love so quickly?"

"Well, as you said, their ship isn't very big. They would be in close company."

His brilliant laugh filled the room. "You are the queen, the ruling highness, of not answering simple questions, but I'm not letting you discount this one. It's personal now isn't it?"

"What?"

"Maybe I'm not making myself clear. Do you think Vivian and Felipe could fall in love so quickly?"

"I, I don't know."

"Did it happen to you? Let's say between you and Jason. Did you fall in love with him immediately, or did it take awhile for your feelings to develop?"

Cocking a brow, she considered not answering. "My situation was unusual and has no bearing on Vivian and Felipe."

"I've never been in love. I thought about it a time or two, but if you have to think too hard about something, it can't be real. You see, I have no frame of reference. How did you fall in love?"

"J.C., I really don't want to talk about this."

"Please, I need your help." Reaching out, he gathered her fingers into his. "I'm not trying to pry. I just want to understand." There were some people who threw out the word please with anything, parroting their parents' wishes of saying please and thank you like rote little puppets. Then there were other people who hardly used it at all. J.C.'s simple please touched her more than an entire diatribe could ever persuade.

"I was pretty messed up, and when I woke in the hospital..." Fara paused and swallowed down the knot growing inside of her throat, "...I was doped out of my mind. It took a few weeks to be really aware. Jason came to see me regularly, bringing me books or magazines he scrounged, or maybe even stole, from the others in his unit. One day he brought me a flower. It was little more than a weed, but I hadn't seen a flower for almost a year. I don't have a clue where he got it from, but the gesture was very sweet. After I stabilized, they sent me stateside for more complicated repair jobs. Jason and I emailed each other over the months until he had leave. I went to Fort Bragg to meet him. We got married the next day, and he shipped back out three weeks later. There was nothing about it that was usual."

"Can you think back at the first time you thought of him as husband material?"

A hearty laugh escaped before she could stop it. "I didn't. His proposal caught me by surprise, but it was a good surprise, while it lasted. Unfortunately, the pain of loss is equal to the joy of love, but they don't cancel each other out. Both sensations are equally vibrant and ever present." She sobered. "I guess in some ways it does parallel what happened to Vivian and Felipe, except I do believe they fell in love at first sight."

"I think so too." His eyes had softened even more, resembling chocolate getting shiny just before it melts. "When I imagine them together, the air sizzles with energy. It's like I felt it while we were role playing."

"Yeah, me too." Closing her eyes, she nodded. "The words just flowed. I didn't have to think about it at all. It just happened."

"We're off to a good start. I'd hate to lose the momentum."
He stood up and stretched. "Ready for round two?"

At the return of the phrase, Fara's brows rose inadvertently.
She kicked off her shoes and walked to the center of the small
room. "They would still be on the ship. The Captain had
invited them to join the officers for dinner every night. Vivian
finally convinced Sister Marguerite that she was being rude to
refuse the Captain's hospitality, especially since he was a good
friend of Vivian's father."

"When did that happen?"

"I would think a ship captain would know the ship builder."

"So how did you determine Vivian's father was a ship
builder?"

"I ... I don't know. It just seems right." She pressed long
fingers to her temple, and the ring shimmered.

He moved to her side. "Something wrong?"

"No." She looked up at him, her eyes glowing like the green
gem. "I just know. It's in my head."

"Well, it works so keep going."

"Vivian dressed in the gown she brought for her cousin's
wedding, but the Sister wouldn't move away from the door until
Vivian changed into her modest gray dress. Although she
sputtered and moaned, she would have worn sackcloth if it
meant an evening outside of the confining cabin."

"That will take too long and really has no bearing on their
love story. It doesn't pop."

"Okay, we'll scratch that part." Fara fingered the ring.
"According to table etiquette, the ladies were interspersed
amongst the gentlemen according to rank and age, and just as
Vivian had anticipated, the arrangement allowed her to sit beside
Lieutenant Cordova." With more vehemence, she twisted the
emerald ring on her finger, which heated, radiating light as
brilliant as the sun spilling through a break in heavy clouds. "As
Vivian expected, they received every courtesy from the dear
Captain, whom was a good friend of her father. Captain Ortiz
would visit every time he was in port. He wasn't the only
captain who would do so, but he was definitely the kindest.
With every visit, Captain Ortiz would bring a token gift to

Vivian representing a port of call. They were little treasures, like a shell or thimble, which no one other than a silly girl would keep as sacred riches in a little wooden box."

J.C. drew out two chairs and sat, pulling Fara reluctantly next to him. "I imagine this talk about ships and cargo is not very amusing."

"On the contrary," she grinned with a sincere elegance she did not possess naturally. "I'm quite comfortable discussing ships. They're a way of life in Cadiz."

Realizing they were missing some characters, J.C. stood, and puffing out his chest assumed a commanding position. "The Captain says, 'Señorita Dufrense could probably teach you a thing or two about the design and inner workings of a ship Cordova. Her father built most of the armada. I have known this young woman since she was a babe, and she just keeps becoming more beautiful. You are the image of your mother, Señorita.'"

She wanted to laugh at J.C.'s comical impersonation, yet Vivian's character was stronger, forcing its way to the forefront. Heat rose to her cheeks, and she fanned herself. "You honor me with the compliment, for my mother was a grand lady."

"The Captain turns to the Sister at his elbow. 'The Holy Order has kept these two pearls of virtue safe I see. Not an easy task, not even for a Holy Sister.'"

Fara didn't stand yet lowered her voice to sound softly aged. "When Colonel Dufrense left for Puerto Rico, he entrusted his daughter, Marianna, to my care and suggested her cousin join her for company. Oh, gracias a Dios, I am a woman of patience, yet I will bless the day when my task ends once they are safely delivered to the altar."

"So are you betrothed as well, Señorita Vivian?" The Captain's quick question shot across the table.

"No, my father graciously promised to consult me in the matter, and of course, I trust his word."

"It's no wonder he sent you to Las Monjas, but I would have imagined him sending you to court. If you were my daughter, I would be casting an eye above the merchants to the noble class to find a husband, such as your uncle has managed for your dear cousin."

J.C. changed his voice, adding a lighter Spanish accent, and sat back in his original chair. "Although I hate to disagree with your logic Captain Ortiz, I don't think Señorita Vivian would enjoy life at court. All of the music and dancing."

She cocked her head questioningly. "I love music and dancing."

"'Then you must join us after dinner for some frivolity. A calm sea must be appeased.' The camera zooms in quickly on the Captain who winks, exchanging an unspoken message with his second in command. 'Our esteemed Lieutenant is the son of Viscount Cordova, an icon at the Royal Palace in Madrid. Once Felipe tired of the gaiety, he chose the sea as his new mistress. I would imagine his favor at court will serve him to receive his own commission soon. When does your father launch his next Catalan?"

A flash glinted in the hotel window, yet there was no sound of thunder.

"Señorita Vivian?'"

"Oh excuse my momentary lapse, Captain. Would you honor me with your question once more?"

"I would expect the next of your father's ships to be under the command of our esteemed Lieutenant. I noticed they were laying the decking while in Cadiz. When does it launch?"

The reflection in the window brightened, shining with the brilliant light of an early moon. Fara noticed it out of the corner of her eye, a change in the image. Details emerged. The walls of the ship's cabin grew three dimensionally, surrounding the images of the occupants sitting around the table, like a movie scene backdrop.

"Señorita?"

"The date hasn't been determined." She pulled her eyes away from the window. "I would surmise at least three months."

Again, the glow commanded Fara, drawing her back into the hypnotic flow. The Captain was there in the glassy image. He turned to look at her directly, speaking to Fara as if reality was in the reflection, rather than in the hotel room. "Why such a sad look to stain such a lovely face? Oh don't worry my dear; your father will await your return before launching her. He claims you carry the sea's blessings."

"My father displays his kind and generous soul by saying such things. However, the King may not share his mind. I'm sure he will insist on conscripting the boat to service before I return, for I promised to remain in Puerto Rico through my cousin's wedding."

"Felipe drew a quick breath and then tried to hide it behind a sip of wine." J.C. pantomimed the action, but in the reflection, the goblet glimmered. "You'll not be sailing back with us?"

"I know the ways of ships Lieutenant Cordova, and none stay in port that long. The Immaculata will be under sail long before I am able to return."

CHAPTER 17

Strangely feeling the unwelcome ache of the couple's impending loss, J.C. rocked forward and up onto his feet, giving his head a shake. "It gives good information, but the scene doesn't pop. Most of that info can go into a short narrative. What do you think?"

"It defines the timetable and identifies the characters, their relationships, and that Lieutenant Cordova is the son of a viscount." Fara also rose, stretching her shoulders, and he resisted the urge to touch her.

"Being the second son puts Felipe in a precarious position. He'd have no claim to any of the lands or wealth associated with his family, which is why he went to sea to seek his fortune. It would be a good match for him to marry a wealthy merchant's daughter."

Fara tipped her head and sighed, "So you think his interest in Vivian is monetary?"

"No," he smiled at her sudden dismay. The look on her face clearly said she wanted to believe in love, yet he still wasn't convinced what she felt for her late husband was a good definition. Maybe she wouldn't be willing to fall in love with him, but she had no choice with Vivian, who would fall in love with Felipe. With a little maneuvering, J.C. would align the parallels, using the paranormal connection to his advantage. "I think love brought them together, but back then marriages needed to have sound reasons on both sides. Felipe brought a noble bloodline, while Vivian brought a thriving business. Did she have any brothers?"

"No, Vivian was an only child."

J.C. wished she would look at him, but she seemed obsessed with twisting the ring. "Do you?"

"Have siblings? No." Fara raised her eyes, and they were cloudy and distant. "Well really I don't know. I was adopted."

"I had an older brother, but he drowned in a neighbor's pool before I was born." He went back to the computer and typed in the characters. "What about young Tomas?"

"Marianna's younger brother. Definitely no pop there."

"Yeah, I agree, at least not to our audience's demographic. The boy can be a stand-in without lines." J.C. swiveled. "Ready to go on?"

"Sure," she glanced at her watch. "It's a little after ten. We've got time."

He rubbed his palms together, scraping them hastily. "Okay, since we're scrapping the dinner scene, we still need them to be on the ship. It's that same night, and they're on deck. Lanterns give off a soft yellow light. Music rises with the drum and fife, or better yet the chords of a Spanish guitar. We take an establishing shot of the two young ladies dancing. And we cut to a medium close up of Lieutenant Cordova intently watching a junior officer dancing with Vivian. When the song finishes, Felipe makes his move and invites her aside for a sip of wine. Whenever he's near her, her loveliness overcomes his rational senses, and in many ways, he's thankful for the Sister's measured gazes. Felipe only knows how to court for seduction, but he never courted for matrimony. He was right to have taken the Captain into his confidence, who diverts Sister Marguerite at the most opportune moments. The elderly nun declares it's time for her charges to be abed, yet the Captain distracts her by asking her to lead the evening prayers. Felipe uses the moment to secret Señorita Vivian toward the helm." J.C. wrapped his arm around Fara's waist and led her across the room toward the broad window. "Reluctantly, he slides his arm from her waist and takes her hand where her pulse is beating quickly, hoping it is an effect of being alone with him rather than the thrill of a stealthy escape. 'Have you ever sailed a ship, Señorita Dufrense?'" J.C.'s hand tightened as the power from the ring radiated, drawing them back into another time, another mind.

"Yes Lieutenant." She glances into his eyes and giggles, "You didn't expect that answer, now did you? But not one truly at sea." She continued, "My father brought me with him to the christenings and initial jaunts out and then back to harbor. Father always sails his ships before anyone else." Absently, Fara slipped her fingers through J.C.'s chin-length hair. "When I was little, he would hold me by the waist and allow me to hang onto the grips of the wheel, of course only when there was a fair wind and gentle sea, but to me I couldn't imagine more power flowing through my hands."

"In a symbol known only to the brotherhood of man, Felipe barely casts his eyes to the side, and the mate steps away. He guides Vivian to the wheel, and folding his hands over hers presses the front of his body to the curves of her long back." J.C. turned Fara and followed suit, amazed at how well their bodies melded together, and then he saw it, the storybook reflection in the window. The fanciful display was truly the ship and the historic characters, taking the images directly from their minds, or perhaps in reverse. The detailed scene didn't startle or scare him. Instead, he relaxed, allowing the two worlds to blend within him, feeling the intensity both men shared. He wanted Fara just as intently as Felipe desired Vivian.

Felipe spoke quickly to distract her from the intimate contact. "I know exactly what you mean. I especially love a heady wind when the ship heels to my command. The power is divine."

"Is that why you decided on a career at sea?"

The scent of the sea roused J.C., but he didn't resist the migration across time. He settled nicely into Felipe's character, as comfortably as putting on a favorite pair of shoes. "I had few options. My elder brother inherited our father's titles and lands as was his right. As the second son, I needed an occupation worthy of a nobleman, which included being a commissioned officer the army, navy, or joining the clergy. I couldn't imagine marching or even riding all over God's good earth, and I especially couldn't see myself taking a vow of celibacy."

"Oh," Vivian squeals, casting an admonishing glance over her shoulder. "You are a rogue."

"At court, I was a rogue of the first degree, but the sea has taught me patience and values, and there is much in timing, especially when trimming the sails to cut into the wind, or while courting a beautiful woman." Felipe brushed the back of her ear with his nose and felt Vivian quiver. He laid a soft kiss on the delicate flesh and others down the length of her neck.

With a gentle sigh, she relaxed against him, and her voice flowed just as fluidly. "Please, you mustn't."

"I desire you more than life itself, and I see the attraction in your eyes and hear enticement in your golden voice. Admit it Señorita, I tempt you too."

Her body stiffened along with her voice. "Lieutenant Cordova, I will not allow you-"

"You misunderstand." He cut her off, and with a glance at the dear Captain who raised his voice in ardent prayer, Felipe whispered in her ear. "I have the utmost respect and am asking to court you."

"Although I have spent my adult life cloistered away, I understand the underlying nature of a man's transient interest. I will not be a conquest, Lieutenant." She whispered vehemently.

His brow furled into a solid line of intent. "You will be my conquest and yield to me, but you misunderstand. From this moment, I insist you call me Felipe, and I will call you Vivian. And sometime in the near future, I plan to call you wife. Let me court you, and once we reach Puerto Rico, you may tell me whether I have your permission to ask your father for your hand."

"Are ... are you asking me to marry you?"

"I am asking for time to convince you to accept me for your husband." Releasing a hand, he shifted his weight back and turned her until their bodies were as close as before, yet now chest to chest. He pressed his lips to hers for a brief instant, for the prayers had concluded with a resounding Amen. "So what do you say my dearest Vivian?"

"Vivian Dufrense," called from the distance, yet neither of them spoke the words.

"Vivian, please give me at least some answer, an inkling as to your mind. Hurry for Sister Marguerite is coming up the stair."

A shy smile creased her lips. "As requested, I shall give you my answer once we reach Puerto Rico, Felipe."

No more than a breath from the heavens swept past them, fluffing unseen fingers through Felipe's hair. "Say my name once more."

"Felipe Luis Morgan Cordova, I will allow you to court me, properly of course."

Another gust blew, this time firmly enough to finger the sails. "You are our godsend my lady. Hold onto the wheel, for here comes another. You are about to sail the Immaculata." Just as she grabbed the wheel, a swoop of power engaged the ship. Felipe swayed with the movement of the deck underfoot, and the unsettling motion rocked J.C. back into the present. He cleared his voice and then continued as if the shift in time didn't occur. "Felipe calls orders to the crew, who spring into action to release the mainsail and harness the wind. His hands steady Vivian as the power in the ship grows, coursing through them with delight. He says, 'You do hold the power of the wind, my lady.'"

"Vivian Maria Concepcion Dufrense!" The reflection of the older woman was crystal clear. While holding onto the short railing of the heeling ship, the nun yells again. The fingers of the wind grab her black veil, tossing it and the white coif into the breeze, freeing her long white hair. The Sister runs trying to snatch it before the sea.

Firmly slamming back into the present, Fara stiffens at the sight in the window. "It's her. The lady I keep seeing is Sister Marguerite."

Stubbornly holding onto the flowing memory, J.C. continued. "Felipe's hands gently let loose of the grips. Poised to grab it again, yet he's amazed at his lady's strength. He watches her stance widen, bracing against the force. 'There, you are doing it Vivian. You are sailing her, full sail, across the sea.'"

"Vivian looks over her shoulder, and her focus wavers. Felipe lunges behind her to grab the wheel and rams his body into the back of hers." J.C. held Fara tightly, pressing his rock hard length against the cleft in her softly rounded ass, and smiled when Fara inhaled sharply, not as Vivian, rather herself. "Never had a man wanted a woman more. Sexual thoughts sear through his mind, playing across his face, branding his expression with the desperate need. With a single arm around her waist, he spins Vivian to face him." Pausing as if for dramatic effect, J.C. panted, his rough breath coursed over Fara's cheeks. In the next shivering instant, he bent his head to take her lips, and she leaned into the embrace, sliding her arms around his neck and entwining her fingers into handfuls of thick, soft hair.

Power radiated around the couple, encapsulating them in a heated bubble of ardor. His body ached, wanting her obsessively. Drifting within her fresh scent of coconut and lime, the scent of sexual arousal rose from their bodies, filling the aura surrounding them.

J.C. wanted to taste her, all of her, before sliding between her thighs. Crazed with the thought, he battled between where and how, and finally determined to carry her to his bed. With the plan defined in his mind, he broke the contact to sweep her into his arms.

In that faint moment, Fara nimbly jumped back, well out of his reach. With smug contempt, she said, "I think that would make a good point to break for commercial, don't you?" With exceptional agility to stay out of his reach, she swept over to the computer. "It definitely will keep the audience's interest through the commercial break."

His groan echoed through the extremely still room, and steeling himself enough not to explode, he finally looked at her. The mischievous gleam in her narrow eyes made him realize she was exacting a modicum of revenge, and yet the underlying tone was playfulness, not anger or loathing. Seducing her would not be easy but would be certainly rewarding.

Following her to the table, he set his hands on the back of her wooden chair and watched her compose the scene. "You have an incredible memory."

"For a short time I can manage complete recall, which is why I carry the notepad, so I don't lose specific details." She tapped the enter key twice to jump into the next cell in the format. "Hold on, I'm almost done."

"Great dialogue. The stage direction and shot selection need some work."

"That's why we're a team." She didn't pause the typing while talking, doing both unbelievably well at the same time. "Are you still angry to be working with me?"

J.C. didn't answer right away. He pulled the other chair over next to her and waited until she finally looked at him. "I wasn't angry. I was startled."

She stopped typing and raised a brow.

"Well, okay, I admit I was angry but for the wrong reasons. Once I got the picture and got to know you, things changed. I'm glad to have you as my partner, and I think we're off to a good start." He glanced at his watch. It was after midnight. "It's getting late."

"Yes, it is." With a quick green flash, Fara's eyes darted to her doorway, and J.C.'s followed. The bedroom was awfully dark. The turndown service must have closed the drapes.

He hoped she was wondering the same thought that had been screaming inside of his head since their last kiss. God, he wanted her to invite him to sleep with her, but if she didn't suggest it, he wasn't going to lose the ground he had gained tonight. Shelving his ardent need wouldn't be easy. Neither would be falling to sleep. But he would force himself to do both.

CHAPTER 18

Opening the blinds brought little solace to the extremely dark night, which was darker than the mere absence of light. A shadow encased the world. Distant thunder rolled sharply across the happy sound the frogs made chirping to each other, scaring them into a quiet repose. Gradually, the tiny frogs found their voices, resounding through the darkness until the next shudder of thunder impacted their hiding places amongst the branches.

The odd experience from the scene lingered. In all of Fara's years of training and even during exotic missions, she had never experienced anything as bizarre. Perhaps she was losing her edge. The more likely and logical answer came from the bump on her head, but she'd been knocked out before and never saw visions. And it wasn't just her. J.C. had seen them too.

What the hell was happening?

More than simple curiosity drew her to look at the bedroom window. Some inner need compelled her. She let her eyes relax, like looking at a three-dimensional picture, waiting for an image to spring out of the patterns; however, the hazy reflection remained steadfast and true to this world. A flash curled horizontally across the sky, sizzling through the cloaked void. Normally, lightning storms thrilled her, but tonight the sporadic hoary brilliance made the blackness in between seem even darker. The rains hadn't come yet, and while listening for the first drops, she checked the small clock radio on the nightstand; it was well after one.

She tried to push how much she wanted J.C. out of her mind, but her need was resistant and indelible, craving him to kiss her again, to hold her, and make love to her. He sparked emotions a recent widow shouldn't feel.

Fara thought she had loved Jason, yet the bond to her husband had never tingled down to her soul, daring it to feel. If she opened her bedroom door and went to J.C.'s bed, they would make love rather than have sex, which scared her most of all. Love would bring him too close, and she had to protect him from the curse she carried since she was brought into this world.

She didn't know much about her life before being adopted, and the pieces didn't fit neatly together. She was born in Egypt, apparently to a Christian woman, who died in childbirth. Catholic nuns arranged the adoption. Her new parents were Americans, kind, and gently spoken, upper middle class, with more to do than time to do it in. They were both stock speculators and started their own brokerage firm between Fara's gymnastics and piano lessons.

Then in an instant, the world collapsed.

Late on a winter's night, a drunk driver jumped the median on the freeway. Fara was in the backseat and screamed as the front of the airborne Buick burst through the windshield of their Volvo. With her agile reflexes, Fara dove for the floorboard and survived. Somehow, amidst all of the breaking glass and twisting metal, she heard her parents' final choking breaths.

Fara woke in the hospital, alone, all alone. Of course, there was an instant outpouring of cards and well-wishes from her friends at school and the congregation at church, but no one really cared, at least not enough to take her into their own homes.

Her skin chilled, and she pushed the memory back into the dark space inside her soul, as dark and turbulent as the churning night sky. She cuddled the downy pillows as she used to do and watched the sky while she slowly locked away the dislodged memories along with her feelings for J.C.

She couldn't afford to love.

After taking over an hour to drift to sleep, something scraped her awake, more than a sound and less at the same time. The sensation rubbed its way along Fara's nerves and zipped into her subconscious mind, slicing into the dark dream of searching the market where pungent and heavy odors clung to the air. Jason stood at the end of the narrow aisle, nearly hidden behind baskets hanging from the metal pole of a merchant's booth. The darkness ambled closer, consuming every detail. He just stood there, waiting for it to come. Similar to Alice's Cheshire cat, he faded until even the bright smile was gone.

An electric jolt hit her nervous system again, rousing her enough to realize she was in a hotel room. The sizzling energy pressed against her skin and heat radiated through the close-fitting air. Something must have been wrong with the A.C. A low hum indicated the unit was on.

After absently throwing off the sheet, the overwhelming need to protect herself made her instinctively reach for the handgun she always kept under the pillow. Realizing she wasn't armed, vulnerability leeched into her. She scooted up against the headboard, wrapping her arms securely around her knees, and concentrated on finding out what could have set her off. The nightmare still lingered in her thoughts, and the darkness was there, waiting to consume her.

Lightning burned through the clouds, and the impact of thunder immediately rattled the world. The strike was so close the scent of ozone charged the wake. Now fully aware, Fara supposed lightning must have struck just outside of her room, sizzling through the humid air and waking her with the sudden dispersal of electricity. Her heart rate slowed at the plausible justification, but all hope of it being a natural occurrence fled instantly.

The emerald emanated a soft florescent glow. Rising with the storm, the ring grew warmer along with her body. The heat continued escalating with the rising brightness, one feeding off from the other, spiraling in intensity. As the amassing energy crept over her flesh, the fine hairs lifted and drew toward the banded waves of heat coalescing in waves near the foot of the bed, rippling through the radiant green light like lazers threading through undulating smoke.

The sky filled with nearly incessant strikes of lightning.

She faintly detected something within the whirling color, coalescing out of the eerie green with a few whispers of blue or purple, at times a lively yellow and rose. The scent of ozone grew smoky and pungent, burning within her nose and throat.

When the next series of lightning flashed, Fara saw the detail of the Immaculata floating on the undulating sea.

Too late to run or even try to move, her body evaporated one cell at a time. Her essence danced and sparkled in the unnatural light like dust motes in the sun. The calmness lasted only seconds before diving into the churning storm. Her spiritual essence swooped down toward the stormy sea, slowing only once she spied Vivian slipping through sheets of driving rain. Fara followed her below deck, and beyond control, slid into the countenance of the vibrant Spanish beauty.

The Immaculata cut through building diagonal waves, slapping and smashing in riotous cacophony. Deafened by the endless roar, Vivian held onto the railing with both hands to ensure she did not slip down the soaked stairs. The belly of the ship was close and dark, carrying scents of cargo and men, pungent yet not offensive, at least not at this level. Deeper within the bowels of the ship, conditions would be worse. With a cautious glance at the sound of low voices within the hold, she stepped off from the bottom stair and still kept a firm grasp on the railing to remain upright while the sweeping gales tormented the vessel.

Since she received the secret note on the breakfast tray, she only could think of spending time alone with Felipe. Every day over the past week, he behaved as an upstanding gentleman, knocking upon her cabin door at the appointed three o'clock hour to promenade her around the deck with Sister Marguerite two steps behind them, hanging on their every word. He would bow and lay several kisses upon her hand, but he had not met her lips since the night the wind swept the Immaculata back on course. Yet even without kisses, every time he touched her, every time their eyes met, she experienced a tug within her chest and another more deeply seeded, where surging emotions tied into knots. If Sister Marguerite would have just relented a little in order for Vivian to steal a kiss from Felipe's gentle lips, she would not have resorted to sneaking off in the middle of the night, worse yet in the middle of a storm. If discovered, her reputation would be destroyed, and yet she waited, prepared to risk everything to be with him.

Alibis flew through her mind as quickly as the rain over the deck. If noticed, she would say the rocking of the ship made her queasy, and she went for a walk on deck when the rains hit in earnest, causing her to seek cover at the base of the half-deck stair. Although the plan settled her mind, her sensibilities were alive, tangibly jolting her emotions as readily as the lightning pierced the night sky, and her inner need resonated with the thunderous roar.

Unless the storm cast them off course, they would make landfall late the next day. This would be their last night aboard ship, their last chance to be alone. With each passing hour, Vivian became fretful of what awaited her in Puerto Rico. The past few years had muted the hostile effects of the bitter argument between her father and uncle. Although the two men supposedly mended their rift, she knew her uncle's reputation. Whatever had been said harbored within his heart and anchored his hatred. Once at the fort, she would be under his absolute control.

Her heart beat harder until the pulsing in her ears drowned out the storm as well as the sanctimonious warnings from Sister Marguerite. Vivian had dutifully obeyed for far too long, first her father and then the nuns. Her uncle would be the most stringent of them all; however, she was not yet under his thumb. For tonight, she would only obey her heart and mind, which were in steadfast agreement.

True to his promise, Felipe had treated her as a gentleman. However tonight, Vivian didn't want to be a young lady of upstanding character. She wanted to be a woman in the true essence of the word. She could not live for another moment without touching him, or better yet feeling him kiss her and touch her with all of the want in the world. He charged her with power, compellingly brilliant and unexpectedly frightening at the same time, stirring new emotions she had to experience to understand. There would be time to repent. She would chastise herself for being weak and then confess her sins. Regardless of the penance, the stolen moments would be worth enduring the punishment.

With a bang as loud as gunfire, the hatch at the head of the stairs slammed shut, and more than just darkness crept down within the cover of shadows. Panic skipped in her breast, instantly transforming her bravado into insecurity. She could no longer make out the details of any solid shape, so when a quick arm seized her waist, she shrieked, which the next vibrant clap of thunder masked.

She pushed her palms against a damp slicker covering a well-muscled chest. "Felipe? Is that you?"

"Who else would you be expecting?" His lovely tenor voice creamed over her skin moments before his fingers joined in, rubbing up and down her arms and then her spine. His hands continued coursing over her slick skin sending shivers through her, but she wasn't cold. "You're soaked to the bone. Perhaps you should return to your cabin."

"Your note ... don't you want to see me, alone?"

His chest vibrated with a deep chuckle. "Well then, let's get you warm and dry. Come with me to my cabin."

Her rebellious resolve evaporated just like the rainwater from her skin. "I cannot go to your cabin. You realize that." She prepared to march away, yet suddenly there was nowhere to go. Biting her lip, she turned defiantly. "I am in no mood for your teasing."

"I'm not teasing you." He drew her closer with the hand still upon her back. "I have made my sincere intentions perfectly clear, and now, my dearest Vivian, I need to know your answer."

"Here and now?"

"No, this is not an appropriate place to discuss such things. Come with me." He drew her closely and started down the dark hall. The ship pitched underfoot, but his experienced stride worked in rhythm with the waves.

She could not make out a single detail of his face or body, or even the walls which she knew had to be near. Her only grip on reality was the arm banded about her. "How can you see?"

He balanced to and fro, continuously leading her forward. "I have walked to my berth a thousand times under even worse conditions."

"Your berth!" Vivian stopped, but it didn't matter. He turned into a sheltered room and closed the door behind them. His touch left her, and she was alone in the dark. The world swayed, causing an uncomfortable shift in perception. For a moment she didn't have her bearings, up and down meant nothing while the world rolled and plunged. Her head became light, and her stomach uneasily lurched.

A few seconds later, a spark grew into flame touching the room with a faint yellow glow, and the flame brought with it a welcome return to normalcy. His room was small yet extremely neat and oddly smelt of dried herbs and tea. He closed the glass door of the sturdy lantern, and as the light left his hands, the lamp swung, casting tumbling shadows over the simple surroundings.

A wild slurping whistle preceded the boat lurching aside, tossing Vivian from her feet. Before she hit the wall, Felipe lunged and snagged her into his arms, twisting to absorb the impact. Panting, she laid fully against him, her limbs tangled between his own.

"Vivian," he stroked the curls from her face. His usually soft and gentle eyes were focused intently, making her extremely aware of every breath she took. "Are you hurt?"

She shook her head tentatively, not able to summon the ability to speak while their bodies were so intertwined.

Gently, he scooped her into his arms and deposited her onto the swinging berth supported by sturdy chains. After hooking the bed onto the joist of the inner hull, he left her to sit alone while he removed his oil-skin slicker. But, those physical insecurities did not last for long. There was no room in her swirling feelings to worry about the storm or her surroundings. His shoulder-length hair hung in wet ribbons, wildly framing his broadly chiseled features.

In a sweeping motion aided by the rolling waves, he slid to his knees and gathered her hands within his. "I've been going mad not knowing your mind, and with Sister Marguerite's constant interference, I have not had the opportunity to ask for your decision." When she didn't reply, Felipe continued. "Will you marry me Vivian?"

"We are not yet at Puerto Rico." Her attempt at levity didn't lighten his serious mood; instead, his countenance only hardened.

"Don't toy with me, not about this." Grabbing the support chain, he leaned closer, hovering over her. "I love you."

Her chest tightened and expanded all in the same instant. From the gripping epicenter, heat radiated throughout her body. "Oh Felipe, I hoped ... I needed to hear ..."

His brow furled. "Tell me your decision."

"When we spoke on deck, which now seems so long ago, I told you the truth. I have never given my affection to any man. Actually," she felt her cheeks blush, "I wasn't sure what love was, what it felt like, and yet every day..." As her voice faded, she turned her gaze away.

His calloused hands gripped her shoulders firmly. "Go on. Tell me."

"Every day, something has changed within me. My thoughts always circle around to you. I yearn to be with you, to touch you. When I think of you my chest tightens to the point where I can't breathe, and..." Feeling her cheeks flush, she inhaled, not sure where her babbling was headed.

The corners of his lips curved toward a smile. The harshness softened. "And?"

"I feel something else. Something I can't explain."

He lowered his mouth and found her warm lips. "Tell me, how that made you feel?"

She blinked innocently. "I don't know."

"Try Vivian." His hands fluttered up her sides and brushed the outer camber of her breasts.

"Oh!"

"Tell me, Vivian. Or I will continue to add influence until the sensations are clear."

Insecurity tinged his name. "Felipe?"

He muffled the sound with an eager mouth. While allowing one hand to roam lower, the other rose to cup her head and strengthen the press of his kiss. Even through the layers of the durable cotton, she felt the heat of his hand and the power of his fingers spread over her rounded form. Drawing her even closer, her thighs had to part as he gathered her body ardently toward his.

She relished in the quickening sensation pulsing through her body, melting beneath the onslaught. His tongue danced against her lips until her inevitable moan escaped, spreading her mouth ever so slightly, yet the brief opening was enough. His tongue entered the soft warmth, and she moaned again, longer and stronger than before, leaving her wanting as he finally pulled away.

"Tell me now, Vivian."

She closed her eyes tightly. "I ... my body melts, and I want to remain in your arms forever. You make me weak and feel strong at the same time. I ..." Her eyes flashed open. "How does it make you feel?"

A grin spread, twinkling in his eyes. "I feel weak and strong, at the same time. I yearn to hold you and never let you go. I want you Vivian Dufrense, body and soul, forever to be mine, only mine."

She heard tell of what men and women do under the cloak of night. She distinctly remembered the act being labeled "sins of weak flesh." Until this moment, she couldn't comprehend how flesh could be weak. The depth of her will was a sense of great pride, but was not pride also a sin?

The storm's recumbent waves incessantly slapped the side of the ship, and the sound roused something unknown, another infant emotion desiring to break into this world.

Now with both hands cupping her bottom, Felipe drew her body to the edge of the berth and into vibrant contact with his straining erection. Heat burned through her body, coalescing in a glowing knot between her legs. The longing ached, insistent and overly bold.

Her lace collar quivered in his hands as he raised it over her head. The simple gray muslin had no adornments except for a row of white buttons down the front of the bodice. His lips found her neck, and with pliant and gentle urging, she arched. The tiny buttons strained. With little more than a touch, the first opened.

She clasped her delicate fingers over his strong hand, forcing it into her cleavage. "Felipe, no, we mustn't. It's a sin."

"What I feel for you is divine. Don't worry my love. I will wait to claim your virginity until our wedding night, for you will marry me." The determination in his voice resounded, clearly stating the definitive conclusion of what he had asked only moments ago.

"Yes, I will." She didn't know where the words came from or how they even formed, for her mouth was so very parched. "I love you."

He cupped her jaw in one hand, cradling her face. "Say it again."

The waves, the thunder, the incessant creaking of the ship, none of them were louder than her three tiny words. "I love you."

Felipe drew her head against his, touching their foreheads gently. "Oh Vivian, I fell in love with you the moment I kissed you at the bow. Then and there, I knew."

"What did you know?" She threaded her fingers into the damp locks of hair and brushed them back from his face.

"That you were the jewel I had been searching for all these long years. I would never do anything to harm you. Do you trust me?"

"Of course I do."

"Then all will be well." His hands lingered on the final button for only a moment before sliding under the bodice, cupping the fragile curve. Felipe audibly groaned as his hand arched her breast upward. Tipping his head, he met the delicate rise with his lips, teasing the flesh until her nipple rose proudly. In broadly sweeping curls, he ran his tongue over the taut peak.

Vivian never knew such exaltations existed. Breasts were just another body part, like a hand or leg, yet now as he closed his lips over her and suckled, shooting vibrations coursed through her, again coalescing into the aching knot. Beyond her control, her back arched, raising the throbbing need ever so slightly. Suckling harder, he drew upon her breast fully. The firmness of her nipple pressed against the roof of his mouth while his tongue coveted the lower curve. Vivian trembled.

Leaving her flesh, he took a breath slowly and then started again, leaving her right breast heaving while the left learned of the forbidden pleasure. Swirling emotions filled her, and she writhed within the embrace, unwittingly thrusting against him. With a gasping breath, her head fell back, arching her breast upward to accept his mouth fully. While reeling in the delight, she closed her eyes and melted into the sensual onslaught. Her stirring emotions were so omnipresent she didn't notice his touch until Felipe's fingers crested the top of her stocking. His grip on her breast was so firm she wasn't able to pull away. The broad palm stroked her inner thigh, causing the coalescing mass of nerves to tighten even more.

Although her thighs squeezed against his body, Felipe's hand continued its slow path and slid over the light fabric guarding her chastity. His groan echoed vibrantly when the tight curls slid under the fabric covering the delicate contours of her femininity. Inhaling a shaky breath, he continued stroking where her heat converged with innocence. A squeal escaped Vivian's lips as he squeezed; the bound nerves pulsed under his palm. In tandem rhythm, his fingers massaged as did his mouth, slowly at first and then growing in mutual intensity.

Vivian's breath backed up into her lungs. Internal excitement drove her forward, reaching out for something she didn't understand. She wrapped her fingers into his hair, pressing his face even more resolutely to her breast charged with radiant life. Her hips lifted and thighs spread of their own accord. Her emotions spiraled, surging higher and higher, rising radiantly until all of the breath she had been holding exploded into a scream. The surge coursed through her in a torrent, ripping open her soul, baring it for Felipe to hold.

Reluctantly releasing his hand from her hidden prize, he wrapped both arms around her and then gently released her breast. In a husky voice, he whispered, "That is only the beginning my dearest Vivian. I want you to remember how I made you feel, and once we are united in the eyes of God, I will teach you more, giving you pleasure beyond imagination, beyond what you just experienced. Before you leave me," he swallowed, "before we must part, promise me you are mine and mine alone."

Vivian was surprised to hear her own voice so strong and sure. "I would rather die than love another. However long it takes, I promise to wait for you."

CHAPTER 19

A distinct hum rolled under the cacophony of light and sound challenging the night. Still dazed with the drugging effects of deep sleep, J.C. stumbled into the shared parlor, and for a moment stared at the window which gleamed with nearly constant lightning strikes, yet even while blazing with fury, the display lacked the other-worldly glow.

The odd sound continued, like the steady hum of an electric razor. The thought struck his mind, and a broad smile awakened his sleepy face. Fara was enjoying a party of one. Unable to resist the temptation, J.C. opened her door without knocking.

A blizzard of cold air blasted his bare chest along with a shock of static electricity. The entire room glowed with green light, fluorescent yet muted at the same time. Fara was huddled against the headboard with her legs drawn against her chest, panting as violently as an animal running for its life. She stared forward.

J.C. drew closer and turned to look at what she was seeing.

The coalesced glow formed the bodies of two lovers, clinging in deliberate embrace. Felipe's mouth was upon Vivian's breast, and his hand had just slipped under the folds of her skirt. Vivian trembled.

The anachronistic lovers were compelling, yet Fara's delicate scent was in the air, light and airy with a hint of coconut. The aroma slid inside of him, braiding the strings of desire across the ages, drawing him into their disturbing ménage-a-quatre. J.C. shared Felipe's thoughts and Felipe his, for at the moment they were one and the same. Desire licked his body, his aching erection stretching against the thin confines of his cotton boxers. He glanced again at Fara, and fear crept past his charging need. "Fara, can you hear me?"

Breathless panting continued through thinly spread lips while her eyes stared blankly ahead at the lovers embracing in the unearthly light.

"Shit," he edged closer, resisting the need to slide into bed and entwine Fara in his arms. Carefully reaching around the cone of light, he tapped her shoulder. "Fara, you alright? What's going on?"

Still there was no answer, no change of posture, not even a blink from the motionless green eyes. The ceaseless hum continued, and compelling ardor filled the air, magical and mystically linked across time. Before J.C. lost his own sensibilities to the heady mix, he slid under the radiant projection of light emanating from Fara's ring and drew against her side. With the back of his index finger, he touched her cheek, sliding up the feverish flesh.

"Fara," he patted her cheek lightly, "come-on baby. Wake up."

A shudder of panic fed his pulse. Grabbing her shoulders, he shook her, still without response. Suddenly overcome at a loss of options, his impulse seized her face in his hands and planted his mouth against hers, allowing the feverish and covetous craving to linger and feed his pounding need. Instantly, she unfolded into his arms with the same yielding ease as a morning glory embracing the dawn.

The hum grew louder, drawing him into the swarming mass, penetrating his mind, permeating his soul. Too close to capitulating to his baser instinct, he drew upon his last ounce of will, "Fara, this bond with the past has to stop. It's too dangerous."

"No," whispered across time. "Not yet. I don't want to leave you." The voice was not hers, rather an echo arching into their world.

Although J.C. fought against Felipe's quest for control, slowly, piece by elemental piece, he felt himself disappearing into the green mist, joining the surging waves and churning desires. His hands and his mouth were no longer his own. He was the first man to touch her, and being at the gate of the delicate barrier was almost more than he could bear. If he took Vivian

136

now, she would have no choice other than marry him, but he gave his word, as a gentleman. Even while fighting an inner battle, he continued adding influence until she crested the peak. The glowing energy of a virginal orgasm pulsated through time itself. Flamboyant colors burst through the room, brilliant and mesmerizing, electrical jolts dancing in the ribbons of light.

Breaking free for an instant, J.C. realized he was facing Fara in the same repose. With a decisive burst, he thrust his hand over the ring, snuffing out the pulsating connection at the cost of his own flesh. Like a disjointed marionette, Fara collapsed in his arms.

The vision was gone. The tense buzzing silenced. Only a single storm lashed at the windowpane.

He stroked her face, but Fara did not respond. Lying lifeless and still, not even breath escaped her lips. Straddling her body, he checked for a pulse.

Smoothly and calmly her arms and legs wrapped around his body, drawing him down on top of her until he was in intimate contact. Her lips found his, and she fed upon him, nibbling and biting the rounded edges of his mouth. Even more sensually arousing, her fingers twirled through J.C.'s hair, grabbing and releasing fistfuls, pulsing in the same quivering rhythm as her mouth and now writhing body. With the vibrant rubbing, his erection slipped through the boxer's fly and encountered flesh, so soft and desirable, compellingly hot.

Desperate for self-control, his hands clenched, yet before he even realized it, his erection was sliding inside smoldering heat. Fara's channel was so snug, as if the crossover in time caused her to share Vivian's virginal integrity. Gently, he worked his way inside, feeling her flesh expand and accept him. The moisture in her channel grew with each of his strokes until she consumed his length just as he remembered. Slowly and deliberately, J.C. slid from her and hastily pulled the boxers off his legs.

She raised her hips and spread her thighs widely, luring him back inside her channel, and he completed the stroke until his straining erection was buried to the hilt. He closed his eyes, relishing in the moment. Too many of his former lovers complained he was uncomfortably large, yet now he had found his match in too many ways to deny. His erection strained to pump her again and again, but he resisted the manic urge.

Those glorious emerald eyes flashed open, wide with desire. "Don't stop. I want you." She spread her fingers on each cheek of his butt and drew him deeply within her channel. "Make love to me. Fuck me. Whatever you desire, I'm yours for the taking."

Even if the meaning of her words hadn't lured him forward, the siren's power within her voice compelled him to slam himself into her. "Anything?"

"Yes," she writhed with the impact. "Yes, anything, anywhere, any way. Take me. I'm yours."

Resisting his urgent desire to bury himself again, J.C. withdrew. "I want to kiss you, to taste you."

Obediently, she lifted her deliciously long legs and set each in turn on top of his broad shoulders. Her heated aroma filled his awareness. He wished there was light, at least a little in order to see her spread before him, and then lightning lit the world with a shuddering display. With touch as his guide, his mouth fed along her smooth thighs, nibbling and licking at will. Her flesh was still searing hot, steaming her readiness into the close air. As he neared her prize, his tongue lingered, tasting the rich flavor of her body, which was just as satisfying as he had imagined. Curling the tip of his tongue into her channel, he outlined the petals of flesh where they converged. Repeatedly he licked her broadly, and she rewarded him with elemental shudders, playful preludes of intensifying arousal.

Having feasted upon her dewy moisture, he raised his chin and braced it upon the orifice, allowing the underside of his tongue to shimmy over the tip of her clitoris. Although the bud was already thick and hard, it grew with the touch, extending even higher and broader.

Writhing with mounting pleasure, she grabbed fistfuls of the sheets, pulling them from the mattress, winding the fabric around her hands until they were bound. "Give me more."

With an expert shift of his body, he pinned a forearm behind her knees, driving them tightly against her torso. With tongue and teeth, he entangled her with a vigorous rhythm. Continuing to drive her with his mouth, he braced more of his weight against her thighs and pressed his available hand to her quivering flesh. He started with only a single finger, drenching it in her well of desire. In such an intimate way, her groan reached him more so through the vibration within her body than audibly. Searching, he found the coarse ridges along her inner pelvis and purposefully pressed and rolled his fingertip over the sensitive rise. He didn't think she could spread herself any more widely, yet he felt her open and then constrict little by little within the mounting impulses. He felt her longing, her desire, her aching hunger. And then she burst like a wave hitting a rocky shore, the orgasm crashed into him, into them both, dragging them under in the corporeal tide. Erotic spasms coursed between the sensitive folds in a syncopated rhythm, and then he bit her bud, not hard, yet not softly either, adding sufficient pressure for her to scream again.

Panting J.C. rose slightly, yet he wasn't done, not by a long shot. His erection throbbed, on the edge of release, and he ignored that need. While she was still spread before him, he dipped two, then three and four fingers into her, kneading the final quivers of her orgasm from her. The drenched moisture dripped over his fingers. "Do you want more?"

"Yes. Take me." The siren quality of her voice compelled him.

Although in fantasy he wanted a woman to allow him to enjoy her absolutely, he never had had the opportunity, until now, until Fara. He withdrew his hand and cupped her slippery flesh. Her orgasm had made her even wetter until a steady flow of glittering liquid coursed out of her and down the slim valley. Following the line that gleamed even in the stormy light, his fingers slid back and forth over the rises and falls, from her anus to her bud and back again.

Fara moaned as the ardor rose. He inhaled the desire, tangibly rising from her flesh, and like a wild creature of the night, responded instinctively. On the next pass of his hand, he paused over her tight ass, rolling his fingers around the muscular opening drenched with the river of moisture. While she kept moaning yes over and over again, J.C. dipped his fingers in her drenched pussy to remoisten them, and then returned, sliding slowly into the tighter channel.

This was the first time J.C. had ever fingered a woman in the ass, and he almost came with the erotic pleasure. Fara was so tight, yet open and willing. He pushed his finger all the way within her, and she screamed "yes" so loudly it rang in his ears as her inner muscles gripped him with her lust for more. He added another finger, slipping the two back and forth against each other while within her. As he slid out, he threaded his thumb into her vagina and pushed inside of her again, massaging the delicate membrane separating the two openings. He squeezed and pulsed, gently at first, yet as her ardor grew so did his. Her channel was getting wetter again, straining, waiting for the full effect of the yearning to mature. Within moments, she arched. The orgasmic pulsations coursed through both openings, tightening in quivering spasms.

Again, he felt his urgent need rise. For a fleeting moment, he thought about coming on her, showering over his hand, and then it just happened. His hot white essence rained over her exposed and open flesh. His body convulsed, urging the final drops to release, and he started to knead his hand within her depths. He withdrew his fingers enough to feel the thick liquid slide down and pushed back within her, smacking his hand against her bottom, spanking his essence inside of her.

Writhing in ecstasy, Fara came quickly, erupting with the final whack of his hand. So intent upon spanking her inside and out, J.C. didn't realize he had grown hard again, firmly erect as if he hadn't ejaculated at all.

Releasing her, he rocked back onto his knees. "Have you had enough?"

"No." She rose onto her elbows; those green eyes burned, challenging him. "Have you?"

His body was tight with need, and he wasn't going to hold back. "Just getting started."

She continued the paused sit-up and then scooted down, easing her body between his legs. With a feline flair, she licked him roughly, up one thigh, across his testicles, and down the other.

"Will you take me in your mouth?"

Wetting her lips, she moved her head into position. He cradled her head in both of his hands, and her silky hair streamed through his fingers. Her lips touched him first, sliding over the crowning ridge, and then her tongue licked the tip, suckling against it, tasting it like a lollipop.

"Oh dear God," he whispered more so to himself rather than her. "If I hadn't already come, I would have lost it. Shit, you do that good."

She couldn't speak, but he felt a smile pull her lips. With her hands cupping his ass, she eased him forward, taking him until his glans bumped against the back of her mouth. He had always worried about hurting a woman during oral sex, but on the next stroke, she relaxed her throat and allowed him to slide within her, not with his entire length, but enough for him to receive the full sensation, more than he had ever been given before. As they worked back and forth, her throat muscles slowly constricted over the bulbous head, adding a snap or pop to the withdrawing slide, yet when he entered her, it was smooth and wet, so very slippery and close. The rhythm grew, slide – pop – slide – pop. Before he knew it, she had taken more of him within her. He could feel her breathing in time with the thrusts, her breath coursing over the tip on its way in and then out. Closing his eyes tightly, he arched into the sensation, and she took all of him. Pure pleasure rippled through him, making him as rigid as he had ever been in his life. He opened his eyes to watch her ruby lips slide back and forth over the entire length of his straining shaft. Lost in the hypnotic sight, he burst without a moment of warning, without an ounce of control. She held his butt firmly, planting him deeply inside, allowing him to erupt down her throat until he was completely spent. He slid from her, and she took a deep breath while wiping her mouth with the corner of the sheet.

Once he could find enough breath, J.C. leaned forward, kissing her, forcing her back onto the pillows. "That was fucking incredible."

A wise smile curled the edges of her lips which were dark and plump from the contact, and a devilish twinkle gleamed in her eyes. "We're not done yet."

"No, we're not." Hovering above her, he tasted her breasts, softly at first, drawing the flesh lazily into his mouth.

"Harder," she whispered.

With her nipple still between his teeth, he shook his head no. "You gave yourself to me, remember? I'm going to take you how I damn well please."

Writhing beneath him, she arched her back, forcing her breast into his mouth. Her dreamy voice purred, "Then take me damn it."

"Exactly my plan," the words vibrated through her flesh. The smooth slope below the nipple slipped under his teeth, but as he encountered the aureole, he bit down and drew her nipple higher with a deliberate pull. Once again, the ardor rose tangibly, and Fara cooed as if she fed off from the lust.

His hands grasped her breasts forcing them together to form a line, and he slid his tongue across and then down into the valley. Upon that simple act of penetration, his body prepared once more. Without hesitating, he spread her damp thighs. The head of his penis found her slick and rosy flesh without assistance, sliding fully into her in a single strong and defiant stroke. She was even hotter and wetter, if that was even possible. He squeezed his eyes closed and started to stroke her. The rhythm was hypnotic and compelling the last of his seed to rise.

"Please," she begged, and repeated the word twice, each degrading into a lower growl. "I want more," she answered his thoughts.

Tangible heat rose from her flesh, inside and out. Her feminine muscles snatched at his length, as readily as her fingers seized his butt muscles constricting and releasing with the rhythmic thrusts. Her wetness eased the way. Inch after long inch packed within her, stretching the compact space with driving passion. He rode her hard on the edge of harsh, thoroughly addressing her yielding need. He became lost in the ardor and felt it again, something more than just lust, more even than love; it was intangible, consuming, feeding upon their sex.

The dense knots of control tied within his resolve unraveled bit by bit with each full stroke until she rose up, pounding her hips into his. He could no longer control the biting need. Both succumbed to the union, their bodies moving in unison, forming and molding into a single being with a single-minded purpose. They culminated upon the same stroke, screaming as they held onto the incendiary moment, the white hot flash darting like the lightning still crashing through the sky. As their bodies relaxed into the melting passion, the heavens also calmed, leaving an echoing reminder of the storm rolling off into the distance.

Resounding in his chest, J.C.'s heart expanded, heating until it was on fire. For a fleeting second, he thought he might be having a heart attack as the desperate feeling developed into more. Devotion flowed within the enthusiasm, commitment within the fervor. Still deeply within her, he lowered his body until he felt her chest rise and fall.

"I love you." He whispered, hoping she would hear it, and at the same time, hoping she wouldn't.

She stirred, while a purring hum coursed through her throat. "I love you."

He hadn't expected that reply and wasn't quite sure what to do now. He slid from her, and she rolled over. He cuddled her closely, spooning his body against her luxurious curves.

CHAPTER 20

Getting old sucked. His body ached from a day of sun and a night of rum; even his joints were disagreeable. With a groan, he opened the sliding door and stepped onto the patio into the almost rosy glow of predawn. The glass closed with a dull thud before the man growled into the cellphone. "This better be God-damned important."

"They know." The smooth voice gave no hint of inflection.

Edged fully awake, he searched empty pockets for cigarettes. "What the hell do you mean?"

"They found the disks, both of them."

Without coffee or a cigarette, how in the hell was he supposed to deal with this? "How can you know that? The disks could've been defective."

"We tracked two active signals last night, both to El Convento. They were arguing about her going alone to the fort. She saw Vivian."

"Are you sure?"

"Yes." The androgynous voice continued, "She noticed the irregularities in the file and then discovered the disk. She is more than she appears which bodes well for our success. While they were out, we searched their rooms, and the ring wasn't there. We need that woman and the emerald one way or another tonight."

"You did it then?" He couldn't keep his voice from shaking. "You initiated the ceremony?"

"Yes."

"Is Juan Carlos prepared?"

"He will bend to our purpose." The call ended with shaking fingers. Setting the phone on the wicker patio table, he went to brew some strong coffee. The coming hours would demand it.

CHAPTER 21

The drapes were still open as dawn rolled into the sky. The young light moved across Fara's eyes, challenging her lids to open. Realization dawned even more slowly than the day. The covers were in their normal state of morning disorder, but they weren't ripped from the corners and thrown to the floor.

Easily sliding from the sheets, she went to the bathroom. After such vigorous sex, there would be tell-tale signs, but nothing was sticky or even sore. J.C. was a big man, the biggest she had ever known. After their first time together, she felt a little cramping, but today she was fine. Either her body had adjusted, or the memory was just too incredible to be real. It was one thing to have sex, even kinky sex, but she had never given herself over to a man, not ever.

Life had taken a sharp turn into the Twilight Zone ever since she met J.C. at the fort. What she needed to do was clear her head. She went to the dresser and put on black nylon shorts, a sports bra, and a thin black cap-sleeved t-shirt. Drawing her hair back, she threaded the pony-tail through the back of a black baseball cap and then pulled on cushioned socks and her running shoes.

Just the thought of running made her determination rise. She was reaching for the door when she stopped. If she didn't tell J.C., they would have another fight, no need to go through that again.

Going to the small adjoining door, she gathered her thoughts and put a pleasant smile on her lips before knocking. "Hey J.C., I'm going out for a ..."

The door opened abruptly. His eyes were as red as the smoldering end of the cigarette clutched between the fingers of his right hand. "Where are you going?" He inhaled a lazy drag.

Stunned, only one thought popped into her head. "These are no smoking rooms."

"We're in Puerto Rico. Nobody gives a shit." He blew the smoke out over his shoulder rather than into her face.

She realized how stupid that had sounded. "How long have you been smoking?"

"About three or four minutes, give or take a few." He eyed the stub. "Don't seem to last like they used to."

"Yeah, well. I'm going out for a run. Be back in an hour."

He shoved a shoulder into the doorframe. Finally his chocolate eyes found hers, filled with pain and doubt. "You're going jogging? In San Juan?"

Taking a single step toward the exterior door, Fara glanced back over her shoulder at him. She knew better. Every time she looked at him, she remembered how he brought her to orgasm again and again. "No. I'm going running in San Juan."

"Like hell." He shot past her, physically blocking the doorknob with his body. "It's not safe."

Approaching cautiously, Fara stopped when she felt the heat radiating from his body, stirring the deep memory of her bizarre dream, fully bringing the clinging need abruptly to the surface. "I need to clear my head. There's so much going on that I don't understand. I've got to get it together before going back to the fort."

"*We* are not going to the fort, not yet anyway. Let's let them wait it out." He reached out and took her hand, smoothing his fingers over her knuckles. "Maybe they'll tip their hand."

Whenever she was alone, she thought she could resist him, but any hope of that shattered when she was with him. The shimmer of emotion curled into her voice even while she was trying her damnedest to control it. "Good point, but I still need the run."

"Then I'm going with you." Releasing her hand, he brushed past her. "Give me a minute."

CHAPTER 22

J.C. emerged clad in a pair of cut-offs and a muscle shirt, stopping short when he realized Fara wasn't in the room. "Shit!"

"What?" Looking even fresher, Fara breezed in from her bedroom.

"Nothing." He shoved his hands into the front pockets and shrugged. "I thought you bailed on me again."

"I wouldn't have done that." Her eyes scanned his odd attire, but it was all he had with him. "You don't strike me as the exercising type. You have one of those rangy bodies that's naturally buff."

"So, do you like rangy and naturally buff?"

"Yeah, it suits you. Come-on." She headed for the door.

With a springy step, he made it there first, and in a gentlemanly manner, ushered Fara into the hallway. "Do you run frequently, like marathons and stuff?"

"No," she adjusted her cap, "I started running in the Army because I had to, and then in Afghanistan to stay alive. Now I run because it gives me time to think. When I hit my stride, everything comes into focus. I sometimes discover new solutions to complex problems."

"Definitely have some of those." At the end of the enclosed corridor, he turned her to the left and opened a glass paneled door. "This is the way Puerto Ricans exercise."

The room was tiny, especially for the size of the massive flat screen TV, which two treadmills, a recumbent bike, and a stair-stepper faced. "Which one do you want?"

"This one." She walked to the treadmill against the wall, and he stepped up on the other. "You should stretch first."

"You first." He hated trying to sound like nothing was going on, like nothing had happened. Here they were, both of them pretending. The small talk was tearing him apart.

"I did while you were changing." She tapped the control panel expertly and started walking. "I normally walk the first half-mile as a warm up."

Not wanting to admit he didn't even know how to turn the damn machine on, he twisted, leaning against the padded handrail to watch her swing her hands in rhythm with long and deliberate strides.

She looked over at him. "You're not going to even walk?"

"I'm giving you a head start." Flipping his fingers through his hair, he struck a pose, rugged and surly, something James Dean would have been proud of.

"You've never done this before have you?"

"Nope," he crossed his arms. "There have been a lot of firsts lately."

Fara's eyes darted to him and then covered her overt reaction by hitting the red pause button. "Here, let me help you." She leaned over and adjusted the speed to level three. "Just hit the start button when you're ready. You adjust the speed up or down with these." She pointed out two triangles. She reengaged her unit and bumped it up to a nine. The belt roared into action, and her feet drummed into a complimentary rhythm.

Slowing down the pace one increment, he was able to keep up with a lazy saunter, which allowed him to watch her. The long ponytail bounced back and forth, making her look younger, really young, like not legal young. Her strides were sure and long, and she didn't hold on as he did. He tried letting go of the padded handrails, but the motion of the belt seemed to be off-kilter, throwing off his balance.

Fara stared straight ahead, concentrating on the wall under the blank screen of the TV. J.C. thought about turning it on, but the sound of the machines caught his attention. The hum vibrated into him, reviving the memory of them together last night, and his courage swelled. "The sound they make makes me think of what happened last night."

Still in stride, Fara's face shot toward him. Now out of rhythm, her ponytail swung wildly. "What happened last night?"

He hit the red button, front and center, and his unit stopped. "Your ring was humming, just like while on the street, but this time, it acted like some kind of projector of their last night on the ship. Felipe told Vivian he loved her." In the growing pause, he could see Fara thinking too much to deny her involvement yet started to doubt whether she would talk about it.

"Vivian went to his room, and they made out." Her words beat with the footfalls. "Even though people back then were prudish, they would still make out."

His heart skipped; she did remember, at least that part. "They weren't the only ones."

Before answering, Fara turned back to face the blank TV and bumped up to the maximum speed into an all-out run. Her strides strained to keep up with the spinning belt. "What do you mean?"

He shouted over the whirring hum and the constant footfalls. "You were in some weird trance. I tried waking you, but whatever was happening had a hold of you. I finally broke the connection by putting my hand over the ring." He held up his palm that had an oval burn mark. "Look at my hand. Fara. It was real."

Violently she hit the red bar and stopped before facing him, taking a few deep breaths. "That part might have been real, but what followed wasn't or couldn't."

"How did you come to that conclusion?" About halfway through, he dropped the volume of his voice to be appropriate within the sudden silence.

"There wasn't any, ah, evidence. Our bodies didn't..." Even though her face was flushed with exertion, it still blushed.

Waiting for her to continue, he finally had enough and grabbed her hands, leading her from the treadmill with a hop down onto the floor. "What do you remember?"

She tossed the question back at him. "What do you remember?"

J.C.'s frustration rose, but instead of swearing he squeezed her hands. "We were together last night."

She tossed back her head to look at him from under the brim of the baseball cap which had scooted a little too far forward. "Define together."

"You know what the hell I mean." With a single step, he closed the distance and forced her back against the wall. "Do you want me to go through the step-by-step details? First, I was over you and was amazed at your level of flexibility. I kissed and tasted and then touched you in both your..."

"Enough," she cut him off.

Instantly, adrenaline charged his system. "You do remember."

"Yes, but it wasn't real. It couldn't be real. It was a fantasy, a dream, a very vivid and fantastic dream we shared. We both woke up in our own beds as if nothing had happened."

"Yeah, that part caught me strange, but whether or not it was with our bodies or just in our minds, it was fucking real."

"Literally." A brief smile broke across her lips. "But if it didn't happen to our bodies, it didn't take place." She patted his chest with both of her hands. "This is real. What we had last night was just some hallucination, a vision..."

"...Of what we both really want." He finished for her and gathered her hands again, holding them tenderly. "I told you that I love you, and you replied..." His eyes narrowed. "What did you tell me Fara?"

"Fuck!" She closed her eyes, and to shield herself even more, she tipped down her chin for the low brim of the hat to hide her face.

He squeezed her hands hard, then let one go to lift her chin. "Was it true? Do you love me?"

Her eyes were narrow green slits, hard and unreadable. "What I said in a dream doesn't matter."

"It matters. To me it matters a hell of a lot. Jesus Christ, I don't know why, but I do love you, whether you're Aphrodite incarnate, a stubborn ex-military jock, or a studious note taker. I meant what I said in the dream or whatever the hell it was, just like you. You said you love me, and you meant it. If that's not true, then tell me now, to my face that you don't." His hands pinned her shoulders against the wall forcing her to look at him.

Her expression was blank, one of those she had to have practiced for years to hide her true feelings. "It's not safe for you to love me."

"Damn it Fara, that isn't what I asked. Tell me straight that you don't love me."

"I don't love you," her stern look hardened until her face shielded every emotion, "and it's for your own good. Everyone I've ever loved has died horribly. If I'm a goddess, I'm definitely not Aphrodite. I am evil, a destructor and reaper of souls, the grand dame of the underworld." Her voice broke.

If he had believed her, his heart would have slammed down to his feet, but he knew she was just too afraid to admit it openly. He waited for her to continue, but the silence dragged on too long. "That's not true."

"Listen to me," Fara grabbed him in turn and shook him sharply, "fucking listen! My mother died in childbirth, and a nun cared for me in an orphanage. While I was still an infant, an American couple adopted me. When I was fifteen, they died in a car wreck, and I was in the car. I heard their skulls crack as the front of a huge fucking sedan came through the windshield. EMS took me to the hospital, but I barely even had a scratch. I became a ward of the state and went to live in a foster home, nice people whose son went to the same high school. Kennedy was a football jock, dark blond hair, sky blue eyes. After a couple of months, we wanted each other, and he took my virginity on a stormy Wednesday afternoon before his parents came home from work. That Friday, he suffered a broken neck on the field. He died right there in front of the entire fucking stadium. A guitarist died from electrocution. While in training, I fell for an Italian who died in a car bomb explosion. Everybody I ever loved has died. I learned to keep sex separate and removed from any other emotion until I met Jason, who caught me by surprise. I hoped since I was half a world away, he would be safe. At his funeral, just before his casket was to be lowered into the ground, his mother screamed that I had killed her son, that it was my fucking fault because I took his mind off from the mission. She was right. It was my fault, just for not that reason. J.C., you can't love me, and I can't love you. You have to get as far away from me as possible."

"It's too late. I can't change it or take it back." His eyes softened, and he wanted to hold her and kiss her now more than ever before. "You are my match Fara. In all of that metaphysical stuff, you're the Ying to my Yang, or however it goes. My parents died in a car wreck. My first girlfriend died of an undetected congenital heart defect the day after I seduced her. I've had meaningless sex all of my adult life. I almost died in Scotland and decided to make each day matter. You and I are the same; we'll cancel each other out."

A change softened her face, easing the creases at the corners of her eyes for an instant before hardening again. "Perhaps literally."

"Then it's our fate, and I'm willing to accept that if it means I can enjoy whatever time we have together." In her momentary lapse, J.C. pressed against her and gently smoothed his lips over her neck, feeling her pulse suddenly skip. "Tonight, we are sharing the same bed, all night long, for real. Ghosts, demons, or whatever may make an appearance, the fucking gates of hell could open, and it won't make a difference. I plan to make love throughout the night and in the morning."

Her cheeks ran wet with silent tears. "J.C., I can't"

"Yes, you can and you will."

CHAPTER 23

The freshness of the storm still clung to the early breeze, cool and revitalizing, but that moment was fleeting as were any of life's pleasures. The morning radiated a little too brightly, signaling the day would become unbearably hot. The abundance of rain was evaporating into visible ribbons of humidity sizzling from the ground. Rob thought he had gotten accustomed to suffocating humidity while living in Miami, but Puerto Rico took the prize, hands-down.

Adjusting the straw hat, he sauntered out onto El Convento's veranda and stopped a moment to appreciate the killer view of the channel where Bajia de San Juan met the Atlantic. While his cruise came back into port, he purposefully studied both forts from the sea. A formidable combination, El Morro guarded the channel and San Cristobal the land and northern coast. Somewhere in that mix was the southern-most point of the Devil's Triangle. He'd have to remind Fara to include that tidy fact in the show's intro.

Breezing out with a brisk stride, Rob brushed past the maître'd when he spotted the unlikely couple sitting near the water. On the surface, it appeared as if they were getting along. Silently he approached and enjoyed the sensation of spying on a spy, or at least a former spy. Although Fara never admitted it, he knew. Rob prided himself on knowing people, and there was more to that woman than what met the eye. He edged closer and overheard the tail-end of J.C.'s question. "... that Felipe and Vivian made love?"

"Some heavy petting, but no penetration." Fara smiled up at the waiter who had to have overheard. "Egg-white omelet, no cheese, coffee."

J.C. closed the menu and held it out. "I'll have the waffles, topped with fresh fruit and whipped cream. Scrambled eggs and a side of bacon."

"Cholesterol will kill you."

"Not if you don't first," he winked, "but I'm pretty resilient."

"Resiliency is a good trait." She tipped her face for the morning sunshine to shine under the brim of a black baseball cap.

"There you are." Rob called out once he realized he wouldn't get any more info from eavesdropping. His familiar voice had their heads turning. "I'm flying back to Miami this afternoon and wanted to check on your progress."

Like a flash, J.C. sprung to his feet, shaking his outstretched hand. "We made considerable headway last night."

He liked the green flash when he caught Fara off guard. It made him feel like he had really accomplished something that not many were able to do. "Good to hear." He cleared his gravelly voice. "I'd love to see the outline."

She replied. "We don't exactly have an outline."

"After concluding the research, we found a flow and jumped right into the script. We have an outline on Post-Its and two of the eight scenes scripted, enough of the details to place an order for the costumes and actors this morning."

"Good, better than I expected since you two got off to a bad start." Rob sat in the chair next to Fara. "I got a call this morning from Señor Muñoz. You apparently worked your magic on him yesterday. He seems quite taken with you." He lightly chuckled, raising a finger to wave over the waiter. "He would be willing to do just about anything to have you visit him again, so I arranged for a private tour this afternoon. There are some very interesting features of the fort you haven't seen."

"I'm not sure what I did to give him that impression." Her words were even yet tight, completely void of her siren wiles. "I'm flattered, but don't need another tour."

"While she was there yesterday, she blocked the locations for the scenes." J.C.'s eyes narrowed. "We need to spend today finishing the script. We've been making progress by assuming the characters' roles."

"Felipe and Vivian."

Fara twisted, and the sun cast a dark shadow off of the brim of her cap. "How did you know their names?"

"I overheard you talking about them heavy petting just now." He hated the shadow covering Fara's face; he needed to read her expression to know what was really going on. "I want it to be hot, scandalously hot."

"Believe me, it will be." J.C. grinned. "They've got it going on."

"Good, good." He felt her eyes scrutinizing him, and even though he wanted to squirm, he held firm. "I still want you to go by the fort today Fara. Keep up the flirting and press on the charm. Keep Muñoz in our good graces until the shoot concludes."

"She's not going there alone again." Visibly reddening, emotion rounded J.C.'s eyes before blooming across the rest of his face. "He bugged us."

"What did he do to make you say that?" He pulled out a cigarette and tapped it lightly against the table, more out of habit than necessity. As he lit the tip, the smoke floated away from them on the morning breeze.

Fara cleared her voice softly. "Not he bugged us as in bothered; rather he electronically bugged the folder he gave me."

J.C. placed both palms on the table. "While Fara was with Muñoz, I met with Eduin Figueroa, the former head of security, and got pegged too. The two men are into this together."

"Into what?" He looked between them. "Jesus Christ, all you two need to do is produce forty-two minutes of program. That's all."

"That's precisely what we're doing." J.C. said flatly.

Fara chimed in, "Rob, do you have any idea why they would want to hear what we come up with so badly?"

"No, do you?" He threw the anger and hostility right back at her.

Her voice assumed its level calmness. "Corporate espionage. Another show wants to know what we're doing?"

"Shit!" He had nearly risen out of his chair with the outburst, and slowly sank back down. "I didn't think about that."

"We were discussing Vivian before Fara found the devices. Even if they got some information to use, we'd still air *Ghost Lovers* first, right?" J.C. shifted in his seat warily.

"Just to be sure, let's accelerate the schedule. I'll send the crew in on Thursday to start shooting. Okay, make some excuse to Muñoz and move forward on the script. I want it tonight."

"We need a ship." J.C. muttered.

Rob cleared his throat deeply. "What kind of ship and why?"

"An 18th Century replica will do, at least for two, maybe three scenes." Fara's voice rose and dropped, making him want to do exactly what she asked.

Before Rob could figure out how, J.C. let the details flow. "From what I hear, there're plenty of novelty excursion boats. We'd get it done in two nights; they're all night scenes except one. I prefer shooting at night rather than trying to match up the day for nights, saves money in post-production. I'll make the arrangements and make sure we come in on budget."

"You always were a lot more stable than Alex." He grasped J.C.'s arm and didn't realize there was so much muscle hidden inside the flesh.

J.C. politely shrugged him off. "Heard anything about how he's doing?"

"Total psychotic breakdown. He still thinks he's Alexander Seton. Lily had been visiting him until he turned violent. The last update said he's being kept sedated." He set his coffee cup down with a rattle against the table. "You don't have any of that paranormal, spiritual bull-shit going on around here do you?"

"If you don't believe in it, why do you produce the show?" Fara asked innocently.

Rob laughed heartily, drawing the attention from several other tables. "I make money sweetheart. Clear and simple, ghosts sell."

CHAPTER 24

Fara's mood had deteriorated, and moody didn't suit her. She considered going back to the gym, but they were on a tighter schedule. Five scenes wouldn't be impossible to write in a day, at least in draft format, but inside she didn't like what was gnawing at her. Ghostly connections. People spying on them. And then the personal issue.

With a sweep, J.C. pulled up two of the yellow notes, "They arrive at Puerto Rico, and then the next one is she meets her uncle."

"Doesn't sound very steamy to me."

"I'm sure we can think of something." He sidled closer, emanating that masculine essence she already knew too well.

Instinctively, she stepped back by the same distance. "J.C., I can't..."

"Yes you can and will." Even quicker than her honed reflexes could react, he seized her hand, pulling her across the room.

"What are you doing?"

"What do you think? We're both too tied up to work."

Anger flinched through her muscles, but she didn't want to hurt him. She tugged just enough to free herself. "It's best then for us to continue because that's exactly what Felipe and Vivian are feeling right now. They petted last night but didn't physically bond."

"Vivian had an orgasm."

She breezed across the room and snagged the phone out of her purse, hoping for a distraction. Perhaps, she should have gone back to the fort. The thought made her flesh crawl but was better than acting on what her flesh really wanted. The desire between her legs was tight and needy. "A virginal orgasm. Those don't happen all that often."

"At least not without her losing her virginity shortly thereafter." His groan was thick with frustration. "Okay, you're right. It will keep us edgy, but I swear I'm going to make love to you before this day is done, which is something I've been waiting to do all my life."

Fara chuckled. "All your life? If we cancel the one from last night as not being physical, we still fucked like wild cats the first night."

"Fucked but not made love. There's a difference."

Yes, there was a world of difference between slow and gentle love and fucking like animals. Warily, Fara met his eyes while remembering how meekly Jason took her out of love. She preferred the fire of lust over that meager showing. Immediately, a wave of guilt capsized her heart.

"I think the two scenes can be combined into one."

"What?" Her mind thought of the two scenes, one with her husband and the other of lustful passion with a man who drove her crazy.

He waved the little pieces of paper in the air. "The last scene concluded with Vivian's orgasm. Now it's the next day. The storm passed. And the ship's in the harbor."

Closing her eyes, Vivian concentrated. "There were two carriages waiting for them at the dock."

"Carriages and horses are too expensive. With the port being so busy, it'll be next to impossible to control the environment for it to look 18th Century." He turned toward the window.

"You know in this light, you look kind of like a pirate." Laughing, she continued to watch him warily, not know quite what to expect next. "So Vivian's uncle doesn't meet them at the dock."

"He's waiting to receive them at the fort along with Don Miguel Antonio de Ustariz, Marianne's fiancé." Regally, he bowed and extended his arm.

Feeling a little silly, she curtsied just like she learned in dance class and glided to set her hand upon his arm, all sweet and genteel. "Captain Ortiz escorts Marianne, so Felipe can escort Vivian."

"With Sister Marguerite close behind."

"Isn't she always?"

J.C. tried to keep his face stoic, but a laugh broke through. "She's holding Tomas' hand."

"The entourage approaches the two Captain Generals who are waiting in Dufresne's office, standing behind the ornate desk." She thought back to the fort and didn't remember seeing a room set up like they required, but they could improvise. "Right after Vivian sees her uncle, close up of Vivian's hand tightening on Felipe's arm."

He glanced at her. "That a girl. Tell details in the narrative, show the mounting anxiety through action."

She never appreciated praise when it bordered on condescending. "She knows better than to speak before being presented, so she and Felipe wait while Jose Dufrense greets and then introduces his daughter to her fiancé, a dour faced man who suffers from indigestion."

"Too long and boring. We'd lose viewers, especially after the orgasm scene. They'll be expecting more." J.C. slid his free hand atop Fara's that was still balanced on his arm. "Those details have to go into your narrative."

"At this rate, there'll be more narrative than acting." She tipped back her head and pulled off the baseball cap in a single motion.

"Jesus, you're beautiful when you do that." Dumbfounded, he stood motionless, just staring at her with wide eyes.

"You're hopeless; you know that?"

"No, hopeful, entirely hopeful." He eased closer, leaning his mouth toward her lips.

"You're not in character, Lieutenant." She giggled as he lunged at her and buried his face into her neck, nibbling aggressively.

Sizzling need suffused her system, choking logic from her mind. The emerald vibrated a barely detectible hum, though deeper in tone. "Mmm," she purred, "your tongue is quite talented."

"Let me show you how I ..." a sudden knock startled them both.

Immediately regaining her composure, Fara answered the door and called upon even more self-restraint to control her surprise. "Señor Muñoz, what are you doing here?"

"Fernando," his name rolled off his tongue, "or did you forget all about me my sweet and beautiful lady?" He grabbed her left hand, examining the ring, and carefully avoiding it, swept a kiss on the knuckle farthest from the emerald.

She could feel the tension explode into the room behind her. "It would be impossible for me to forget." Reluctantly, she stepped aside. "Phantoms opening doors and cold spots. Seems you have quite an active spiritual location."

"I didn't think it was only the ghost that interested you." As Fernando entered the parlor, he stopped short. Even with stiffening shoulders, the finely tailored suit adjusted. "You have company."

"I'd like to introduce my partner, J.C. Calderon. We co-produce *Ghost Lovers*." Secretly, Fara relished in the jealousy flaring in both men's expressions. "J.C. may I introduce Fernando Muñoz, the head of security at San Cristobal."

Using the opportunity, J.C. wedged himself between them on the pretense of shaking the man's hand. "You caught us at a busy time. We're in the middle of writing the script."

Hastily Fernando Muñoz extricated himself from J.C.'s excessive squeeze, and lightly stepping to the side, approached her again. "You said you would bring back the file today. Since you didn't arrive this morning, I decided to stop by and see if you would have lunch with me and then finalize the details for your program."

"*We* had intended to bring the file to you. When Fara and I were together at breakfast this morning, *we* found out our production schedule's been moved up. Fara and I will be working all day, together. Here, in *our* shared rooms."

"He's right." Not able to resist, she smiled at the not so subtle way J.C. tried to reinforce their couple's status. "I'm afraid going to lunch or the fort today will be impossible. I hope you understand."

Instead of her holding Fernando's attention, he stared squarely at J.C. "Well then, where's the file?"

"Oh I left it in the trunk of J.C.'s car after we went to dinner last night. Unfortunately, it wasn't very useful, and I forgot about it. Did you ever notice each page is exactly the same except for the date?" She assessed the minor twitch in his jaw as a revealing detail, but of what, she wasn't quite sure.

After an initial twitch, Fernando's face kept changing, morphing ever so slightly, not enough to really be perceptible, yet enough to be disconcerting. Her senses tingled warning throughout her mind, and her stomach tightened. Rational or not, she shielded herself, a self-induced trance technique she'd learned while in training; the procedure separated the active mind from the analog input of the senses. The last time she used it was steeling herself against the torture during her abduction.

Fernando's eyes visibly darkened, the deep brown turning almost as black as the pupils tightened, and then abnormally dilated. "No, I hadn't had an opportunity to peruse the information. I only pulled it out of the filing cabinet to file the most recent report."

"If you wrote the last report, why was it just like all the ones from your predecessors?" Taking broad steps, J.C. circled like a vulture waiting for its prey to die with an expression just as anticipatory.

"I wasn't really sure what to say, so I copied the last entry." Muñoz didn't move his feet or really seem to turn his head, yet he followed J.C.'s movements intently.

"If the reports aren't important, why did you come here today to get the file?" J.C. finally quit his ridiculous circling and propped himself in the doorframe of Fara's bedroom.

"Well," his hands opened palm up in front of him. "In all honesty, I was hoping to spend some time with Señorita Trotter, but since that's not possible now, perhaps this evening," he picked up her hand and met it with his lips, "I would love to take you to dinner this evening."

Gently, she pulled her hand away. The vibe was more than uncomfortable it was unnatural. "Sounds enjoyable, but I promised to meet a couple of old friends who just happen to be in San Juan. Tonight's the only night we'll be able to get together."

Fernando's face hardened while his voice leveled into an odd monotone. "Perhaps you will change your plans for me."

She heard the subtle suggestion float into the air, filling the gaps between the words. At first, she wondered if she should play along and pretend his mind tricks were working, but given the state of J.C.'s discomfort, playing it straight was best.

"Change your plans Fara. You want to go to dinner. Change your plans for me." Fernando continued to repeat his request with subtle enough changes to make it not sound overt.

She knew exactly what he was doing because she used the same mild hypnosis technique frequently. Particular sounds shifted dynamics of the brain. People didn't realize they were being influenced because they continued to think and plan, yet they were compelled to do what the hypnotist suggested repetitively. The technique worked on eighty-five percent of the adult population.

"No, I appreciate your efforts, but I will not change my plans." Rousing her own skill at manipulation, she replied in kind. "Perhaps another time. Perhaps another time, later in the week." Watching the shock skim over his eyes, she smiled, relishing in how it infuriated him. "Another time."

Fernando acknowledged her skill with a stiff bow. "Another time." He breezed out of the room, banging the door harshly.

A chill ran through Fara when she released her steely emotional shield.

CHAPTER 25

"What the hell was that about?" J.C. didn't like the impromptu visit on a multitude of levels, the most basic being Mr. Smarmy spoiled a good start to seducing Fara, but that irritation was second to the fact Fernando Muñoz wanted to seduce her himself.

"Repetition is a tool hypnotists use. He was trying to compel me to do what he wanted." Fara twisted around one of the chairs and straddled it guy style, setting her chin upon the upper rung between the spindles.

Jealousy was an unfamiliar emotion. The surging impulses sizzled through J.C.'s veins and tightened his voice. "You saying he's like a Jedi with the mind-control thing?"

"Yeah, sort-of, but if he's a Jedi, he's on the dark side." While speaking, she absently separated her long hair into three chords and loosely braided them behind her back. "Did you notice anything weird about the way he looks?"

Filling his eyes on the innocent yet somehow provocative motion, he bit down on the urge to ask her to leave her hair loose. "Like what?"

"Never mind. I've learned never to say anything out loud that would make me fail a psyc eval." She held the end of the braid and started to search through her purse for a rubber band.

"Like he changes slightly when you're not really looking at him?"

She froze, and then her fingers continued. "Yeah, like he's not real, like he's an avatar of something that can't or won't come out into the real world." She shook her handbag and dug again along the bottom. "Shit."

"Leave it down." He took the heavy rope of hair from her and unwound it. Running his fingers through the lengths was sensually arousing and so very intimate. "Leave it down. You look beautiful with your hair down. Leave it down."

Giggling, she swiveled. "Your mind tricks don't work on me, Jedi. I'm in the minority who can't be hypnotized. Believe me; the best of the best have tried."

After arranging her hair behind her shoulders, he knelt in front of her. "Are you ready to get back to work?" J.C. raised his shoulders and squeezed the shoulder blades together, arching his back.

"First, come here. Let me rub out some of the tension." Within seconds, her hands were firmly kneading the tight muscles. "Man, you're stressed."

"What do you expect?" Stretching, he leaned into the swirling motion allowing her strong fingers to dig deeper. "Having another man come in and ask my girlfriend out on a date wasn't easy. I wanted to tear his head off."

She briefly paused and then continued the swirling motion. "Girlfriend?"

Breaking the contact, he twisted around to face her. "Would you prefer for me to say lover?"

Her lovely green eyes held his gaze. "Not at the moment."

His fingers cradled her face and drew her toward him. "Now is the perfect moment." Their lips met, and it was damn good thing he was already on his knees. All of the blood drained out of his head, leaving him dizzy and aching. "I want you Fara. I want you so bad it's tied me up in knots. I'm not going to be able to work until we get this out of..." A vibrating hum stirred his already straining erection. Shoving his hand into his pocket, he withdrew the slim phone with a groan and stared at the screen. "It's my grandfather. He can wait." Disdainfully, he tossed the phone onto the table next to the laptop and swiveled back toward her, wrapping his arms around her. "This can't."

His lips touched hers. The compounded yearning and waiting burned through him in a heated flash. Last night couldn't have involved their bodies, for his need was sharp, on the edge of madness. With both hands, J.C. pulled her t-shirt out of her shorts and slid his hands up her back.

"Don't..." Suddenly his hands were very empty.

He looked at the spot where Fara had been. "Don't what? What did I do?" Yet before the words left his tongue, he realized his mistake. "If you don't want me to touch your back, just tell me. Does it still hurt?"

"No." She quickly tucked in the disheveled shirt. "We can't do this."

"Shit, come-on Fara. I don't care your back has a few scars."

"A few scars?" She spun around. "It's deformed, and I hate it."

"You are beautiful." His cellphone hummed from the table, spinning slightly with the vibration. "And I want to touch you."

"You can, just not my back."

A twisted grin pulled the corners of his mouth at the unexpected invitation. "I can touch you here." He cupped her breast, and then covered them both, squeezing gently. "Let's see, my guess is 34C."

"34B, but suggesting a cup size larger feeds the feminine ego." A smile finally grew across her lips. "You are damned persistent."

"You have no idea how persistent I can be." With a deft move that even surprised himself, J.C. used the next squeeze to grab the shirt and yank it over her head, exposing the black sports bra. He wished she had worn a regular bra, one that he could unclasp rather than pull over her head. "You're incredibly beautiful and sexy." He slid his arms around her waist, carefully avoiding her back while hooking his thumbs in her bra, easing it over her shoulders.

She glanced at the table as his phone buzzed again. "Are you going to ignore that? Could be important."

"Nothing's as important as this." While he bent his head to taste a breast, his hands fumbled with her shorts until he got the tight fit to slide down her legs. His tongue eased around the tense need, teasing the peaks to rise into even tighter points, and he remembered the shared experience as Felipe had tasted Vivian's nipples. The parallel stormed into him, making him want her that much more.

The words barely formed in Fara's open mouth. "We should be working."

With a broad lick, he moaned, "Consider this research." Drawing her panties down, she finally stood before him naked. "Now you're not going to tell me this isn't real, are you?"

"This is very real." Her voice quivered. "That's why I'm scared about where this is going."

"This is going to my bed; although, I've heard there are more creative ways than making love in bed." He grinned, watching her reaction, but it wasn't what he had expected.

Her eyes had fallen, looking squarely at the massive erection straining in his shorts. "I don't know if ... what you expect."

"You know exactly what I expect." At first he thought she was joking, but her face was anything but humorous.

"That's not what I meant. Last night we did things, well, I don't know if I can do for real."

His brows arched while easing backwards, drawing her toward the open door to his room. "Like?"

"Don't tease me." An odd echo puddled back in time, and the emerald ring hummed low and steady. "You know very well what I'm talking about. I did things I'd never done before."

"I'm not teasing." He threaded his fingers into her loose hair, allowing the silken strands to slip through his fingers while his lips found the groove above her clavicle. His tongue eased into the warm valley. He reached her throat and whispered into her heating flesh. "I won't ask you to do anything you don't want to do."

"I know, but J.C. we shouldn't..." In contrast to her words, her fingers slid into his shorts, guiding them from his hips. While absently licking her lips, she followed the shorts to the floor and knelt in front of him, pulling down his boxers. The skin of his penis was dark and velvety, drawn tautly over the straining core. Her mouth grasped him near the base, nearly biting into the sensitive flesh.

"Holy shit," his head fell back, and his penis arched even higher. Fara's suckling reached the straining head and rounded the crown with her tongue. He reached out and cupped her face, holding her head away from him as he knelt down too. He met her eyes and filled with longing too sharp to deny. Richly and warmly, he brushed his tongue over her lips and then kissed her.

The emerald's soft tone grew until humming filled the room, distorting the perception of time in hazy waves. Lifting her left hand, they both stared at the green glow, whose rays slid like foggy smoke across the timeless sea. The tendrils glided softly over their bodies, caressing gently while enveloping them into the past.

Every door and window in the large room was open, allowing the sea breeze to flow; however, from Vivian's perspective, the air was hot and tense. With each step forward, her hand tightened on Felipe's arm, squeezing until tension gripped her entire body. The last time she had seen her uncle she was only a girl, yet imprinted memories of that day stayed with her for the past seven years. Vivian never told her father she witnessed their fight. Never in all her life had she been as scared as when the point of her uncle's cutlass scratched across her father's neck. When he received the letter requesting Vivian attend Marianne, he would have refused his brother, but Vivian's ardent desire to accompany her cousins to Puerto Rico softened his heart enough to accept his brother's apology.

Now as still and cold as marble, Vivian waited at Felipe's side, growing visibly paler. Her steadfast will dissolved, afraid she might faint while waiting for Jose Dufrense to complete the introductions between Marianne and her future husband. Staring down a straight and hawkish nose, Miguel Antonio de Ustariz's narrow eyes scrutinized Marianne. Once they fell upon Vivian, his serious expression broke into a smile.

Captain Ortiz completed their introductions, and Felipe led Vivian to the edge of the room. "You look pale. What if we take a walk and some air?"

While Dufrense affectionately greeted Tomas, Felipe led Vivian into the corridor and down the narrow back stair. The winding stone staircase ended at the field level. Every eye turned to admire Vivian. Men outnumbered women on the island ten to one, and in the fort nearly fifty to one, so even the homeliest of women were sought after prizes. News of Vivian's beauty had spread faster than plague, and already more than a hundred men hurried out onto the practice field to witness the rumors and found verity rather than exaggeration.

"You are quiet." Color started to rise in Vivian's pale complexion.

"I want you to return to Spain with me." Felipe walked slowly, squeezing her hand softly.

With the same vehemence of the concussion from an exploding bomb, "Vivian!" shot across the grounds, blasting its way over the damp and trampled earth, silencing all.

Vivian's uncle strode toward them with an armed escort on both sides. "I ... I'm afraid, Felipe. Please don't leave me." Tears swelled but didn't spill down her cheeks until Jose Dufrense grabbed Vivian and shook her until she was loose of Felipe's hold.

Her uncle growled. "How dare you leave your audience until you have been excused!"

"Sir, I apologize, for it was not Vivian's will, rather my own." Felipe clasped her other arm, trying to draw her back under his protection, but Dufrense shoved the girl aside harshly. "After being confined aboard ship for three weeks, I thought a walk would help her acclimate to life on land."

"I shall determine what is best for my niece, Lieutenant, and you may address her only as Señorita Dufrense." The General shoved her shoulders downward, forcing Vivian to fall onto her knees.

"Uncle please," tears ran freely down her cheeks but had not yet entered her voice. "Felipe and I ... I have given him leave to use my given name."

Her uncle's foul breath contaminated the fresh breeze. "And I as your guardian remove that right."

Felipe took only a single step forward and was suddenly confronted with the point of a cutlass. "Captain General, might I have an audience with you to explain. My intentions are entirely honorable."

"Your intentions are perfectly clear and interest unwelcomed." Dufrense balanced the tip of his sword at the hollow of Felipe's neck.

"Uncle, please you misunderstand. Felipe is the son of Viscount Cordova and..."

"Stupid girl." While keeping his sword in place, Dufrense scowled at Vivian. "I know who he is, for whilst at court, Felipe Luis Morgan Cordova gained considerable notoriety for his seductions. Nary a woman was not at some time in his arms. You are too young to understand the ways of men, especially the likes of this man. Even this walk will soil your reputation. He's not to be trusted."

"Felipe has treated me with utmost respect." Although Vivian's nerves were frayed, she drew upon her resolve, even while muddy soil soaked into her finest dress. "Upon Felipe's return to Spain, he will be meeting with my father to ask for my hand and then with the king to seek his blessing."

"Are you telling me you have consented to become his wife?" Without looking at Felipe, Dufrense forced the sword forward until the tension bowed the blade.

"Yes, I have agreed for him to..."

In an instant, Dufrense's palm connected with Vivian's face. The glowing pain snapped suddenly, but the sting was not nearly as acute as the anguish growing within her soul. He swung the sword toward Vivian, which dredged up the hideous memories of the fight with her father. "You have no right. The moment you left Spain, you became my ward, my property, and shall do as I command. Get to your chambers and attend to Marianne." He motioned to the one of the soldiers. "Take her upstairs."

The men on the field silently parted while the soldier dragged Vivian away in disgrace. She twisted against the man's grip while her heart broke. She loved Felipe. She would always love him.

With a nod from the Captain General, the other man at arms moved into position next to Dufrense. "Lieutenant Cordova, I forbid you any communication with my niece or any other member of my household. Vivian is the only child of my elder brother, who is a successful merchant. I am certain you are well aware of that fact, for although lecherous, you are not stupid, and neither am I, nor my brother for that fact. I consider it my solemn obligation to inform him of what I know of your character." He motioned to the soldier. "Escort him to the gate and make it clear he's not permitted to return."

"Wait ... a moment ... please ... Captain General." Felipe resisted, digging his heels into the soft turf. "I do not deny while at court I was young and coveted the favor of ladies, but I never forced a woman to do anything against her will. I left that life behind seven years ago. I have since repented my ways and truly seek Señorita Dufrense's hand as my wife. I have done nothing to sully her reputation. Her innocence is as intact as the day she stepped aboard the Immaculata."

"If I suspected otherwise, I would have you thrown in the dungeon rather than from the fort, but you try my patience. If I ever lay eyes on you again, I shall do worse." Dufrense waved another man over, but before the additional soldier arrived, Felipe strode toward the upper gate of his own accord, each long stride leaving an impression in the mud.

Vivian gave up the struggle, and the soldier eased his grip. Breaking free of his hold, she ran up the steps of her own accord and down the hall, stopping only once she realized she didn't know which room was intended for her use. Marianne stepped out of a doorway. Before Vivian could react, Captain General Dufrense grabbed her by the hair and dragged her into the next room on the right.

The bedroom was large and more than adequately furnished; however, Vivian didn't have time to acknowledge such things. The man's backhanded blow fell swiftly, and she shrieked from both surprise and pain. Off balance, the girl landed in a heap upon the circular rug. Warily, she gazed up toward the reddened face, creased harshly with turbulent anger. She wanted to say something; however, she was not acquainted well enough with her uncle to know which words would calm rather than reignite his wrath.

He stood with his feet spread in a wide stance, commanding all of the space around him. "Women are all too eager to corrupt their virtue with a man who spins a desirous web. Did you allow him any favor?"

Vivian's eye stung from the latest blow, causing a stream of tears to flow unchecked down her swelling cheek. "I did nothing. He treated me as a gentleman should."

"As her dueña, I guarantee Vivian conducted herself appropriately." The ageless voice of Sister Marguerite carried upon the gentle breeze blowing through the still open doorway. "Lieutenant Cordova also acted in accordance to proper decorum and did her no harm."

"No harm? Just being in that man's presence is a sin. He sullied many a virgin, including Constance," his voice broke and then began again, "my intended. I did not learn of Felipe Cordova's treachery until our wedding night, when I discovered my bride had lain with him. The Pope himself warranted our union annulled; however, my brother regarded my actions against the girl too harsh. The incident also dissolved our brotherhood. By the time I learned of Cordova's treachery, I was too late to exact my revenge upon his head, for the jackal joined the King's navy to escape me."

Sister Marguerite sidled closer to Vivian. "There was no way for this child to have known."

"It does not matter. The sin of lust is the same in thought or in deed, and her penance shall be delivered now by my hand." He swung the coat from his shoulders, and his man stepped up to catch it. A small crowd of the elite guard had gathered, and the shortest of the men placed a switch of green bamboo into his outstretched palm. Tense fingers curled around the rod.

The first blow landed with a hard thwack, and Vivian's scream echoed through the open balcony. Through the communal silence all could hear the swish of the rod before it landed with a thud upon the girl's flesh, a heartbeat before the next curdling shriek ripped the air.

Sickened to witness such unspeakable evil, Sister Marguerite bent next to the huddled form, and with the gentlest of touches, helped the girl to the bed. The Sister recalled Matthew 5:45 and verbalized the passage, hoping it would gift some solace. "That ye may be the children of your Father which is in heaven: for he maketh his sun to rise on the evil and on the good, and sendeth rain on the just and on the unjust alike."

Once the men filed out of the room, Sister Marguerite stripped off the layers of the ruined dress. Her restrained breath relaxed once she loosened the corset. Clearly, the disagreeable device had guarded the flesh, distributing the vibrant depth of the lashes across the whalebone grid, significantly mitigating the damage. In comparison, the skin across Vivian's shoulders was welting in vibrant streaks where the lashes directly encountered tender skin.

Sister Marguerite wetted a cloth, laying it across the worst of the rising damage. "Trust in the Lord our God, king of Heaven and -"

"What in the hell are you doing?" The words clung to the air heavily.

The Sister used a moment to cover the girl's body with the muslin sheet. "I am tending to my child, for I promised both her paternal father and the heavenly Father to watch over her."

"Get out." Dufrense didn't move from his position in the doorway, yet his command clearly permeated the space.

Vivian's chin rose, nearly clearing the pillow, but Sister Marguerite's hand stroked the back of her head, guiding her face back into the downy softness. "I will leave her only once I have completed my duty."

"Your incompetence is done, over. I blame you even more than the stupid girl. You of all people should have kept that abomination away from her. Instead, you encouraged their lascivious desires."

"Sir, I can guarantee that I was never more than a few feet away from your niece at all times. Lieutenant-"

He cut her off abruptly, spitting the words through gritted teeth. "Do not dare say that name in my presence."

She nodded her ascent. "The man did not make any attempt to burnish her reputation. He behaved honorably, in this circumstance. Do you not think he could have repented his sins and mended his ways?"

"No man should ever be forgiven the defiling sin of taking another man's jewel, one that a woman can only give once in her lifetime."

"That is for our Lord to decide, for to err is human to forgive divine. The Lord will judge us all in the end."

"Get out, you vile white-haired witch, before I have you burned, for no woman who honors God would be able to defend the devil."

"I know my own mind, and my soul is unstained. I do not fear you or your wrath sir for the heavenly Father protects and keeps me." After gently patting Vivian's hair, the Sister stood. "Since you are so certain that man's intentions have tarnished this child, I request to take her to the convent and have her confess and repent in the holiest of ways."

"She will not set foot outside of this room until the Immaculata sails from the harbor."

"Then at that time, I will claim her for my keeping." Sister Marguerite nodded while passing.

CHAPTER 26

The event had been so real Fara's back relived the sharp agony. At least Vivian's flesh was not whipped into tatters, but the welts from her beating would not fade for several days, maybe even weeks. Even though flesh eventually healed, the underlying wounds did not. The parallels were too close, too intimate to be mere coincidence that had drawn Fara to this place and to this shared reality. Who else would have known how Vivian felt at this moment? Yet Fara had been tortured only in body, while Vivian's anguish cut beyond mere flesh. The man she loved was a rogue. Even as her damaged wounds swelled, she still loved him, which hurt more than any beating ever could.

Scooting away from J.C., Fara quickly rose to her feet. Her stiff knees had dark red patches from where she had been kneeling, which made her wonder how long they had been huddled together. Ignoring the physical discomfort, she continued to her room and grabbed her robe from the hook on the bathroom wall just when a knock pounded on the hallway door.

J.C. pulled on his shorts and got to the door first. "Look, it's…"

"Why haven't you answered my calls, Nieto?" Angrily, Eduardo Calderon stormed into the room and stopped short as he noticed the discarded clothing in the middle of the floor. "Something terrible has happened."

"What?" She didn't care that she was only wearing the short satin robe and strode into the room. "What's happened?"

"Eduin Figueroa is dead." His voice didn't change. The noticeable anomaly caught Fara's attention. People with this heightened level of excitement would have a tinge of fear, even resentment or remorse.

"What!" J.C. paled, and his tone broke as was normal human behavior.

"Sometime last night, someone broke into his house and stabbed them with a butcher knife." As he continued, Eduardo sank into the closest chair weakly, but again his actions were anomalous with the strength of his voice.

The edge rubbed Fara the wrong way, raising her hackles. "Them?"

"All of them. The entire family. Only Andres wasn't there. He came back to San Juan for work today, leaving Sarafina and the kids at the lake. They're all dead." Eduardo pointed his finger at J.C. "The police are looking for you. I'm surprised I made it here before they arrived. They'll be here any minute."

Indignantly, she stabbed her fists on her hips, revealing the inner curve of her breast, and the hem rose precariously close to the uncovered juncture of her thighs. "They can't possibly think J.C. had something to do with this."

After assessing the striking woman a little too clearly, Eduardo's face fell into his hands. "I told them we left together, but they say they have evidence."

"J.C. was with me last night. There's no…" Another pounding fist shook the door.

"Shit!" J.C. grabbed his shirt off from the floor and struggled into it.

"We'll be able to figure this out. Don't do anything stupid until I get back." Scooping up her clothes, Fara stormed into her bedroom.

The sound of the bedroom door closing echoed with the burst of the other door opening. Several male voices all started talking rapidly in Spanish. Listening carefully, she overheard them telling J.C. he was needed for questioning. Anticipating them to do a complete sweep of their rooms, she tossed the bra onto the bed and pulled on the top and shorts, realizing her underwear still had to be somewhere in the parlor. She wanted to retrieve the handgun she always kept under her pillow, but she had to leave the Browning behind on this trip. Damn handgun laws! But blazing into the room armed might get someone killed, and killing a cop wasn't on her to-do list today.

Quickly assessing the room for any other potential weapon, she knew time was running out. Grabbing her cellphone from the bedside table, she dropped it into her pocket. Realizing her only weapon would be her wits, she had to keep her head to make this work.

She swung open the door, and only three of the armed men swung their nine millimeter standard issue in her direction. An instant adrenaline rush sizzled into her senses, gratefully washing away Vivian's residual emotions. Without being told, Fara threw her spread hands out in front of her. "What's going on? I was in the bathroom and heard all the noise."

"Who are you?" The shortest man demanded in Spanish and approached her. If his uniform wasn't authentic, it was a damned good imitation. This scenario could be legit; if so, beating up a cop could end up badly, for all of them. If they were on the take, the consequences were still bad, but here, probably most of the cops were corrupt. Only if they were impersonators could she kick their asses and get away with it. Although her body itched with adrenaline anticipating a good fight, she held back her inner instinct and weighed the options.

Smiling coyly, she testing the situation. "Look, if we were making too much noise, I'm sorry. Okay I got a little carried away, but when sex is this good, a woman should scream." She spread her arms. "See we didn't do anything to damage the room."

The tallest man wore a loosely-fitting white linen suit rather than a uniform and smiled genuinely while his dark eyes swept over Fara's feminine form. He resembled J.C. in the overall shape of his body, but this man's face was scarred, from either a really bad case of acne or even chicken pox. Although he couldn't be considered handsome, he had an inner confidence. "I apologize Señora, but this isn't about the noise."

"Then, what is this about?" The print on his ID badge was too small to read from a distance. Batting her eyes, Fara stepped forward, easing past the policeman who had yelled at her until she was next to the well-dressed man. Using her peripheral vision, she noted his name was Franz Gomez, the hotel's chief security officer.

He continued, "The police are here to request Señor Calderon's assistance in solving a case."

"With guns drawn? It looks rather suspicious, Mr. ..." she leaned closer as if to read his ID, allowing her hand to linger on his arm. The telltale scent of cigarette smoke drifted along with his body heat. Realistically, he kept his jacket on to cover the fire power he carried. Fara then extended her hand, brushing it across the front of his jacket. He was wearing a shoulder holster on his right, which indicated he was left handed. She assumed he had a smaller weapon wedged in his belt at the hollow of the back or perhaps strapped to his inner right calf. "... Mr. Gomez. Why are you here?" She was a good head shorter than the man, but she affected an ominous pose.

He smiled again, this time widely enough to reveal a perfect set of teeth that were so white he could shoot a toothpaste commercial if his face hadn't been marred. "I am the security manager of the hotel. However much I dislike the police barging in to harangue my guests, I must assist them in such a situation."

"I'm Fara Trotter, and this is J.C. Calderon and his grandfather, Eduardo Calderon. What can we do to help?"

The angry officer started to speak, but the hotel agent held up a hand and waited for silence before he continued. "Where were you last night Miss Trotter?"

The word miss grated on her edgy nerves. "Here. I went to Fort San Cristobal in the afternoon and met J.C. here around five. We worked for a couple of hours here in our rooms before going out for dinner and then returned here to the hotel."

"When you say worked, what were you doing?" The short man asked in heavily accented English.

"J.C. and I produce a TV show. We were writing the script. It's in the laptop." She shrugged while motioning to the table. "I can show you if you don't believe me."

"When did you finish?"

Even if she couldn't have seen the man, she'd have known he sneered, just through the prolonged effect of his slithering words. Regardless what language, power-hungry cops all share the same tone, especially those on the take. If they had been legit, they would have formally identified themselves and quoted Miranda. Still their uniforms and badges looked authentic, but she needed a closer look.

"I noticed it was getting late around midnight, and we worked here for almost another hour before going to bed. J.C. was here the entire night." She caught his eye and nodded slightly, hoping he was committing the details to memory.

The cop in charge failed to notice the exchange. His eyes were dull and glassy; either he was tripping on some psychedelic or under the power of a hypnotist. If the cops were hypnotized, the practitioner was good, unbelievably good, to have so much control while out of physical proximity.

The man sneered again. "How do you know he did not go out the door of his room?"

"Because he was here, in bed with me." Given enough time, Fara could roll him; perhaps she could roll all of the men in the room, especially since they were already under the influence of persuasion. She dropped her voice and smoothed through the words, inflecting a hypnotic cadence. "We made love, for a couple of hours, here before falling asleep, and J.C. was here, in bed with me. The last time, I remembered looking, at the clock, it was almost four, and he was here, in bed with me. I'm a light sleeper, and would have woken, if he had left the bed, so he was here, in bed with me. When he did, get up in the morning, to use the bathroom, I woke, and he came back to me, in bed with me. We made love again, before going to the veranda, for breakfast, where we met our executive producer, Robert Hartz. He was flying back, to Miami today, and touched base, to check on our progress. We shared the details, of the script, we wrote yesterday. J.C. was here with me."

"I will corroborate their story with the wait staff." Mr. Gomez nodded. "Anything else?"

She touched his sleeve again, adding physical contact that added to the effect of the persuasion. "You can prove J.C. didn't leave the building. You must have security footage, of the entrances and exits, of the building. J.C. didn't leave the building. Prove J.C. didn't leave the building."

Someone behind her clapped his hands, breaking down the psychic walls she had formed. Fara spun instantly but couldn't tell who did it.

"The rear cameras are offline. The repairman's coming in the morning. There's nothing I can do." The soft edge left his voice, and Franz Gomez refused to make eye contact.

"Juan Carlos Calderon is coming in for questioning." The uniformed officer motioned to the other policemen who each took up a position, flanking J.C. on both sides.

Roughly, they tugged his hands behind his back and cuffed them. "Fara, I had nothing to do with this. Abuelo and I left their house while everyone was still on the patio. I left before Andres did."

The short man moved toward the door. "Are you saying Andres Figueroa killed his own family?"

"No!" J.C. struggled. The officers grasped his arms, and the one on the left drew his weapon and pointed it at J.C.'s head. His throat bobbed with a deep swallow. "I've known Andres for years. He's a good man and would never do such a thing."

"If you didn't kill them and he didn't kill them, then who did?" The cop's tone was stilted, as if repeating practiced lines.

At the edge of reason, J.C. yelled, "I have no idea."

"Regardless, you are coming with us for questioning." The stumpy one waved toward the door.

"You can't do this. I can prove I was here around four because I checked into that room," J.C. motioned with his head, "that one, that's adjacent to Fara's."

"Wait," Fara held up her hand as her mind wheeled, seeking any other alternative. Even if she could seize a gun and start shooting, J.C. would get shot before she could kill them all. "I need to see your badge?"

"What?" The short man stepped back.

"I need to see your badge. I have the right to ask you for your badge and the right to verify you are a foresworn peace officer before releasing any information, or in this case, Mr. Calderon, who has the right to remain silent until an attorney is present." She held out her hand. "Now, show me your badge."

With a grunt, he pointed to his chest. "I don't need to do anything for you Puta." He shoved past her and grabbed the door, holding it open for the armed escort.

Instantly her blood pumped in hard bursts. Seething within self-imposed restraint, she jumped into the doorway, blocking it with her body. "You're not going anywhere until I have verified you are real cops."

The short man got up into her face. "I will arrest you on obstruction."

Defiance surged through her. "If you're going to arrest me, it will be for damned more than obstruction."

Throwing back his head, he spat at her while another officer grabbed a tazer. In less than a heartbeat, metal barbs dug into Fara's abdomen. The current stormed into her nervous system, singeing rational thoughts from her mind and wrenching a scream from her throat. While the sound hung stiffly in the air, her instinctual nature emerged with the ferocity of a raging tigress. Channeling the electricity, her muscles burst with speed, landing a left jab into cop's ribs and a right hook just under his chin. She was still on her feet when another sting hit her thigh. Her legs crumpled and head spun. As she fell, a hand reached for her with a large silver ring on the third finger.

CHAPTER 27

True to her promise, as soon as the Immaculata had sailed out of the harbor, Sister Marguerite claimed Vivian. With a tear-stained bible in one hand and a rosary draping the other, Vivian followed the Sister through the crowded streets. Daily routines paused to catch a glimpse of the woman who bore the wrath of Captain General Dufrense. Regardless of their whispers, Vivian maintained a serene composure and continued toward the convent, reverently in step behind the Sister.

The great wooden doors were open, allowing the breeze to slip through the sanctuary, sedately as a whispered prayer. Complementing the fresh scent of the sea air, the heady aroma of ageless incense clung to the dark wooden walls. Morning prayers had concluded, and reverence commanded the vacant yet never empty place, for Vivian believed God lived within its holy walls.

Out of habit as well as piety, the women genuflected upon one knee and formed the sign of the cross. The motion soothed Vivian's troubled soul, which became lighter still after her confession to the elderly priest. She spoke the truth regarding how impure thoughts had lit an inferno within her soul yet did not discuss her moments alone with Felipe. Vivian didn't know how to describe the burst of ecstasy Felipe's touch had lured from her body. Better to wait and confess once she could verbalize its meaning. Her maidenhead was intact, so their momentary indiscretion was only that and not a damning sin.

Just outside the confessional, Sister Marguerite waited to lead Vivian from the sanctuary to the inner garden of the priory. Two kneeling benches draped in white silk stood a few feet away from the stature of the Holy Mother. The shade of blushing flowers in exotic shades of pinks and purples cascaded along with shoots of golden blooms. The heavenly scent caressed the garden just as tangibly as did the songbirds' tribute to the glorious morning. The serene beauty was even lovelier, and as Vivian reflected, even more appreciated after four days of cloistered absence from the world.

Crossing herself again, she knelt and started reciting the rosary to the Holy Mother. The mantra softened her pain and enriched her resolve. Belief not only in the sanctity of prayer but also for the eternal love safely lodged within her heart revived her spirits, filling her once again with hope. No one could take that from her, not her uncle, not her father, not even her king, for true love was divine.

Intently focused upon remembering the sight of the sails unfurling to catch the persistent wind, she prayed for the Immaculata's safe passage and for her father's ability to understand how she could love such a man. Her intense desire did not make sense, but nonetheless was real and very much a part of her. Even though she had prepared a letter penned in careful script, there was no opportunity to send it to her father. Perhaps, the lack of a formal statement would be viewed as a testament to her seclusion and abuse. No doubt Felipe would describe the situation, yet he did not know, nor could he understand, the true weight of the hefty punishment Dufrense levied upon her.

She crossed herself and prepared to rise, but Sister Marguerite's warm hand rested upon her shoulder. At the edge of Vivian's vision, a flash of sun glinted off polished steel. A flood of emotion arose. With a deep breath, she prepared to admonish her uncle's guards for sullying such a holy place, but once her eyes rose, the sight was too improbable to be real. In full regalia of his station, Felipe advanced and swept down upon a knee onto the flagstones. Until he clasped her hands within his, she thought him a hallucination rather than flesh and blood.

Her breath huffed through parted lips. "I saw the Immaculata sail."

"She left with the morning tide." His rich voice was true and deep, resounding within her sensitive nature.

"Then what are you doing here?" Her heart skipped out of rhythm, first with joy and then from fear. "If my uncle…" She couldn't continue, knowing what would happen should they be seen together.

"I swear he will pay." Gently his gloved fingers circled, the silky fabric slipping easily over the backs of her pale hands. "When the King hears of his ill treatment of my wife-"

"Your wife?" Despite her resolve, Vivian's eyes widened, and she pulled away from his touch. As her heart twisted, the rosary twisted in her hands just as intensely. "You, you have married?"

"I have told you on more than one occasion it is my sincere intention." Following the scalloped edge of the lacy veil, he stroked her cheek. Upon reaching her chin, he raised her hollow gaze. "Vivian, you cannot possibly tell me you desire to remain under that demon's keeping."

Confusion glazed her mind. Clearly, this all had to be a dream. She would wake in the dark and close room and fill her lungs with stifling air to renew her prayers. "I saw the Immaculata take to sea, so went my heart and hopes, for at least you were safe. By staying behind you risk your safety, your very life."

"Then pray tell me what other course..." He stopped when the elderly priest touched his shoulder.

Father Jacob's dark yet gentle eyes regarded them both. "My son, perhaps you should pose the question to the lady and make her your bride before discussing other, ah, complicating details."

"Your bride?" She had to be delirious. This was so improbable it couldn't be real. Surely, her mind had formed another fantasy of how Felipe would rescue her and take her off to Spain.

He nodded and then fixed his warm brown eyes upon hers. "I pledge my love and my life to you. You are my world, and I will never covet another. Vivian, will you take me as husband this very morn?"

As little whispers fluttered through her nerves, the garden awoke. Birds took flight, and leaves rustled. Then everything settled. The wind quit blowing. Everyone, everything waited with anticipatory patience. Vivian closed her eyes as her arms enveloped Felipe. Before she could think of any words, his lips sought out her mouth and found his answer. After their embrace parted, Father Jacob cleared his throat and started the ceremony by blessing them into God's keeping.

CHAPTER 28

Fara didn't fear pain. Every ache and twinge told her she was alive. Not even a thread of light found its way into the close dampness, but she didn't require light to know she was in the belly of San Cristobal. The age-old decaying scent was close yet not foul, as if many years had passed since this place was an active prison. Now the damp musk clung to the memories of what had been.

Twinges raked through her muscles, still stinging with the tazer's electrical overload while sluggish from the sedative from the dart. The combination was bad, like being high on uppers and taking a handful of barbiturates. The effects definitely didn't cancel each other out. Rather they fucked with the body, pulling the inner tides each in its own potent way.

Even with the muscular disorientation, she worked her way up onto two unsteady legs. The binding under her knees was firm but not tight. The enemy underestimated her. Men normally underestimated women, especially in combat situations. Centuries of being the fairer sex led to distinct advantages. The enemy would let down their guard and not prepare for an all-out assault. During her tours of duty, Fara was rarely on the front lines, only when situations degraded quickly did she engage in direct combat. While in full gear, she was virtually indistinguishable from her male counterparts. The Taliban assholes didn't even know a woman killed them. If they had, their egos would have collapsed around their sexist ideals of women being weak and second-class. In the sandbox, at least in the parts she had witnessed, women were little better than dogs, used for breeding to replenish the unending fight.

Leaning against the stone wall, the slimy dampness soaked through her shirt. Disregarding the seeping sensation, Fara wiggled the muscles in her right calf with undulating twists until the flesh rose over the strap, and with just as much patience, she worked the binding down the other side, eventually stepping from the fabric band one foot at a time.

The longer she was in the darkness, her other senses became more acute, actively trying to make up for the temporary blindness. The heavy aroma was an identifiable mix of algae and mold, mingled with the sharpness of old urine, all layered thickly with decay. Breathing steadily through her nose in a calming rhythm, she crouched low, working her bound wrists from behind her back to under her butt, legs, and past her bare feet. Grasping the cotton bands with her toes, she tirelessly tugged and pulled, but the knots refused to loosen.

Holding out her bound hands, she felt her way. The rocks were rough, but not rough enough. If she had hours, she could rub the binding against them; unfortunately, her wrists would rub raw in the process. She continued searching and finally found a rusted bolt sticking out from the masonry. Spreading her hands as widely as possible, she rocked the fabric, feeling it give a thread at a time until she worked her small hands through the widened gap.

Without any external stimuli, she was unclear how long she had been in the cell, yet as she stretched her fingers, the numb swelling clearly stated more than an hour, perhaps two. For a moment, she contemplated leaving the gag in place, for if she was discovered, she could pretend to be bound completely. Regardless of whether she was gagged or not, she would have to fight, and her mouth provided another weapon with words or teeth. After untying the gag, she licked her dry lips with a tongue as rough as the Afghani desert.

The gag hung limply in her now throbbing fingers. She stared at it, as if she could see it physically. No one was near. No one would hear her scream. Why then would they gag her in the first place? Unless, someone was near.

"J.C.?" Fara whispered hopefully into the darkness. Stretching out her fingers, she encountered the edges of a door and then a small barred opening near its top serving as a window. Pressing her weight against the aged wood, the door didn't budge. Working her fingers across the rough surfaces, she didn't feel any latch or other device. She tried to reach through the bars, but the bolt was too low. "J.C. can you hear me? If so, make a sound. Rub your feet on the floor, moan, do something to let me know where you are."

A drip echoed vacuously through the empty complex, and she contemplated diminishing alternatives. Then the darkness moved, and a rush of hoarsened breath blew down the corridor, brushing across the black stones. The sound grew in definition, a faint sound of scraping as if claws dragged along the wall, as a bored child would pass along a fence with a stick.

Silence grew thickly once more. Nothing but the few droplets of water falling onto the floor resounded around the maze of halls. Yet Fara held her breath, knowing something waited. The air around her suddenly turned cold and even more stagnant, as if death itself sniffed her scent off from the back of her neck. Death would definitely know her scent. Perhaps that momentary recognition would be her salvation.

Near the intersection of the passageway, a gray dead glow contrasted within darker smoke. The form shifted again, not something in the darkness, rather the darkness itself. The smoldering fell away in heavy chunks only to disappear before reaching the ground, as if recycling back into the dark billowing body.

Fara's every sense edged acutely aware, and then she heard it again, scraping in the approaching shadows, expectantly hollow and drifting through the rising formless void. Exhaling a whispering breath, the shadow inked the darkness into an even deeper black. The mass paused on the other side of Fara's door, and she instinctively backed away, sensing something completely disassociated from her verifiable senses. This awareness was lower and deeper, perception of something out of her past, yet just beyond the reach of conscious memory. Recognition flared. This was the thing which lived on the other side of life, what some would term a dark and injured soul. Time and space were damaged here, the way a bruise darkens the skin, and through that wound, something abnormal had pressed its way into this world.

Contrary to natural instinct and diligent training, she closed her eyes, shutting off the tangible need to focus on the intangible. Forcing herself into a meditative state, she opened her proverbial third eye and knew the creature. She had known this entity from her very first moments in this world, for she was born out of the darkness, ripping the flesh of her mother in a rush of pain and blood.

Instead of the revelation causing fear, the knowledge was comforting. For too many years she suspected the curse she carried was more than a mere stain of evil upon her soul; it was her soul and embodied her flesh, just as dark and injured as what stood before her. The government recognized this unholy gift and developed her into a lethal weapon by drawing out the hidden forces to make unsuspecting men divulge their most guarded secrets.

She sniffed the air, recognizing the fetid odor of the underworld. Too many times, she had unwittingly traveled to the edge of this dark realm, standing on the fragile lip of nothingness, and now the darkness awaited her on the other side of the cell door. It was what children feared under their beds and made adults' hearts pound in the dead of night shifting at the edge of their vision. Her enemy was identified and targeted, an enemy only she could defeat. For one had to know thy enemy to defeat him. And in the end, they were one and the same. She was the harbinger of death, a reaper of souls, kin to the shadow of death opposite the door. One day, she would share its fate.

Using the lowest and gentlest tones in her vocal range, she whispered to the void, singing in wavering tones, calling it forth until its sweeping breaths drew even closer to the chamber's door. As it approached, Fara sensed the maleness of the entity. He was bound to this place, forever to guard, yet now he didn't guard an escape from the cells. He guarded a passage, a bend in dimension.

Loneliness and desperate servitude bound the spirit to the life the man had once led. She kept singing, drawing his presence to her, letting him know he was no longer alone. Once she gained his full attention, she repeated in a chanting rhythm for him to open the door. Never doubting herself, she continued to the point of hoarseness, and then finally the bolt slid with a grinding thud. The door swung on rusted hinges, weeping the disruption. Having expended his energy to affect this world, the darkness withdrew. The poor soul would never find eternal rest until the cause of this anomaly ended. How many other souls were trapped here?

With the edge of her hip, Fara forced the door wider until she could slip through the slender opening. The hardness in her pocket pushed sideways into her flesh. Apparently, no one had frisked her, or perhaps her abductors thought a cell phone would be useless within the deep bowels of San Cristobal.

Ducking under the rusted framework, she cautiously stepped into the equally narrow hall and stopped before she touched the back of the iron-barred gate at the juncture. This was the opposite side of the gate she had seen on the monitor. If opened, security would notice. She envisioned the young man informing Señor Muñoz of the movement. Fara sensed him watching the unwavering monitor. He would gain pleasure hunting her through the labyrinth.

"J.C.?" Fara whispered cautiously but couldn't sense him or any other living soul.

Experience told her there was always more than one exit, and she headed in the opposite direction. Once out of sight of the camera, she carefully opened her phone. Not quite time for sunset, but well after the fort was locked down for the night. Of course the phone had no reception, but the soft greenish light lit her surroundings as had the emerald. She grabbed her left hand. The ring was gone. Brushing her fingers over the spot, round and rounding again, she visualized the emerald and called it forth, yet the ring too was silent.

CHAPTER 29

Any outward signs of the storm were gone. The only remnant was brilliant heat visibly shimmering off the pavement in hazy ribbons. Under any other circumstance, the clear sky would have filled J.C. with contentment, but not today, not as the police car crept down Calle Sol without sirens or lights.

His inner thoughts churned with sickening clarity. The vision of Fara crumbling to the floor and the hotel's security officer dragging her back into the room were ever present.

His grandfather stayed behind. At least they didn't suspect him of the grisly murders. J.C. couldn't imagine how anyone could take a life, and especially not a child's. Only a madman would do such a thing, and they thought he was that madman. Hopefully, Fara would contact the studio's attorneys. After the incident at Fyvie, he knew the suits on a first-name basis. He would wait for them to arrive before answering any questions. Fara gave him a good alibi. Albeit a little stretched, it was the truth.

The ominous gray wall grew until it effectually blocked the sun. As the penetrating darkness obscured the shining world, the sky itself paled into a sickly shade of amber. He leaned toward the window, craning his neck to get a better view. The cloudless sky continued to darken as the sun slipped into the shadow of the earth. While flying in from Miami, he remembered reading about the solar eclipse. It was March 20th. Today was special, for not only was there an eclipse, but also a new moon and the vernal equinox. Three celestial occurrences rarely combined, and the tension of expectancy was in the air.

After sharing the latest of the emerald's visions with Fara, J.C. had lost track of time and didn't know when the cops dragged him from the hotel like a common criminal, but at this point, it didn't matter. Day or night, eclipse or full sun, he now knew where they were heading, and it wasn't the police station. The fort was claiming him, once and for all, after fifteen years. He sighed as an odd sort of contentment filled his soul. This was it. Realistically, he had only been living a half-life since the incident, as if part of his torn soul remained there all these long years.

Shifting, he leaned back against the vinyl-covered seat. Closing his eyes, he instantly saw Fara's face. She represented the only part of his life he really wished to continue. He never was one for religious affiliation. Actually he never even remembered going to church as a child, yet he knew God would hear him if his prayer was sincere, so silently, he prayed to keep her safe.

CHAPTER 30

Jail cells covered the left wall of the stone corridor, while only one was on the right. Vivian peeked inside and whispered for J.C. Just beyond the lonely single cell, the wall jutted out with another low, almost square-cut door, and just beyond a set of stairs circled down toward the lower depths. Even though Fara knew she needed to go up, perhaps the stairs would lead to another connecting corridor. The next moment, an icy hand seized her ankle. Twisting as she lost her footing, she landed and rolled immediately back onto her feet. Her available hand clenched into a fist as she crouched into a fighting stance. Her heart beat strong, ready for combat.

Directly in the center of the floor rose a solid door made of arched convex steel. Laughing at herself for imagining a ghost had grabbed her, she pulled on the handle and opened the hatch to the abused wail of rust and time. The heavy sound resonated, lingering in the damp air. Instantly a hazy vision slid into her mind of a man's hand grasping the edge to keep from falling into the pit. His fingers found purchase just before the jailor slammed down the hatch, clipping off the digits above the second knuckles. The man's wailing scream added a chorus in the air to the current shriek of the rusty metal, mixing the two worlds, the two times.

After the startling vision faded, Fara stood alone in the dark on the edge of the oubliette trimmed in darkness, wondering what in the hell had just happened. The sound of the scream was so close to the rusted noise of the hatch, logically the two had to be the same sound. The second, more human sound, was just a misplaced echo. She absently nodded, an echo in time was absurd, but logic and sanity didn't rule this place.

Having to make sure the sound wasn't from J.C., she laid on her belly, extending her phone, but the light couldn't part the shadows far enough to provide a glimpse of the bottom. She called out, and the echo repeated his name. Not the same sound at all. In one way she was ecstatic, yet disappointment trimmed her elation. Clearly, the cops hauled him into the station. They could hold him for twenty-four hours without charging him. Hopefully, he kept his mouth shut. She blinked at the cellphone in her hand and wondered if Eduardo Calderon had thought to call the studio. But deep down, her gut feeling told her the cops didn't take J.C. to the station. Even though they had been together only for a few days, Fara was tuned into him, and something abnormal was happening.

Examining the room at large, she inspected the wall where three loops of steel were permanently set into the masonry, clearly intended to secure manacles. The one on the right still had a piece of the coarse chain clinging to the metal heavily pitted with rust and age. An ancient pin-style lock held onto half of a metal cuff. The lower loops were complete, intended for ankles, which would have kept the prisoner firmly against the wall and upright at all times.

Kneeling, she touched the links of chain, and images of the damned emerged. Most were men, yet a few were women, all beyond the point of redemption, save one. With a flash, Fara saw Sister Marguerite in chains hanging limply, lifelessly with dried blood staining the tangle of white hair. The nearly transparent jailer hit the holy woman with an equally translucent rod. His only defined feature was his grin, broad and white, generating its own radiant light exuded from the perverse pleasure.

This was an imprint, a glaring bruise of the damage levied here over two centuries ago. Whatever happened punched a hole in time and space, leaving haunting memories to reside as a mutilated reminder, a warning for those sensitive enough to recall their presence. As Fara approached, the ghostly impression did not change. It resided here, forever entombed within San Cristobal's walls. Just when she was convinced there was nothing more to it, a curl of energy descended, tangibly filling the space with static, as if an exposed wire suddenly sizzled dangerously close with high voltage. Electricity charged across her flesh, raising the fine hairs over her body.

As if the power reached in and squeezed, Fara's heart skipped a beat as the specter gained more clarity, increasing in physical substance. The woman's chest rose and fell with shallow breaths. A sound mumbled from beneath the spoiled veil of disheveled hair. Fara wasn't sure whether she really heard the sound. As she discounted it, the woman moved again, raising her chin off from the withered chest.

This was how Sister Marguerite died. The shriveled image was clear enough, for no one could have recovered from this desiccated state; however, the pale eyes opened, emitting the salvation of eternal life, strong and vital. Perhaps like the different levels of hell, there were varying degrees of being a ghost. There was no doubt the woman Fara had encountered at the oddest times was a ghost; except her eyes were real, human real, not some swirling orbs of foggy purgatory. Sister Marguerite's eyes shone with strength of spirit, as if God's light shone through the woman, consolidating His heavenly power. The woman smiled, again fortifying her withered appearance, and extended a hand unfurling fingers that had remained closed for centuries. Inside the leathery paw was a ring, the one Fara had seen in the vision she had shared with J.C. inside the jewelry shop, the male match to the delicate jewel she had purchased and only recently lost. The emerald glimmered, casting a warm glow from which the darkness withdrew.

Internally torn, Fara didn't know whether to take the ring or not. Sister Marguerite was not evil, yet physical contact clearly opened portals that perhaps should remain closed.

Within the silence a voice rose. Having studied other ghost shows, Fara knew an E.V.P. or electronic voice phenomenon was a sound unheard at the time yet appeared on a recording. This was the opposite. Well, perhaps it would record, but she heard this sound from lips that did not move. "The key to salvation belongs on his finger."

Fara wasn't afraid of the sight, for she had seen death and destruction, bodies drying in the sun when there was no one left to bury them. She had seen fear in every form, some caused by her own hand. Yet none of those negative emotions embraced this moment. Warmth and kindness drew Fara to reach for the ring, and upon making contact, humming filled the world.

CHAPTER 31

Dressed in a tattered cloak of the holy order, Felipe carried his head low and humbly, effectively hidden within the shadows of the oversized hood. His wife, also adorned as a servant of the Lord, rode atop a beast scarred from years of hard burden. Sister Marguerite's logic that such an animal would attract little attention was valid, yet he grieved his bride was derogated to such embarrassment. The lovely Vivian deserved an elegant mare with a gleaming white coat and long flowing mane and a wedding gown made of silk, trimmed in pearls. However, just like the horse, her plain gray habit and rough cloak served their purpose, for the sentries barely looked upon her as they passed through the city's gate.

Relief from the fight Felipe had anticipated for days poured from him, and after rounding the second bend in the road, he allowed himself to look once more upon his bride. His heart tightened sharply at the humbling sight. "Vivian?"

"Shh," her soft voice wavered nervously, "soldiers are coming. You must yield and let them pass."

Biting back indignation, he led their beast from the road and begrudgingly bowed his head as the patrol galloped past. Sprays of fresh mud flew in the riders' wake, splattering his robe. The daubs were barely noticeable since they were the same hue as the worn brown cloth, but the riders' careless disregard was infuriating just the same. Although he wanted to admonish them against the unnecessary affront, he remained in character, impatiently waiting until they rounded out of sight. "How do the clergy bear such affronts?"

Leaning forward, she whispered; even though, they were once again alone. "Think pious thoughts."

Boldly daring to stop while still so close to the city, he turned and stepped closely enough to brush against Vivian's legs, which were both facing him since she refused to ride astride. Light and irresistibly sweet, her feminine scent drifted, making him desperate to know his wife. "I cannot think of anything other than tasting the flesh of my bride."

Since leaving the security of El Convento, Vivian frequently glanced at the horizon. Again checking carefully back toward the fortress, she didn't dare meet his eyes until she was certain no others were near. "Have you so quickly forgotten?" She hesitantly touched his cheek, visibly reddened from the combination of heat and anger. "During my cloistered days of penance, the memory of how you suckled upon my breasts made the time pass more bearably."

"As I said, that was just a prelude of pleasures to come." His hand slipped below the hem of her robe and caressed the outer curve of her lower calf. "Did you confess our intimate indulgence to the priest?"

Grasping a handful of mane for balance, she twisted slightly, turning her knee outward to encourage his touch. "No."

"You surprise me." Momentarily forgetting his frustration, he chuckled while his hand explored the opening between her legs. Sliding his fingers up to her knee, he still didn't encounter the tops of the plain cotton stockings. "Why not?"

"I didn't know how to phrase the deeds without going into detail of how my body shuddered with pleasure while your hand cupped the gateway to my chastity and your mouth suckled like a babe." Her eyes briefly caught the midday sun, and a flash of green glinted from under the shadowy hood. "Now that you are my husband, when will you claim my virginal prize, my jewel meant for none other?"

He whispered a prayer for patience, more to himself than to Vivian or even the Heavenly Father. How he yearned to lay her upon the soft grass, which fragrantly rolled in the swelling breeze, but any delay could cost them dearly, especially the delay it would take for him to teach her how to accept him in order to minimize the unavoidable pain.

Groaning with frustration, he resumed his position next to the beast's head and led the scarred work horse back upon the equally scarred road. He picked up the pace and marched at a jog. The faster they made their way, the sooner they would rendezvous with the Immaculata and the sooner he would be able to lay with his wife. Even though she deserved to be bedded upon a downy bed draped with gossamer veils, his meager berth would have to suffice. He could still picture her there on that stormy night, swaying within his embrace. Oh, how he had wanted her, and the memory came to life in his loins. Pushing the thought from his mind, he tried to focus on their journey, for without its safe completion, he would never know his wife's internal charms.

Settling into the uneasy bouncing rhythm, Vivian leaned forward and threaded both hands into the horse's mane. She moved as low as she could to be closer to Felipe. "I'm sorry if I disappoint you. I did seek absolution for impure thoughts, which I thought would suffice. Did you confess our intimate indulgence?"

"Dear Lord, Vivian, you do not disappoint. Rather just the opposite. You are a virginal vixen, a rare combination truly without compare." He glanced back to view her reaction, and the hidden scabbard tangled in the rough robe, nearly tripping him. He cursed, which led to other malevolent thoughts. "Most of my confession regarded my desire to steal the life from your uncle." His robe caught again, and with a frustrated curse, he slowed.

Vivian leaned back onto curve of the saddle and adjusted her robes. "Would you mind if I walked awhile? I've never been comfortable atop a horse."

He lowered her to the grassy rise in the center of the road, using the moment to hug her tightly. Despite her attempt to cover the discomfort, pain brushed over her eyes. Immediately releasing her, he heated with his own selfishness. "I never even asked if you were well enough to ride."

She held onto him firmly. With the advantage of the height of the center rise, she rocked up onto her toes and placed a quick kiss upon his hooded lips. "I am well enough to ride. I just don't like it." After casting another quick look for anyone approaching, she giggled, "And well enough to be ridden, which I desire more with every passing breath. Felipe, I want you to continue my instruction in the ways of love, for you, as you put it so ingeniously, to taste my flesh." She gazed off toward a meadow, golden with wildflowers. "Would you chase me if I ran off into the field?"

"We don't have time for games. I would have to carry you back and set you once more atop this flea-bitten relic." Securely he led her forward with an arm about her waist, careful not to touch the healing welts.

"When are we going to...?" Her voice drifted.

"Consummate our marriage? Good God Vivian, I have never heard of such an eager bride." For a moment, he dropped the horse's reins and tossed back the priest's hood with a single hand, for he refused to let loose of her. How he wished he could shed the priestly robes, for neither their enthusiasm nor the topic matched their costumes. Although he knew Vivian was not a nun, the sheer fact of her wearing a habit made their discussion awkward and even more taboo. "I don't think you understand..." Looking upon her keen expression, he momentarily lapsed. He roughly rubbed his face and then massaged dry and tired eyes, for he had not slept well since the Immaculata docked in San Juan harbor. He delayed, trying to think of a way to put her off without putting her off completely, for developing a woman's passion was a delicate and thoughtful process. "What would a goodly and pious Catholic girl know of such things?"

"I did not always live in an abbey. In Cadiz, there were plenty of women who met the sailors when ships came into port. They would retreat to a back alley and in full view of my window-"

Turning her chin toward him, he marveled at how beautifully her eyes caught the midday sun, as green as the emerald he had placed upon her finger, and he wore its mate upon his own, a token of his solemn promise. "If it wasn't a thousand degrees outside, I would think you're blushing, and I would certainly hope so." Felipe couldn't help but grin at her sudden discomfort. "You shouldn't have witnessed such things. At times, people act little better than animals. You are a lady and I a gentleman. You deserve wine and music, perhaps a few lyrical sonnets, and then a very large and soft bed." Trying to keep his hands off from her was straining his patience, and to busy himself he removed the water flask out of the saddle bag and prolonged the drink. He extended it to her, but she waved it off.

"Are you saying we must wait until we reach Cadiz?" Disappointment hung heavily in her softly spoken words.

"You deserve the best this world can give," with a gentle caress, he brushed a wayward curl of ebony hair back under the white hood and again reminded himself to respect her costume as a representation of her virtue, "but I would go insane to sleep alongside you and not know you as wife. My quarters aboard the Immaculata, however inadequate, will be our bridal suite. As a gift, Captain Ortiz has given me leave from my duties for three days."

"Three days. Will it take so long?"

Despite his resolve to keep thoughts of taking her from his mind, a quick chuckle broke through the heavy air, which had stilled as the heat continued to grow with the lingering day. "What do you know of the marriage bed?"

"Verily, only the single lesson you shared with me. Yet I have heard-" her eyes drifted off into the distance.

"You may always speak to me openly without fear or shame. Tell me." He expected her to continue to avert her eyes, yet to his surprise, she faced him.

"A man spreads a woman's thighs and fits himself within her. The channel bears a holy seal that may only be broken once in a woman's life. It is the mark of her purity, and when it breaks, it causes a flash of pain, yet later, the act brings untold pleasures." Her confidence did not waver or words hesitate.

He stopped dead in his tracks. "Who told you such a thing?"

"Is it not true? When I returned to Cadiz this past season, I inquired of the cook who carried her seventh child. Did she tell me false?" Vivian hesitated and then thrust out her chin in an indignant pose. "I paid her a good amount of coin for the information."

They were walking too closely for pious clergy and too far apart for newlyweds. Ensuring the road and adjacent sugar cane fields were empty, Felipe drew her closely to his side, feeling the curves of her body pressed against his, and continued down the road. "She told you true, although rather indelicately. The act of love is beautiful and does bring incredible pleasure when delivered gently and lovingly."

"And will it take three days?"

Imagining her in his arms repeatedly making love for three days and nights, his britches tightened uncomfortably. At least the holy robe hid his overt interest. "Definitely, at least three days."

"Oh, I had no idea." She kept walking steadily as if discussing intimacy was matter of fact. "What of meals or perhaps a respite for water?"

"You are ever practical my lady. Refreshments are definitely part of the celebration, and I stocked my personal pantry with the best the island had to offer in anticipation of our blessed event." Gazing upon her hooded form, his eager eyes gained powers, penetrating the layers of worn cloth. He watched her graceful body walking down the road naked. Fully knowing his imagination fueled the image did not matter when her flesh rosily tinted with heat, and even pinker nipples bounced ever so slightly atop rounded breasts. Although he had never seen her fully unclothed, he had felt her hips and the curves of perfect thighs and knew his imagination was an accurate premonition of delights awaiting discovery. "I think we should ride awhile and make better time."

"Oh please not so soon." She tried to pull away, but he held her.

The tugging interplay excited his mounting enthusiasm, and his uncomfortable erection stretched even more tautly against the restrictive lacings of his britches. Drawing Vivian closer, he felt the curve of her breasts against his chest, and his fantasy continued as if her bare flesh pressed warmly into his skin. "Are you now trying to delay the consummation of our marital vows?" Rough with need, his voice rumbled in his chest.

In a huff, she tried to pull away again yet failed. "Have I not spoken plainly and my interest been overly bold?"

Easily, he lifted her astride the saddle and then immediately swung up behind her, drawing his wife to him with an arm securely cinching her waist. The saddle was more than snug for the two of them, but instead of discomfort, he reveled in the proximity. Spurring the horse forward, Vivian's rounded bottom rocked with the gentle motion, curving perfectly against him. Every thought glazed with desire, and he could no longer try to imagine her as a nun. Vivian was his wife and her fruit very ripe for the picking.

"What has fueled your bold interest?" When her only answer was a sudden breath followed by a sigh, Felipe brushed her cheek with a tiny kiss. "Vivian, answer me plain."

"You shall discover all about me soon enough. Such as, I am overly curious; everyone who knows me understands that fact. What no one knows is how deeply I have felt the compelling womanly need. Even before my body developed fully into a woman, internally I yearned for something I did not comprehend until you so expertly channeled my emotions into that wonderful explosion, as if my entire body had prepared for that moment all these long years. I'm still not quite certain the how or why of it all, which I anticipate you will share with me. Well, my initial inquiries on the subject made my father suggest continuing my education at the convent, where none had knowledge of physical love. Whenever I broached even a mundane question about a man's expectations, I was instructed to pray vigorously, yet the sensations kneading within me continued to ripen. Then, I spoke with Cook who apparently knew the business." Vivian twisted to look at him. "I don't want you to think me brazen, for that is not the case. I have followed all of the rules of decorum devoutly. That is until I met you."

Treasuring her unreserved manner, the warmth of love radiated throughout Felipe's consciousness, drawing him closer to her than he had ever been to another person. "I have met brazen, and you are not."

"Cook was hesitant out of fear of reprimand from my father, but coin loosened her tongue as did my word never to let him hear of her tutelage." She continued her glance long enough for him to drink in the strength from those glorious green pools. "At first I was fearful, upon over thinking the act of someone entering my body, yet the more I thought about how many couples marry and then beget children, it could not be a terrible or fearful act. Do you have children, Felipe?"

"What?" Instantly fighting against the innate reaction to avert the question, he tried to relax.

"My uncle admonished your behavior severely. Apparently, you took the prize of his intended, which was the foundation of his rage. After knowing so many women at court, I would assume your issue took purchase, for that is what creates children, is it not?"

Quietly he answered, "Yes, it is." Momentarily, he contemplated this odd turn of events, yet his wife was not a usual bride, nor would he desire her as much if she were anything less. "Do you want me to answer honest and plain?"

"Of course. Whatever existed in your past has turned you into the person you are today, and you pledged your faithfulness never to covet another. I believe you."

"As you should, for my love has never been given to any woman other than you."

"How can that be?" She struggled to turn fully, but he held her. Still, the motion rubbed him vigorously, inflaming his desire nearly beyond control. "Did my uncle lie when he said you had bedded many women?"

"Bedding a woman and loving her are not the same. During my tenure at court, I gained a reputation, and like many tales, started with a core of truth. Take the case of your uncle's intended."

"Constance."

"She did not want to marry a man twice her age, so she used me to nullify their contract, a fact I discovered over a year later upon my return to Spain, though I didn't realize your uncle's resulting umbrage."

Contemplative, Vivian sat quietly. "You still have not answered my question, husband."

"No children I am aware of." With a sweep of his forearm, he lifted her, shifting her sideways, across his lap.

"Does that mean we will not have children?"

"No. As you can feel, my interest is fully functional and perfectly capable of fathering children. I just never received word if any of my lovers conceived." Instead of cradling her waist, Felipe's hand slipped lower, cupping her rounded bottom, angling her body toward him until he could watch her expression and read her reaction. "Life at court is complicated. Once a woman produces a male heir and at least one other, her husband is less inclined to take to her bed, so she seeks physical companionship elsewhere. If she does find herself with child, the usual remedy is to seduce her husband and then declare he has conceived another child within her womb." He leaned aside and switched the reins into his right hand while his plan took shape. "I have pledged my fidelity to you, and I do expect the same in return Vivian. I will be a good husband, and I need a good wife, a faithful and loyal wife. Many men will seek out your interest, not only for your beauty, but also because you are mine. You must resist the temptation which will lessen once we take up household together."

Her body stiffened. "You will not be staying with me in Spain?"

"I'm afraid not, my darling, which pains me deeply." Using the momentary stillness, he slipped his left hand under the habit and gathered her legs, bending her knees over his left thigh, and continued his quest, sliding higher until he encountered her rounded hip.

Vivian, so encompassed with the news, did not protest nor notice for that matter. "Where then shall I stay? And with whom?"

"When we arrive in Cadiz, we'll learn much in that regard. If your father acknowledges our marriage, you may choose to remain under his roof. If he disowns you for marrying without his consent, we will seek out my brother and request for you to remain at our family's estate outside of Madrid." His hand was nearly at the juncture of her thighs before she reacted to his caress. Seeking out her lips, he stifled her exclamation and rounded the top of her bloomers, quickly untying the bow and drawing them low enough to run his fingers into the moist lower curls. "I want to stay with you Vivian, desperately, but my commission lasts two more years, which is when I had planned to marry. Meeting you at this juncture was not expected, however welcomed. Unless the king provides special dispensation, I must return to sea, but my sincere hope is I leave you expecting. Upon the return of my next voyage, I hope to see you blushing with child. Do you want children?"

"Whether the Lord blesses us with children or not is out of my control." Vivian hitched one knee over the pommel of the saddle, widening the spread of her legs to accept his intimate caress, and relaxed against his torso. "What I am able to declare is that I am a willing participant in their making. When you held me upon your berth and scooted my body to the edge of the bed, I was hoping you would take me, and then I was proud you did not, for I wouldn't have had the will to refuse you. You make my body teem with emotion in such a way I never knew existed."

As soon as they entered the tree cover Felipe had been anticipating for the last half-mile, he slid his fingers between her delicate petals. Soft and moist, they spread for him naturally, like a flower blooming. Nuzzling his lips against her ear, his tongue rounded the delicate channels just as his fingers rounded the circular opening to her inner treasure. "I wanted to take you then, oh so very badly, but I gave you my word. Now you are my wife, and our union is not only sanctioned but also mandated to seal our vows. I will instruct you in the ways of pleasure. You will want me to touch you and enjoy your body in ways you have never imagined."

"Oh, Felipe." Vivian lids grew heavy with the breathy words and closed.

His fingers continued to circle, and Vivian's body arched, so effortlessly, so naturally offering herself. The angle of her body was perfect, the spread of her thighs wide just enough for his hand to slide fully against her. As he continued to explore her inner offering, he convinced himself if she misrepresented herself, as brides had a tendency to do, he would love her unconditionally, unwavering in his devotion, for he would love her forever.

Vivian shifted ever so slightly in order to raise her mouth in offering. Ravenously, she opened her lips and brushed her tongue over his, nibbling and suckling as he had taught her ever so briefly. A hum pulsed through her, tangibly radiating into Felipe. With a matching low moan, he slipped his finger deeper. She was so tight, yet wet and welcoming. Her body organically craved his touch and responded without fear or shame.

Excited beyond any woman he had ever experienced, his mouth went on the offensive, conquering the kiss Vivian had started, driving his tongue even deeper. With a matching intensity, his finger arched forward, driving into her feminine passage, encountering the hidden veil.

Felipe's mind ran wild. Despite all of his sexual escapades, he had only once decanted a virgin and that was during one of his initial encounters, an act of less than satisfying merit. Yet this was special. Vivian was special. The long-awaited jewel he found at sea was a sexual nymph, a goddess of physical love, and she was his alone. Hot desire burned through his mind, erasing any rational thought, and he could no longer control himself. He added another finger, preparing her body for when he would truly claim her.

Feral thoughts raged to have her straddle him and then enter her. He never had a woman atop a horse, but just before he turned her body to fit his purpose, he opted for a more traditional way to take his wife. Her desire and fulfillment was more important than creating another scenario to add to the journal of his sexual exploits. In fact, the moment he took his wife would be the end of his novel deeds. He would never share Vivian, not with anyone, not even through words put to paper.

In time with the rhythm of his fingers, she rocked her hips, which matched the sway of the horse. Each time his fingers encountered the barrier, and each time she unpretentiously accepted him, willing him to continue. Heat jumped and rose within Felipe. His embrace tightened. Fingers charged forward, breaking the seal.

She squealed but did not pull away. Her eyes flashed open with the sting and stared at him full of challenging emotions.

"The pain was inevitable my love, yet still tortures me. You will thank me once we reach our marriage bed, enhancing your satisfaction of the actual act of physical love." His fingers were still deep within her. When the membrane broke, her inner muscles clamped tightly, and now as her body slowly relaxed, the channel was slick and warm, so very inviting, too inviting. He was at the edge, ready to dismount the horse to mount his wife, but she deserved better than to be treated as a common strumpet. Reluctantly, he withdrew his hand, and a fine coating of her virginal blood covered his fingers and even anointed his ring.

"The pain was brief. Felipe, I want to continue…"

In unison, the couple turned toward a rumbling sound approaching through the shady woods. The horse was standing still, near the edge of the road chewing clover. Reluctantly he lowered his wife to her feet and then followed, leading the horse along the muddy path. They encountered the wagon hauling a load of vegetables to town. Both Felipe and Vivian were once more set into their holy roles and accepted the gift of food from the simple merchant.

CHAPTER 32

The vision faded. As Fara's resolve returned, she wrapped her fingers around Felipe's wedding ring. She left the Sister to her transitory fate and continued down the only exit. At the base of the staircase, she encountered a barred door. The metal frame was pitted with age and flaking bits of rust, similar in design to the other gate, but this latch was complex, with handles on both sides of a central bolt-type hasp. Reluctantly she touched the handle, and as anticipated, sensed the past. Two jailors stood, one on each side of the door, which required them to work the latch in tandem. Even then, the handle was worn and splintered, like this section of the fort was decades older than the upper floors.

After securing Felipe's ring upon the dog tags she still wore around her neck, she slid one thin arm between the rusted bars and moved the latch a half-inch at a time, progressing bar by bar, until the tongue finally slid free of the reinforced indentation in the wall. Oddly without any rusty hesitation, the door swung toward her, and she stepped into another hallway with multiple doors, four on the left and five on right. Nothing was evenly spaced, adding to the distortion of the labyrinth.

She sensed something. "J.C. is that you?"

Not receiving even a breath or a scuff in reply, she continued. The passage was so narrow Fara had to turn sideways. These cells resembled the one where she awoke, but the doors were smaller, barely shoulder height. Even though people were shorter back in the day, a man would still have had to stoop. The main hasp was rusted shut. She crouched and opened the mini door on the bottom by throwing another bolt, which complained its use with a loud, scraping groan. Extending her hand, the light from the phone seeped across the room that was barely wider than the door, and maybe three feet deep. Contrary to the shortness of the door, the room was about six feet high. Pushing herself back to her feet, Fara raised the phone toward the ceiling of the hallway, which was taller. The difference would leave a crawl space over the cells. The odd proportions made her head reject this as reality; rather, it was more akin to a morbid Wonderland where nothing was as it seemed.

The thought triggered the memory of another movie she watched when she was just a girl. Unlike Disney's depiction of the colorful Wonderland, this film was black and white, about an evil house where no walls were exactly upright and no doors were truly squared. The irregularities set the stage to trap or even consume souls. She didn't remember the film's name, but she did remember its message. The irregular design of Hill House had as much to do with the malevolence as did the evil deeds done within its walls. "Whatever walked there walked alone."

San Cristobal was just as foul and just as abnormal. She wished she had forced J.C. to tell her what he had seen, for it still existed in this tainted place. That had to be what she felt, yet unlike Hill House, this malevolence didn't feel alone.

Moving forward, the narrow hallway opened onto a rectangular room with an equally proportioned rectangular table exactly in the center. The craftsmen had to have made the massive wood and metal table within these walls, for there was no entrance to accommodate the substantial structure. Beyond worn, the surface was scarred and gouged. Those splintered boards still bore shackles for the neck, wrists, and ankles nailed in place with immense iron spikes wedged deeply into thick wooden slabs. Dark and irregular stains splattered the stone floors leading away from the table back toward the cells, and another palette on the opposite side of the room spread toward another gate.

After her capture by the Taliban, Fara was kept blindfolded. She never saw the table the men shackled her to, yet she remembered being forced facedown and then chained upon rough wood, her arms and legs stretched to their maximum tension without being disjointed. When Jason and his team rescued her, they pulled off the blindfold. After being crushed for days, her eyes could barely see. What came into focus first was the vision of her dried blood splattered across the floor.

Again, the odd parallel overcame her senses. Here the stains were thick with runoff where hundreds of years of blood coated the table and floor. She reached out then stopped, not willing to risk another link. Whatever resonated from the slab would have no bearing on finding a way out of the labyrinth or finding J.C. These stains were old. If he had been here, none of this could be his blood.

On the walls, torch holders were spaced evenly above the stone ledge designed to hold tools to eviscerate and maim while keeping the victim alive for as long as possible. Although interrogative methods had developed with the sophistication of technology, nothing replaced the fear of physical punishment. Even though the tools were long gone, dried blood outlined the length and breadth of each device. Some were curved, others blunt. As she reached out to touch the broadest stain, the ring around Fara's neck heated against her chest.

CHAPTER 33

For the ancients, spring rituals celebrating the equinox ensured the sun would once again seize dominance of the sky from the winter moon. As an expert navigator, Felipe understood the seasonal ascension of the stars and the timing of celestial occurrences. Although he did not believe they marked supernatural portents as did primitive man, the rarity of celestial alignments made them special, and tonight of all nights bore witness of not only the vernal equinox, when day and night held equal purchase, but also the anticipated lunar eclipse. This was the first time Felipe had heard of the events occurring in conjunction.

While anticipating the rising moon to light their continued path to the east, tiny dots of light flickered on the hillsides like lost stars, and behind them darkening the verified celestial objects was El Yunque, the blessed peak sailors used to identify Puerto Rico when arriving from the east. Felipe was hungry and weary, yet continued knowing their destination neared. The scent of the sea carried upon the night. Although they had glimpsed silvery water several times throughout their journey, the northern coast was too rugged. Captain Ortiz sailed to the most accessible port of Fajardo on the eastern shore, the closest port that could accommodate the draft of the tall ship.

Slumped toward the horse's neck, his bride was dozing. The nun's habit clung to her, outlining curves despite the garment's designed intent to hide any womanly rise and fall. Vivian had no other clothes with her, none of her possessions. She left her world behind and now was entirely in Felipe's keeping. He liked the thought of Vivian being his to have and to hold, to dress and to adorn. To demonstrate his love, he would shower her with gifts from around the world. With every journey, the loveliest and most exotic would become hers.

The white rim of the secular veil reflected the infant rays of the newly rising moon, appearing to glow like the shining halo of the Virgin herself. His wife was no longer a virgin, yet he had not made her a woman in the total sense of their union. Just like this night, she was trapped in between.

Vivian looked young, like the portrait he had seen in her father's home. With her eyes closed, he focused on her lips, full and rounded with high tulip peaks. Even in the silver monochrome light, they retained their touch of red, soft and velvety as a rose petal. The signs of her Uncle's beating were still visible on her face, darkening cheek and eye. Sister Marguerite described the depth of the welts, which would require weeks to heal.

Felipe had to remind himself when Vivian was in his arms to treat her not only as a virgin but also as an injured soul. Weighted by the heavy thought, his lustful desire settled.

Darkness set behind them hours ago. Once he believed no one would be able to distinguish his form upon the road, he shed his disguise. The unbuttoned white shirt billowed with the growing breeze, whipping the ends around his body. After spending the sweltering day hidden under rough cloth, he welcomed the touch of the wind passing over the fine sheen of perspiration clinging to his chest, heightening the sense of freedom. But they would not be free until they left the island. By now, Dufrense would have sent guards to retrieve Vivian when she did not return to the fortress. Hopefully not before sunset, yet regardless of the hour, once Dufrense discovered Felipe had eloped with his niece he would have sent several riders in pursuit.

Instead of focusing on the ever-present possibility of soldiers overtaking them, Felipe concentrated on what they would do once they arrived in Spain. Naturally, they would seek the blessing of Vivian's father first. He had met the man once, well over a year ago, when he accompanied Captain Ortiz on a visit to the ship builder. The Captain had a gift for Vivian and was disappointed upon discovering she was no longer living in the city. If she had been home and Felipe had met her that night, would he have been bold enough to ask her father for permission to court her? A stranger question, and even more important, was whether Señor Dufrense would have given his consent. Felipe's reputation had spread throughout Spain. Any father in his rightful mind would have kept his eligible daughters away from him, for Felipe courted for his own pleasure. Never had marriage crossed his mind, at least not until meeting Vivian.

Felipe was at court when Vivian's uncle received his commission from the king to supervise the completion of San Cristobal, so the sailor had preconceived expectations of Dufrense's elder brother. Yet during their visit, Señor Dufrense seemed to be a man of genuinely pleasant spirit. Their host was older than Felipe had expected. The proper man was courteous and cordial, inviting them into a drawing room equally as sociable. Above the mantle was a portrait of an exquisite dark-haired girl, who could have been no older than ten or eleven, and after meeting Vivian as a grown woman, Felipe realized the artist had not exaggerated the dazzling green of her magnetic eyes. Some girls are charming beauties, yet lose their allure as they mature, while Vivian had ripened into womanhood splendidly. Across the room, to the left of the doorway, stood another portrait, seemingly of a trim boy in a fencing costume, long of leg with dark hair pulled back at the nape. Something about the portrait drew Felipe closer. When he asked about Señor Dufrense's son, both of the older men laughed, revealing the identity of the boy was none other than Vivian Dufrense.

Captain Ortiz had brought him a gift from Mexico, a distilled libation called tequila. In Felipe's experience, there were two kinds of drunks, jovial and hostile. Señor Dufrense was the former and drew upon great witticisms with odd references once inebriated, while the man's younger brother was the latter. Felipe had witnessed the putrid animosity Captain General Dufrense levied upon others in equal measure. Drunk or not, the man was lethal.

Felipe glanced again at his wife whose body now slumped fully upon the horse's bowed neck with her cheek resting on folded hands. So delicate and fragile, it was amazing she survived the beating. Fresh anger rose, and along with it, a surge of renewed hatred for Vivian's uncle, whose quest for power and control had to stem from being the second son. Also a second son, Felipe knew the bite of that jealousy. The fact Hernán received everything was not easily dismissed, yet years at sea washed away the resentment. Felipe's last visit to his family's home, Hernán's home, was congenial. Even with their past mended, certainly no one would expect Felipe to return suddenly with a wife. Deep within his heart, he knew Hernán would receive her, and upon learning their situation, would offer his new sister-in-law sanctuary. Hernán's wife was only a few years older than Vivian, and although Carlotta was born to the gentry, she did not overshadow Vivian in either look or manner. He wondered if Carlotta was still without child, a fact which wore upon his brother. Although their rivalry had ended, Felipe would love to declare paternity first, especially of male issue. If his brother never begot an heir, the title would naturally flow to Felipe's son.

The realization warmed Felipe's body. That was it, the real reason why Captain General Dufrense didn't want Vivian to marry, for if she begot an heir, the ship business would never flow to Jose Dufrense and subsequently to young Tomas. The Captain General would have discouraged any suitor away from Vivian. In Felipe's case, Jose Dufrense had the excuse of Felipe's interlude with Constance.

He internally groaned. All this trouble was seeded upon her, and he had never truly been attracted to the young woman, whose face was long and angular with a body slightly too thin and weary. In hindsight, his ego brought him to regard Constance, for he and his brother were competing to see how many women they could bed in a single year. He laughed despite the serious consequences his indiscretion caused, for he had won their bet by nearly double, yet in the same stroke provided his future enemy fuel for vindication.

Jerking awake at the sudden sound, Vivian lost her balance and slipped from the saddle. Lunging, he caught her while off balance, and they both tumbled. She landed on top of him with her hands splayed across his chest.

CHAPTER 34

Only one bar remained on the phone's battery charge. The hesitant glow barely spanned the room. Roughly fifteen feet opposite the stairwell, a massive iron gate arched across the entrance to a long tunnel. The craftsmanship appeared ancient, as if the construction would predate Columbus' initial ocean crossing. In anachronistic opposition was a large electronic lock welded upon the left side of the double swing door.

Fara had expected the foul odor to be stronger here, but oddly the scent was welcoming. She inhaled again, this time through her mouth, tasting the flowery aroma against her palate. There was something else hiding under the pleasant smell. Once she identified the pretense, the tangible awkwardness intensified, flooding out the sweet calm with something malicious and painful, raising the hairs on her arms and at the nape of her neck.

Listening intently, she heard nothing. In other parts of the dungeon and stairwells, hell, even in the cell where she woke, there was always a sound, water dripping or a rodent scratching. Even the wind let its presence known while breathing through the tunnels. Here, there was nothing. No echo. No wind. No life. The dead silence was an anomaly unto itself.

Staring into the arising darkness, her eyes tried to focus, like something was there. A whisper on the edge of hearing, the drift didn't carry sound but rather disturbed the surrounding air. Holding her breath, her ears strained. There. There was something low, under the range of normal hearing. Gurgling. Whimpering. Suffering. Pain. They were there, a blending mix of them all. She had heard those sounds too frequently not to recognize them now. This was the real dungeon, the one from which no one returned to know the light of day.

The sight resonated in Fara's recent memories. This was the tunnel on the monitor, what she had mused was the death tunnel, where tortured victims were taken for removal out of the sight of others. Certainly most were slaves. In a society where the majority of the population was enslaved, even a vocalization of uprisings would be treated with blistering seriousness. San Cristobal provided a daily reminder of the consequences of insurrection.

Craning her neck to locate the camera, she leaned against the gate. A shock coursed through her, similar to static discharge, but not exactly. There was power, but not that of regular electrical current. She grabbed the bars with both hands and felt the subtle vibration. The faint edges of her senses perceived whatever hummed through the gate was not of this world. Normally, she would close her eyes and try to analyze the feeling, but she wanted confirmation the tunnel was monitored. A tiny red light flashed, revealing the location and a brief hint of the rugged stone wall.

Why was a security camera recording footage of an empty tunnel? But the tunnel wasn't empty. The darkness shifted, and Fara sensed something there, waiting and watching, judging her every move. The gate wasn't to keep someone out; it kept something confined, something strong enough to require both a force field and bars.

Steadily the greenish light from her phone continued to fade, and Fara's eyes adjusted. Soon, all too soon, it would be gone. Practicality and training kept her calm while options flashed through her mind at a startling pace. The wooden table was the only thing she had seen that would burn, but she had nothing to ignite it. No accelerant. No lighter or matches. Hell, she didn't even have a piece of flint to strike. Panic embraced a single quick flutter of her heart. She had been in worse situations, albeit with more tools to work with, but she would find a way. There was always a way.

Before the final ohm failed, she noted the detail of her surroundings. The gate was one stride forward, and the lock two small steps to her left. An indention about fifteen strides down the tunnel could be a doorway. There would be no escape through the tunnel without opening the gate. Using her last few seconds of light, she knelt in front of the electronic lock, which was unlike any she had ever seen, and that was saying something. She touched it, and the hum connected with a charge of residual voltage. The lock was the source of the force field. She keyed in 8-4-6-3-1-2-4-8, the code the security guard had used. The red light continued flashing. Then she tried B-4-t-i-m-e-2-b which according to the electronic map had unlocked all of the locks in the complex, save one, and this had to be it.

Quickly she turned to face the staircase, putting her back toward the gate, rechecking every wall to ensure there was no other means of escape and for any jagged edges that would cut her while groping her way. She would have to go back up the staircase to the torture chamber. Her back crawled at the thought of inadvertently brushing against that table.

The uneasy challenge stayed pushed in the back of her mind that sometime soon, whoever locked her into the cell would come looking for her. It wouldn't take too long. Although being found would solve her immediate problem, it wasn't a good solution, not really a solution at all. At least she was dressed in black and barefoot and would be able to move relatively undetected. She could cat and mouse for a while, twist into the shadows and hide until she identified the enemy and perhaps why he wanted her in the first place. Apparently, the emerald ring wasn't the only thing he needed, or else he would have killed her while she was unconscious. And she was pretty damned sure the "he" was Fernando Muñoz. The dungeon and tunnels had that same feel of something incomplete, transitory ... *waiting for something or someone to show them the way.*

Fara stopped. That phrase resonated oddly in her memory, and then the recollection hit her. It was a line from *Hotel California.* Even though her mind was definitely twisted, she had never driven a Mercedes Benz or liked pretty-pretty boys, and she was sure as hell going to leave.

Pulling herself back to the moment, she stared at the failing phone. Again Fara ran through options, perhaps she could create a connection between the phone and the lock, cycling through combinations. Shit, that was a long-shot even with time. She ran a hand over her brow, swiping at the stress-induced sweat. Before she came to any potential solution, darkness grew, encroaching inch by inch until only lingering obscurity remained. More than just dark, the shadows were once again tangible. They drifted, caressing her exposed skin with cool strokes. The cold waves intensified until they literally pulsed from the tunnel, washing over her in intervals with a rhythm as consistent as a heartbeat.

Not out of fear, rather the temperature change, she physically shivered. The abnormal presence surrounded her, cloaking her in its absence of light. The sensation of being wrapped in the burqa and physically bound pressed inside her mind, but with equal resolve, she pressed the evil memory back into her own hidden shadows. Whatever was out there would use her fear, perhaps even feed from it to gain corporeal strength. Regardless of what might happen, she would not show fear. Fear was a weakness, a mind-killer, which she had used against her enemies, but refused to be leveraged against herself.

"Abib's New Moon awaits."

The entombed silence had been as pervasive as the chill, so the words, even those so smoothly spoken, cut into her awareness. Muffling a squeal of surprise, she maintained control. The massive gate stood between her and the voice, and the lock was on her side of the gate for a reason.

The sound was not really a voice. The resonance was off, distorted, as if the thing on the other side wanted to portray itself as human, but was not. If she had audio equipment rolling, she'd dissect the sound and determine what was anomalous, out of range. Only through peeling back the layers would she find the underlying source. That was it. This wasn't a single voice. It was an overlay of multiple voices all speaking in unison. The words carried the same resonance as did a choir, all voices rising to be one.

Disconcerted with the realization, Fara focused on the overly smooth diction, one that breath did not seem to propel. Her mind reeled with exhilaration, along with her internal longing to do something meaningful. Her entire life primed her for this moment. "Who is Abib?"

"*And the Lord spake unto Moses and Aaron in the land of Egypt, saying this month shall unto you be the beginning.* Today marks Abib's arrival."

Listening carefully, this time she noted the variation, the slightest overlap of multiple voices, which gave the sound curling smoothness. "You quote ancient scripture."

"I have seen the ages, waiting, always waiting. As I am, I shall forever be." The voice continued to approach until she could almost see the detail of a broad figure, clearly not that of a single man, more like the composite of those who were speaking with shared words. Defining the absence of light, the definition of the shape was darker than the surrounding obscurity. "Scripture confirms all, for one does not exist without another."

"One?" Proud the sound of her own voice was clear and effectively scoffed, she gained even more confidence. "I sense many more than one resides within this existence that faces me."

"I am legion, for we are many."

"The story of Gerasene Demoniac is shared through many of Jesus' disciples. Why don't you tell me your version?" Again, she kept her breathing even, heartbeat controlled. Her training served her well; no sign of weakness escaped.

"I have no need." The smooth waves swept over her like a calm sea.

Felipe's emerald ring was on the chain about her neck yet tucked out of sight within her tank top. She didn't need to see it to know its presence. She hummed along with its growing resonance, creating her own composite sound. She wanted the entity to know she was not alone; another power fed her, reinforcing her resolve. The siren's song continued to rise with the intonation of the ring. When the heat became uncomfortable, she pulled the chain, and a glow, however meager, illuminated the immediate space. The creature shrank back from the light and sound. A peculiar sheen shimmered off from the undulating surface, as if it too was just a manifestation, something not in its true form.

"What do you need?" Fara's own composite sound enveloped her.

"I have no need, for all I require come to me. All pass through the darkness. All come to me." The vocalization repeated exactly as before, like it had been recorded for playback, yet it resonated closer once again. The words transported energy, the cold waves she had felt earlier, or perhaps the waves transported the words. Regardless, the shivering energy was tangible, and anything tangible had a physical source and physical weakness.

During her training, she learned to shield, to bring up defenses to protect her mind, to detach what she did from who she was. Although the waves continued to emanate from the tunnel without being attached to words, she stood firmly defiant. This shit-head of an entity would not roll her, not today, not ever. The ring's protective glow grew brighter, encasing her in light, increasing her resolve.

"I taste your power." The entity had stopped its encroachment, maybe even backed up a step.

"How about I cleanse your pallet?" Adding additional focus to her mind, she visualized the opposite of cool and smooth. Her own crackling wave released, forcing blistering emerald fire down the tunnel. Akin to something she could only equate to a form of sonar, she saw the burst outline the mass.

According to the darkly menacing manifestation, she prepared herself to see something hideous, like the medieval drawing of St. Anthony plagued by demons. Instead, the outline of the true figure was considerably smaller, humanoid, shiny, and reflective. The disparity struck her senses, and her mind processed quickly analyzing her opponent, who presented itself in the image of what was expected, rather than what was real.

A low and broad chuckle not only emanated from the tunnel, it resonated all around her, reverberating off the small chamber's walls. "The taste of your power is sweet. I will savor your soul."

A genuine laugh curled out of her, and the creature shrank back again. "You're too late. I lost my soul long ago. If you're able to find it, let me know and then we'll negotiate."

Multiple legends existed of shape shifting demons that took on the characteristics of what you feared the most. The concept was ancient. The most recent term was a doppelganger, which would also explain the odd appearance of Señor Muñoz. Either he was a real man overtaken through manipulation or a psychic projection. Fara had touched his arm. It would take a hell of a lot of energy to project that, so logically he had to be human, or at one time was human. If Fernando was a puppet and the creature was behind a force field, who was the puppet master? The person who brought it food? She was probably the special on tonight's dinner menu, but ain't no chicken being served tonight.

"Fara?" The familiar voice sounded behind her. At first, she thought it a trick, a mind-fuck the creature conjured out of her memories, but then her name repeated, along with the sure sounds of athletic shoes hurrying forward.

She turned her head, and her eyes widened despite the stinging glare from the flashlight shining in her eyes.

CHAPTER 35

The uneasy dream was still clinging to the edges of Vivian's mind, distorted images of her home in Cadiz, empty and barren. Black shrouds draped the mirrors. Dried leaves scattered across the floor, blowing away from her bare feet as if her presence embodied the wind. She wandered familiar halls listening for the sound of her father's voice. There were no sounds at all, nothing, not even the endless curling of the sea.

Suddenly, the silent world erupted in argument.

With a bright flash, she was inside a different home, palatial with a Y-shaped staircase rising from the center of a huge marble foyer. Two male voices rose in equally harsh tones, quickly debating. Back and forth, the quarrel raged. Although she didn't understand the words, regardless of how acutely she listened, she knew the fight was about her. Just as she approached the wide double door, the floor gave way, and she fell, encountering flesh.

Vivian's hands slipped upward over Felipe's muscled abdomen, sliding into tense curls of dark hair upon his chest. The sleepy glaze quickly left her eyes. The realization blinked through her senses, and instinctively she attempted to pull away, but he clasped her wrists.

"Oh," her eyes blinked again. "I-" she glanced around at their surroundings; nothing but fields extended in all directions. She was in Puerto Rico. The stupid beast of a horse stretched its muzzle down to her, staring at her with disdain. "I fell off the horse."

He inhaled deeply, causing his chest to rise under her palms. "Yes, you did."

Vivian blinked again, and the dream faded. "You caught me."

His dimples drew deeply with the smile despite the dark and hazy growth of beard. "Not quite. You fell on me."

222

Still fuzzy, her mind was slow to process, and inadvertently her fingers spread. His flesh was warm and soft, yet cool and firm at the same time, a confusing combination. She had never touched a man's bare chest. Realistically, she had never even seen one up close. Many times sailors would load or unload cargo bare-chested, yet from a distance the sight didn't evoke the stirring sensation now swimming within her. But this wasn't just some burly sailor, Felipe was her husband. She spread her hands wider, allowing the silky curls to unfurl and caress her fingers.

He released her hands, and the caress swept over the rises of his chest. His abs tightened and hips rose, brushing her with his sudden erection.

Completing the forward motion, she met his lips, feeding her inner need. In between each lengthy kiss, she whispered her husband's name, and then once again met his mouth while the vibration still tingled upon her lips.

A groan rumbled within his chest. "We have to keep moving."

The vibration stirred her fledgling longing even more. Lying on top of him was so very intimate, closer together than they were riding together in a single saddle, closer then when she sat upon his berth. His britches pulled tautly against their seams. The rising stiffness pressed against her sensitive flesh, and her body reacted as it never had before. Sweeping waves melted within her, culminating in the tight bud Felipe had awakened aboard ship, making her covet his intimate touch. Now there were no barriers to their intimacy. This time they were married. This time she clearly knew the marvelous sensation awaiting the culmination of their intimacy. This time she was ready to take him within her.

His eyes shone in the mystical light transforming the night sky into unnatural shades of amber. Distracted, Vivian looked at the shadow passing over the misshapen moon. Perhaps she was still dreaming.

She bent low and met his lips. Tentatively she extended the tip of her tongue. Stroke for stroke, he met her eagerly. With her confidence empowered, she caressed the warm moisture of his mouth. The pressure inside of her continued to mount until her breath coursed in tiny gasps.

With a hand cupping the front of each of her shoulders, Felipe lifted her until their lips separated. "Oh my darling wife, not here, not like this. Although I adore you and will go mad if I don't culminate my passion, we must stop." Her mouth tried to descend upon his again. "No, Vivian. It's not much farther. Come, we must continue."

Resuming the motion, he lifted her body from his completely. The tired stress had disappeared for a moment, but now, his features tightened, gazing down the road. Glancing over her shoulder, she saw it too, a fleck of light jumping in the distance.

Instantly, Felipe arose. After a single long stare, he pulled her to his side. "We have to go." In a single sweep, he lifted her atop the drowsy beast and swung up behind her. A harsh kick woke the horse into a bouncing trot. With more effort, he finally got the animal into an ungainly run.

She held onto the saddle's pommel with both hands. Her breath fought with the timing, never knowing when to inhale or exhale. Each wild bounce forced the wind out, and with a gulp, she swallowed more in, nearly choking on the gasps. How she wished he would slow down. With the syncopating breaths, she forced out, "It could be ... just some ... random travelers."

"Dear God, I hope you're right, but who else other than soldiers and outlaws would be traveling at night?"

"We are."

"And we are outlaws."

"Outlaws? We've committed no crime."

"I've eloped with the Captain General's niece, stealing her away for my nefarious needs. Even if he had heard of our marriage, your uncle will do anything to stop us. We have defied him publically, and Captain General Dufrense is the law. You and I, my darling, are outlaws." He glanced back. "Your uncle would love to hang me."

"Hang you? For what?"

"All of this affair could be construed as piracy. I stole you." With the diminishing distance, the single glow was now four distinct lights. His arm tightened around her protectively. "If they are soldiers, I want you to run, run as fast as you can on this relic until you reach Fajardo."

She had just enough breath to tint the words with indignation. "I will do no such thing!"

"Vivian, listen to me!" Under his breath, he swore. "This is no time to argue."

"We can both go hide in the sugar cane and let the horse continue down the road without us. They will never find us." Chancing another glance, the riders galloped at full gait.

"They will block the port at Fajardo and confiscate the Immaculata, endangering her captain and crew." Drawing her against him curve for curve, he rocked her body in rhythm with his, pressing tightly against her and inhaled. "If we stop, I have to fight. I am competent with a sword."

"As am I and will fight at your side." She leaned into him. "I refuse to run. Where would I go? I could not return to San Juan. I could not continue to the Immaculata unimpeded. I have no home, no money, no useful skill to earn a living. Without you, I am nothing." The sickly feeling of her dream crept back in, like oily smoke contaminating her resolve with a filmy despise.

"They might kill you." His voice broke. "I cannot, will not, take that chance."

"I prefer to die with you than return to my uncle." She inhaled with a gasp and then clung onto a renewed resolve. "If he does not kill me, he will make me wish I was dead. I'm leaving this island with you, one way or another, in body or spirit."

"There has to be another way. I will not endanger you." The torches were gaining, and he spurred on their pitiful beast. They had to be close to Fajardo, but only darkness loomed in the distance. "I'm sorry Vivian. I knew there was a risk, but I thought the plan would work. The distance to Fajardo is significantly longer overland than by sea."

She didn't listen, so focused on the potential fight, knowing all those long hours training with a sword would one day have a purpose other than to please her father's need to treat her as a son. "I know how to use a sword as well as any man."

"No! I forbid it." But his words weren't audible over the driving hoof beats.

With the torrent of sound, so grew the expectation in her breast. Her heartbeat pounded within her ears until the crazed hoof beats drowned out even that internal noise. Frightened, their poor farm horse stumbled, and then the crazed mounts surrounded them, foaming sweat pouring from heaving sides. The confusion and commotion reined their beast to a new master's bidding. Men shouted above the slice of swords being unsheathed. The sickly night sky instantly shimmered with torchlight and steel.

CHAPTER 36

"J.C.! Jesus, where the hell did you come from?" The ring on Fara's neck burned hot, nearly searing her flesh. To be safe, she had tucked it back into her shirt before she had turned. Instinct told her to throw her arms around J.C. and kiss him soundly, while training told her to step back. "How ... how did you get here?"

"All pass through the darkness." Echoed more so inside her head rather than audibly hearing the words. "All come to me."

J.C. cast a hesitant glance toward the tunnel and then tugged her forward. "Later, we've got to get out of here."

She hesitated, trying to determine if he had heard the creature. Once again he pulled her; this time his fingers crushed around hers. His hand was cold and clammy, a classic symptom of fear. Instead of forcibly removing herself from his grasp, she permitted him to lead her up the stone stairway. The landing opened to what she knew was the torture chamber, but she didn't get much chance to focus on shapes in the darkness. They continued up another flight and then through a passage she apparently had missed in the waning light of her phone.

Never making a misstep or taking a wrong turn, J.C. led her from one corridor to the next so quickly that despite her refined sense of direction, she was disoriented. Although he was leading her toward the main part of the fort, her senses were still in overdrive. To navigate so efficiently, so confidently would require detailed knowledge of inaccessible areas of the fort. Although he had been here a few days ago, he hadn't been to any of the non-tourist areas for over fifteen years. There was no way he would remember such detail.

His grip relaxed, and she dug in her heels, stopping short. Her hand slipped through his fingers. "Okay, enough. I'm not taking another step until you tell me what the hell is going on."

Although the design of the fort channeled light, the hallway was dark, except for his flashlight whose beam jittered up and down the corridor. "What are you doing here?"

"Rescuing you. I may not be some Special Forces jock, but do I have some skills." He swung the flashlight, temporarily blinding her. Snagging her wrist, he tugged her along, knowing exactly where to turn into a mid-level corridor that traversed several other openings.

At the fourth arched double-swing door, they passed into another hallway and continued for about fifty feet. The corridor then forked. Again without hesitation, he helped her over the chain that corded off this section. He drew her to the left past an assortment of open rooms that displayed period swords, flintlocks, and uniforms which she remembered from the tour. At the end there was a small stone landing where a stairway curled tightly, definitely designed to be defended from above by sword. Openings in the shapes of crosses allowed the fresh sea air to pour through the narrow casements.

Fara twisted out of his grasp, and this time lunged out of reach. "I'm not taking another step until you tell me what happened. Where are the cops?"

"Hassling someone else right now." He surged forward, trying to snag her wrist, but she evaded, backing down two steps. "Jesus Fara, just shut up and come with me."

Felipe's emerald burned so hotly she squirmed, and her intuition hummed even louder than the stone. "J.C. please," pushing her hands onto the tops of her knees, she panted as if exhausted while devising a plan, "let me catch my breath. We should be safe here for a few seconds."

"No, we need to keep going. My grandfather's keeping the security guard busy, so I can get you out. Shit Fara, come on!"

"We will, just a minute. Remember how thirsty I got while running? You don't happen to have any water, do you? Like this morning when you miraculously produced that bottle of Evian." She tipped her eyes up to assess his expression. Her heart pounded, yet not even a hint of deception tinted her words.

"What the fuck? Did the tazer blast your memory or something?" His voice resonated like a guitar whose string was ready to snap. "I pushed you up against the wall and forced you to tell me what we experienced last night. I still swear it was real. Regardless, dream or not, it was the most incredible sexual experience of my life. There's something about you Fara. You do something to me. Something no other woman has ever done before. It's like you're magic." The flashlight's beam had swiveled with the motions of his waving arm, punctuating and slicing with the words, and then it stopped. His arm dropped, and the light glowed alongside his shoe. "Shit!" He backed up the stairs. "What happened to you? What the fuck happened to Fara?"

"Nothing. I was just making sure you were really J.C. and not some look alike or clone or something. The last person I expected charging in to save me was you."

"What the fuck is that supposed to mean?" The light swung up into her face, blinding her.

She blocked the glare with a forearm. "You went ape-shit over leaving your car in the parking lot. I didn't expect you to come anywhere near the fort at night, never mind creep around down in the dungeon."

"I was saving you. I thought you would be fucking grateful." He kept the beam pointing directly at her.

"Tell me what you saw that night."

"What night? What the hell are you talking about now?" He pushed his back against the curved inner wall. He was wearing the same ratty gray t-shirt which was tucked into only one side of his baggy khaki shorts. Even in the weird light, Fara could clearly see the funky Puerto Rican tourist belt they had purchased together. If this was an imitation of J.C., it was a damn good one.

Although she tried to keep her face impassive, a single brow rose of its own accord. "The night you and Andres came here. The night you stole your grandfather's keycard. The night you saw something in the dungeon. I think I saw the same ghost, demon, hell, I don't know what the fuck it was. It appears in whatever form will fuck with you the most. That's why I need

229

to hear your version. If it's not the same thing, then there's even more going down."

"I don't know what you're…" Suspicion narrowed his glazed eyes.

Throughout all of this time in the dungeon, seeing apparitions and meeting a doppelganger, Fara felt the first curl of fear, and with it, the emerald's power started to rise, flowing out and engulfing her in pulsing green light. "The first night we were together you told me about how you and Andres snuck in here. What did you see J.C.?"

"Damn it Fara, what the fuck are you talking about? I never snuck around in here. My grandfather would have killed me if he ever caught me doing that."

Her mind swirled through the possibilities. The most reasonable explanation was someone erased his memories of that night, just like what happened to his friend, Andres, which would mean they had gotten to J.C. Fara's heart skipped faster as the taste of fear matured and coldly slipped up her spine.

CHAPTER 37

The horses pranced in an agitated mob, pushing and shoving just as readily as the men. Hands tried to grab Vivian, but she slapped the man swiftly with the ends of the reins. He cursed and pressed his hand to the bloodied welt on his cheek as another drew a pistol. Drawing upon her years of training with a battle-weary fencing master, she calmed the instinctual urge to panic, and subsequently channeled that same energy, energizing her mind and heightening her senses.

In a flash, the night exploded around them. First one, then a second pistol fired. One of the balls hummed past her left ear and the remnants of the sound buzzed inside her head. Just before the first shot, Felipe had leapt at the soldier, kicking him from his horse. The glint of steel preceded the second shot, which sliced the torso of the gunman a mere second before he squeezed the trigger. With the second blow, Felipe stabbed his sword into the man's chest.

Another horseman grabbed Vivian from behind, but the fool held only fabric. She twisted within the nun's habit and faced the blackened grin.

"I just won me a hundred pieces of silver." The words rolled out of his mouth like drool.

With an imperceptible shift of her eyes, she concentrated on the hilt of his sword sticking out temptingly toward her. Once she made the decision to engage, she was committed to her actions, acting and reacting just as her trainer had drilled. *Engage, parry, do not falter. Stay on the offensive. Keep the advantage. Leverage your blows.* More so through instinct than cognitive will, her hand flew forward, unsheathing the blade from her adversary's scabbard. The look upon his face fluctuated from glee to surprise to anger within an equal number of heartbeats. She continued to watch his expression as his own blade sliced up under his ribs to pierce his heart. The man's final heartbeat quivered through the sword and into her hand. Nothing could have prepared Vivian for this moment. No amount of training. No amount of focus. She had just taken a life.

She did not watch the man fall, for she heard the slice of steel and knew Felipe was engaged in combat. Turning her attention to reassess the scene, the final guard on horseback had been cheering on his two friends and had not even noticed her kill the man with the blackened smile. With a minor shift of her body, the farm horse turned, and she was within range. Not even a tinge of remorse flowed as she thrust the blade into his side. Only a poor soldier would lose vigilance to all fronts during a conflict.

Behind the mass of ever shifting horses, she slid to the ground. The sound of her feet encountering the dirt was too loud for her liking, but only the dead were close enough to take notice. Edging the long way around, she followed the increasing strikes of metal.

Stealthily, she rounded the beasts, staying low. The nun's habit blended with the dark ground, and even though her loose hair flowed in the steady breeze, it was even blacker than the eclipsed night. Smoother than a shadow, she crossed the road without detection and knelt behind the far edge of the wheel rut, waiting for the moment to strike. Monsieur Garamond said there were only two types of battles, those won and those lost. Exquisite form and impeccable honor were for exhibitions. He taught her real battle used every advantage, including kicking, punching, and biting, for correct style would never win an equally matched contest.

She marveled at her husband's prowess with a sword. Facing multiple attackers was exponentially dangerous, and Felipe's body moved with the grace of a large predatory animal, muscles flexing, always balanced, even under the onslaught of two blades. Although he should have been exhausted from traveling all day and most of the night, he drew upon an inner strength, engaging the soldiers with vigorous might, as if feeding upon the glory of battle. He ducked, and the taller man nearly struck his own ally. During the momentary lapse, Felipe elbowed him in the face as he rose, causing the soldier to stumble back and then attack with blind vengeance.

Fully engaged, the three men turned first one way and then another; their ebb and flow continued to wash them toward Vivian as surely as the workings of some inner tide. She waited patiently, blending in with the uneven terrain. Only once the soldier's booted foot passed within inches of her concealed arm, she uncloaked the sword and plunged it upward, expertly passing just under the lowest rib and pierced the tall man's lung. With the sword still in his side, he twisted and a scream of both pain and surprise pierced the night. She held on to the weapon with both hands, using her low position to advantage. The sword sliced deeper, biting into the lower rib. Twice Vivian tugged and finally dislodged the sword. In the next second, she drove it home again. This time the man was facing her, so she had no trouble locating his heart. As if weightless, he collapsed slowly, crumpling directly in front of her with glazed eyes fixed upon the modest grin of his feminine slayer. So entranced by the dead man's eyes, Vivian didn't see the final blow Felipe levied upon his distracted opponent who nearly landed on top of the staring soldier, which jostled the unseeing eyes toward the dirt.

CHAPTER 38

Not once in his lifetime had Robert Hartz been a pushover, but when his dazzling beauty of a girlfriend requested more time on the island, he didn't refuse. Although he knew not returning to Miami would cost him money, he delayed their flight for two days and now watched the sunset from the balcony of his hotel room. Puerto Rico was famous for its sunsets, and this one didn't disappoint. The thick clouds from the afternoon storm were now on the far western horizon. The sun illuminated the vaporous layers in variable hues of gold and red, and where the density thinned, immaculate rays pierced the heavens. The light dimmed until the night claimed the sky.

He could get used to this. If he checked his blood pressure right now, it would be the lowest in ten years, maybe twenty. Propping his bare feet up on the railing, Rob took a puff off the Cuban cigar and savored the full-bodied smoothness. The exhaled smoke curled for only a moment before the breeze caught it, tearing it into long bands that drifted toward the dying sunset.

He twisted the ashtray. Rob wasn't accustomed to fidgeting. To him, it was wasted effort, and any effort he put into something would be expected to pay a dividend. Although he knew what was bothering him, he didn't want to acknowledge the odd tug of intuition.

When he left J.C. and Fara, they were speaking to each other in a business-like way, appearing even friendly. Even though his producers' skirmish appeared mended, the tickle of intuition still bothered him, and its true cause waited, just on the edge of his cognizant mind. Rob wasn't the kind of man who believed in any supernatural or preternatural phenomena. He didn't need to believe.

He never told anyone, especially since Lily's mom was a ballsy D.A. and would sue him for negligence, but he knew when the shoot was going awry in Scotland. He felt it deep within his gut. Hell, E.S.P. was for fortunetellers with crystal balls, but somehow he tied into the moment and knew his crew was in trouble.

Regardless of how regal the sunset or how sexually satisfied he was, he felt that same unease again, like a finger prodding his eternal soul. It churned even stronger now and had something to do with that damned fort. He told himself he was just projecting J.C.'s aversion to being there at night, but that was a goddamn lie.

Rob threw the cigar into the ashtray and watched it smolder away at least $10 of the $100 stogie. No one ever would dare call him a chicken, a pussy who was afraid of the dark. He was going to damn well prove nothing was awry with the location. They would start shooting, and he was going to ensure that happened, right on schedule. *Ghost Lovers* couldn't survive another incident like Fyvie. Even with a masterful spin, another location blowout would ruin him.

Shifting in his chair, Rob put his feet down and leaned forward, resting his elbows on his knees. The dying smoke drifted into his face, and he waved it away.

"Hey baby, ready to take me to dinner?" Carolyn's sweet southern drawl rolled over him.

He was so lost in his own bullshit he didn't even hear the door open. "Yeah doll, I thought we'd go to the Blue Parrot and then make a stop by the San Cristobal fort. I kept back one of the access cards and thought we could go around and take a look see."

Carolyn stomped her foot. "Do I look like I'm dressed to go sneaking around some dirty old fort?"

Rob turned to look at her. God, she was radiant with flowing hair that glimmered with reddish highlights. The matching metallic fabric clung to her breasts and followed the rest of her glorious curves all the way down to polished pink toes. "You look too good to even leave this room."

"I don't care how often your little blue pills can keep you going.   This time I'm hungry, and you owe me dinner." Affecting a pout with her full lips, she pointed a pink manicured finger toward him.   "And tube steak isn't on tonight's menu," she winked, "at least not until later."

Rob laughed and went to put on his shoes.

CHAPTER 39

A tide of emotions pulled Felipe toward the bodies at his wife's feet. At the edge of exhaustion, he stumbled, nearly falling upon the corpses. "Vivian! Oh dear God. Are you hurt?"

"No." Shining tears slipped down his wife's cheeks. "I was just saying a prayer for their souls."

Stunned, he slowly gazed from the innocence still in his wife's eyes to the experienced sword in her hand. A confusing combination of cold chill and warm pride mixed through his veins, just how salt and fresh water glide over and apart in swirls before ultimately mixing into one. "You killed two fully-armed soldiers."

Vivian nodded passively while looking upon the dead. "Three, if you allow me the tallest man. You had injured him, but I'm the one who ran him through." She tossed the bloodied steel next to the bodies. Her eyes glittered despite the eclipsed moon, and then widened. "Oh, you're injured."

Felipe went to wave her off, but she was quicker. She ripped the ruined sleeve and slid it from his arm. In a consistent sequence of motion, she expertly wrapped the cloth around his upper arm to staunch the flow of blood. She pulled the knot, and he flinched. "Where did you learn to do that?"

"At the convent." She innocently blinked up at him. "I apprenticed with Sister Berta, the healer. I learned to bandage many types of wounds. Once aboard ship, I will bind your cut with clean cloth after dressing it with ground arrowroot. That is if you have some. Otherwise, a tobacco poultice laced with strong wine will staunch infection, yet the blood flows more freely using that method."

Even though his hands were bloodied, he reached out and caressed his wife's cheek. All of the pride and happiness in the world were within that single caress. "I definitely have strong wine, but I doubt much will make its way into a poultice. We will both drink our fair share and then focus on more important details."

"But your arm…"

He interrupted, "Just a scratch. I've had worse." Pulling her close, he kissed her forehead and then her damp cheeks before finding her supple mouth. Love coursed through him as electric and mystifying as a sudden storm, and just as turbulent. No amount of bounty or victory had ever made him feel this good. Despite the battle-weary exhaustion, his body hummed with the exalting power of life and hope. While continuing the tender embrace, he allowed his mind to slip once again to their future, of hearth and home with children, their children running through the halls. Children made from love as well as passion with his wife. How strange the world was. Only a few weeks ago, he had not contemplated any of those elements or associated them with his future, yet here they were. A loving wife was in his arms, and soon a child would grow within her womb. Yes, a brilliant future…

Blistering pain burst within Felipe's side simultaneously with an explosion charging the air. With a battle cry, he pushed Vivian out of the line of fire. She stumbled over the bodies and fell, tumbling into the ditch.

From the tree line, at least twenty riders emerged, all heavily armed with pistols and flintlocks, apparently stolen from the British. Even in the distorted light, Felipe recognized the pompous hat of Captain General Dufrense.

Felipe clutched his sword, balancing it, testing its weight, but it was no match for the pistol extending from the man's hand. Dufrense was lethal with a blade, but even more so with a gun. Felipe's heart beat faster, and wet heat flowed thickly from the bullet hole in his side.

The rider approached at a nonchalant pace. Only once within twenty paces did the man speak. "You have stolen something that belongs to me, and I have come to reclaim my property."

In a dark burst of speed, Vivian darted into the road.

Despite the feverish pain, Felipe felt the torrent of fear even more strongly. "Vivian, no!"

She fell to her knees in supplication. "Uncle, please do not do this. I beg of you. Felipe is my husband."

"Is he?" The man's cold gray eyes glared along the barrel of the flintlock. "Well then, consider this an annulment."

An explosion of powder lit the brittle night.

CHAPTER 40

The Caballero was the highest level of San Cristobal, nearly one hundred and fifty feet over the charging surf. Even though Fara was an expert climber, she knew there would be no escape on that front, at least not unless it was a last resort. The stone masons set the blocks smoothly. Although she had climbed the inner wall with little difficulty, the exterior would be altogether different. Incessant waves kept the blocks moist, and when wet rock met the tropical sun, algae grew. One slip and Fara would repeat Vivian's leap onto the jagged rocks.

Rapidly, her assessment swept to the concrete observation post. Although it looked worn and aged, the young ranger said this had been added during World War II. There was nothing up there other than three flagpoles which stood like barren sticks across the moon. Even though the new moon didn't reflect any light, the darkened circle was visible and abnormally large. Of course, the distortion was an illusion. This whole fucking place was an illusion.

Since setting foot upon the Caballero, the ring hidden under Fara's shirt had gone silent. No hum or luminescence, not even any glowing heat radiated from the stone. The magical properties ended as mysteriously as they had begun. Perhaps it meant she no longer needed it, but that didn't correspond to the anxiety charging her system into overdrive. Every sense, every nerve was wary. Something had happened. She felt the disturbance within her soul, a painful reminder of what had been in another time, the connection to the broken past. She preferred the glowing, burning heat singeing her skin to this new emptiness. The ring's vitality reminded her of life and love, and now that it was quiet, she was coldly alone.

The connection to J.C. was broken too, and even with him at her side, she felt isolated. Even worse was the empty feeling of vulnerability, inside and out. There was no cover, no egress from this perch above the city. Coming up here was a bad idea. Her narrowed gaze landed upon J.C., and even though she tried to maintain control, her temper flared. "Where do we go now?"

He tipped his face up to the security lighting, and the wash highlighted his features within the bizarre sodium vapor glow. His face was the same in a relative way, but he looked older. "We wait here. We come to the Caballero, and we wait here."

Something was off. Those weren't J.C.'s words, and there was no way in hell he would be so patiently relaxed while at the fort, especially at night. The only person who could have rolled him so thoroughly had to be a masterful and accomplished hypnotist, yet to remove J.C.'s most terrifying memory wouldn't be easy, even for the most artful of practitioners. That serious therapy depth started with trust and built over sessions. Even if it had been several hours since the altercation at the hotel, no one had enough time to accomplish that, especially with his annoyance toward Fernando Muñoz's attempts to lure Fara away earlier today. There was no way J.C. would drop his guard enough to allow Muñoz access to the most hidden and painful memories of his life. That ultimate hypnotic control just didn't exist, especially rolling someone whose worst memory had scarred him for life.

"J.C.?" The name twisted harshly off of her tongue.

"We wait for my grandfather; we're supposed to wait here. We wait here. I'm surprised he's not here already. Maybe he had to go back."

"Back where and to who?" Fara spun around at a sound. It was barely more than a scrape, but the noise kicked her already overburdened senses into hyper drive. Something wasn't right, not right at all. "It doesn't make sense."

"Jesus Christ Fara, let's not get into this again. We wait here." He stomped, while making fists against his thighs. His hands opened and closed, pulsing in time with the sound of the waves.

She sidestepped his sudden advance and headed toward the double doors. The clear decision and certain movement took her focus off J.C. and made her feel a little better. Surely they would be locked, but she had to try. It was better than heading back the way they came. When they were on the staircase, she had that odd feeling of being watched, as if something lurked just out of sight within the shadows. She tried to remember if the stairwell went down to a lower level, but J.C. was pulling her so quickly, she didn't notice. The only place she remembered was the dungeons, and she definitely didn't want to end up back there anytime soon.

As she neared the large wooden entrance, she remembered the motion sensor. If someone was in the control room, she would have about three minutes to get down the hall and into the main complex. Once there, she could find cover and avoid capture. If no one was in front of the monitors, she should have enough time to make it to the exterior door before security could be dispatched and arrive at the location. But the nagging feeling again swirled; someone was watching.

J.C. hurried after her, intercepting her arm as she reached for the handle. "Fara, don't. We wait…"

She snapped, "Yeah, I got it, we wait here. But this part of we is me, and I'm not waiting. You wait all fucking night if you want." As she stared into his blank eyes, acute pain poisoned her heart. She didn't know what happened to him but didn't have time to contemplate those details now. Every instinct told her to escape was to live.

Shoving him aside, she tugged on the handle. The door swung open, effortlessly and silently, perfectly balanced on well-oiled hinges. The hall was dark and long, impossible to see the other end. Not being able to see down the hall affected her wary senses even more than when she stared into the tunnel. With a sudden urge to run, she bolted into the corridor. Moving with a defined purpose made her feel more control. She stopped short; the doorway at the opposite end opened in a wash of light.

Immediately, she ducked inside the closest door. The room was cold, like an air conditioner had been left unattended, pumping for hours on end. Fara knew where she was. She turned just in time to see the face of Vivian Dufrense appear in the mirror, but unlike her previous encounter, the ghost slipped through the reflective oval membrane and into this world.

Tendrils of smoky haze flowed, gaining in density until the pooling vapor coalesced in the center of the round rug, twisting and binding around itself. The apparition continued to form out of the churning mist until the woman stood tangible and real. If Fara had not known the ghost, she would have thought this was a living person until Vivian lifted her drooping chin. The churning mist either cloaked the once dazzling emerald eyes or had consumed them; either way, the orbs were reduced to puddles of gray swirling voids.

"Vivian," Fara's mind swirled as quickly. "What's happening? Why are you bound to this place? Can I help you escape? Is Felipe here with you?"

If Fara hadn't known Vivian's story, she wouldn't have believed this spirit was Vivian Dufrense, for the woman was nothing like her former self. The once glossy black mane held visible chunks of dirt which matted the hair into stiff chords. A pale face peeked through the disheveled jumble, but not even the shaggy mess could hide the glaring bruises and dried blood. Ageless tears left brittle streaks down the edges of darkly hollowed cheeks. Grief and misery filled the space before the first word even slipped from the blackened corpselike mouth. "They are coming. If you stay here, you will share my fate."

"Who are they?"

"Many." The ghost's head turn quickly toward the door. "They are coming."

"Shit!" Fara couldn't hide and get away with it. The room was big, but not that big. Certainly, they would search it. Dislocated joints on a gnarled finger pointed the way.

CHAPTER 41

J.C. waited. He didn't know why. He didn't know for how long. He just waited on the Caballero and stared through the open door. At the opposite end of the corridor, a single ray of yellow light spilled in a wide arc across the carpeted runner. A darkened shape stood in the open doorway, and an arm reached out.

The scene struck his memory, pinging his nerves with flashes of a creature, tall and scaly, with swirling smoky red orbs for eyes. Like a demon straight from hell, the creature walked upright on abnormally long legs ending in cloven hoofs. Thick mats of hair covered its lower body, leaving the human chest bare to show off a masculine build. Its bulging head was broad and inhuman, like a shape shifter gone bad, stuck between two forms. Two thick, foot and a half long horns grew from its forehead, curving upwards into razored points.

The memory was gone, and his body broke out into a cold sweat. On some level he remembered, but his clouded mind refused to see.

Electric lights switched on, making the abnormal appear normal once again. The lamps were like authentic candelabras, appropriate for the period, but instead of flames, the bulbs were designed to flicker as if burning. The soft light cast lovely shadows over warmly finished tables and evenly spaced chairs meant to offer comfort between the lavish rooms.

His grandfather passed into the corridor with Señor Muñoz following a step behind. J.C. wanted to shout to Fara, warning her they were heading in her direction, but he couldn't. Like a thread of smoke captured by a lonely breath of wind, the words were gone. Only a dull thudding remained in their fleeting wake. He tried to remember, but concentration caused pressure to build inside of his head, aching and throbbing. Only once he gave in did the pressure subside until there was nothing, and in the nothing, he found comfort.

Eduardo Calderon beckoned with his hand, and J.C.'s feet instantly sprang forward, obeying the command, only then leaving the Caballero and entering the grandiose hall, as if this was the first time the thought had come to mind. Midway, he approached the two men, and as a single unit, the trio turned into a bedroom. The balcony door was open, and the sheer white curtains wafted gently with the breeze.

An abnormal chill clung to the disturbed air. In the doorway, the cold stirred with the moist warmth of the hall, causing swirls, swirls like when fresh and salt water meet. J.C. focused on the thought that wasn't his own and wanted the pressure within his head to go away. He even raised a hand to press against his temple. It took him several moments to realize there was a woman in the room who was small, and the black dress hung on her frail frame. Even though the dress was long, rips in the fabric exposed portions of the pale torso, parts that most women kept covered.

Señor Muñoz and his grandfather were talking to her rapidly in Spanish. When she didn't answer any of the men's questions, they started arguing between themselves and with her, shouting the name Vivian. The girl's expressionless face turned toward J.C. He couldn't keep from staring at the swirling foggy eyes, and the hand that had been pressing against his temple fell to the small scar on his abdomen. Instantly his mind rebounded into his own cloudy memories, jumping over some invisible and undetectable obstruction.

Here, right now, a ghost had appeared in front of them all. She had to be Vivian Dufrense, but this image was nothing like the vibrant woman from the visions he shared with Fara, the visions the emerald brought to life. Thinking of the emerald further cleared his mind, and the memories became more vivid. How he and Fara interacted in the light of the emerald edged out the dullness, and as he focused, his mind continued to clear. The pressure lessened. Where was Fara?

Even though J.C. didn't really hear the words, his feet moved to the order instantly. Every square inch of the spacious bedroom was exactly as Fara had described, but that memory was distant and took conscious effort to recall. This was definitely the room where she came with Fernando Muñoz, where he tried to seduce her, and she tried to seduce him. Fueled by jealousy, the heat in J.C.'s body rose degree by degree, burning at the invisible bond that held him.

CHAPTER 42

The iron brackets supporting the shallow balcony were rough. Coarse flakes of rust bit into Fara's palms. She avoided the impulse to move her hands into a new grip; if she did, more cuts would open. Blood started to flow down her forearms, trickling a thick path of crimson over straining muscles. Ignoring the instinctual impulse to staunch the bleeding, she held on even tighter while her bare toes felt for a gap in the stones, any cranny to find purchase. There was a fissure, not much of one, but enough to take some of the stress off her arms. Even with the improved distribution of weight, her hands throbbed with the quickening pace of her heart.

She studied the approaching footfalls, counting the steps and identifying their rhythm. Two sets of leather soled shoes snapped against the hard floors. Barely detectible, she felt more than heard the third. The metal vibrated, at first minimally, but then the steps pulsed through the aging structure. Someone commented about the doors being open. She cursed silently. As soon as she had swung over the ornate railing, both doors caught the breeze, and she didn't have time to go back. She barely had the chance to hide under the ironwork as it was.

Leaning forward, she pressed her body against the stones, hugging the solid warmth. The wall smelt of endless summer, pungent remnants of tropical heat. The scent triggered her memory of her first visit to San Cristobal, the day she climbed up the wall to look at the surf, the day she met and seduced J.C. Closing her eyes tightly, she refused to give in to the heartache and focused on the tangible pain of the metal cutting into her hands. The throbbing travelled down her arms and into her shoulders, but instead of giving into the immediate need, she used the sharp edge of sensation. Anytime she brought herself to the thought of escaping, the thought of leaving J.C. behind was stronger. While he was under such strong mental control, she couldn't save him, at least not with his cooperation, but abandoning him to be collateral damage caused another kind of anguish, one she didn't want to acknowledge. It cut deeper than the rusty metal ever could.

Squeezing her eyes shut, she breathed and concentrated. The first step of survival was to develop a plan. Develop a plan. Develop a plan. Her inner voice repeated the phrase until it shut out everything else. There were two possible points of escape, one, scaling down the fifty-plus foot wall, two, climbing back up onto the balcony and leaving the way she came.

Footfalls circled and then approached again, stopping nearly overhead. "Where is she?" The ever-smooth voice oozed through the open balcony door, speaking in old Castilian Spanish. "I command you to speak."

Silence issued from the room, but it wasn't calm or contemplative. Tension grew, filling the space with a difference kind of noise, the type of disquiet that resonated in the soul.

"I am your master, the keeper of Maboya to whom you are indentured." An angrier voice cut into the night. "You will obey me."

Fara assumed he was speaking to Vivian, and when she didn't answer, the other man directed a hushed question to his cohort in English. "Do you think it's because of tonight's power? Abib's New Moon calls upon the energy of the dead."

"The girl belongs to us, for all eternity." Although spoken in a similar low tone, the terse words bit off from the man's tongue impatiently.

"Her power's spent. This girl won't do. We need the other one, the one J.C. loves."

The chuckle was low, yet crazed. "We'll finally control Maboya. Yes, a legacy for all eternity."

Inside Fara's head, the same phrase screamed. Although the voice didn't seem to be his, the phrase was. Only one man used that phrase frequently, repeating it in cadence and flow, and now she understood why it was so important.

Her mind couldn't process logically, but at the moment, logic didn't rule the world. Her memories jumped across the last few days, like an errant ping pong ball. The way Eduardo Calderon's face looked when Fara spoke Vivian Dufrense's name should have been enough to change him from her nice to naughty list, but she trusted him because J.C. trusted him. Eduardo was his grandfather for Christ's sake.

Eduardo Calderon had the proximity and the trust required to roll J.C.

He had the proximity and capacity to kill the Figueroa family.

The ranger had access to all of San Cristobal's secrets, which he alluded to during the tour. She wasn't paying close attention when he said something about San Cristobal hill being sacred and tied to the Taíno's god, but she was certain he never mentioned the name Maboya. She started listening actively when the practiced speech went into the torture and subjugation to the point of genocide. There had been true loathing laced in with the historic account. Eduardo mentioned so few of the Taínos survived that those of the original bloodline were rare; however, J.C. was a descendent of the Taínos.

Her cheek came away from the wall. Certainly, Eduardo wouldn't do anything to hurt his own grandson, especially when he needed to continue the legacy, and to continue the legacy, J.C. would need to father children, with a Taíno woman. Before she could stop it, a thin band of jealousy twisted around her heart.

Steps approached once more. She pressed her cheek back against the stones. The soft-soled shoes stepped onto the small balcony, which groaned from the weight. The metal brackets sagged, and Fara dug in her toes even harder to maintain her precarious balance.

"Fara?" J.C. called out right above her. "Fara! Where are you? Come-on, it's time. My grandfather's here. We need you."

So J.C. was there, joining in with the hunt. The basic pretext of hypnosis was that no one could make someone do something outside their normal parameters or inherent beliefs. Even though he wasn't making his own decisions, it still didn't diminish the feeling of betrayal, on both their parts. She abandoned him, and he turned against her, equal treachery and disloyalty. The memory of his words, "You and I are the same" echoed vacuously inside her heart.

"Fara..." this time her name slipped along the sudden curl of a breeze, which brushed past her skin before being pulled out to sea. She savored the invisible touch as much as if J.C. had run a finger down her cheek. A single tear crested the corner of her eye. The drop didn't smoothly slide down her cheek. It stopped and started, making her feel every centimeter of its progress.

"She's not in here." Inside the room, a man stomped his foot. "Vivian appeared as a decoy. I guess the foolish girl didn't want to share her position serving Maboya with anyone else." The rough laughter nearly drowned out three pairs of feet moving away from the balcony. "Check the other rooms and turn on the search lights."

There was no way Fara could save J.C., but perhaps she could save herself. With at least three men searching the rooms, she would have to be a magician to slip out unnoticed, which left repelling down San Cristobal. With ropes and carabineers, she would consider it fun, but freeform descent wasn't easy, especially on such a smooth surface. Every time she pushed fingertips into a new hold, the rusty cuts bled, making her grip slippery. Her toes were little better, the way they throbbed made her wonder if she had any toenails left. She certainly didn't feel them; the nubs were sort of squishy as they braced into the stone. At least the physical pain brought clarity, crisp and precise, which was much easier to deal with than emotional pain that always rolled subversively. She had to keep her mind on the climb; every part of her body had to be working in harmony to succeed.

Her toes reached across the gap in the levels of San Cristobal, feeling for a cranny to find purchase. She had tried to descend as vertically as possible to be in the visual shadow of the tiny balcony. A renewed volley of shouts resounded from within the building. Then, a man stepped onto another small veranda. Motionless, she clung to the blocks of stone. This part of the fort had to face west because the blocks were baking hot. Even with the blistering discomfort, she remained until the footfalls retreated.

Although Fara's internal awareness knew she was certainly within a few feet if not a yard or two from the adjoining wall, she stopped the descent once again when she heard J.C. call for her from yet another bedroom. His voice resonated with heartfelt despair, ripping open the aching void within her once more. Blowing out a silent breath, she peeled her body away from the rock while her fingers and toes continued to burn. With the next reach, she encountered a ledge. When both feet touched down on solid stone, she clung gratefully to the wall. Feeling the air course in and out of her straining lungs made her feel better. The feeling was normal, and right now normal was peachy. Unfortunately, she knew normal wouldn't last for long.

After a few seconds, she calmed her pulse and refocused. The penchant darkness of Abib's New Moon was both a blessing and a curse. Fara couldn't see the ledge, but no one would be able to see her either. Finding her internal center, she balanced on the flat of her aching foot. The hours studying gymnastics had paid off many times over, and again, she put the skill into practical application. Visualizing, she relocated to the practice beam. Big red pads surrounded the low balance beam on all sides, making her feel safe. She had fallen more times than she could count, but each only wounded her pride, never her body and especially never her fortitude. Although she wasn't Olympic material, she used the lessons to maximize her skill. Over and over again, she placed one foot and then the other, brushing the edges as each step swung forward. The sound of the surf grew, and then mist moistened her face, bringing her back to the present.

Dropping to a squat, she extended her hands and felt forward, encountering the edge of the exterior wall. One more step and she would have tumbled into the sea. Noisily the next wave rolled in charging and churning. The force pounded up the wall, and salty spray hit her face, stinging her eyes. She stopped herself from sweeping her arm or hand. Salt water was better than blood, and the stinging would dissipate.

She remained motionless, allowing her senses to collect clues as to her location. Glancing up, the security light on the Caballero glowed about sixty feet above her. Anger suddenly roiled within her, casting rosy energy throughout her system. How could Eduardo Calderon roll his own grandson? Why?

The old man needed J.C. for something tonight, as well as her. Their fates had converged for a reason. Instead of dwelling on what that could possibly be, she pushed back those burdensome details and concentrated on immediate needs. In the dark it was hard to judge how far above sea level she was, but it couldn't have been more than twelve to fifteen feet from the sound of the surf and the amount of spray. High tide. She was a strong swimmer, but skill and speed were no match for the power of the sea. Waves never tired and always won in the end.

Taking a full breath, she focused once again. This was the northern wall. To her left was west. At the end of this wall was the northwest corner of the fort and freedom.

Using the same method, she continued along the upper edge of the seawall. Erosion must have undercut the foundation, causing even the wide wall to lean slightly toward the sea. The joints in the masonry weren't close or smooth, so she continued cautiously, feeling her way forward.

Counting her steps might have been mundane but kept her mind occupied. When she had reached thirty-three, an electric pop sounded across the complex. A circular beam instantly lit a broad point on the parade grounds. She purposefully fell onto her belly, pressing herself against the rugged surface until she became part of the wall itself. The brilliant beam brushed over her and continued across the casements, sweeping back a few seconds later to illuminate the expansive grounds.

Springing to her feet, Fara started counting again, but not her steps. This time she noted the seconds until the beam came back to her. Eighteen. So, roughly every eighteen seconds she did the drill of fall flat, lay still, and once the light passed, she got up and scurried. By the sixteenth cycle, her body complained against the abuse, but she jumped up and moved ahead again.

CHAPTER 43

There was no explanation. J.C. saw Fara run into the hall. They searched all of the rooms thoroughly. Upon entering the closest bedroom to the Caballero, he immediately stepped out onto the narrow balcony. Grasping the railing, he squeezed the iron, trying to remember which room she went into, but the concept wouldn't develop fully within his mind. His heart wrenched against the thought of her having jumped from one of the rooms. The internal vision of her lying broken in a bloodied heap made his stomach curl, especially with the distressed appearance of the once pristine Vivian Dufrense. He didn't want Fara to share her fate.

As he searched from room to room in the upper residential wing, Vivian stayed close, sometimes following, sometimes anticipating his next move. Regardless, the ghost lingered, hampering his search. He did whatever he could to avoid her, but she constantly was blocking his way, staring at him with those gray swirling eyes. Whenever he did look, a strange internal pull grabbed him, edging him toward something, but he still couldn't remember what it was. Yet the disquiet was there, dark and malevolent, on the edge of recollection. Each time he almost remembered, but not quite.

"Find Fara," sang in his brain.

"Fara!" He screamed into the night, allowing his charged emotions to course within her name. He waited hopefully for several seconds, and then dropped his head down to his chest. Closing his eyes, he waited, hoping to hear something, anything, but just like his other attempts, no one called back. He turned to leave and just like in all the other rooms, Vivian's ghost manifested, leaving no egress from the veranda.

"Why are you doing this?" His frustration mounted. "Move out of my way."

The ghost dissolved into nothing right in front of his eyes. Under any other circumstance, that would have freaked him out, but not tonight. Too much freaky shit was happening to make a ghost disappearing seem weird. Even without Vivian in the room, supernatural power charged the air, tangibly making his skin tingle. The sensation was similar to the tingly numbness in a limb falling to sleep, but this sensation coursed through the night, attaching itself to any living thing. And Fara was out there in it, alone on the darkest night he could remember.

Nothing seemed right or normal. Even the insects had disappeared. Puerto Rican mosquitoes were infamous, as well as potentially dangerous. Dengue fever outbreaks were all too common. Andres' dad nearly died from it back when they were in high school. Señor Figueroa was in the hospital when J.C. and Andres snuck into the fort. The memory shimmered. He stole his grandfather's keycard and...

The bitter pulsing started again, drumming inside his mind, "Find Fara."

He focused through the bitter pain and sort of remembered them being in the center of the hotel room. Fara was in his arms, her scent so warm and inviting with the exotic blend of coconut and lime. He sniffed the air and could almost smell it even now. He had been seducing her, successfully, and the ring started to hum. Gaining clarity, his faculties also gained momentum. They experienced segments of the past. This time, Felipe and Vivian arrived at San Cristobal.

"Find Fara," echoed in his head.

"Stop!" J.C. fell to his knees in the center of the ancient bedroom, pressing both palms against his ears. The pressure built, throbbing inside of his mind, but he refused to give in.

"Find Fara." He ignored the chanting voice. "Find Fara."

Going back again through time, J.C. forced himself to remember. He had touched her back, and she sprang out of his arms. She said he could touch her, just not there, so he palmed her breasts.

He set down the flashlight and looked at his palms, remembering how her heated nipples pressed against his skin. His tongue had tasted the hard points, and he could now feel how his lips held each peak, while her scent drove him mad. She dropped to her knees and undressed him. Suddenly, the heat of her mouth grabbed him, nearly biting his erection, not quite enough to hurt, but definitely enough to get his undivided attention. She always seemed to know just how far to go.

Her ring had started to hum, but that wasn't the only sound.

He ignored the pain in his head and insisted the idea develop. Something else hummed. His phone! That was it. His grandfather was calling. There was a murder, no, murders. The cops charged into the room to arrest him. Fara tried to distract them, but the mean one tazered her. She hit him. The cop on his left extended a long barrel, but instead of exploding with the shot, it only made a small whoosh. A dart hit her, and Fara collapsed.

His head started to hurt again, making the memories fade, but stubbornly he continued. She fell in the doorway, and his grandfather and the hotel hombre pulled her back into the room before the cops dragged him off. He remembered being in the back of the police car and...

His thoughts scrambled and mind went blank.

"Find Fara," mumbled from his lips.

He growled and hit the bedpost with an open palm. Dust wafted off from the canopy and filled the room with motes that twinkled in the beam of his flashlight lying upon the bed. He didn't remember how it got there. He didn't remember it leaving his hand.

A gaping hole was inside his head. He felt it diverting the course of his analog thoughts into pixilated digital images, dropping pieces of the picture out at will. The next memory he had was finding Fara in the dungeon. The gate. Not just any gate. He had seen this gate before, a long time ago. His hands were sticky and feet sore, but they kept going and going through dark tunnels. J.C. had reached up and touched a huge wooden table. Just when he managed to pull himself up enough to look over the edge and see what was fitted into the wood, his mother grabbed his hands and yanked him away. An argument ensued between his father and grandfather, something about birthright and duty.

The harsh words scared him. He had tugged out of his mother's grasp and ran into a round staircase. He felt the stones with his fingertips as he circled down. The bottom was dark, very dark, but he kept running until he bumped into a gate. A curl of power coursed into him, and he saw a face in the dark, a face with glowing red eyes.

"Find Fara! Find Fara! Find Fara!"

J.C. screamed and grasped the bedpost to keep from falling.

CHAPTER 44

Fara glimpsed street lights, but instead of elation, a curl of fear challenged her. Even once she escaped, what would she do? The cops were on the take. While under the influence of his grandfather, J.C. wouldn't corroborate her story. The hotel would be watched, and she didn't have her key. She had no money, no shoes, no underwear, and was bleeding. Glancing at the endless dark sky, she whispered a prayer for rain; otherwise, they would track her by either the visible bloody prints or the scent of blood.

The breeze lifted fresh cigarette smoke that had to have been lit with a match since sharp phosphorous tinged the initial scent. Inching toward the end of the wall, she edged just far enough to get a clear view of a single man standing guard. The street light reflected off from his white linen coat, which stood out against the night. The glow was beautiful, brilliant, especially after endless hours of darkness.

Franz Gomez fidgeted with a traditional pack of matches, the kind with a thin cardboard flap. Even with the lit cigarette pressed between his lips, he continued to light match after match, watching them flare and burn down, waiting until the very last second to litter the stub onto the cobblestones.

A sound from the cemetery across the street drew his attention. It was little more than a scrape, but enough to cause him to turn. Like a panther, Fara pounced from the wall, landing squarely upon his shoulders, and he fell face first into the street. Remembering he was left handed, she pinned that arm and pressed his body into the pavement with a knee firmly in the small of his back. Even though she felt the small pistol nestled under his belt, she reached for the bigger one in the shoulder holster first. It was a Browning, exact same model as her weapon of choice.

Expertly she flicked off the safety, and then casting her gaze from side to side, searched for a place to secure her captive. There was an easy end to this, but Fara had enough blood on her hands. Worse yet, she didn't want to end up in jail, especially a Puerto Rican jail.

"I don't want to hurt you, but I will if you don't cooperate." The same unnatural brushing sound carried again on the breeze, and Fara glanced for cover while removing the little pistol from his belt. With a gun in each hand, she finally crawled off the hotel security agent. "Up."

Whenever she bested a man who prided himself on being a badass, each one, regardless of their race or creed, had the same look. Franz Gomez was no exception. His cold eyes curled up, over her body, tensing upon meeting her weighty gaze.

Fara answered the unspoken question waiting in those constricting pupils, "No, it's not you're bad. I'm just very good."

The toothpaste smile glowed just as brightly as the jacket. "When I first saw you, I thought you would be good, just not in this way."

She chanced a low chuckle. "Behave, and we might find that out. Now move nice and easy." He dropped his arm, and Fara clucked at him. "Up, on top of your head where I can see 'em. Now straight ahead, into the cemetery."

The surf pounded against the island, adding a lulling hush to the palpable tension. It definitely was high tide, and the exploding waves lifted salty mist into the air. The moisture swept over the wall and lapped into the graveyard, leaving tendrils of heavy mist to drift just above the ground and encircle the monuments. The ancient markers were in good condition despite the weathered ravages of age. Countless storms had swept over the island, and from the pounding, some of the headstones leaned slightly askew. In the darkness, she couldn't make out any of the inscriptions to determine just how old the graves were.

Following her curt and precise directions, Franz led the way. They moved silently and said nothing extraneous as they continued deeper into the venerable locale. An old cemetery commanded reverence and exuded a special feel of peace and tranquility of lives lived to their fullest and now at eternal rest. To Fara, the exception to that state of normalcy was Arlington. Although perfectly respectable and definitely praiseworthy, the National Cemetery had an incomplete feel of all those lives having been cut short. She would have buried Jason in a private cemetery, but his mother insisted his wish was to be with the brotherhood. Just thinking of Gladys caused Fara's hackles to rise, but there was more cause for the hairs on the back of her neck to tingle.

A flash of movement caught her eye at the edge of her peripheral vision, but she didn't look. The mist pouring in from the surf shifted. Yet that explanation didn't hold up when a thread of radiant mist flowed up from a grave whose headstone was small and nearly cracked in two. Sensing the male manifestation on a deeper level, she now knew what Eduardo Calderon meant. She just didn't expect such a literal interpretation of how Abib's New Moon would call upon the power of the dead. And, the dead answered.

Franz stopped, staring at the ethereal sight. Even in the poor light, she watched the robust face go pale. Another willowy streak rose nearly alongside his leg. This time the luminescence was opalescent, while the one from the next grave had a tint of methane blue.

Urging Franz forward wasn't difficult. The man was as eager to get out of the cemetery as she was. Behind them, the misty swarms twisted and doubled-back upon themselves taking corporeal form, just like Vivian had done only an hour or so ago. Fara sensed the ghostly transformations continuing as they exited through the other gate and emerged onto a back street.

Even if she wasn't such a bloody mess, there was no way she could waltz into the hotel through the front door for a myriad of other reasons, so with a pistol wedged against his spine, Franz Gomez led the way across the back parking lot and toward the rear door. He motioned to the camera set-up nestled in a crook of the awning where a bird had made a nest amongst the wires.

"You will be caught on the security footage." His deep voice seemed to come out of nowhere and everywhere at the same time.

"Earlier, you mentioned the rear entrance surveillance was out of operation until morning." She pressed the gun a little harder, just to remind him who was in charge. "Open the door."

The man did as she commanded, but just as quickly went to pull the door shut behind him. The pneumatic hinge had to be new and consequently slow. Instantly, she wedged a foot into the door jam and shouldered into the opening. As she slipped through, she noticed they were alone in the short back hall and shoved Franz into the wall, wedging her left forearm against the top of his throat, just under the jaw, effectually constricting the flow of air through his windpipe. A few unintelligible syllables fluttered from his lips.

Fara wanted to yell at him, to curse and swear until all of her inner frustration was released, yet she kept that power bottled up, reserving it until needed.

"Move." Although she whispered the single word, it wasn't soft. Neither was the gun once more wedged into his ribs. This time she hoped it left a bruise.

Regardless of the situation, she always had the uncanny sense of angling the barrel directly toward the heart. Because of it, her partner gave her the nickname of Lady Dracula, and the fact she was a sexual vamp played into it as well, which he also knew personally. She needed only one shot, either way, to get to a man's heart. The thought of Guy Carver pulled back that inner shield, exposing her for a second. That was all it took for his car to explode, another victim of her curse.

Shaking off the ugly memory, Fara pushed Franz around the corner and into the main corridor. Of course just a few seconds later, a couple approached, exchanging the normal flowing words and giggles lovers include in the repertoire of foreplay. Before they got too good a look at her, she shoved Franz against a door with a thud. She planted a brutal kiss upon his mouth, all the while balancing the small gun between their abdomens. Of course, she made it a good show. The tourists even broke their pre-sexual repartee and commented briefly about skanky Puerto

Rican hookers, but their attention quickly diverted into another topic once they reached their own room.

Although rankled, Fara preferred to be considered a skanky whore rather than an assailant who was using a man's own gun against him. As soon as the door clicked and the giggles deepened, she exchanged the guns and pushed the barrel of the Browning up under his ribs. "Now that was a good boy. Keep acting this way and you may actually survive the night."

"You wouldn't kill me," he licked his lips. In a huskier tone, he continued, "But there are other things you want to do with me. That was quite a kiss."

Cynically yet with a seductive edge, Fara chuckled, wrapping her other arm around his waist to wedge the small revolver. It nearly disappeared in the folds of his jacket. She could unload the six chambers of the .38 snub nose and probably not take him down completely, at least not immediately; although, the wounds would finally catch up with him in the end. "I've killed many men, so many I've lost count."

"Do you always kiss them first?"

"Sometimes." She stopped in front of the suite's door. Franz didn't move until she shoved the gun even higher. Once he finally winced, she smiled. "Open the door Slick."

Fara expected him to make a move once they entered the dark parlor, but he didn't. She clicked the three-way bulb only once and immediately noticed her purple underwear still lying on the floor in the middle of the room. He noticed it too and scooped up the boyshorts. Allowing the soft lace to flow over his fingers, he felt the fabric gingerly and then inhaled against it deeply. "You are quite a compelling woman, Señorita Trotter."

"Señora Trotter."

"So, what does your husband think of your line of work?"

"My husband is no business of yours, nor is my choice of occupation." Keeping the barrel of the Browning pointed at him, she waved the index finger of her other hand in a tiny forward circle. "Strip."

"Excuse me?" His eyes widened quizzically.

"Take your clothes off. Right here. Right now." Although this was one of her undisclosed fantasies, she didn't allow her perverted pleasure to show. Her eyes remained narrow and wary on an otherwise blank face. C.I.A. were the best at blank face, and Fara had learned from the best.

Slowly, calculatingly, Franz folded his arms in front of his chest, absently flexing his muscular build. He had to use more than just the exercise room at the hotel to stay in that kind of shape. "And if I refuse?"

"I'll knock you unconscious and do it myself."

"Now where's the fun in that?" As he shrugged off the jacket, the threaded shoulder muscles worked with feline grace.

But Fara concentrated on other things. The shoulder holster was the old-fashioned kind, made of leather and buckles instead of lightweight Kevlar and Velcro. His fingers lingered on the buckle, pulling the strap tighter in order for the tongue of the buckle to release, and his muscles flexed under the tension. Anyone who wore a rig knew it intimately, every strap and buckle. Instead of watching what he was doing, Franz's eyes stayed on Fara, and she witnessed the transformation. His breathing became deeper. The harsh tension in his face relaxed and then intensified, yet in a different way. The corners of his eyes curved up, and the lids widened. Franz licked his lips and tossed the holster on top of the jacket.

"I said strip." The words were still curt, yet now she blended in some wile. Just a taste of it smoothed between the words. "Lose the shirt."

The buttons were small. Even with big hands, his fingers were nimble and opened each one easily. Feeling the edge of the fabric between his fingers, they slipped down to the next button. He reached his waist, and the shirttails came out of the waistband with a rough tug, exposing a glimpse of well-muscled abs. He shrugged out of the fine linen, dropping the lavender shirt on top of the leather holster. He just stood there, defiant and proud. The only softness in that body was the look in his eyes.

She chuckled softly. "Normally when men don't want to take off their pants in front of a woman, there's a reason. Either you have a hidden weapon or you are embarrassed about the size of your cock. Which is it?"

That perfect grin lit his face, broader and brighter than ever. The nimble fingers unbuckled the leather belt and slid down the trousers. He still wore his shoes, and when he leaned over, she stopped him with a cluck.

"Stand up, hands up." With a quick sweep, she snagged the back of the wooden chair and swung it in his direction. It rattled as if it might fall, but didn't. "Sit."

Sidling up to him, the tension built. This was the dangerous part, but she still held the advantage. Under normal circumstances, her reflexes would be so acute that she wouldn't worry about a sudden attack, but tonight her body hurt. She knelt in front of him with difficulty but didn't let it show. Provocatively slow, she untied the polished wingtips. Then, one at a time, she slipped the shoe off from his foot with one hand while the other slid up his sock and onto the broad calf. She selected the left foot first purposefully to ease her fingers into his flesh, massaging and kneading him into a lulling distraction. Even his clasped fingers slipped a little down into the dark curly hair. When she switched sides, her fingers encountered more leather.

This time when Fara pushed herself to her feet, she couldn't keep the grunt of a complaint from edging its way through clenched teeth. Taking a step back, she aimed the Browning. "Follow my directions exactly. With both hands pull up the bottom of your right pant leg." She waited and then cooed, "Good. Unbuckle the strap and then toss the knife to me still in the sheath. If I even see a glint of metal, I'll shoot you. And, believe me, I'm a very good shot."

After unbuckling the rig, he held it out for a second and then tossed it directly in front of her dirty and abused bare feet. "I bet you are very good at a lot of things."

"Be, the best that I can be." She sang the recruiting tune and bent to pick up the casing. It was a little tricky to press down the release and pull the blade with a single hand, but she managed. The polished metal glimmered in the light. "Nice one. You have good taste in weapons."

Franz only lightly laughed, but his eyes twinkled merrily. "I also have good taste in women. You are a compelling beauty, Señora Trotter. I would like to know you better."

"What like close friends? Very close, intimate friends." She took a step toward him, allowing her eyes to meet his. "Now stand up and finish the job."

Instantly, Franz shed his socks one at a time, released his belt, and unzipped the fly. He stood, and the trousers fell to his ankles. With another calculating glance, he pulled down the loosely fitting boxers that just so happened to match the lavender of the shirt. Fara had to give credit where credit was due; the man had style.

A skitter of interest flit through her system. "Well, you definitely have nothing to be ashamed of." She smiled, taking in the larger picture without wavering the aim of the gun in her hand. "Now into the bedroom."

His face lit up. "Do you realize this has been a fantasy of mine for years now?"

"Umm," she hummed, "is it now?" The sexual curl between the words flowed and filled the space between them. She followed him into the dark room but didn't turn on a light. She could see him well enough from the light in the parlor. "Get on all fours, beside the bed."

The athletic man stopped and glanced back at her, but his eyes weren't scared. They gleamed with building passion. "Why?"

"I have a bag of toys. I want you to get them for me, nice and easy."

His muscles flexed in his thighs and buttocks as he did what she asked.

She thought about having sex, not out of need, but to prove a point, a very logical point. Before her interlude with J.C., she had been celibate for months. She had calculated and then executed the fulfillment of a private fantasy to seduce a total stranger and just take him for her pleasure. Because of all that, perhaps her attachment to J.C. wasn't real, perhaps she projected an attachment onto him out of some weird sense of self-propriety. If she took another man, she would prove to herself, one way or another, whether she really loved J.C.

Overthinking sex usually wasn't her problem, and whenever she was this close to a naked man, physical intimacy was a foregone conclusion. Although her inner nature should have been tingling, there wasn't any heat rising inside her body or expectancy quivering in her loins. Whenever she got horny, her clitoris would swell and grow with the need, even pulse with it, which is why she always brought herself to orgasm through manual stimulation before taking a man. The clitoral climax was such a vibrant prelude to intercourse, and guys really liked watching her do it.

Whenever Fara thought about sex, she would develop that inner need. The aching would want, no it would demand something firm to push its way inside of her, yet here was a man with a great body, kneeling by the side of her bed, following her every instruction. What woman wouldn't want to have sex with him?

Instead of picturing herself over him, taking long strokes to enhance her own pleasure of hitting those internal, most intimate pressure points, her mind envisioned J.C. and what he looked like when she was on top of him with pleasure written all over his face.

"Got it. Now what do you want?" Franz backed out from under the bed and glanced up at her with a saucy smirk.

Seeing the small backpack, Fara refocused. "We're going to play a little game, Slick. Do you want to play with me?" She added coyly.

"Can't you tell?" Franz rose, in every interpretation of the word. He was taller and more muscular than J.C., but not bigger in that most intimate way, yet still big enough for her to enjoy the ride.

"I like what I see Slick. Put the bag on the corner of the bed and then climb on up." She watched him, wanting to feel excited, willing her body to want him. "That's right all the way up to the headboard. Oh Slick, you do know how to play." Again, she breathed power into the words. When he reached for her, she slapped his hand purposefully hard, "No! Now wait for me like a good boy."

Using her peripheral vision to keep him in full view, she dumped the contents of the backpack onto the bedspread while still covering the man with the gun. Various shiny objects fell out, but she knew exactly what she was looking for. With a single finger, she hooked the two sets of handcuffs and rocked them gently back and forth. Licking her lips dramatically, with as much tongue showing as a late night porn star, she edged closer. "I hope you are going to be a good boy and play my game with me. Here are the rules. You do what I say. That's it."

"If I don't?" He wanted to fill his voice with macho bravado, but the devious twinkle in his eyes gave him away.

She shook her head, ticking little clicks with her tongue. "Then, I will have to punish you."

His penis darkened, the tip growing even broader. He looked at his erection and then rolled his dark brown eyes back to hers. "Which do you prefer, good or bad?"

"Either way Slick. I'll let you decide. Do you like pain?" The question reverberated inside of Fara's memories. She had said that line to many men, too many to count, but it was never sexual in nature, until today.

A single brow rose. "Not particularly."

Her breathy whisper carried more seductive power. "Fine, then I expect you to be a good boy. Cooperate, fully and completely, and I promise to be nice, very, very nice." She touched the pink tip of her tongue to the center of her upper lip and drew it back into her mouth slowly. "Are you ready to start our game?" Purposefully, she over-articulated the words with her best Marilyn Monroe impersonation.

"Oh yeah, baby." He held his hands out, wrists side by side.

"One at a time, Slick. One at a time. It's too nice a job to rush." She clicked one cuff over the powerful wrist and attached the other end around the narrowest curve of the carved bedpost. "Tight enough?"

"Oh yeah." The scent of desire poured off his bronzed skin, and he bucked his hips up, making his erection bounce stiffly. "I'm ready. Can't you tell?"

"Ooh, I like what I see. Now give me your other hand." She clasped the cuff over it, but even with the muscled breadth of his shoulders, the cuff was a little short of the other bedpost. "You will get the full benefit of my intentions if you are fully stretched." The final word curled off her tongue. "Scoot over for me, oh yeah, just like that Slick. Give me what I want. Ooh, what a good boy."

Even though he stretched, the cuff was still just a hair too short. Surprisingly strong, he pulled his hand out of her grasp to tug the pillow out from behind the small of his back. He then scooted over again until his arms spread across the entire width of the broad headboard, stretched as tautly as possible. The corded muscles pulled thickly, showing the incredible definition of his powerful shoulders and chest. The edge of the cuff scratched tightly over the wooden post but finally closed with a secure click.

Stepping back, Fara assessed her conquest. Under any other circumstance, she would have reveled in having dominion over another human being. Even got off to it. But not tonight. The tension had taken its toll. Inside and out, she hurt. Every laceration throbbed with the rhythm of her pulse along with a humdinger of a headache. Her next priority had to be caring for herself, but she needed to finish securing her captive, ensure he would behave. Hotel walls were thin.

Walking on the outside edges of her feet helped a little. She hobbled to the dresser and looked for something to use as a gag. Instead of just pulling out a stocking and walking back to the bed, she wanted to stir her emotions. She needed to prove this to herself. Even with her body being a little abused, there was no excuse she couldn't get her libido to rise.

One piece of clothing at a time, Fara undressed in a quiet and subdued striptease until she stood nude. Playfully, she brushed her cheek with the nylon, allowing the slippery smoothness to caress her skin. She draped the black stocking back and forth, over her face and neck, shoulders and breasts, all the while watching Franz's expression in the mirror, waiting for him to comment on her scars.

His eyes were large and glossy, edged with that expectant look men get right before sex. Shallow pants coursed through his open mouth, and then he quickly licked his lips. "Dear God woman, you are damned sexy."

Not breaking out of Lady Dracula's persona, Fara approached the bed, and gingerly climbed over the footboard, poised between his powerful legs. She didn't fear him trying to hurt her, at least not anymore. Franz was hers to do whatever she wanted, and her mind ran through the possibilities.

With a flick of her wrist, the lacy upper edge of the thigh-high drifted along the inner curve of his calf, and slowly, ever so gently, the silkiness smoothed over his flesh. The hair on his legs was thick, tensely curled. Purposefully, almost painfully slow, the naturally tanned flesh under the curls reacted, trembling as the stocking passed. The quivering wave followed the silky movement, all the way up the sensitive flesh of the leg's inner curves and back again.

With an audible thump, he tossed his head back against the wooden headboard. "Oh yeah baby. I've never had it so good."

"I'm just getting started." Scooting forward on her knees, she worked her way toward him until she was nestled close to the juncture of his thighs. She had played once like this with Jason, minus the bondage. Still, he had a similar reaction. Something in a man just loved a woman draping lingerie over his body.

Concentrating on the area directly in front of her, she couldn't help but stare at his erection but didn't touch him there with the stocking, no not yet. Brushing the silky fabric up and down over his testicles made his pulse course visibly along the anxious veins.

In a broader sweep now, Fara started stroking him, allowing the fabric to slide over his entire length, back and forth, forward and aside. As she brushed over them, his testicles rose and quivered within their fleshy sacks.

Opening his eyes, he tipped his chin toward his chest, rising and falling with rapid breaths. "Jesus woman ... you're going ... to make me ... oh, shit!"

Continuing the rhythm, brushing him in consistent waves, Fara inhaled the scent of sex and absorbed its circling power. Men had called her a succubus, and perhaps there was a kernel of truth to it. "Show me what you got Slick. How far are you going to fly? Show me. Come for me. Show me now."

Called forth by her power, a thunderous groan shuddered through the room as the masculine essence exploded from his body. His abs constricted and rippled with the inner thrusts propelling the thick streams, arching into the air and then landing onto Franz's torso. The earthy scent rose while his penis released its final shudders, quaking out the remaining pearly drops. Still breathing in deep, panting breaths, he dropped his head back against the headboard again. "Ah Dios, que una suena."

His comment about this being a dream touched Fara's softer side. Even with a scarred face, Franz was an attractive man with an exceptional body. In the dim light, the semen draped over his torso like a broken string of pearls. At first, she thought about running her fingers through the glossy strings, but she just watched as rivulets formed. The tiny streams flowed down the natural slopes of his body, and some congregated in his navel and along the ripples of his abs.

"Oh my Slick, you were pretty noisy on that one. Although I like it, I can't have someone calling hotel security, now can I? That would spoil our fun." Wrapping each end of the stocking over her painful hands in several twists, she pressed the light yet strong fabric to his lips. Without any hesitation, they parted, and she pulled the stocking just tightly enough to be secure without being too tight to bite into the corners of his mouth. Twisting it behind his head and then back, she tied it off with a knot filling his mouth. The stocking's ends hung like a giant black mustache. His eyes grew wide, and she licked her lips. "There now Slick, you're ready for round two of our game. But before it's my turn to play, I have to clean up."

CHAPTER 45

The bedroom was dark and the night abnormally cool. J.C. glanced over his shoulder into the empty room. Even though the furnishings were elegant, they weren't right, didn't match somehow. Why, he didn't exactly know. But tonight, nothing was right.

Just like before, he didn't remember setting down his flashlight. This time it was on the highboy dresser with the beam shining upon the old tapestry hanging on the wall. Oddly, the brightness didn't reflect or even spill onto the floor. The fabric absorbed the energy, invigorating the detail of the depicted scene, almost bringing it to life. Although faded with time, the embroidery's colors and texture still clearly illustrated the bloody carnage of battle. Bearing down on horseback, soldiers in Spanish Morion helmets brandished steel swords against peasants, whose only weapons were wooden spears. Hundreds if not thousands of fallen bodies littered the battlefield. Only a few natives remained, and they congregated in front of the mouth of a low cave in the rocky terrain. From within the steaming fissure a creature rose from the darkness, emerging into this world. The giant beast's torso was shaped like a human male, but instead of skin, red pebbled scales formed impenetrable armor. Like a page right out of Dante's *Inferno*, the broad inhuman face had two twisted horns growing from its forehead, curling to razor-sharp points. The scourge's legs were abnormally long and covered in dense curly wool. Although menacing in its own countenance, in a clawed hand, it carried a giant scythe as if torn from the Grim Reaper himself.

The sight drew upon something within J.C., challenging memories to rise. He had seen that beast; more than once, he was sure of it. As the memories churned just outside of his recollection, a chill climbed his spine, and the hair rose on his body.

The flashlight moved.

Quickly he swung toward the dresser. In his mental disarray, he hoped something was there, and in another way, he hoped it was just another hallucination. Glittering in the beam of light, particles formed and coalesced. Dumbfounded he just stared as a dark-haired beauty took shape. She was Vivian Dufrense, and he nearly leapt with joy at actually remembering something.

A hum filled the room, and with his head pressed between his hands, he fell to his knees. Mirroring his position, Vivian wrapped her fingers into his, and her unearthly chill crept into him. On that tremble, the unending darkness opened, consuming him in a vortex of Vivian's making. When the spinning stopped, J.C. stood alone on top of a rocky rise.

The thunderous rush articulated the thrust and ebb of the waves, and each part of the never-ending cycle carried its own specific allure. The rumbling built up momentum and then hung expectantly in the air for a moment before crashing into the rocks. The associated roar carried the concussion of the impact, and once spent, hushed out in a frothy whisper, inviting another wave to claim its place.

Although the fresh sea scent was close, the metallic stink of death tainted the air. Just like the tapestry, bodies laid strewn as if sown from the land. The few natives remaining fell back toward the fissure in the earth at the base of the giant stone hill. Although few in number, the men's voices rose in unison charging the moonless night with ethereal power while chanting "Maboya, Maboya, Maboya."

A resounding crack shook the night when the barrier between the dimensions shattered.

Fully emerged, the creature moved swiftly on the spindly legs. With the first sweep of the scythe, the beast unhorsed a Spanish soldier, cleaving the animal and man atwain in the same stroke. Both of their screams clung to the air along with the resonant zing of the scythe. Then, in a coordinated attack, four foot soldiers in full armor charged. The scythe sung again. Crushing the fallen bodies under a cloven hoof, the creature screamed its delight into the night. Raising its claws in a sweeping motion toward the sky, the northern sea rose into the blackened sky. Of biblical proportions, a tidal wave charged upon the land. As the flowing surge gurgled back out to sea, it swept the lowlands clean of bodies, dead and living alike. Of the fortunate few, one rider and then another retreated toward the other side of the peninsula where several ships waited in the bay, and very soon all of the invaders followed suit.

Maboya stood at the mouth of its cave staring toward the ships.

Time must have passed, but not for J.C. From his vantage point, instantly a battery of men carrying torches snaked their way from the harbor back to the battlefield. In the flickering light, he recognized the man leading the procession. On the horse behind him was a girl. Her loose black hair spilled over her otherwise naked body, making the bindings at her wrists and mouth stand out in contrast to her pale skin. The leader pulled her off the horse and dragged her forward, toward the immobile red giant. Her heels dug into the ground, and she even fell. The Spaniard didn't care. With his hands clasped around the binding at her wrists, he kept leading her until she was within twenty feet of the steaming fissure. The Spaniard bowed roughly toward the devil and then extended a huge raw emerald. Instead of the beast accepting the stone, it shied away from its light.

Recognizing the power, the one Spaniard remained, while the others in his entourage had immediately turned and snaked their way down the rocky slope back toward the docked ships. The sharp-faced man turned the stone over in his hands, mesmerized by the glowing light.

Grunting, Maboya turned and regarded the girl, who had fallen to her knees in sobbing supplication. With his great snout, he sniffed her hair and then lingered on the thatch between her legs, taking deep breaths of her feminine scent. Overcome, the girl fainted. Gathering her into his human arms, the beast retreated back into the fissure from whence it came.

Still with the emerald in his grasp, the Spaniard followed at a safe distance until he was certain the beast had returned to hell.

He turned to follow his comrades, setting sail with the outgoing tide.

Six Taínos had remained and witnessed Maboya's strength. Deep in prayerful supplication, the men thanked their god and dedicated their lives and the lives of their descendants for generations to come to serve their savior.

Accompanied by only the wind and the dead, J.C. remained on the rocky hill staring at the crack in the earth. Behind him the surf washed on the rocks, making the same patterned sound, exactly like the fort on San Cristobal hill. San Cristobal hill. The battle of San Cristobal hill.

J.C. sucked in a breath and gazed down at the battlefield. None of the textbooks discussed the last stand of the Taínos against the Spanish. When his grandfather told him the story of Maboya smiting the intruders, the bizarre account was a weird fairy tale, dark and foreboding, the Taíno version of the Brothers Grimm. His grandfather knew all about this, but how?

A fracture across dimensions existed under the hill, creating a physical passage or portal between worlds. The Spaniards built the fort on San Cristobal hill, supposedly for the terrain, but also as a show of power and a clear reminder of the Spaniards' unrelenting might. They thought Maboya was Satan. What better way to entomb Satan than to build tons and tons of rock over the top of the portal to hell?

The wind changed, and a fresh breeze blew a cool wash over J.C.'s face, enlivening his senses. Closing his eyes, he allowed the exaltation to flow unchecked, and power coursed through him, humming into his veins. The last time he felt this good was after he and Fara had that wild night of sex. Like hell it wasn't real. He had to find Fara. Taking an even deeper breath, he called for her at the top of his lungs.

"We can't find her boy."

J.C.'s eyes shot open at the sound of his grandfather's voice. He was back in the bedroom of the fort, kneeling on the floor.

"Nieto, you okay?" Eduardo knelt at his side. Putting an arm around J.C.'s shoulders, the older man helped him to his feet.

He glanced around the dark room. "Where's Vivian?"

"Fara, where's Fara? You need her, to join with her. I have others searching." Eduardo clasped his hands over J.C.'s and stared into his eyes. "You must prepare. Go downstairs. The ceremony is beginning."

The glint of green caught his eye, and the calm fled J.C.'s mind. "That ring. That's Fara's ring."

"Go downstairs. Prepare." Eduardo repeated.

"How ... how did you get her ring?" He stepped back and bumped into the bed. "What have you done to Fara?" His head filled with the sound of the surf.

"You need Fara. You will have Fara." Eduardo clapped his hands. "For all eternity."

"For all eternity," repeated from J.C.'s lips.

CHAPTER 46

The cool bath water soothed Fara's bruised and abused body, but nothing could soothe her anxiety. A turbulent battle waged, good versus evil, right against wrong, survival opposed to death, or at the very least freedom pitted against indentured servitude, for all eternity. Damn him!

Logic screamed for her to go straight to the airport and get off this accursed island. Her job was to produce a television show, not save the world from the coming of Maboya.

Sinking into the water, she closed her eyes, and although she wanted to find peace, the final images of Vivian and Felipe's life vividly appeared. Since the connection ended abruptly, Felipe had to be dead, leaving Vivian at the mercy of her deranged uncle. Since her battered ghost was within San Cristobal, Dufrense had to have brought her back to the fort and quite possibly sacrificed Vivian to the beast. He expected Vivian to be a virgin. In a way she was, just not quite. Perhaps that distortion caused enough disruption to lose control of Maboya, enough to bring him into this world, but not control him. She scoffed out loud. If that was the case, then what the hell did they want with her? Certainly, they knew she wasn't a virgin.

Sweeping up handfuls of water, she splashed her face allowing the coolness to flow over her eyes and into her mouth. The sting made her remember, and she stared at the deep cuts crossing her fingers and palms. This was fucking real. Virgin or not, they needed Fara for something. The words she overheard while under the balcony stayed with her, resonating inside of her, *"We need the other one, the one J.C. loves."*

"Shit!" She spat the word out with the mouthful of water. Although she wanted to leave J.C. to his psycho grandfather, she couldn't. Underneath it all, under all of the layers of keeping herself safe from what really scared her, the time had come to fess up. She loved J.C., and love came with responsibility. She had to go back. Even if she couldn't save him, she wouldn't be able to live with the guilt if she didn't try. It was better to die than to live in the shadow of cowardice. Guy had taught her that.

Consigned to her fate, Fara stood. Droplets rolled down her torso, dripping from the ends of her fingers and gliding down her legs. Ignoring all of that, she dried the dog tags first. Only one was hers. The other belonged to Jason and was the only memento she had. Then she carefully polished Felipe's emerald ring, rubbing the stone in hypnotic circles. With each revolution, she gained more focus. Once set onto her path, she wouldn't withdraw or ever surrender. Achieve the objective or die. Finally, her head and her heart were in agreement.

Wrapping the extra-large towel around her torso, she stepped out of the tub. Her feet had stopped bleeding. Most of the toenails were broken, not as badly as she supposed, so she had clipped off the worst of the rough angles. With a couple of pairs of socks, she would be able to get around in her jogging shoes just fine. The cuts on her hands still oozed a mixture of sebaceous fluid and blood, but not too badly. Without a care as to the mess it would make, she dumped out her toiletry bag and almost laughed aloud at the tiny white box. What in her right mind made her think this was a sufficient first aid kit?

She wrapped her palms with gauze and used the cheap knock-off adhesive bandages to hold the ends in place. There were only four bandages left, leaving her to prioritize which of the several cuts to cover. Limited mobility was always a liability, so she left the joints exposed and concentrated on the largest and deepest gashes between the knuckles. Thankfully, the bleeding had done its job and cleansed the wounds of any rust particles. She'd lived through worse, and bleeding a little now was better than dying later because of not being able to pull a trigger or hold onto a knife. But she changed her mind when she saw the tube of instant glue. It stung like a son-of-a-bitch; still, one at a time, she squirted the liquid into a cut and held it closed, careful not to inadvertently glue her hands together. Now that would be a sight.

With her hands throbbing once more with brilliant pain, she opened the door and stopped short. Strangely, she had forgotten about the naked man handcuffed to her bed. His dark eyes shot toward her, staring at her violently with a mixture of annoyance and allure. He was a fine specimen, yet just like before, she had no inner need to seduce him. A few days ago, she would have taken him for the hell of it, but not today.

"*Shit*," she scolded herself silently. She had lost her edge, her impartiality. Although she had been faithful to Jason while he was overseas, other men had tempted her. She had gone out drinking and dancing, even singing karaoke, but she stopped short when she started to heat and yearn in her own personal way. Dear God she had been tempted!

Unsettling guilt swept swiftly through her. She had wanted to love Jason, deeply and sincerely, but wanting to love and loving were very different. She didn't know how different until now.

Fara stared blankly at Franz envisioning J.C. in his place. If he had been the man on the bed, she would have climbed on top of him and... Instantly, she felt the heat pulse between her legs and a flutter deep within her loins.

Franz murmured and kicked his legs wildly. Each in turn, he pulled against the cuffs.

"Hold on Slick; don't be doing too much of that. You'll rub your skin clean off." She sidled over to the bed, realizing her thoughts had played across her face. "Don't take it personally. Under other circumstances, I would have fucked you and enjoyed it. I'm involved with someone. More than that, I'm in love with him." It helped by saying the L word out loud, which was something she hadn't said often or used lightly. With Guy, it was her deepest regret. That wasn't going to happen again. "I've got to go save him, so I'm borrowing your weapons for the evening and have every intention of giving them back to you when I return. If I don't come back, well ... regardless, you'll be okay. Housekeeping will find you during their morning rounds, and I'll leave the key to the cuffs over here by the TV. They'll think you're into kinky sex, rather than I jumped you and well ... rather than what actually happened. We'll keep that just between us, but if you feel compelled to share the real story, go ahead.

Your choice. If I'm not back to release you, it won't make a damn bit of difference to me what story you come up with."

Pulling the towel off with one hand, Fara stood before him naked. Franz quit struggling, as his eyes widened until the dark irises were merely an extension of the pupil. She climbed over the footboard, just like J.C. had done their first time together. Realistically, it was their only time, but at this point, she kind of liked the idea of their intertwined fantasy. Giving herself over to J.C. had been the most erotic experience of her life. She had never had that level of trust with anyone, not even Jason, whom she trusted with her life, but not her heart.

After wiping Franz's abs clean of his own residue, she spread the towel and draped it over his lower torso, tucking the edges under his hips. "This way if the maids find you, it won't be quite so," she searched for a good word, "revealing."

From that point, she disregarded his presence and dressed quickly in black on black. From the discarded contents of her utility bag, she discovered the pair of workout gloves she had packed as an afterthought. With her hands swollen from the abuse, they fit snugly, which made her feel much more confident of her grip if she had to climb the wall. Coiling her hair, she rolled it up under the black baseball cap she had worn that morning while running. Taking a single glance in the mirror, she quickly checked her hair. While pushing a wayward strand under the cap, the fine hair on her arms started to tingle, standing up with static current. She shook off the sensation and left the room, but before swinging the door completely shut, she froze.

"It's you." Fara knew how lame the words sounded but couldn't think of anything else to say.

"I stayed in this room, for a few days anyway." Sister Marguerite turned away from the window and walked across the parlor with as much substance and vitality as any living person.

Focused on her mission, Fara squatted in front of the pile of clothes and picked up the shoulder holster. "Why are you here?"

"Why are you here?" Sister Marguerite replied in kind. "You could have just left the island."

"I could say the same of you. You're not bound to this place, at least not like Vivian." Fara's gaze rose slowly to meet the ghost's regular looking eyes. "You look better than you did a few hours ago in the dungeon."

"I needed someone of physical substance to remove Felipe's ring from the fort."

"Yeah, about that. I've got Felipe's right here." Fara patted her chest and then went right back to making the necessary adjustments. Once buckles had been in position for so long, they were almost permanently affixed. Her fingers were stiff with the glue and the gloves, making the tactile work even more difficult. "The ring you sold me, well, someone stole it, took it right off my finger while I was out cold. I assume it was Eduardo Calderon."

"He's Maboya's keeper. He needs both emeralds to complete the rite. Since he stole your ring, I stole his."

A chuckle passed through Fara's lips while pulling the final buckle to the tightest hole. "That's not very sisterly, Sister."

"You met the demon?"

Fara smiled from the nun's clever avoidance. "Yes."

"And do you know what it is?"

With a grunt, Fara pushed up to her feet and started shrugging into the shoulder harness. "Shape shifter or a kind of a doppelganger. I'm not sure whether it really shifts or whether each person just perceives it differently. Maboya reflects whatever scares you the most. At this point, I don't care what it is, or what it turns into. I'm getting J.C. out of there."

"Juan Carlos is his grandfather's chosen successor. Calderon and Muñoz placed listening devices to determine if you had discovered their involvement. Eduardo needed more time with J.C."

Fara had already come to those conclusions. "To fuck over his personal will." Even after adjusting the straps as tightly as they would go, the rig was still too big, yet better than nothing. She needed a place to secure the big gun. Just like Franz, she slipped the snub nose into her belt at the small of her back and then slipped on a black hoody to hide both. Instantly, her skin beaded sweat, but she kept it on, better hot than being spotted and stopped by a trigger happy rent-a-cop. That thought triggered another. The guard with the AK47 was close by. Quickly she calculated her odds at disabling the soldier and getting the weapon without being noticed by anyone on the sidewalk. She shrugged and felt the harness shift. Although she would feel better with an assault rifle, she had enough fire power to do the job. A massacre was not the plan. Right now, she needed stealth and cunning. Slip in, and then slip out with J.C.

She pulled out the chair and started to strap the dagger to her left calf on top of the Spandex pants. Someone would need to be looking pretty damn close to notice it from a distance. If he was that close, he was close enough for her to take him out. Once complete, she twisted toward the sister. "You never answered my question."

"Which question was that?"

Fara sat back with a huff. "Why are you here Sister?"

"Why to help you of course." The elderly nun rose without any signs of stiffness of age. At least there was something to look forward to in death.

"Like you helped Vivian and Felipe?" Instant regret burned through her. "Look, I'm sorry. I'm grumpy because I'm sore. I shouldn't have said that. You weren't the one who killed them. It's as irrational as my mother-in-law blaming me for Jason's death. I didn't kill him, and you didn't kill Vivian or Felipe."

"No, but my idea set them upon the path." Sister Marguerite walked into Fara's personal space and placed her hands on the curve where Fara's neck met her shoulders. Energy exuded from the touch, filling her with a different type of warmth, more energy than heat. The pain instantly melted away. "Felipe could have set sail, just like you could have flown off. And just like Juan Carlos, Vivian was doomed the moment she set foot in San Cristobal."

"Why?"

"Her uncle and Ustariz discovered San Cristobal's secret from one of the Taínos they tortured, and they targeted Vivian to use as the required sacrifice. Vivian Dufrense didn't commit suicide. They killed her in the dungeon and then threw the body out of the garita. The next day when the watch discovered her, the surf had done so much damage no one was any the wiser." The power in the pale eyes dimmed. "That beautiful young girl didn't deserve to never reach the gates of heaven. I vowed to God not to rest until I deliver her soul."

"What of Felipe?"

"Dufrense left him face down in the road. They were so close to Fajardo. Close enough for Captain Ortiz to hear the shots, and at dawn, he sent scouts to see what happened. They buried the body at sea on the return voyage to Spain. Ortiz never again set foot on Puerto Rican soil."

"So Felipe's at rest?"

"Even with a proper burial, a tortured soul will linger and seek resolution. His spirit waits for Vivian outside of San Cristobal's wall." Sister Marguerite rose and took Fara's hand, leading her toward the door. "We can't save one without the other."

"Shit," Fara sighed. Her simple plan to go in, kidnap J.C., and get the hell out of the fort had just gotten a lot more complicated. "So what do I have to do?"

The elderly hand was warm and strong, filling Fara with confidence. "You are not alone. Do not fear."

Lightly touching Franz's access card and keys that were already in her pocket, Fara opened the door and peered into the hall. "I'm not afraid."

"It would be more accurate to say you do not fear for yourself. Do you know why you didn't die in Afghanistan?"

Fara set a finger to her lips and quickly led the ghost toward the backdoor, remaining silent until they slipped into the waning night. "I didn't die because I was saved."

"That's right." Sister Marguerite squeezed Fara's hand and suddenly they were in the old cemetery.

"Damn. You've been able to do that this entire time?" Indignantly, Fara scolded. "I wish you had told me. It sure would have made my escape from San Cristobal a hell of a lot easier. Can you get us inside the same way?" With a tip of her head, she motioned toward the fort, but lost her train of thought when her tilted gaze landed on several fully-formed ghosts.

Sister Marguerite nodded pleasantly to the apparitions. "No, too much darkness shields the fort. When God's light came for me, a crack in the portal remained open. Only I can come or go from San Cristobal in spirit form, so you will have to find your own way inside."

Unable to figure out something clever to say, Fara pointed toward the souls. "Are they good, bad, or indifferent?"

"Mostly indifferent. They are waiting. Tonight is Abib's New Moon, a rare celestial occurrence during which the unclaimed dead are able to rise from their graves and seek salvation." Sister Marguerite waved them toward the sky. "The gates of heaven are open and waiting. Join your loved ones. Your work here is done."

The hair on Fara's body sizzled, just like when Sister Marguerite arrived, but times ten to the tenth power. Static electricity charged through the cemetery and filled the air with the scent of ozone. At first Fara thought the brilliant glow was the search light from San Cristobal, but this was light and yet at the same time wasn't. Pure energy was a better description, which shone with all of the colors of a rainbow, like multicolor glitter swirling in a gentle vortex.

One at a time, the earth-bound souls connected with the light, became one with it, adding their own special luminosity to the brilliant collective glow. As each one ascended, the burst of energy charged the atmosphere, adding another rolling wave to the ever present sound of the nearby surf, amplifying the thunderous roar until it was the only thing she could hear, the light the only thing she could see. Just when she thought it couldn't get any louder or brighter, the portal dissipated, the opaque becoming sheer until then it was gone completely.

Still bristling from the residual energy, she stared at the spot where the heavens had opened and accepted those few wayward souls. After all of the transgressions against mankind she had committed, hope for redemption existed. One day the light may yet come for her, but she didn't plan for it to happen tonight.

She trained her focus onto the fort. At first, she thought the outline of a human figure was just some weird anomaly, how bright light sometimes left residual images. Still, even as her vision cleared, there was a man waiting, just outside of the gate.

CHAPTER 47

The security card was generic, just a plain white tag without any logo or insignia. Not even a damned arrow indicated which part needed to touch the sensor. Rob stared at the card and then the gate. His eyes narrowed sharply as the process rotated back to the sensor at the side of the short driveway. Once more, he pressed the card hard against the sensor on the short post. Nothing happened. His eyes made the circuit again. Flipping the tag over, he tried the other side.

"Shit!" He had chastised himself, even called himself a scared little pussy for turning around. Twice. Finally he got up enough balls to drive up to the gate, and now the fucking card wouldn't work. He would have to call that shit-head Muñoz in the morning and complain. A tense grin full of malicious intent stretched across his face. He would charge the son-of-a-bitch for a half-day delay. Yeah, that would teach him.

Slamming the car into reverse, Rob gunned the motor and zipped back out onto the road. Where that car came from he didn't have a clue. Damn Puerto Rican drivers! He thought Miami was bad, but this place, Jesus, it took top prize. Almost got him killed.

He should have stayed with Carolyn. Certainly, doll-face was spending his money in the casino at a rapid rate. Still, gambling was never his bag. Winning was great, but losing, well, the bitter feeling lingered far too long. The odds were in favor of the house, so the chances to win were too slim for his taste.

Everything in Rob's life was calculated down to a work-benefit or a cost-benefit ratio. If something wasn't clearly in his favor, he just didn't do it. He had made it to a point in his life where he didn't have to anything he didn't damn well want, which included going into a moldy old fort. But now, instead of it being his choice to walk away, the damned fort wasn't letting him in. The irritation of being denied outweighed the former sense of fear. Hell, he wasn't really that afraid. Once he shrugged off that creeped-out feeling, exhilaration had taken its place. The fort reminded him of the settings in the Saturday matinees he had loved so well. This old fort could be Frankenstein's Castle or Carfax Abbey, even the fortress of Dr. Moreau. There was still enough of the dreamer inside of him to keep a kernel of imagination alive after all those years. No one really knew about it. He didn't dare let anyone know his deepest-darkest, and this fort had secrets too. At least J.C. thought so, and Rob was now determined to find out what they were.

He glanced at his watch but couldn't read the face of the gold on gold Rolex. Punching the button for the light on the roof, he noticed it was nearly midnight, the witching hour. Would a secret clock chime the twelfth hour and then open all of the doors?

Wistfully, Rob just sat there in the middle of the street, staring at the fort. J.C. was afraid of this place, especially at night. How in all blazes could he get up in J.C.'s face for being a pussy if he couldn't get inside and prove there was nothing supernatural going on? Entering the fort had now become a challenge. Hell or high water, he would find a way inside. This was his only chance to explore an abandoned fort at night, and he was damn well going to do it.

Another car swerved around him. This time the asshole had the balls to honk. Rob threw the car in gear and tail-gated within inches to the end of the long block, allowing a string of curses to flow unchecked as the ass-hole in front of him ran the stop sign. The release was short lived. San Cristobal's tall, gray wall curved to the right, reminding him why he was here.

From what he remembered in his original discussions with the parks department, there was an upper entrance. If the front door was locked, try around back. That was Rob's motto. Damn well made him the man he was today.

The hill was abnormally steep, and the motor of the cheap rental car complained. Damn it if both sides of the street weren't full, bumper to bumper, not even a gap to park in. At the edge of his sight, he spied an indention in the wall near the very top of the hill. He eased into that driveway and rolled down the window. At the canted angle, he couldn't quite reach the security sensor cemented in at the edge of the stone wall.

A little too close to swing open the door more than a foot or so, he had to wiggle his way out of the car. Before both feet touched the ground, every hair on his body stood straight up, including the implants. His hand swept back from his forehead, checking the strands of hair which cost him an arm and a leg. He turned toward the sensor once again, and a tingle rose icily up his spine. A flash of light swept across the gate and then along the inside of the seawall.

His eyes stung. A few seconds later, it swung back again, but this time he shielded his face with a forearm. "What the hell?"

"They're looking for me."

Twisting, he jumped, along with his heart which landed in his throat. His stinging eyes couldn't focus, but he recognized the sultry voice.

"What the hell are you doing here?"

Fara's face developed into a series of hard lines, making her look much older. Even her normally dazzling eyes were mere slits and focused suspiciously upon him.

"You were supposed to go back to Miami." With a huff, he exhaled the tight breath he had been holding. "Jesus H. Christ! What the fuck are you doing sneaking up on me like that?"

Before the search light could sweep the gate again, she edged them to the angled side of the wall. Once hidden in the shadows, she whispered, "You won't believe..."

Pulling back from her a step, he looked her down one side and up the other. "What the hell are you wearing a sweatshirt for? It's a hundred degrees."

Looking down, she nodded and unzipped the hoody. The shoulder snagged on the loose-fitting gun, and she had to lift and then tug to get the fabric freed.

"Damn, what you doing? Going into battle or something? I've seen cops with less firepower." He regarded the other two who now approached and hitched a thumb in their direction. "Who are they?"

She pointed to the man whose dark shoulder-length hair fluttered in the slight breeze. "This is Lieutenant Felipe Luis Morgan Cordova."

"Don't you think he's a little short to be playing the role of the hero?" Rob pressed a palm to his forehead. "Let me guess, the old broad is Vivian."

"Hardly," the woman stepped forward and extended her hand, "I am Sister Marguerite Vincentia Yorlay Montenegro."

Confusion never set well with Rob, but someplace deep inside told him not to touch her. "You in the show or just going for a tour with Rambo here?"

Fara pushed him back against the wall roughly. "Just shut up and listen."

He sucked in a deep breath, which his first ex-wife said made him look like a stuffed Thanksgiving turkey, but he didn't care what he looked like. He wasn't about to take any shit from anyone.

Fara didn't seem to notice. She just kept on talking in that harsh whisper. "The situation is bad. I don't care if you believe me or not, but this is what's going down. J.C.'s grandfather is the head of some weird cult, and he has J.C. hypnotized, has the whole lot in there hypnotized. I've never seen anything like it before, but that's beside the point. They're preparing a ritual in honor of this ancient Taíno god named Maboya, and it has to be done tonight. It's Abib's New Moon, a night when the dead can walk the earth."

While Fara took a breath after nearly running together all of the words together, Rob jumped in. "I smell a load of bull-shit."

"I only have until dawn to get in there and rescue J.C. before he's tuned into Maboya's newest human servant." Her face tightened. "I suggest you get in your car and turn around. You have no business being here right now."

"No business!" The search light streaked across the top of their heads, and she pushed him firmly against the hard wall. "I have more business to be here than these two bozos."

"I don't know how you're going to take this, but both of these people are ghosts." She pointed to each in turn. "This really is Felipe and Sister Marguerite."

"Now I know you've been smoking some of that island weed! These are a couple of actors. You knew I was coming because of me trying to get in the other gate, so you snuck out here and are setting me up for some stupid practical joke." He snapped his fingers. "*Gotcha.* This is a *Gotcha* set-up. Well, it's not going to work doll, not on me, not tonight, not ever."

"I knew you wouldn't believe me. Just a waste of my time." Fara shrugged him off and turned to Sister Marguerite. "Can you take Felipe inside with you?"

The white head drifted side to side slowly. "No, I told you, I'm the only one."

"I can't go in. Not even tonight. I've been trying for hours. I have to get Vivian out of there." Gritting his teeth, the intense frustration curled within Felipe's deep voice. He leaned closer to whisper in Fara's ear. "Have you seen her?"

"Yes, I have." Shoving her hand into her hip pocket, she pulled out Franz's security cards. The second one released the gate. After the next sweep of the light, she grabbed Felipe's hand and bolted into the fort. One moment Felipe was there, the next her hand was coldly empty.

"What the fuck?" Rob shouted from behind her.

With a groan, Fara turned and hurried back to the secluded edge of the driveway. "Shit! Felipe, where are you?"

Foggy ether started to take shape in front of them, not far from Rob's car. At first glance, it looked like steam curling from the radiator, but then a corporeal form developed from the condensing mist.

"How are you doing that?" Rob craned his neck skyward searching for cameras. This was some projection. Damn, they were pulling out all the stops to scam him.

"Vivian," drifted from translucent form.

"A real elaborate set up," Rob whispered through a gaping mouth. They even included audio feeds in the grill of his car.

As Felipe developed substance, the handsome face contorted while the body continued to writhe. Wounds opened and then closed, as if the man had to pass through death once more in order to reenter this world.

Rob approached and stuck his hand into the condensing fog. It was cold, cold enough to make his fingers instantly numb. Dropping to his knees, he felt the ground. Even in the dead of night, the stone driveway still held the heat of the day. "How are you doing that?"

"I already told you. He's a ghost." Grabbing the back of his collar, Fara pulled Rob back into the relative safety the wall provided. "If I were Felipe, I'd be pissed if someone kept running their hand through me."

He inhaled sharply. "Why you..."

She put her hand over his mouth, while deadly intent stained her eyes. "Not now. I don't have time for macho bullshit. I've got to get inside with or without Felipe." She faced Sister Marguerite, "We have one more shot before I go it alone. Do you know how to overcome this?"

The older woman shrugged slightly. "Try the ring."

"I already have the ring." Fara replied blankly.

"Not you." Marguerite motioned to the man who had now completely formed, and the tiny woman walked to his side. She brushed back the dark hair that had fallen into his face. His expression was intense, filled with powerful years of waiting just to be denied once again. "Give it to Felipe."

Fara nodded, and after giving Rob a sideways glance, released him. At first, he planned on verbally berating her for disrespecting him, but the anguish in Felipe's expression was real. Rob looked at the hand he passed into the foggy form. It still was a little numb. Suddenly, the delicious steak he had for dinner rumbled near the top of his stomach. This was fucking real.

Slipping off the necklace, Fara pulled the ring from the chain and held the emerald in the palm of her hand, extending it to Felipe.

It was the largest green rock Rob had ever seen outside of a museum. The stone glistened, reflecting the light of the street lamp across the gem's facets. For a moment, he didn't think Felipe was going to take it. The man just stared at the ring and then a tear fell down his cheek. He never cared much for men showing weakness, but this was different. The way Felipe looked at the ring was reverent. Now filled with tears, those dark eyes gazed at Fara as he slid the ring onto his finger. Instantly a hum encased them, drowning out the rush of the surf.

Squeezing the dog tags for just a second, Fara took a cleansing breath and then pulled the chain back over her head, tucking them safely inside of her shirt. Swallowing hard, she looked straight at Rob with a blazing glare. "Now do you believe me?"

"I ... I don't know what to believe." He was amazed the words passed through the dry lump in his throat.

"If you really want to go inside, I can use a diversion. They're not expecting you, so it will throw off their plans, perhaps long enough for me to grab J.C." She cast her eyes over Felipe who was staring wistfully at the gate. "Long enough to grab J.C. and Vivian. Rob, you can go waltzing in, claiming to be here for whatever reason you had to come tonight. Keep the search light on you, giving me enough time to run along the inner part of the wall rather than over the top. I don't want to have to repeat that stunt if I don't have to. Just don't mention me." She snapped her fingers in front of Rob's face. "You haven't seen anyone recently have you? Fernando Muñoz, Eduardo Calderon, J.C.?"

Rob just stared at her.

Fara huffed, "Are you even listening?"

"Yeah doll, I heard you. I create a diversion. I haven't seen you, and no, I haven't been anywhere near anyone."

"Whatever you do Rob, don't mention seeing me." She grabbed Felipe's hand. "Come-on, let's try this again."

"Wait!" Sister Marguerite laid a cool hand on Fara's shoulder. "Although I can't transport you inside, I can help. Follow the northern wall to the end of the parade grounds. There's an outer building. About ten feet southwest, you'll find a trapdoor. I'll open it for you and then guide you to the dungeon. That's where they are at the moment."

Fara briefly nodded before taking off at a full run, hand-in-hand with Felipe. They broke the plane of the gate, and the air rumbled, fueling a burst of energy. The concussion from the invisible explosion was just as violent as a blast from dynamite yet didn't make a sound. Knocked off of his feet, Rob watched with amazement while the couple continued running until they disappeared into the dark shadow paralleling the wall.

Gritting his teeth and with his heart beating double time, he walked boldly into the fort and waved his arms, calling out at the top of his lungs for J.C. Butterflies fluttered in his stomach for the first time in dozens of years, and he enjoyed the crazy rush of adrenaline when the spotlight blinded him.

CHAPTER 48

Whenever Fara entered a combat situation, her mind slowed and senses heightened. Methodical steps flowed in logical order. She concentrated on tactical objectives, poised to make instant adjustments while opportunities developed or situations deteriorated. Even during the most desperate of circumstances, she never panicked. So, why was her stomach churning and heart beating so fast?

Focusing on the tangible, she had been in San Cristobal four times, and each occurrence led her to discover new areas, adding definition to her mental recall of the fort's internal structure. Even with her last visit being more bizarre than any of the previous encounters, she gained knowledge and definition of the fort's inner workings and connecting points. But this mission wasn't a simple get in, locate the hostages, and then get out. If she couldn't grab and go, how far was she willing to engage?

Deep down, Fara instinctively knew she would kill if she had to, but she no longer had governmental immunity. Certainly Puerto Rican bureaucrats wouldn't appreciate the stranger than fiction story of an ancient god with perpetuating generations of human servants who bent the will of others through mind control. Jesus, she still had trouble believing it.

She crouched low and ran across the soggy grass, forcing the consequences from her mind. She was going to reach her objective; even though, her plan had changed at the last minute. While in the bath, she decided to retrace her steps from the Caballero and infiltrate the security room. That vantage point provided centralized observation of both internal and external areas and offered the best opportunity to locate J.C. while identifying locations where there were too many guards to infiltrate without killing someone. Now she had a scout, one that was able to appear and disappear at will. Sister Marguerite knew the fortress, including all of the hidden tunnels. Fara wasn't clear on the ghost's boundaries or limitations. Under normal circumstances, she wouldn't have trusted an untried ally, but there was nothing normal about this. Something within her trusted Sister Marguerite on a very internal and basic level, and having help was better than going alone.

When the concussion of the blast shuddered through time and space, Fara had expected Felipe to disappear. Instead of the concussion hurting, it energized her fortitude while she continued to cling to his hand, pulling the dazed man toward the wall. In Afghanistan being against a wall was bad, where automatic weapon fire would cut you in two. But here, it made sense, and she hadn't seen any heavy-duty firepower, at least not yet.

With each stride, the humming tension became tangible. She hoped the ring was generating the sound and not something inside of her head, or worse yet, something inside of the fort. Immediately after the concussion of breaking the ethereal plane and entering Maboya's domain, the normal sounds of the outside world stopped. There was no surf, no wind, no birds, no insects, no nothing, only the constant hum. Even the sound of her own breathing was muted, hidden or absorbed by the power that held dominion here. That same power is what kept poor Felipe and Vivian forever apart. They were parts of the puzzle which had to be solved before any of them would be able to leave.

Fara heard a sound. She gave Felipe the signal to stop, but he either didn't see her or didn't know what holding a fist in the air meant. With his next step, he ran clean into her. Swallowing the grunt from the impact, she glanced back. They had covered more ground than she estimated.

A shout had broken the humming bubble. The voice wasn't clear enough to determine the source. The spotlight was fixed on Rob, and three men were running across the parade grounds toward him. No other movement was perceptible, ahead or behind. She put her lips directly against Felipe's ear, but before she whispered, she absently inhaled his masculine scent of the sea and earth. His being here wasn't supernatural. His presence was as natural as the perpetual motion of the waves that had to be churning on the other side of the wall. "You need to watch me. Do what I do."

"I have to find Vivian." His voice was hoarse, choked with emotion.

"We stick together. Better our odds." The need to keep moving churned within her breast, so she took a deep breath and let it out slowly to reduce the mounting stress. She couldn't keep forcing Felipe forward and needed his willing cooperation. "I will not leave here without your wife."

As if he understood more than just the simple words could convey, his dark head nodded. "And your man, J.C."

Her man? Dear God that was it, why this was so much more complicated than other missions. She had lost her emotional detachment. What would she do if he was already Maboya's pawn? Squeezing the thought from her mind, she whispered, "We will get them both out, I promise."

She didn't wait for an answer and this time trusted Felipe to follow without holding onto him. Again, her body crouched low to the ground. She inhaled in time with the steps, counting as she often did to keep her mind in neutral.

Again, optimism slipped into her when she saw the dark outline of the storage building. Rob had given her enough time to meet their first objective. When she first saw him at the gate, she experienced the sinking fear Eduardo or Fernando had gotten to him first, but the distraction was bold. If she was lucky, maybe they had five minutes until Rob fell under their control and talked. A lot could happen in five minutes.

Darker than just dark, the night was devoid of light, as if whatever power controlled Abib's New Moon absorbed all of the power held within the heavens. Following the structure, her hand skimmed along the smooth stones, which she had treated as a balance beam a few hours earlier. Just as the Sister described, the domed storage building loomed on the edge of the inner grounds; oddly, Fara hadn't even noticed it earlier.

Determining southwest was a challenge. Fara's inner compass was usually reliable, but tonight her innate ability felt off kilter. Even if she had an actual compass in hand, she doubted it would read true. The Devil's Triangle was infamous for magnetic disturbances, and the southern point of the abnormality landed squarely on San Cristobal hill. Perhaps whatever happened here centuries ago caused the rift initially, flooding the northern Caribbean Sea with the anomaly.

Pushing the unproductive thought from her mind, Fara pressed her back to the large hut and concentrated. She should be facing west. Turning a few degrees to the left, she walked ten steps and dropped to her knees, ignoring the warm mush while her fingers spread through the tangled grass. The turf was shaggy and dense, growing into a thick groundcover over swampy dirt. About a foot and a half to her left, a dull suckling sound lifted through the turf, leading her to the spot where Sister Marguerite tried to open the hatch. The grassy carpet barely gave under the pressure. This turf wasn't regular grass with single blades, oh no; it had to be the most interwoven tangle of devilish tendrils.

Felipe bent close. "Hurry, they're leading him this way."

In time with the sloshing rises, Fara wedged her fingertips under an exposed edge and strained, focusing every ounce of strength and determination. Through the now minute wedge, there was a glow, an illumination of pure light, celestial, and divine.

"Fara…" Felipe hissed. "Hurry."

"Shit, take the edge." Once his fingers replaced hers, she jerked out the knife and sawed through the tangle of roots and grassy vines. Even once she freed three sides, the turf was heavy and refused to release the buried hinges.

Fara and Felipe pulled together with a force of will not to be denied and lifted the wooden square back as far as it could possibly go. With a knee, he braced it open. "Go, go."

Lying on her stomach, she wriggled backwards into the small opening, which even at its widest would have been a tight squeeze. Crunching into a pike position, she bent her body toward the wall and found rungs, which groaned their complaint of having to support weight after years of abandonment. With a final wiggle, she eased her chest and then the Browning through the hatch. After her head ducked below ground level, she switched on the halogen penlight clenched in her teeth and saw the curved top of the old and heavily rusted metal ladder. If any of Maboya's supplicants knew this hatch existed, they wouldn't consider checking it. Certainly, it hadn't been used since World War II.

Supporting herself with a single arm hooked around a rung, she held the hatch while Felipe worked his way to join her. Once in corporeal form, he apparently didn't have the ability to disappear at will. Thank God, he wasn't a larger man. That too gave Fara a moment's blessing. Even if the guards did think of checking the hatch, no one larger than Fara or Felipe would be able to fit through the opening. The men would have to go around, wherever that may be, which bought them more time.

Once inside, the hatch closed with a sloshing complaint. Instantly sparkling with the same energy that had welcomed the displaced souls in the cemetery, Sister Marguerite waited just as patiently at the base of the ladder. The illumination made their descent down the twenty-three rungs much easier, and once on solid footing, they followed the Sister lower still, down a straight staircase into the true bowels of San Cristobal. With each step, the stale air became heavier and damper, carrying a lingering fetid decay. The putrid scent was all around them, clinging to Fara's clothes and her hair. The musty heaviness made the narrow walls feel that much closer, but still they continued their steep descent. For only a moment, Fara worried the scent was methane, but she continued. She didn't have a choice. There was no going back.

The small landing at the bottom of the staircase wasn't designed for three to stand side by side. They faced a single door, and Fara motioned to Sister Marguerite to check out the other side.

Felipe physically pushed past the women and threw open the latch. "I take the lead."

Instantly, Fara shushed him. Silence was their friend, and there wasn't time for macho bullshit. She didn't know how much he had gleaned over the years as a ghost, but once they got out of here, she was damn well going to give Felipe a lesson about the feminine revolution. Not now. They didn't have the time. Maybe, two minutes remained, three tops before Rob talked.

The stench definitely originated in the room behind the door, but what was rotting wasn't apparent. Even with the Sister's celestial glow illuminating the open space, Fara waved the penlight down the walls and into corners before moving inside and latching the door behind them. The room was huge and barren except for something large and shiny set into the stone floor. After ensuring they were alone, the thin beam reflected off an irregularly shaped metal tub recessed into the masonry. Despite the ever present moisture and countless years of neglect, the brass or bronze was a brilliant golden color. Fara knew the copper content would oxidize into a greenish sheen. But what other metal could this be? Certainly the vat wasn't made of gold. The tub was about ten feet across and four feet deep with an irregular circumference of roughly beaten edges. It would have taken hundreds of pounds to create something of this size, even for just an overlay. A few feet further, there was another, almost identical to the first, but the irregularities in the not quite circular shape were even more pronounced. Whatever these were used for, they were certainly made by hand, hammered a long time ago. She guessed this was some sort of bath, but there was no identifiable source of water or drain for that matter.

Perhaps the odd insecurity coursing through her came from the room being so large and open. The vulnerability increased with the sense of being watched. Unsettled, she conducted another sweep and worked her way gingerly across the room. Perhaps the odor was truly gas, and it was eating away at her rational mind. The putrescence certainly was causing her eyes to water. Nothing else was in this room, only the two glistening metal tubs set into the floor. The walls weren't oozing. The arched ceiling was intact. Fara didn't have a clue where the stench was coming from, but at this point, it didn't matter. She pulled up her shirt and breathed through the fabric, ignoring the burn inside of her throat. Felipe gave her a side-long stare but didn't say anything about exposing her midriff and bra.

At the opposite end of the room was a narrow corridor, and she darted inside before Felipe could assert his machismo. Each step she took only added to the tension, increasing her unease. The scent of rotting flesh was lessening, but she felt the burdensome weight of San Cristobal filling her inner ears. They were deeper than she had gone earlier, even lower than the dungeon.

The floor was flagstone, or perhaps slate, and sloped at a minor degree. Even with the durable tread, her running shoes skidded on the slick surface, and she caught herself with a hand on each wall. After nearly falling twice, she walked her hands along with her, bracing her steps. The walls kept getting closer, and it wasn't just her perception. The dimensions were physically getting smaller and darker. Not that her flashlight was dimming. No, the darkness was sturdier, more resistant to the light. Even the heavenly glow from Sister Marguerite couldn't penetrate this blackness more than a few feet.

Fara stooped even lower than when she was running along the perimeter wall, and still her scarred back brushed the ceiling. The rugged stone construction was nothing like the smoothly fitted blocks of the superstructure. These stones had been gathered, not hewn, and stacked with mud-like mastic mixed with smaller stones to form primitive cement. Apparently whoever crafted this didn't have many tools but made up for it with ingenuity and good old-fashioned geometry.

The trio continued downward, and the ominous pressure increased. Finally, the light penetrated the final few feet of the tight shaft. At the end, the corridor narrowed even more to a small door, about half the size of a regular doorway, yet at least twice the size of the hatch in the grass. The once sturdy wood was splintered, with a latch fashioned from a piece of brittle wood that fell into a wooden trough permanently set into the knobby masonry. At one time, there was a handle, something small and flexible like a leather thong which had deteriorated a very long time ago.

She lightly touched the not quite round hole in the bar. Since she abdicated Felipe's ring, she hadn't received vibrant images of the past, and right now, she was grateful. Even without the ring, her senses perceived something not quite right.

"Wait," Felipe whispered. "Let me go first."

Sister Marguerite disappeared.

With a contemptuous glance aimed at Felipe, Fara pressed a finger to her lips. He had no idea she had more combat experience than he did. Even if he had fought pirates on the high seas, she had killed more men, but that wasn't something to brag about. It was a total she wanted to forget. Each life she took had stained her soul.

Sister Marguerite manifested inside the shaft only a heartbeat before the door quaked with a sharp impact.

"Holy shit!" Fara jumped backwards, landing against Felipe, and they both fell back as far as the cramped space allowed.

Even mostly rotten, the door was still thick, with broad, horizontal V-shaped hinges that crossed every board. Still, the thin metal blade cleanly cleaved through the upper boards, extending nearly a foot through the wood. The silver blade shone, glistening in the meager light. To account for the lift and descent of penetration, the blade would have to be not only curved but also have a handle, something long, like a scythe.

The blade retracted and hit again. This time lower, snapping through the latch like a toothpick. The concussion rang through the narrow corridor. Along with the zing of the curved blade humming from the impact with the hinge, Felipe's ring joined in the chorus. The emerald's glow permeated the tight space, filling it with green light.

Hissing as if acid splashed the metal, the blade reacted and withdrew. Simultaneously whatever was on the other side of the door yelped, then unnatural silence saturated the space, but Fara knew better than to move. She felt it there, waiting on the other side of the splintered wood.

A rushed and hoarsened breath snorted through the now gaping crack in the door, sniffing at them like a bloodhound, in multiple short inhalations for each long and pronounced exhalation. Once it had gained their scent, the presence shuffled a step back from the door and started to laugh. The mirth gurgled deep within its throat, growing into a guttural chortle until even the door rumbled with the vibration. Within the rumbling blew in a single word, "Fara."

The creature's breath reacted with the stones. She hoped it was just imagination, yet serious condensation started to build. Tar-like ooze continued until it was seeping out of the rocks, filling the recesses between the stones before gaining enough substance to flow. Stench surrounded them with a heavy sulfurous reek.

Glancing up the shaft, ooze covered the floor, eliminating the option of retreat. Pushing up to a crouched position, she warily regarded the door. If the hinges didn't give under the demon's scythe, certainly they wouldn't be able to force them open.

The pitch flowed down the wall and over their legs. She expected it to be moist and heavy, for that was certainly how it smelt. Her fingers ran through the substance, but it didn't really have any. She stared at her fingers and skimmed them over each other tactilely, trying to feel what wasn't there. More like air than even fog, the pitch was the embodiment of darkness.

"Was that Maboya?" Fara whispered to the Sister.

The white head nodded. "Maboya changes form, but you already knew that. Trust your instincts, not your eyes."

Her mind ran through the possibilities with associated probabilities for success. She lifted her shirt again, but it did nothing to lessen the stink. "Can it harm you?"

"It can absorb my power to become stronger, leaving me bound to this place."

"Like Vivian?" Felipe leaned forward, balancing himself with a hand on Fara's back.

Her scarred flesh crawled. God, she hated that. Grating her attention back from worthless self-pity, a scraping started, faintly but quickly grew. Her teeth gritted, clenching against the sound. She remembered her fifth grade teacher who would run a single fingernail down a chalkboard to get the class' attention, but this was even deeper and longer. Instead of gaining in intensity, the screeching retreated until only a faint echo remained. The sound finally faded completely, and uneasy silence grew once more. The walls stopped oozing, but still there was no going back. Instead of feeling trapped, Fara's senses lightened. The tunnel led up to the dungeon. She patted her pocket full of security cards and would deal with the gate when the time came.

It only took one glance, and a moment later the Sister's ethereal glow coursed through the cracks in the wood. "Clear." She whispered.

Squatting in a very awkward position, Felipe lowered his shoulder. With one broad hit, the splintered boards fell away; however, the rusted hinges endured, as they would for at least another hundred years.

The opening was larger, but jagged and still much too small. Bracing her foot against the wall, Fara broke off the next board with a punch from the heel of her hand. For a time, she had forgotten about the cuts. Even though it hurt like a son-of-a-bitch, she still squeezed off a smile at Felipe and then wiggled through the space between the hinges and into the tunnel. For the first time in what seemed like hours, she took a deep breath. Not that the air was any better, yet being out of that confined space was both physically and mentally liberating.

The transitory moment of triumph was short lived. The tunnel was more than just dark, filled with the same black fog shifting tangibly. Fara jostled the penlight and then held it up to her face. It was on and just as bright as earlier, but the paltry glow barely extended an inch or two.

Silence laid just as heavily as the darkness. Fara had admonished Felipe too many times for speaking, but now she needed reassurance someone else was there and extended her hands, circling in each direction. "I can't see a damned thing. Are you there?"

A bubble of light grew within the otherwise impenetrable darkness. In the center of the glittering orb, Sister Marguerite stood with her hands outstretched. Intense concentration lined her otherwise flawless complexion. Even with the Sister's illumination, Fara couldn't discern which way led up toward San Cristobal, but then she saw it. Squatting next to the ragged line, her fingertips lightly touched the divot in the stone, easily a half-inch deep. Casting her penlight along the marred surface, the scratch flowed like a ribbon into the unending shadows. The creature left a trail, which meant he wanted her to follow.

She removed the Browning and clicked off the safety. Feeling the weight of the two pound gun, she wrapped the palm of her left hand under her right, not wanting to take a chance her grip might falter. Even with the pistol safely tucked in her hands, unease gnawed in her gut. She held her breath while a tingle climbed her spine. Something wasn't right. The air around her suddenly felt even heavier, and a chill clung to the churning mist. Something was there, manifesting behind them in the ethereal mist.

Spinning around, Fara saw a glow of misty eyes taking shape within the recesses of the tunnel. The gray contrasted against the black nothing, but only slightly, as if whatever was there wanted to remain hidden. The figure didn't approach or withdraw. The darkness swirled around those two fixed orbs like dark matter being pulled into a dying star.

CHAPTER 49

The sharp metallic screech echoed through the enclosed space. The sound vibrated down the tunnel, amplifying its chilling effect. Immobilized, J.C. stared through the gate. Something was there in the darkness. If his grandfather hadn't been standing with a hand on his shoulder, he would have run before the echo subsided. Eduardo squeezed his shoulder reassuringly, but the gesture didn't make him feel any better. Despite the words circling in his head that everything was going to be alright, the churning in the pit of his stomach told him otherwise.

The scraping stopped within a few feet of the gate. Inside the pregnant silence, something hummed. More than really hearing the sound, he felt it. The minor vibration coursed through his body, jiggling into his memories, loosening them, not quite enough to remember, but lurking irritatingly close. He clenched and released his fists alongside his thighs. His hands gripped so tightly that the edges of his roughly chewed nails bit into his palms.

Humming had something to do with Fara. Regardless of how scrambled his thoughts were, he remembered Fara. God, she was beautiful with flowing hair and those dazzling emerald eyes. The emerald. His eyes flew across the room and landed squarely upon his grandfather who had approached the electronic lock. His left hand extended toward the darkness. Holding it out like a shield, the green glow hummed, keeping the edge of the darkness at bay.

Using his other hand, Eduardo pulled the retractable key chain away from his belt and swiped the security card down the side of the lock. While he punched the code, J.C. started to back up while keeping his eyes fixed upon the gate. Something shifted inside the tunnel. The form was blacker than its surroundings, a bruise on the skin of the night. A sharp scent rolled out like an invisible fog, heavy and sulfurous, catching in his nostrils. Approaching out of the fog, red eyes grew into giant orbs like exploding stars against the spatial void.

Still with the ring outstretched toward the interior of the tunnel, Eduardo grasped one side of the gate and then the other, swinging each wide. His deep voice resonated odd words. The rhythmic tone repeated, and then echoed again, over and over, generating its own humming. It wasn't English and definitely not Spanish. Still, somehow, J.C. knew the words. He had heard them a long time ago. He listened. It was his grandfather's voice, and then at the same time, it wasn't.

With each chorus, J.C. shuffled another step back until he encountered the wall. The firm stones gave him a point of reference, some semblance of normalcy while trapped within this nightmarish subsistence. Inside of his head, up and down were relative terms, but now actually feeling something solid, his mind grasped onto that tidbit of reality. The stairs were to his right. The other men were up one flight. Rob had joined them just before he and his grandfather came downstairs to... to... J.C. struggled. He knew, but instead of the recollection being blocked, he didn't want to acknowledge the truth. He didn't have to. Ten feet of truth walked through the gate on two cloven hooves.

Like a feral animal issuing a warning, a guttural growl resonated. The ring upon his grandfather's pinky finger glowed with power, and Maboya bowed his broad head. Approaching as cautiously as a zoo keeper would a grizzly bear, Eduardo fastened a shackle around the beast's neck and then snapped the chain, proving its strength. Even during the creature's subjugation, those hot eyes never left J.C.

Inside, numbness froze him into a state of immobility, yet the sudden shock of seeing his worst nightmare lifted the dark cowl from his veiled memories. When he was six, he met the demon. After the encounter, J.C.'s nightmares flowed in chants with words he didn't understand. Even in dream, shadows choked the air, surrounding him with the rancid scent of the underworld. Awakening in a cold sweat, he sought comfort from his grandfather who would be beside him and stare deeply into his eyes, speaking the same strange words over and over again. Only once they bubbled along J.C.'s unwitting lips, his grandfather clapped his hands, masking the memory.

Now open, his memories flowed, called forth from their obscure mental recesses. Suddenly he was fifteen, he and Andres were running, lost in the twisting corridors. Having to double back, they missed the connection and emerged into the tunnel. They were in the lowest recesses of the fort, where the oldest tunnel flowed into the earth. From those subterranean depths, they heard steps clopping with the impact of hooves rather than boots or shoes. They ran. The something stalked them, step for step, lingering in the dark to conceal its true form. But it was there. They heard long snorting breaths following them. They found the staircase and then passed through the dungeon. A beautiful light appeared. The silvery white orb led them through the maze and back up to the security entrance, but the creature was there, anticipating them.

"That stone is weak." The bull head turned its heavy glare upon Eduardo.

Jumping back to the present, J.C. blinked. The demon's voice was just as sharp and eerily arcane as he remembered.

Eduardo tugged the chain once more to prove its strength. "Strong enough, and soon I shall recover the other. With both stones, you shall bend fully to our control."

The beast's rumbling chuckle resonated with all of the entrenched contempt from prolonged captivity. Turning with two lunging steps, the demon suddenly stood before J.C., nearly touching but not quite. The head bowed, almost impaling J.C. upon the twisted horns, and using its great snout, inhaled his scent. The muzzle sneered, not in a grimace, rather savoring the moment. Saliva flowed, drooling thick white slaver from the broad sides of its jaws. Its pointed tongue slipped over jagged teeth and lapped the moisture from the jowls to taste the scent collected there.

It was exactly the same as that fateful night with Andres. While his friend was fighting to release the outer door, Maboya approached J.C., just as close with its hot breath reeking of rotting flesh. Pinning him between its horns, the demon's long tongue extended, nearly wrapping around J.C.'s leg, sliding upward, scraping the flesh with cat-like roughness. Only once it had scraped every drop of perspiration from his flesh, the tip slid inside the legs of J.C.'s baggy shorts to prod his genitalia, obscenely hefting the weight.

J.C.'s hands opened and closed. Just like that night fifteen years ago, his fisted hand rose of its own accord and bashed the creature just below its ear. This time though, Andres hadn't busted out the security glass in the door and released the lock from the other side, giving J.C. opportunity to escape. This time, he had nowhere to go.

Maboya took the blow and didn't react negatively. Rather, what could be surmised as a smile creased the foul snout. "I let you go before because you were not complete. Now you are a man. I have your scent and hers. Your skin reeks of your mate, yet she has another man's essence upon her skin." The chortle resonated through the confined space even after Eduardo yanked the chain, making Maboya's back-hinged knees stumble a half-step.

Instantly, its mirth changed. The beast turned upon its master.

CHAPTER 50

Within a single echo of a heart-wrenching sob, the misty eyes faded, retreating into the tumbling darkness, but Sister Marguerite was faster. The spirit grabbed the girl before she could disappear into the void and held her firmly. Illuminated by the celestial light, Vivian appeared nothing like her former self. Shaking sobs raked through the emaciated form whose torn rags barely covered the abuses of her worn flesh.

"Vivian?" Even standing next to the man, Fara could barely hear Felipe's heavy whisper, yet the girl's weary head perked and turned the full brunt of those lost eyes upon him.

"Go away. Don't look upon me." Another shadowy sob choked the words. "I belong to the beast."

"Oh dear God Vivian, it is you." Felipe rushed forward, embracing both ghosts in his sturdy arms. "It's been so long. I've searched and waited. I never gave up hope of finding you." He turned Vivian to face him, and his eyes unleashed tears that had waited for centuries. "You are my wife and belonged to me before that beast laid any claim."

The *belonged to me* part rankled Fara, but she kept her feminist sarcasm to herself. Their love had been so strong it survived death, who was she to judge. A thin slice of remorse slipped through her, and melancholy etched her happiness. She stepped back, physically and emotionally, retreating a safe distance as to not contaminate their reunion with her solitary bitterness.

Felipe's large hands rounded Vivian's face, holding her firmly while kissing her forehead and cheeks, chin, and then lips. The large emerald on his finger hummed, filling the space with power, from which the darkness retreated. Binding her in his arms, he cried with deep choking breaths. "Oh my God, oh my dear, dear God. Thank you for finding it in your grace to deliver us back to one another once again."

Silently, yet vibrantly, the light from Sister Marguerite grew, and upon the completion of Felipe's fervent prayer, the force of the emerald and the heavenly light combined, flowing with intertwining tendrils of energy. The pearlescent and jade curled into ringlets, encasing the couple within the braided strands. As the reunited lips met, the pure white light and the green enchantment combined, exploding with divine ignition.

The unexpected concussion flung the Browning out of Fara's hands. This wasn't the first time an explosion knocked her from her feet. She prepared for the impact, planning to expend the force with a slap or a tuck and roll, but she didn't hit the wall or the stone floor.

The blast knocked the air out of her lungs, and she struggled for breath. But, there was no air. A void of nothing surrounded her, enveloped her in darkness. Trapped, she struggled, kicking and punching. Regardless of how precisely delivered were her well-practiced blows, there was nothing tangible to hit. Nothing to fight. No air to breathe. The pressure within her head grew, aching for oxygen, and then even that need faltered, along with the strength in her burning muscles. The pain melted, yet she still wouldn't yield. Flashes of her former entrapment blindly wrapped around the mental bindings, yet she refused to succumb to the blackness. The enmity closed around her, squeezing with the force of a giant snake. The new pressure caused new pain, bruising and then crushing. She was losing the battle, losing her strength. Her mind faded. One final thought trembled, a silent prayer for J.C. to survive this endless night.

Time was lost to the darkness; what felt like minutes might have been hours. Fara realized she was breathing. Real air coursed in and out of her lungs in steady sweeps. Instead of moving or groaning from the plentiful aches, she laid motionless. It was so hard not to open her eyes. Every impulse told her to open them, but playing possum gave her an advantage.

Assessing her body internally, nothing hurt any more than it did before, with the exception of a ferocious headache. Her hands or ankles didn't suffer from any biting tightness or undue weight, and her mouth was moist, definitely not gagged. She was on a hard and rough surface. Something poked her in the back. Even through the scarred flesh, it bit sharp and hard.

In the next breath, she inhaled the scent of open flames, not sweet like candles, rather fingers of oily smoke twisted through the air. She listened, tuning her ears to hear the separate crackles of each flame. Localizing the sounds, there had to be at least two torches per wall. Each was equally as loud, pretty equidistant, which would mean she was in the center of the room.

A humming started close to her head, four maybe five feet away. She didn't need to see the gem or its greenish light to know the emerald was calling. Humming in the same key, audible voices joined, using the sound as a chorus would use a tuning fork. Carried on the edge of the hum, chanting started.

Fara fought the reaction to move, to jump up and engage the enemy. She would increase her odds of survival by taking a few more breaths, regaining her strength.

There was a voice. One she recognized but couldn't immediately place. He was behind her. That same man had her ring and started the chant. Other masculine voices repeated the call. The differences between the voices were minimal, but even when raised as one, she noted the subtleties. Seven men surrounded her.

The chant rose fervently, and she opened the eye closest to the table which her hair partially covered, imperceptibly peeking through dark lashes. Although she only saw a mere slit of the overall room, the sight validated her former perceptions and added one significant realization. She was in the dungeon.

The vibrations resonated in the thick boards of the wooden table. She blocked the rising visions of what had happened in this very spot over hundreds of years. Still, her blood ran cold as if the souls of the consumed dead touched her with their final breaths. Forcing the thought out of her mind wasn't easy, but she focused. She had to stay sharp to avoid their fate.

Only one of the hooded figures was in her limited line of sight. His head bowed toward her, the hood completely obscuring any recognizable features except for the masculine chin covered in dark stubble. Fara didn't recognize the pronounced dimple.

The odd hardness continued to dig in the sweep of her back. Outside of her control, her pulse leapt, visibly beating within her throat. Jesus! They hadn't frisked her. Perhaps the knife was still in the ankle holster too.

Taking two deeper breaths, she charged her body with much needed oxygen. Leaping to her feet, Fara grabbed the gun from her back. The smooth movement was sudden enough to hide how she palmed the small gun.

None of the men moved or acknowledged her in any way. The only man whose face was not covered in a white ceremonial robe was Rob. He stood outside of the circle in the corner of the room. He looked drugged, staring forward and seeing nothing. His chest rose with a ragged breath. Before she could ascertain more, the chanting stopped. The man at the foot of the table pulled back his hood, and the dark upon dark eyes of Fernando Muñoz glared upon her. "Welcome Dalal, we have been awaiting you."

The chanting rhythm changed, combining the names. Maboya and Dalal. Dalal and Maboya. Back and forth, the names twisted and at times combined.

Dalal was a word Fara recognized. In Arabic, it meant a seductress who bewitched men and lured them to their deaths, similar to a siren, but Dalal could work her magic on the land as well as at sea. She was a temptress who drove men mad with passion and made them forget their holiest of vows, damning them with sinful pleasure. When a man ejaculated inside the Dalal, she would consume more than just his semen. Dalal absorbed his soul. In Afghanistan, Fara's captors called her Dalal instead of her name, which helped them intertwine her existence with the crimes they had accused her of committing. She didn't buy it then, and she certainly didn't subscribe to it now.

Circling atop the table, Fara turned step-over-step, assessing the enemy's strength. Still, the men did nothing. No one advanced. No hands reached out. She stared at the robed figures, wondering which one was Eduardo Calderon, the keeper of Maboya. If she restrained him, she would stabilize the situation.

Suddenly the men's hands clapped, punctuating the chanting names. Maboya, clap. Dalal, clap. Maboya, clap. The process went on, picking up speed as the men started to turn, rotating around the table in a counter-clockwise spin. Instead of turning with them, her eyes remained fixed upon a single point. As the men passed her, she noted their hands. Each wore a bulky silver ring, which matched the one she noticed on Eduardo Calderon and Fernando Muñoz. Thinking back, even Franz Gomez had one of these matching signs of their indentured brotherhood.

The fifth man rotated in front of her and clapped his hands. A glint of green sparked on his pinky finger. Fara's palm started to sweat around the gun still hidden in her hand. One quick shot and it would be over. Eduardo's hold onto these other men would break; the mass hypnosis brought to an end. But if she killed Eduardo, J.C. would never forgive her. She would save him and lose him in the same stroke. Each of these men had families, someone to care for and who relied upon them. She didn't need any more blood on her hands. There had to be another way.

In a leap that was beyond human, Fernando Muñoz jumped onto the table. Flinging his robe off in a crossed sweep of his arms, he stood before her in full glory of his natural element.

"Dalal, finally you are mine, for all eternity." The former harmonic discord layered in his voice was gone. Only a single voice spoke, filled with energy and certainty.

Her mind slowed, focusing on his areas of vulnerability. A quick blow to the throat and then a knee to his groin would incapacitate him for at least sixty seconds. But what would she do then? Escape? Hell, she'd already done that once and came back.

She thrust out her chin defiantly. "I belong to no man."

The creature's chuckle arose, so profoundly deep, that the force rippled through Fernando's washboard abs. It also affected other parts of his anatomy, making the horse cock hanging between his legs rise firmly. "I am not a man. I am Maboya."

"I am not Dalal. I am a woman." With another quick sweep of her eyes, Fara searched but didn't relocate the man who had the emerald. Shit! "I don't know why you would want me. You need a goddess, someone who wouldn't leech your power but add her own to make you even stronger."

"Wisdom, but not truth, speaks from your lips." Fernando's intense gaze penetrated her emotional shield and made her visibly tremble. "You, my dear Dalal, are a goddess, the daughter of Astaroth and Megaera Alecto, born from the land of our ancestors. I've awaited your coming for centuries, and tonight, Abib's New Moon marks the change in tide. We shall dominate the world."

Fara laughed, turning slightly to expand the area within her peripheral vision. "We're going to dominate the world from Puerto Rico?"

The dark features furled. "Do not mock me."

"I'm not mocking you. I'm just being practical." There, she located a twinkle gleaming like a tiny green beacon at the head of the table once more. "And I appreciate your interest. I do." She sidled closer with her eyes gleaming. "I've been a lot of things to a man, but a goddess hasn't been one of-"

Using the heel of the gun, she struck Fernando in the throat and followed with a kick squarely to his erection. He stumbled off the edge of the table but landed on his feet; instantly, the dark eyes blazed red. With a twist, she cartwheeled across the table and rounded off outside of the circle, directly behind Eduardo. She pressed the gun tightly to his ribs while yanking off the hood, grasping a handful of hair in the process. The man's head yanked back with the force, exposing his neck for a deathblow.

"J.C.?" Fara chilled. Using the last bit of breath in her lungs, she mumbled, "Shit, J.C. What have they done to you?"

Releasing her grip, he straightened, staring at her blankly. "I am Maboya's keeper."

Pain and anger combined. The vibrant energy churned, unleashing her wrath. "What have you done to him?"

"J.C. fulfilled his destiny and replaced his grandfather as my keeper." The naked man pointed toward Rob, who was shackled to the wall. A flash of recognition flared in Rob's eyes. Near the his feet lay a prone figure. Eduardo Calderon couldn't have been dead for long, for his skin was just now turning ashen.

Fara hauled back and slapped J.C. squarely across the face. "Wake-up." She hit him again, "Snap out of it."

With as much feeling as a cold android, J.C. turned his eyes toward her. They were no longer warm chocolate pools. The color had changed to near black, rimmed with red around the pupil. When she swung for a third time, J.C. intercepted her wrist, squeezing with a strength that was not human. "You belong to Maboya."

"Fuck! Don't do this. J.C.!" Fara twisted, but his grasp was superhuman. In her other hand, the gun weighed heavily. If he had been any other person, she would have pulled the trigger, but she couldn't shoot him. Her weakening resolve echoed into her softening voice. "Don't do this. For the first time in my life..." She shifted her thoughts. It was too late to tell him she loved him. This thing wasn't J.C.

The ring glimmered on his pinky. Palming the short pistol, she hit him squarely in the back of the head. Her heart shattered as he crumpled to the floor, his head barely missing the edge of the table. Instantly, she fell to his side and pulled the ring from his finger. She slid it onto her hand and focused all of her inner force on the ring. The emerald didn't hum; it rang with power.

Barely perceptible over the pervasive ringing, Fara heard laughter. Fernando was back on top of the table and was laughing at her. "You're too late. Abib's New Moon has risen as have I. Come to me Dalal."

J.C.'s chest rose with a breath, a bittersweet fact which gave her some solace. The blow didn't kill him.

Quickly coming back to her senses, Fara hitched a thumb in Eduardo's direction. "That mother-fucker stole my ring. If you hadn't killed him, I would have."

"Eduardo knew it was coming. Blood lust must be fulfilled to join the circle." He pointed to the man whom Fara had seen first, the one with the dimpled chin. He responded to the nonverbal summons and uncloaked. "Just as Andres took the life of his father to assume his role. In his case, the lustful enthusiasm overflowed, and he couldn't stop."

"The taste was so sweet." Andres' face was glazed, blankly devoid of any emotion.

"They no longer control me, rather I now control all of them." Hidden within Fernando, Maboya chuckled again and waved his silver ring over his head. All of the men's robes fell away, leaving them naked and exposed. "Each assumes his place through blood."

Fara pointed at Franz. "How did you get out of my handcuffs?"

A devilish grin beamed from the pox-marked face. "Maboya is strong."

"Tonight Dalal, you join with me, and we join our power as one," Fernando tipped his head toward the shackled man, "and toast our union with blood."

Two of the naked men dragged Rob to the table, eventually fastening the kicking and screaming man into the shackles wedged securely into the wood.

Unnoticed, J.C. had risen, and with Andres, each seized one of Fara's arms, holding her tightly between them. The men dragged her forward until her lower abdomen bumped the table.

Now with the ring on her finger, Fara had no choice; the psychic images flowed through those who had seen their final moments of the living world upon this slab. Thousands of visages. Mostly men, but some were women, and then there she was. The wide-eyed innocence of Vivian pleaded toward Fara, aware and conscious of what was happening. The scythe's silver blade rose. Fara twisted the ring from her own finger and shoved it onto Vivian's.

The world exploded in a titanic burst, throwing everyone from their feet, except Fernando; the man-beast barely staggered. Yet the distraction was enough for Felipe to appear. Raising Vivian to his side, the couple stood on the table encircled in celestial light. Vivian and Felipe's hands joined in glowing harmony, resonating with the power of the reunited rings.

The creature roared and swung the scythe, yet Felipe's resolve was greater and grabbed Maboya's blade, stopping it in midair. The moment the ghost touched the staff, the silver blade glowed with the emeralds' power.

Maboya squealed with shock and pain, releasing the staff. Triumphantly, Felipe extended the scythe overhead, and with one broad and swinging stroke, stabbed the point of the blade through Fernando's heart.

Emerald sparks flew from the wound, like Chinese fireworks gone bad. The ethereal pathway opened, but this time it wasn't pure and shimmering. Gray ashes churned in a vortex of fire.

The creature writhed, distorting the visage between man and beast. Maboya struggled, grasping and clawing to keep hold of this world. His countenance swept through the manifestations he had assumed over his tenure in the physical plane, finally reverting to the original form when the Taínos summoned him from the fracture in the earth. The bullish head bucked and thrashed, horns twisting wildly. The cloven hooves smacked the stone floor with hollow thwacks. Claws scratched the air, struggling to hang onto its dominion. A single pointed nail found purchase in the wooden slab, wedging deeply into a narrow crack between the aged boards. For several long heartbeats, Maboya lingered, hanging between the worlds.

Maniacal screams resonated and then sharpened as the vortex constricted in deep gulps. Like a giant anaconda, the maelstrom tensed and released, consuming Maboya inch upon inch. The creature's shrieks resounded, echoing throughout San Cristobal. Those same shrill echoes distorted in the turbulence, whistling as the vortex tightened to ingest the beast. The swirling tendrils of fire caught Maboya's horns and twisted the neck back. The snout snarled open, revealing hideously yellowed fangs and writhing tongue. Lunging with his final ounce of will, Maboya struggled to find more purchase on the wooden slab than the single claw, scratching deep fissures. Pieces of the table gave way, flying for only a moment before being incinerated to swirling ash. With a final pulse, the vortex lunged, consuming the beast.

The world didn't calm. The vortex expanded once again, sucking all remnants of Maboya from this world. The naked men struggled, grasping onto whatever was closest, yet the power was too strong. Two flew into the mouth of fire; their screams reduced to ash. Then another three twisted against the vibrant suction, fighting for naught, holding onto each other as if that could save them. The day they assumed their place in the circle had sealed their fates.

The vortex swung, and Fara seized Rob's arm just under the shackle. Flakes of ash twisted and burned, singeing her face and hair. As best she could, she shielded Rob's body from the hellfire. She thought of J.C., and her heart skipped. Raising her chin, her face was inches from his own. His body bent toward the vortex. Releasing one arm, Fara caught J.C.'s shoulders just as his grip faltered. Drawing upon all her physical, spiritual, and emotional might, Fara tucked him toward her, wedging his naked body between her and Rob.

In Afghanistan, her consciousness had reverted to a safe place within herself, to a state of self-induced hypnosis, but this was too sudden and too vibrant to prepare. Rancid flames licked Fara's back, incinerating her clothes and blazing over the scars. The fiery tendrils lashed her anew, akin to the Taliban's whips and chains. For a time, the scent of burning flesh overpowered the sulfurous reek. The fire consumed, sucking the putrescence into the bowels of hell.

Her grip slipped. Fara's strength was faltering. Her time had come. Suddenly, her thoughts cleared. Only one thing mattered. Opening her eyes to view the face of her man, she placed the briefest of kisses upon J.C.'s lips and whispered, "I love you."

Her fingers slipped free.

Fara winced, preparing for the instant consumption. Instead of blistering into ash, a cool breeze held her, instantly soothing the searing pain. Encased in a pearlescent bubble, she hovered just above the men whom she had been protecting. The flames flickered over them, drawing out the stains evil had impressed upon their souls. The negative impressions lifted like smoky shrouds. Immediately, the vortex claimed the shadowy imprints and closed, tumbling into and upon itself until only a few flakes of ash drifted listlessly in the quieting air.

Fara's bare feet touched the stone floor, and she realized the rest of her body was just as naked. She tried to speak but only a gruff groan left her throat. She swallowed and whispered hesitantly into the dark stillness, "J.C.? Rob?"

Her heart tightened at the silence.

An orb grew out of the nothing, shining opalescent light across the enclosed yet empty space. Two bodies laid upon the charred wooden surface. They were the only ones left. Every trace of Maboya and his minions were gone, including the body of Eduardo Calderon.

Stumbling on unsure legs, Fara approached the intertwined limbs, as if the men were haphazardly tossed ragdolls. They didn't move, not even to breathe. Tears rose to her dusty eyes, and she didn't try to stop them. The streams flowed down her cheeks, cleaning irregular paths through the sooty residue. Her fingers reached out reluctantly, for she didn't want to verify her greatest fear of being all alone once again.

As if sensing her, J.C. turned toward the anticipatory caress, allowing Fara's fingertips to smooth over his shoulder, toward his face. His hair was charred, the long locks damaged beyond recognition, but his skin wasn't blistered, not marred in the least. His eyes fluttered open, once again the color of melting chocolate. The body beneath his rustled.

EPILOGUE

"...Once so lost and alone, Vivian and Felipe fought against elemental forces and overcame all odds to ascend together into eternity." Fara waited with pleasant anticipation while the camera lens zoomed in for a close up. Perfectly timed, she continued, "I'm Fara Trotter. Thank you for joining me in Puerto Rico. On our next episode, *Ghost Lovers* takes you to Italy where local virgins seek guidance from a skeletal bride. Until then, may love fill your heart with celestial light."

The spectacular Puerto Rican sunset drifted behind the shot, adding definition to the backdrop of Old San Juan. With a hand balanced on the big man's shoulder, J.C. peered over Rex who in turn was looking through the camera.

"And that's a wrap." J.C. smiled across the set at Fara who was still on her mark. "God, you're good on camera."

Ruffling her fingers through her spiked hair, she smiled coyly. "You don't think anyone will think I'm a boy with this close cut do you?"

Rob spoke before J.C. could squeeze out a word. "Doll, if anyone thought you were a boy with that voice, they would be reading subtitles."

J.C. tossed her a golf towel to remove the layers of makeup which kept the sweat from shining on camera. "It's not just the way you talk. It's the whole package. You got it going on girlfriend."

"Is she you're girlfriend?" Rex stood and stretched his back, leaning a little to the left to switch off the camera.

J.C. slapped the big man on the shoulder with a resounding whack. "Por cierto, dude, por cierto."

All four lights went off with a pop, leaving Fara temporarily blinded, and she stared in the direction where she heard the men's voices. "What do we do now?"

"Cast party." Rex's deep voice reverberated in the moist air. Fara searched the faces for J.C. but didn't see him. "We're throwing a party? Where? God, not here at the fort."

"Doll, you're invited, but I'm throwing the party." Rob sauntered up to Fara and squeezed her hand. "I've already reserved the pool area at the Intercontinental. We have plenty to celebrate."

Squeezing back, she painfully tightened her grip along with her expression. "Don't ever call me doll again."

"You got it. Anything you say ... Fara." Pulling away, he shook out his hand. "I expect you'll want to shower and change first."

"Something like that." Her vision had cleared and still didn't see J.C. "Yeah, we'll be by."

They completed all of the scenes with the actors on the previous day, so today was all Fara. Intros smoothed into asides then to the conclusion, and she hit each of her lines perfectly. It took longer for the crew to set up the equipment than for her to do her take, which was a good thing. Stories of the fort and the missing men had leveled an unusual mix of anticipation and anxiety. Nerves were tense and higher strung than normal. Now that they were done, she could feel the tension draining along with the fading light of the day.

After receiving accolades from the crew, Fara continued her quest to find J.C. and sauntered around the open equipment cases and spools for electrical cords. Just inside the double doorway, she found him standing in the long hallway of the residential wing. The man didn't turn. He just stared at the other end of the hall.

"You okay?" She approached cautiously.

J.C. hadn't mentioned anything about that night, and even wondered if the fire burned away the associated memories.

"Hell, I don't know." Finally, he looked at her with those glorious chocolate eyes.

"Want to talk about it?"

Uncomfortably, he glanced down the hall. "Not here."

She took his hand and led him into Vivian's bedroom. Strangely comforting, the room felt just like any other, warm and moist, with a slip of a breeze curling through the doorway. The carpet was soft and quieted their footsteps. After leaving J.C. sitting on the edge of the bed, she closed and latched the door to avoid anyone accidentally overhearing their conversation.

"My grandmother called again, wondering if I heard from Abuelo. I don't know what to tell her." With his elbows perched on his knees, he dropped his head into his hands, running his fingers through the equally short haircut until his forehead rested on his palms.

"What do you want to tell her?"

He looked up abruptly. "Shit, I don't know. Fara, I don't remember what happened, but I swear to you I didn't kill him."

"Maboya killed him. He condemned them all." Slowly, as to not jostle the bed, she sat next to him. "You were a victim, J.C. Your grandfather brought this upon himself. You didn't cause any of it, regardless of what happened." The words resonated within her own memories of the shrink saying the exact same thing regarding her abduction and then Jason's death.

"Doesn't make not remembering any easier."

"I know, but maybe it's a blessing. Do you want to remember?"

"Yes and no. I don't think I could live with myself if I actually killed him to ascend to that damned circle."

"Let's look at it another way. Tell me what you do remember."

"I was looking for you. Dear God, I was so worried something had happened to you. I kept seeing Vivian and then had a vision of the Battle of San Cristobal, when the Taínos summoned Maboya. Abuelo brought me down to the gate, and I heard this terrible scraping. It was fucking everywhere. He had your ring and was using it against Maboya, but Vivian's emerald wasn't strong enough to control him."

That sound was something she'd never forget. "Then what?"

"Nothing. It's like a giant nothing inside of my head. The next thing I remember you were touching my shoulder, and I was laying on top of Rob, naked. Now that's something I would like to forget." A brush of cooler evening air slipped past.

Not knowing what to say, she went to the balcony doors and stared out into the night. Sounds of Coqui frogs chirruped and the buzzing of other insects made the air alive, so different than the night of silence. "At least do you think Vivian and Felipe are at rest?"

"I don't think so." His voice sharpened with sudden nerves.

Fara turned, and her heart dropped. Both Vivian and Felipe stood before them, hand in hand. "I hadn't seen any of you since, well since Abib's New Moon. Why haven't you crossed over?"

After placing a kiss upon his knuckles, Vivian released Felipe's hand and glided toward the balcony. She approached so closely, Fara felt the tingles of her ethereal form. The ghost whispered, "We have a favor to ask."

"I'll do whatever I can." Fara also kept her voice soft and low. "Tell me first, do you know what happened to Eduardo Calderon? Did J.C. kill him?"

A line of pain winced across Vivian's eyes, which Fara now realized were as green as her own. The ghost glanced over her shoulder and spoke loudly enough for all to hear. "The beast consumed his keeper when he assumed control. J.C. didn't harm anyone, which is why the portal didn't take him. He never truly ascended to the circle of the damned."

Visibly, J.C.'s shoulders straightened.

Vivian continued, "Even taking a stranger's life leaves a stain, but to kill someone close forms an indelible bond to evil. The hellfire consumed all evil, leaving not a single remnant of Maboya's influence behind. He is gone from this world. The portal closed, for all eternity."

"Thank you." Fara touched the ghost's arm and gently slipped through the opaque but not physical form, the consistency of a heavy fog. "What can I do for you?"

The color in Vivian's cheeks glowed rosily. "You shared so many of our personal moments ... well you must realize then ... Felipe and I ..."

Each word had become softer and softer until Fara had to lean in very close to hear the faint whispers. "Felipe and you, what?"

"Before we leave the physical plane, we want to ..." the ghost averted her eyes, "... to enjoy the pleasures of a married couple."

"Oh," Fara smiled broadly but kept her chuckle at bay. "I understand, but what can I do?"

Holding a quick breath as if she were about to jump into a pool, Vivian suddenly slid inside of Fara's physical body. Instead of feeling cold or even uncomfortable, lovely warmth radiated, energizing Fara's senses until she even shared Vivian's sensual hunger.

A moment later, Vivian slipped back out. "You and J.C. are lovers, are you not? Will you allow us to experience the act of physical love while within your bodies?"

"Yes, we're lovers," after a brief hesitation, she opened her palm toward Vivian and beckoned the ghost to follow her toward the bed. "J.C.?"

"I know that tone your voice gets when you want something. What have you two been whispering about?" His overall countenance glowed with relief.

Standing next to him, Fara still wasn't sure how to broach this new subject. She wasn't into sharing, and this took the concept to a whole new level.

"Vivian and Felipe have asked a favor, and given the situation, I would like to, yet I really want you to be in honest agreement." She hesitated, but then continued in the same melodious tone. "They never consummated their marriage in the physical world and would like to use us as surrogates. It would be similar to when we experienced their petting aboard the Immaculata."

"You were there." Felipe perked incredulously. "How is that possible?"

Fara shrugged, "How is any of this possible?"

J.C. cast a suspicious glance at Fara and then softened. Releasing a long breath, he shrugged. "After everything they've been through, they deserve at least one night."

"We don't have the energy to manifest for an entire night, but we do have enough for once." Vivian extended her hand to

322

Fara. They touched, and the ghost slipped back inside of her body. The wonderful warmth filled Fara's soul.

J.C. stood and took a half-step toward Felipe. "I will remember, right?"

Felipe nodded and shimmered for a moment before sliding into J.C.

"See it's pretty pleasant." Face spoke with an odd ringing resonance of two voices layered into one.

Also in tandem, J.C. and Felipe touched the women. The rosy warmth glowed, and the awkwardness evaporated. Lingering passion, too long denied, took its place. They lifted the united consciousness of the women they loved into their arms and laid the single form ever so gently upon the bed.

Gentle fingers stroked the men's cheek. "It's a big and downy bed Felipe."

"You remembered, even after all of these years." The rolling voice reverberated in the close space.

"All I had were memories to carry me through the darkness." Arching toward him their lips met, and the temporary transformation became complete.

"Now there is only light and love." Felipe's tongue stroked Vivian's mouth, enticing her lips to open, and slid into the inner softness. Just like their first kiss while at the bow of the Immaculata, the lustful surge held only momentary sway before ripening into full-bodied love. Devotion tinged with accumulated longing poured into that single kiss. With a sudden breath, he pulled his lips from hers. "I've experienced an eternity of waiting. Wishing to hold you. Praying to touch you even just once more."

"And I, while lost in the folds of darkness, held onto the hope of being with you once again." She arched up to meet his lips and drew him closer. "My love for you is everlasting, eternally pledged. Make love to me Felipe. Complete what we briefly started that night so very long ago when you held me to you."

"I claimed your virginity without giving you my full interest." His grin twinkled, lighting his entire face. "If I had known what awaited us, I would have made love to you."

"Atop the horse?" She giggled.

His brows arched, "The thought did cross my mind."

"Mine too. But now there's no horse. No one's chasing us. It's just you and me in a gloriously downy bed. Take me Felipe, and let us join."

Even with his need so apparently aroused, he removed each article of clothing meticulously, enjoying the revealed flesh with his mouth and tongue. With each new discovery, his need grew beyond measure, hammering through his loins. He discovered new complexities, such as zippers and then learned how to unhook a woman's bra.

With her breasts uncovered, his lips found her nipples, high and ready, arching to meet his caress. He had only tasted them that once during their stolen moments aboard the Immaculata, and the memory he cherished for so long didn't do the delicate mounds justice. He kissed and licked, suckled and tasted.

Vivian writhed with each embrace, cherishing his every breath that skimmed her flesh. His lips curled around her nipple once more, and she cupped his head in her hands, pressing him even more firmly, encouraging his mouth to take more while she arched with a moan. He suckled harder, pulling her deeply within his mouth. The bud between her legs ached with the memory of how his fingers called forth her desire. Greedily she craved that fulfillment only he could bring and pressed her mound toward him.

Felipe's mouth left her breasts and with broad strokes licked her abdomen, lower and lower until he encountered her curly triangle of feminine delights. He continued slowly, positioning himself between Vivian's thighs.

"You are a miracle to behold." His fingers glided toward the source of her heat and spread the rich red petals.

At the intimate caress, Vivian's bud tightened, causing her thighs to spread and her hips to lift from the bed. Felipe collapsed upon her but took great care, treating her like the most delicate of flowers. His licks unfolded each petal in turn, until her passage beckoned.

Building with the insistent caresses, primitive sensation coursed through her, coalescing in waves of pulsing need.

Holding her breath, she welcomed the glorious swells, urging them to carry her into acute awareness. She drifted, allowing the memories of their stolen moments to flow and converge with the present. The splendid consciousness spread through her, growing and heating, lingering and tingling deeper and hotter. She was more aroused than while upon Felipe's berth and had an even greater expectation than while in his arms on horseback. His mouth suckling and teeth nibbling was ever so much more than the touch of his hand. Her pleasure mounted, drawing every muscle tighter with tingling expectancy.

Vivian's breath surged in rugged gasps until even breathing was beyond her. Tension escalated, heightening and spreading, until every cell in her body was aflame. Her mouth opened in a silent scream. Glory burst, erupting through her flesh and licking her very essence with ecstasy. As his mouth still held her, Vivian's flesh convulsed in spasm. Nearly rising from the bed, she screamed out Felipe's name in a breathy moan.

He rose over her, laying hard and wet kisses along her stomach and lingered only slightly longer upon her glorious breasts. Looking deeply into Vivian's emerald eyes, Felipe positioned himself at the opening of her channel and pressed inside. His ministrations had prepared her, but still he took great care and entered her slowly. She felt his urgency throb, and it called to her, demanding fulfillment. He slipped out and entered again, working inside of her, allowing her body to open and welcome each stroke. Oh, and welcome him she did.

A guttural moan slipped from Vivian's throat, and her hands slid down his back and onto his butt. She urged him forward, spreading her legs wider, yielding as he continued ever deeper until they fully joined. Their bodies were conjoined as deeply as a husband and wife could be.

His dazzling eyes melted into liquid fire and sparked as she met his steady rhythm. "Oh Felipe," the words coursed through her dry lips. "In all of my imagination, I never expected..."

He stopped and stared down at her, brushing her blushing cheek. "What, my love, what did you expect?"

"This is more, ever so much more. You light my very soul on fire. I never want you to leave me."

Felipe smiled softly and bent low to take her lips in a gentle embrace. Yet as soon as they touched, the blaze of passion sparked anew. His kiss challenged her lips and tongue, drawing upon them in breathless strokes. Her hips raised in invitation, and he drew back. In one definitive stroke, he entered her, sliding all the way inside, bumping their loins at the point of deepest union.

"Oh yes, oh Felipe." She screamed breathlessly. "Do that again."

And he did. Over and over again, he thrust into her passage, and she met him urgently. The hazy glaze of passion consumed her, growing once again, the same yet different. As Felipe rocked within her, he touched the most sensitive of places, areas that had never known sensation. They lit and glowed, charging her body with renewed vigor. The pulsations were bright and shiny, lifting her to a new plane of consciousness, and as they burst, her entire body quaked.

He paused, holding himself deeply within her while allowing her orgasm to crest. Heat poured from his straining flesh in heavy waves along with his challenged breaths. A fine sheen of lust glossed their skin, and the scent of ardor filled the charged air. His member grew hot and heavy while his lips kissed every inch of her face and neck, shoulders and breasts. With caresses as gentle as butterfly wings, his hands journeyed, touching and roaming over her curves, especially the fullness of the lower curve of her breasts. Only after he had certainly memorized every detail of Vivian's physical form, Felipe resumed his rhythmic quest.

Beyond the point to create conscious thought, she sank into the joyful bliss and once again encouraged the sensual gratification to rise. Like an orchestration, the tension built within them both, plucking and vibrating in harmony. Yielding in every way she could give herself to another, she accepted his increasing speed, feeling the escalation of his internal tension.

He arched and with a shout buried himself. The hot surge burst within her, another and then another. The heated force urged her once again over the vibrant edge, and while his body bucked, she clung to the vibrant orgasm. His lust flowed, not giving up until the last of the essence left his body.

Together they slowly sank into the lulling hum of sexual satisfaction. Another hum joined their world, resonating within their minds and souls. The tone flowed into and between the ghosts and separated them from their temporary hosts.

Opening her eyes, Fara expected the world to be cloaked in emerald light, but just as the final edge of sunset drifted across the room, day melted into night. J.C. peered down upon her and brushed his fingers through the damp hair at her temple. Leaning forward to balance on his elbows, he touched the edge of her rosy lips with his thumb.

Once again, J.C. and Fara were themselves, but they weren't alone. Even though the ghosts had crossed into the ethereal realm, their love and devotion remained. They continued to hold each other in every way possible for two humans to be together in united body, mind, and soul.

Unconsciously, Fara's distinct categories for men crumbled. She wasn't sure exactly how it happened, but now it was so very clear and easy to see. J.C. was more than friend, lover, or coworker could ever be. Loving him created a fourth category, a new realm no other man would ever achieve, a mate for all eternity.

Fulfilling and captivating, every cell in her body glowed with life. Threading every wile in her voice, Fara sent out a distinct and tangible impression of that inner feeling intertwined within, "I love you."

J.C. nodded slightly while a flamboyant grin consumed his features. "You must really mean it because you said it me when your grip faltered and you thought you'd be consumed in the vortex."

"You remember."

"Yeah, just now. Hearing you say that to me was all it took. You know they say love heals all wounds, and dear God Fara, I love you."

Lazily, she stretched in her unique feline way and allowed her fingers to skim down J.C.'s back. Rounding the cheeks of his ass, she slipped her hands up his sides and spread her fingers over his chest. Her breath caught, and she felt her face go numb.

"Jesus, what's wrong?"

"Look. It's Vivian's emerald." Slowly, Fara drew her hand away, focusing on the glittering ring clinging to her finger.

Shifting his weight, J.C. lifted his left hand. Felipe's emerald emitted light. As they brought their hands together, the rings resounded with life and love everlasting.

THE END

A Special Preview of *Ghost Sex – Ghost Lovers* book 3

CHAPTER 1

A frosty grip squeezed the inside of Fara Trotter's throat until she couldn't breathe. Inch by inch, the morbid chill spread, and numbness crept into her fingers. She didn't notice her cellphone slipping until it smacked the top of her foot, but the phone didn't matter, not right now. She pressed her eyes closed and then reopened them, blinking twice before daring to look toward the curb.

Guy was gone.

A tinny voice echoed between her shoes. Off-balance, she swooped up her cell and accidentally hit the speaker button.

"Shit!" J.C. Calderon's shouts echoed from the phone with enough volume to carry across the church's small portico. "What's going on? What's wrong? Fara! I knew we should have postponed the shoot in Naples until I could leave Puerto-"

She started talking over him. "I just saw a ghost."

Immediately, he fell silent.

She fixed the phone while bracing her body in the corner where the wrought-iron fence met the building. The solid wall made her feel more stable, and she leaned her head against the weathered stones. Words as rough as the hewn bricks scratched through her throat. "A ghost. I saw a ghost."

Even with the church blocking some of the wind, the steady Mediterranean breeze pushed against her cropped hair. With a rough hand, Fara ran her fingers through the spiked angles.

"Dios mío, not again." He whispered. "How do you know it's a ghost?"

She forced out the truth while trying not to remember. "I saw Guy Carver die."

He didn't reply, but the tension emanating across the phone line spoke volumes. She wanted to shout how she didn't kill him, but in a way she did. That incident verified the curse she carried beyond a shadow of a doubt. And now, J.C. was next. Loving Fara was a form of suicide.

Sick tension lifted from her stomach. The fiery memories of Guy's death were too raw to relive. Taking a short series of sharp breaths, she sought her inner Zen.

She didn't want to go through anything paranormal. Her plan was to get in and get out, just like the missions she used to run, and seeing Guy's ghost instantly filled her mind of those bygone days. Why Guy, and why here of all places?

Thankfully, her assigned escort from the Roman Catholic Diocese beckoned from the doorway and distracted her from the awkward silence. "The church just reopened. I've got to go. I'll call when I get back to the rental house and tell you what I found out about the ghost bride. Chow." She hung up before her co-producer could even take a breath. Immediately she turned off her phone and shoved it through the small opening at the top of her backpack without releasing the drawstring.

Inside the venerable church, golden light drifted from lofty windows, casting slanted shadows. Half of the roman arches glowed while darkness masked the other side. A few short months ago, she would have equated the symbolic division as good versus evil, but now the scene struck her differently. Darkness crept slowly across someone's life and in the end engulfed all, yet some souls remained mired in the transition. Only some were trapped. Others refused to continue into the next plane. Regardless of their circumstances, they were all damned until someone showed them the way.

More rapidly than what seemed reasonable within the normal passage of time, the distinct shadow crept across the central aisle and stretched to touch her arm. An unmistakable sense of cool serenity flooded her awareness. She closed her eyes, absorbing the tranquility. As a girl, she loved bright sunshine, but now darkness gave her comfort. It was where she hid all of her pain and sorrow, including the memories of Guy.

Why would his ghost appear here of all places? He died in Baltimore.

Just that one thought recalled the buried details, replaying the vivid scene in her mind. Even though they only needed to go a few blocks from their apartment, Guy insisted on driving. She left him waiting in the car while she ran into the liquor store. Just after her fingers rounded the tall bottle of vodka, the car exploded. The incendiary blast left no intact remains, but Fara held a memorial service anyway. She invited his family from Alabama, but either they didn't receive the notice or they didn't care enough to attend the service. The small and quiet ceremony didn't have a color guard or twenty-one gun salute. CIA didn't get the regalia; they were invisible, especially in death.

She took one long stare over her shoulder almost expecting to see Guy athletically striding through the heavy doors then gamboling down the stairs. A residual ghost repeated the same events over and over again whenever the circumstances aligned just right. J.C. had taught her that.

Maybe she was just mistaken. Guy was of Italian descent, and a lot of Italian men specialized in Frank Sinatra chic. Quite honestly, she didn't get a good look at him before he pulled down the classic Ray-Bans, yet her intuition resonated on a deeper, intimate level. They were more than lovers, more than friends. They were partners to the bitter end.

The priest touched Fara's arm, and she opened her eyes with a shock since she didn't realize she closed them. His softly spoken Italian was even more reverent inside the sanctuary. "You see, this church is recognizable right away from its four stone columns, but now only three still bear the bronzed skulls." He motioned toward the closest sets of bones with a gnarled hand nearly as grave from age. "You see, they are shiny from the caresses of the devout. Believers in the power of the dead have conferred upon Purgatorio ad Arco the nick-name of Cap'e Muorto."

"Skulls? This is the church of skulls." Fara's senses were clearing, and she recognized the Byzantine architecture surrounding the rows of simple wooden chairs. Centuries ago, the area would have been open, and the parishioners stood or knelt on the hard floor throughout the mass. "That's why the Cult of the Dead meets here?"

"I don't think you understand, Signora Trotter. You see, here in Naples, more so than any other place, the living and the dead have a relationship, a devotion to each other." The priest extended his hand again, guiding her into the light. "During the terrible bloodshed of the war, many lost their lives far away from their families, so their loved ones adopted the remains of another who had died long ago. The devout believed if they helped a soul in purgatory cross into heaven through homage and prayer, the grateful spirit would guide their lost loved one to the gates of heaven. Now in less stressful times, the living asks the dead to bless them with favors in this world."

"Let me see if I'm understanding this right," Italian was one of the many languages Fara spoke fluently. Even though the priest had a heavy Sicilian accent, her confusion wasn't a language barrier, rather a new way of thinking about death, a subject in which Fara was an expert. "Let's say I helped a soul or two ascend to heaven, then it's possible for one of my deceased love ones to pass through the gates of St. Peter?"

"Signora Trotter, do you believe?"

Fara didn't answer and approached the marble altar. Genuflecting upon one knee, she crossed her torso and bowed her head toward the larger than life painting of souls ascending to heaven, then added a silent prayer.

Guy was a trained assassin, but he was a good man and didn't deserve to be damned to wander throughout eternity. Maybe that was it, why he appeared here. Perhaps her assistance to the ghosts in Puerto Rico earned enough supernatural brownie points to help Guy find salvation.

As if able to overhear her soulful monologue, the priest waited until her thoughts ceased to touch her shoulder. She followed him around the gilded front wall and past sumptuously ornate red velvet chairs sitting on a raised dais. A small chamber behind the main altar was noticeably cooler, nearly incased in marble. Dark and rough in comparison, a sturdy wooden slab leaned against the wall, and the priest unlatched a shin-high wooden gate.

The steep stairway descended between narrow off-white walls. At the base of the stairs, a black metal gate stood open. Unlike the corroded gates in Puerto Rico's Fort San Cristobal, this wrought iron was pristine; even though, this edifice had to be at least two hundred years older than the fort.

The air grew thicker and heavy to breathe. She knew it would be stale, but this was different, a combination of dampness and decay found only in places where the dead gathered. And then she noticed something else, not quite a scent, rather an impression. Fara closed her eyes and concentrated on expanding her aura, which in turn fine-tuned her inner perception.

"Mrs. Trotter?" The father's voice jerked her back to the physical world. "This is a place of power. Many find it difficult to cross the threshold. If you want to go back-"

Without any further delay, she passed through the tangible barrier into the hypogeum, and the impression of the amassed dead slid around her body, engulfing her in an invisible embrace. Static charged over her skin, lifting the fine hair on her arms.

The ancient sanctuary stretched below them. She glanced back up the short stairway and then down into the lower chamber again. The depth perspective was wrong. The crypt's vaulted ceilings seemed far too tall to be below the church, like fitting the Empire State Building inside of a bottle. Her fingers curled lightly upon the protective railing, and she glanced down, easily thirty, maybe even forty feet. Without points of reference, it was hard to determine.

Naples was an ancient city, dating back to the cradle of human civilization. As one culture fell, another grew on top if its remains. Compressed layers preserved bygone eras in haunting clarity. This was a prime example.

Father Dominic waved toward the dramatically-peaked arches. "Everything in this place belongs to the Cult of the Dead. In the seventeenth century, plague killed nearly half of the city. Paupers and aristocrats alike met within these walls, joined by the desire to pray for loved ones lost, which didn't discriminate between rich or poor. As many as sixty masses a day were observed for the lost souls to ascend from purgatory. Come, signora, this way."

He led her deeper into the labyrinth of chambers, where several altars and tiered crypts segmented the uneasy tomb. Skulls stared in eternal vigilance, propped up in manmade displays, boasting the bizarre and macabre at the same time.

Posted against white tile walls were photographs of the loved ones who sought salvation or perhaps photos of those who provided the prayers. A few tintypes of people in Victorian-era clothes stood alongside Polaroids which were next to ink-jet prints on regular bond paper. Moisture trapped behind cheap plastic frames made the digital colors bloom, like a photographic embellishment of holy light. She searched the faces hoping to see men who looked like Guy, but not one was a good match, not like the man in the church's courtyard.

Again, the priest waved with a reverent twist of his wrist, "Beyond the long catacomb for the aristocracy are larger rooms meant for burials of people of lower social rank, but all buried here had been believers. Yet over time, the tombs were sealed and long forgotten until the Second World War. As Axis and Allies alike swept across the land, Neapolitans sought refuge underground and rediscovered the nameless graves. The Cult of the Dead continued until 1980 in spite of the fact that they received no support from religious authorities. Rather, the Church ardently opposed the practices as heresy and eventually closed the underground. In 1992, the local cultural association, Incontri Napoletani, intervened. One of our most devout families supports the facility in exchange for personal benedictions."

"That young woman?" So rattled by seeing Guy, Fara had forgotten about the beautiful blond who preceded him out of the church to an awaiting limousine.

"Aleri Caravaggio, the daughter of Donna Elena Caravaggio who is the most powerful woman in the city."

"Why does she come here?"

"This way, I show you." The priest touched her elbow and led her deeper into the crypt where more elaborate shrines with candles and flowers honored the polished remains. Rosaries draped the edges of tiled crypts along with statues of the Holy

Mother and others of winged angels interspersed with haloed saints.

Fara turned, and her breath caught in amazement. The processional leading up to this particular crypt overflowed with fresh and silk flowers, crucifixes, rosaries, and statues. Front and center were two skulls in a rectangular boxy shrine. The one on the right wore a bridal veil. "That's the ghost bride."

"The faithful call her Lucia. She married and only a few days later lost her life. Young women come to her to pray for assistance in finding a good husband. Signorita Caravaggio comes to pray almost every day."

The striking woman was youthful, no older than twenty. When she stepped from the church, the breeze caught her golden hair, and the late afternoon added a glow of radiant fire. The unbound lengths tumbled down her back like a satin waterfall. In all her life, Fara had never seen a woman as lovely. "With her being beautiful and rich, I don't think she would have any trouble finding a husband."

The old man waved a bent finger at Fara. "Not every husband is a good husband."

"I understand that." While staring at Lucia's skull, Fara's memories drifted back to her own short marriage. She and Jason only had three weeks before he shipped out for his last tour in Afghanistan. It seemed so long ago when she buried him in Arlington National Cemetery, but in truth, it was less than three months. In the weeks that followed, her life changed. She encountered ghosts who were all very real. An ocean of bizarre experiences separated her current life from the past, at least until she saw Guy. Just that one glimpse opened the floodgates to those turbulent years she wanted to forget.

"Signora Trotter, kneel and pray. If you believe, you feel the power." The priest backed away from the altar where three white candles were still burning from Aleri Caravaggio's offering. His movement stirred the flames, and trickles of wax let loose, streaming down the sides to form a communal puddle in the center. The wax continued to flow until the three circles touched to form the shape of a clover inside the triangle. Just beyond the trinity stood a brass candlestick pitted with age, strangely dark amongst the light.

The dancing flames reached inside Fara and drew out the frustration of her flight arriving late, the hysterics of the terrified realtor, and then finding the church closed to the public for a private service. Even her short fight with J.C. about his grandmother quit simmering inside of her and drained into the ambient power of the crypt.

While watching the candles, her pounding headache cleared, and she realized how others interpreted the tranquil, almost hypnotic effect as divine. Perhaps it was. After the experiences in Puerto Rico, she knew there was more between heaven and hell than just the souls of man. Inexplicable forces manipulated the living and the dead, of that she had no doubt. There was power here in the catacombs, either infused or preserved by the Cult of the Dead. Regardless, the force was tangible, what some might call magic.

Skirting the tiny table filled with offerings, Fara carefully reached past the candles. Two skulls sat side by side with a silly, dollar-store figurine of a cherubic angel between them. The jaws were missing, and empty holes lined the upper mouth where teeth had once been. Fara's fingers encountered the slope of the skull's forehead just under the edge of the lacy veil.

Brilliant colors lanced her mind, transforming into visions of women in long dresses and men in silken pantaloons. Music drifted, at first lightly with the tones of a flute and mandolin then the rich notes of a harpsichord joined the chorus. In perfect unison, the men lifted the women in a swirling array. From a raised platform, she watched a raven-haired beauty toss her head back for the full light of the candle-lit chandeliers to highlight her classic features.

A singular flare of anger sizzled throughout Fara's awareness. Intrigued by the out of place rush, she wondered who the girl was. At first she looked like Vivian Dufrense, the ghost she helped in Puerto Rico, but instead of vibrant green eyes, this woman's were dark, nearly black, under even darker brows if that was possible, with pale white skin so fair she looked like Snow White.

Fragile. Delicate. Virginal.

With a swirl, the ladies switched partners, and the smile Snow White gave to the next man was not innocent. If the couple were not yet lovers, they soon would be. She curtsied toward the tall and equally saturnine gentleman with a soft twinkling in her eyes. Each toss of her head, caress of her hand, and blink of her lashes exuded sensuality. At the end of the song, he dropped his head and briefly passed his lips over her ear to which she radiantly smiled.

"Signora Trotter?" Her name echoed softly within her head, bringing her back to the present. The priest softly continued, "We started late, and you see, the church closes at dusk. No one, guest or member alike, is allowed in the catacombs at night. Spirits do not rest when observed. We must go, but may return tomorrow."

Fara didn't argue. For some strange reason, she believed him.

Find *Ghost Sex* online.

ABOUT THE AUTHOR

 Sally Swanson is an avid fan of historic ghost stories. Through diligent research and personal travel, she recreates tragic romances with a few spicy twists. The Ghost Lovers' series takes readers around the world and into the spiritual realm where *True Love is Eternal*.

Ghost Dreams – Fyvie Castle in Aberdeenshire, Scotland

Ghost Emerald – Fort San Cristobal in Old San Juan, Puerto Rico

Ghost Sex – Purgatorio ad Arco in Naples, Italy

Ghost Spell coming in 2013

Web www.farlightpress.com

Facebook *Ghost Lovers* Fan Page
www.facebook.com/pages/Ghost-Lovers/241177722588808

Blog http://ghostloversnovels.blogspot.com/